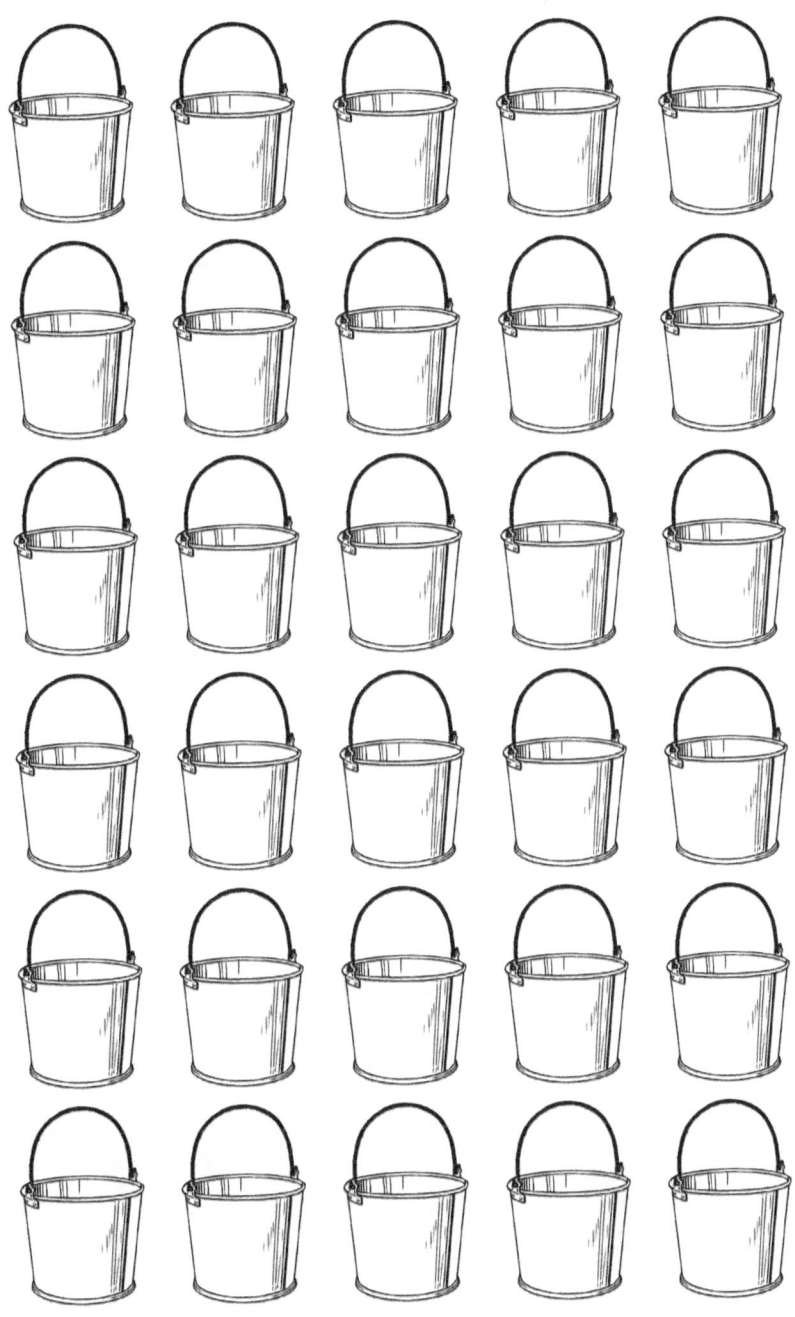

Pure Slush Books

April
May
June
2014

a Pure Slush compendium

First published December 2014
Edited by Matt Potter

Pure Slush Books
4 Warburton Street
Magill SA 5072
Australia
Email: edpureslush@live.com.au
Website: http://pureslush.webs.com
Visit the Pure Slush Store: http://pureslush.webs.com/store.htm

Front cover photograph copyright © Evert-Jan van Scherpenzeel

ISBN: 978-1-925101-46-1

Pure Slush proudly features (both online and in print) writers from all over the English-speaking world. Some speak and write English as their first language, while for others, it's their second or third or even fourth language. Naturally, across all versions of English, there are differences in punctuation and spelling, and even in meaning. These differences are reflected in the stories *Pure Slush* publishes, and it accounts for any differences in punctuation, spelling and meaning found within these pages.

stories by

Guilie Castillo Oriard

Townsend Walker

Derek Osborne

Gloria Garfunkel

John Wentworth Chapin

Lynn Beighley

Andrew Stancek

Rachel Ambrose

Gill Hoffs

Susan Tepper

Jessica McHugh

Shane Simmons

Michelle Elvy

Len Kuntz

Michael Webb

James Claffey

Gwendolyn Joyce Mintz

Stephen V. Ramey

Gay Degani

Sally-Anne Macomber

Mandy Nicol

Margaret Bingel

Darryl Price

Teresa Burns Gunther

Matt Potter

Gary Percesepe

Nathaniel Tower

Kimberlee Smith

Vanessa Weibler Paris

Joanne Jagoda

h. l. nelson

April

The Hunt for Pélagie Solak

by Guilie Castillo Oriard

The inside of Luis Villalobos's Rubicon Jeep feels like an oven preheated for the Christmas turkey, even with the air conditioning at full blast. "Ultra powerful compressor," the salesman said back in December. "Special for Curaçao." Four months later, barely spring, and the island heat has already defeated it.

And Milena – his boss, his lover – has defeated Luis.

As he parks outside the ironwork gate of #74 Jan Sofat, his phone buzzes in one of the central console's cubbyholes. Milena. He's tempted to lower the window and throw the damn thing into the mangroves.

How *could* she?

And how could *he* have been so trusting? Like a fool – so apropos today – he'd been celebrating. A year's worth of compliance work achieved in two months, just in time to meet the FATCA deadline next week. Failure would cost Ehrlich Fiduciary its license. And Luis his righteousness, after all the confrontations with Milena.

But he never expected her to pull rank, go behind his back. Or Wendolyn to fall in with it.

Wendolyn looking at Julissa, her assistant. Julissa looking at the floor. Comprehension beginning to crack wide open. Discovering Wendolyn's loyalties hurt, but what really rankled was her justification – a shabby *It's just six entities, Luis. Only one is domiciled in Curaçao.* She sounded just like Milena.

He locates a bell next to the gate, rings it twice. Six days to fix this. He'll do it himself. No one else can be trusted.

A huge uniformed maid surrounded by a dozen dogs is shouting to make herself heard over the barking. "I already said, sir. Ms. Solak not home."

"When will she be back?"

The dogs push bared teeth through the suddenly-flimsy-looking iron bars. The maid – Jamaican, judging by how her vowels stretch like putty – shrugs. "She have no schedule when she out with the dogs."

Luis eyes the canine Dawn of the Dead swarming the gate. "*More* dogs?"

The maid narrows her eyes. "You not know Ms. Solak well, do you, sir? What business you have to see her about so urgently? You selling something?"

"No, I'm not selling anything. It's – confidential." But he knows he won't make a dent on this Amazon. Besides, he's got a hunch. "Please ask her to call me."

His business card disappears into the folds of the Jamaican's apron. Back inside the sweltering Jeep, Luis makes a note to request heavier paper for his business cards. Something that might provide a full minute of chewing pleasure for a dog.

Weekday car rides mean only one thing for Al. Luis catches him throwing suspicious glances his way from the back seat. "No, bud, no vet. A little work for me first, and I'm hoping you'll help me with that. Then straight-up fun. Sound good?"

Luis heard of this dog beach last month, has been meaning to bring Al. If there's any cosmic justice, he'll find the elusive Ms. Solak here, no gatekeepers except her dogs. Surely she won't sic them on a fellow pet owner? Without the suit and tie, she won't suspect who he is until it's too late. He has the affidavit in the glove compartment.

One signature is all he needs.

A dirt road ends at an inlet cradled between the hillocks of the St. Joris valley. A Ford Explorer, red under the mud spatters, is parked next to a burst of mangroves. That's the only sign of human presence – Ms. Solak's, Luis hopes. Everything else is red dust and brambly vegetation. The surf laps at gritty shores with lake-like softness, hardly audible above the bluster of wind that slams the Jeep's door back on Luis's shin.

"Carajo!" He smothers the more violent curses, limps out and opens the back, hooks the leash to Al's collar. "Come on, bud."

Al's front legs are splayed, head hanging low, ears flat. His haunches are quivering. A lamb next in line for slaughter couldn't look more pitiful.

"Nothing to be scared of, man. It's the beach! Lots of room to run. You *like* running. And the water – nice, cool water – Aw, come on, Al."

Luis tugs on the leash, but Al wiggles back farther and farther until he's pressed against the passenger-side door. When Luis switches to that side, Al backs away to the driver's side. Finally Luis climbs in, intending to bodily force Al's fifty pounds out of the car.

But the dog's whole body is quaking like the worst case of Parkinson's.

"Hey, buddy. Hey. What's wrong?"

Al whines.

Luis holds Al's massive, shaking body against his chest until the quaking comes only in bursts. Then he reaches for his cigarettes. "Bad idea, huh?"

Another whine.

He lowers all the windows, opens the doors on the downwind side in the unlikely case Al decides the world isn't as scary as it seems. He lights up in the shelter of the car and steps out.

Al's whine is pure anxiety now.

"I'm right here. Just stretching my legs. I'd never leave you – Oh."

The dog is peering out of the car at him, head so far down his nose brushes the seat upholstery.

"Is that it? Someone abandoned you?"

Al's ear twitches.

"That's how you ended up a stray, bud?"

But Al isn't listening. Not to him, anyway. Something out by the bay has caught his attention. Then Luis hears it too. Dogs barking. A whistle. He follows Al's gaze and sees six, maybe seven dogs splashing along the shore three hundred meters away. Behind them walks a figure so slight it might be a child. "That can't be Pélagie Solak. I'm sorry, Al. I put you through all this for nothing."

A barking pack won't help Al's anxiety attack. They better leave before the Ford's owner gets back. He closes the doors, turns the ignition, buckles his seatbelt. "We'll try again tomorrow, okay? Maybe we'll have better luck –"

A scrabble of nails on upholstery, a shift in the Jeep's suspension, a flash of black streaking toward the bay.

"Al! No!"

He forgot about the windows.

The dog is racing for the pack, leash streaming out behind him. Low growling carries back to Luis on the wind. They'll tear him to pieces.

"Al! Get back here!"

Damn suicidal dog. He turns the ignition off, lunges out – shit, the seatbelt. Buckle seems stuck, the band of nylon weave tangles in his arms. Then he's out, tripping over his feet, wishing he could fly. "Al!"

18

He's not going to reach him in time. Luis watches in horror, legs pumping as if of their own volition, as the pack engulfs Al with a roar.

A whistle, then a single booming HEY!

Luis and the pack – even Al – freeze. The girl – Luis makes out the hint of breasts in the dog owner's tank top – holds up a hand. Like the miracle of bread loaves, her seven beasts, now tame, back off. She approaches Al. The tip of his tail wags. She scratches his chest, takes his leash.

She's small, wiry, no curves worth mentioning. Her face isn't beautiful, not like Milena's or Wendolyn's – no trace of even the memory of make-up, no sexy lips, no come-hither eyes. The skin is freckled, but the bone structure underneath has aristocratic haughtiness. With a shock, Luis realizes this 'girl' is older than him.

The dogs reach him first. He steels himself, but they barely sniff at his feet before moving on. The woman watches him, waits until she's within arm's length before speaking. "Your dog?"

"Yes." Luis tastes tears in his throat, wants to kick his wimpy self. "Thank you. And – I'm sorry. I didn't – he was terrified, didn't want to get out of the car, and then he suddenly –"

She rubs Al behind the ears before handing over the end of his leash. "He was trying to protect you."

Al licks his hand, looks contrite. Later there'll be teary hugs, but right now Luis's macho pride pushes for sassy nonchalance. "Thanks, bud, but I can take care of myself."

The woman doesn't even smile.

Luis wipes the stupid grin off his face, offers a chastised hand. "I'm, uh, Luis."

She looks at it the way one looks at a plate of cookies after two servings of carrot cake. Luis gets the feeling she has no qualms of politeness; he won't be the first, or the last, to be so slighted. When she does give her tiny –

19

surprisingly strong – grip, he feels the elation of having been found worthy.

"You risked your dog's life to find me, Mr. Villalobos?"

"How do you know my –"

"Francelle called."

"Who's Francelle?"

The woman smiles for the first time. "You met her at my house."

The ground is cracking under his feet. *"You're –"*

"Pélagie Solak, yes. I'll do you the courtesy – no, I'll do your dog the courtesy of listening to whatever you have to say. And then you will leave. Me. Alone."

La Ronde / Annie and Myron

by Townsend Walker

It's three o'clock. Annie sweeps through her office door at PricewaterhouseCoopers, raincoat trailing on the floor. Lunch with Joey ran over. Not lunch as much as finding ways to appropriately thank him for the diamond and emerald bracelet. They both limped out of Room 634 at the Hilton, tired out after three hours lying down.

She pulls out her compact, checks her hair, smooths down her skirt, props up the collar of her blouse. Message light is dancing disjointedly, her assistant pops around the corner, primly announces, "Your client has been waiting," the phone rings.

"Sweetheart baby," the receiver booms.

It's Myron, *Sweetheart baby* is his tag for everyone.

"Where've you been Cuddles? Tenth time I've called."

Annie thinks he only uses "Cuddles" with her, but with Myron, who knows?

"Just got into town, you free tonight?"

Shit. Of all nights, she was planning a long bath looking at her Cartier Panthere through the bubbles.

"Sure, sure, jammed right now. Call you back."

§

Annie's client, an undersized guy compensating with obvious platform shoes, stumbles through the door carrying two boxes, paper falling out in a trail behind him.

"You said you needed everything, here it is."

"Mr. Johnson, I said I need everything from 2013, not since the company started."

He shrugs – weighed down by boxes, and from his expression, a heavy ennui.

"Just give them to me, I'll have someone sort through it."

Annie resented the partners in Newark foisting this local chain, *Dynamic Mechanics*, on her when she arrived from Los Angeles last year. 2014 would be the first and last year for this account. Not that Joey's moving company is much larger, but Joey has contacts and that ineffable something else (she just spent three hours with).

She calls her assistant in, dumps the boxes on him, then calls Myron.

"Great hearing, Myron. You couldn't tell me you were coming?"

"Wanted to surprise you, baby. Here for a month. Finalizing script, checking out locations, getting a feel for Jersey. We're going to see a lot of one another, if you know what I mean," followed by a chuckle.

Myron is a film producer – a cut above B, but not far. PwC is his studio's accountant, as a favor to the Weinsteins. Myron started out with Bob and Harvey; some people soar, others jog. But Myron knows people; they like him, feel unthreatened by his infrequent successes. He introduced Annie around and helped her firm build up a good clientele in the industry. She came to Newark because there was a partner slot open a year down the road; there wasn't in LA.

§

Annie goes home, power naps, showers, dresses (small, black, not too provocative, as if Myron needs help, or she, around him).

Myron's got this tip from a friend for the Adega Grill. Friend of a friend knows the owner, Carlos Lopes. A corner table, low lights, soft yellow walls, Mediterranean feel. *Quiet, so you can talk.*

"It's been a while, Cuddles. Did you miss me?"

He puts his arm around her. He's the stocky sort, put together out of sausages; all curves no angles and his arm more lies on her shoulder than holds it. Surprisingly agile though, Annie's always thought.

"Of course I did, you big lunk."

Myron has a pretty face for a guy, smooth pink skin, twinkly blue eyes shining on her. "So tell me what's up, not the business, talk to me about you, how's my little Annie liking it out here?"

"There's this deal I can use your help with." She moves in closer to him and drops her voice.

"Say the word."

"Client / friend-getting-to-be: his sister is tight with a woman she went to high school, college, worked with, you know like they've been together forever."

"Yeah, yeah." He moves closer to her too, but for other reasons.

"Her husband beats the crap out of her regularly and she wants to get him offed."

"Offed?" Myron shrugs and squinches up his face.

"Offed." Annie is fairly matter-of-fact about arranging a hit job. She's not sure why.

"Where do I come in?"

"You're a friend of Max, who, I've been told, knows people who know people who might be of service to this lady."

The waiter brings a bottle of Dom Perignon. "From Senhor Lopes. He can't be here tonight, but he's told us to take good care of you."

"Didn't I tell you I had an in?"

"So, you see Max lately?"

"Here's the word on Max." Now Myron is whispering. "Got this from an acquaintance in Tijuana. Max is not a person anyone wants to talk about, and me, I don't know a thing. Last deal did not go down well, some Colombians became very upset with our Max, who as you remember also had some Asian connections and may now be either in the jungles of Burma, or if he didn't get that far, is under 60 feet of water off Catalina."

"Good champagne, let's drink to Max."

Conversation stops as the waiter approaches with a plate of calamari. "The first item on the Chef's tasting menu, Lulas a Romana. Bom apetite!"

"So this client you're getting to be friends with: what's his name?"

Annie is hoping Max doesn't get too inquisitive about Joey. Thoughts of the afternoon, feel of Joey's hands, weight of the bracelet. She's not sure she can pull off blasé at the moment. "Joe Leone. Owns a big moving business. Grew up in the area, contacts everywhere." *Maybe that'll justify Joey for Myron.*

"Leone, Leone. Where'd I hear that name before?"

"So you know someone can help this lady?

Two waiters arrive with the fish course, Bacalhau à Adega Grill, fried salt cod with fresh tomato sauce, sautéed onions, shrimp, Spanish sausage, green peppers and bacon. Max sticks his nose in the platter. "Jezzus, is there anything not in this dish?"

"I can't believe someone here in Jersey can't do the job." He waves a fork full of sausage in the air. "You need to go to the Coast for this."

"Might be better though it's not someone local, hides the trail."

"Well, just so happens ..." Myron takes the pregnant pause and fills his mouth with cod.

"That's fantastic! Joey will be so happy." Annie bounces up and down on the banquette.

"Joey?" Myron sputters, cod sticking to his chin. "It sounds like more than getting-to-be-friends."

"Don't get me wrong, you big bear. Joe, Joey, what's it matter? Don't worry."

Myron sits up, takes Annie's hand, squeezes it (harder than affection would call for), glares at her. "I'm not gonna worry, for the next month anyway, then I'll get you moved back to the Coast. That crowd you work for owe me."

Annie's thinking: just when she and Joey are getting close and even making some wispy plans; he's talked about leaving his wife; the bracelet was not cheap, like 50K at least. Not the sort of thing you give to someone you don't plan to spend some time with anyway. Plus, she figures he's into something that's not in the accounts she's seeing. Searching for a stall or at least time away from Myron: "You know it's tax season and I'm working nights and weekends most of the month."

"We'll find time, Cuddles, we'll find time. Leave it to me."

"Can we get back to the hit man this poor beaten up lady in New York needs? Well, actually she's not too poor, offering fifty for the job."

Annie digs in her purse and pulls out a wadded-up slip of paper (*can't be too careful*); recites in a low monotone: "Guy's name is Franklin Lancaster Cabot III; goes by Frank. Works at Goldman Sachs on West Street, downtown Manhattan. Six foot three, 200 pounds, pasty complexion, curly black hair going gray, beak for a nose, Brooks Brothers dresser, loafers with tassels. And Hermes ties, the silly patterned ones. Outside, Prada Aviators, high-end sunglasses, blue tint even in the rain."

"Okay, I got that. But I don't want to hear about this moving guy any more. Seems too small a fish for you, anyway."

"Sure Myron, sure, count on it."

"That's my Cuddles."

Back in her apartment, and alone, Annie texts Joey: "Max in Burma. Found another lead. Gave him a full description (pasty faced, Brooks, shades, etc)."

Joey picks up as the phone vibrates. *Hell,* he thinks, as he reads her message. *Never did tell her the guy is a tanning bed freak.*

Skullduggery

by Derek Osborne

Max didn't tell her about the cancer that night down in Annapolis. He didn't get back to the boat until well after 2AM. The drive from Manhattan took hours. When he came aboard, all the lights were off except for the navigation lamps. Eddie must have turned them on. Rebecca wasn't curled up on the sofa in the salon as he'd imagined, she was in his cabin, sleeping under the patch-work quilt his kids had made for their mother, her dark hair a jumble over the pillows. She stirred when he bent to kiss her and then she kissed him and then it seemed they were there at the airport, two days later, saying goodbye in the car.

There just wasn't time.

As Rebecca promised, *Miami Blue* is taking another break. She's flown out again, this time commercial, they chartered a chopper from Logan Airport and it's well past midnight. She and Anja are having fun getting smuggled onto the island, the airstrip deserted, only the soft glow of the moon casting shadows down Orange Street, the line of little white shops silent as the jeep's tires rattle over the cobblestone. *Gadabout's* tender waits at the foot of the ramp.

"Skullduggery," Rebecca says as Max quietly rows out to the boat. He's bundled them up in sets of red foul weather gear, only their eyes peeking out.

"We're doing skullduggery."

There's something about climbing onto the big wooden boat in the dead of night. Eddie is there at the rail, helping them with the ladder. With his dreadlocks and deep dark skin, a gold ring in one ear, he looks like a pirate. Max and Rebecca practically run to the cabin.

It's late in the day now and they have barely seen the sun. They've come out of the cabin once for lunch and once for tea. Anja and Eddie are playing cook and concierge; they've come back with groceries and souvenirs and now they've gone out again. The salon mantle is covered with tiny lighthouses and hand-painted birds, hats and tee-shirts strewn on the sofa. There's still an issue with the film company that chartered the boat, their shooting schedule delayed again. Part of why they're out of bed is so Max can find the agreement. Rebecca is modeling some of the tees; she's hard to ignore. Max is on the phone reminding the studio they have to pay for the layover. He goes forward and holds the SAT phone down near the anchor winch, pressing a big black button.

"Hear that, Murray? That's the sound of my anchor coming on board." Rebecca has followed him into the locker, a room full of lines and chain. It's one place they still haven't christened. Murray, the studio's guy, agrees to wire the money that day.

Max is feeling okay. Between the Red Bull, Viagra and pain pills his symptoms have disappeared. He's waiting to start the next round of meds once Rebecca goes back to LA. This time they'll be apart almost two months. The doctors warned him not to abuse the regimen during these rallies but he can't help it, he's one of those guys who are naturally fit, born with pecs and a six-pack, a full head of hair (so far, so good), he doesn't look fifty-six. Eddie calls him 'The Marlboro Man'. Last time Max met with his care team they warned him again. He wanted to ask, "What would you do with Rebecca Vasquez standing naked in front of your bed?"

She's standing there now, just across the cabin, light from the one oil lamp casting its shadows, the curves and lines of her body soaking into the dark wood trims. And yes, she's naked. She hasn't brushed her hair and she doesn't have any tan-lines. He loves the two dimples just above her hips, loves kissing them, loves moving down and hearing her sigh. She comes from a place so deep at times he swears it's another dimension.

"What are these?" she says, opening one of the little drawers over the desk. There's a line of seven stretching across like you'd find in an antique roll-top. Each time they make love she gets up soon after and starts to explore. It's why they've had sex in almost every part of the boat.

And it's quiet now out in the harbor. The Newport crowd has gone home. If it had been full season the four of them might have risked having dinner in town, but things are still a bit thin, none of the restaurant lines you'd find in summer. An odd dynamic, safety in numbers, celebrity sightings expected there on Nantucket. "Too much exposure," Anja decided. Seeing her boss disappointed she added, "We'll do takeout." The reason she and Eddie went back ashore.

Rebecca wanted skullduggery.

"The drawers are part of the legend," Max says.

She's holding one of them up to the lamp, exposing the curve of her breast. The drawer is small, the width of a wallet and not very deep, miniature five-panel face and carved ivory pull.

"*Gadabout* has a legend?"

"Oh yes."

She puts the drawer back and opens another. Max likes telling the story.

"The boat was built to help seven sailors find their way home."

Rebecca is looking inside.

"It's written into the bill of sale. Ownership can't transfer until the previous owner's drawer has been filled. The Estate has to approve."

"The Estate?"

"The builder was quite formal, an old New Bedford whaling family."

She opens the first of the drawers again. Above is a set of shelves, Max's personal library. Across the stern are more lockers and shelves, everything raised wood panels, everything deep, dark cherry. Along the port side the big double bunk sits over a pair of captain's drawers. At the foot of the bed a bulkhead returns with an arched door to the private head. The head has a full size tub. Rebecca likes taking baths. A skylight, similar to those out in the salon, lets the stars down into the cabin.

She reaches into the drawer and pulls out a green plastic ring: it's set with a cheap silver shamrock, the toy you might find in a Cracker Jacks box. She tries slipping it onto her finger, too small. She pouts and Max shrugs.

"A hundred possibilities there."

She puts the ring back into the drawer.

The next contains an old black and white photo, a family standing in front of a tenement, light gray stars pinned to their dark woolen coats. Max knows the inscription, *Warsaw, '38, DaDa and Pops, Mom 2nd from left*. Rebecca's eyes tear up. Though she's told him she's Roman Catholic he suspects from other things she has said, the shape of her face, those Mediterranean eyes, her grandparents emigrating from Europe around that time. Maybe they chose the church for protection, who could blame them in those days? She touches the face of the photo, looks over, attempting a smile, then slips it back into the drawer.

Contained in the third is a folded note, tattered and torn, bleeding ink as though it might have got wet.

"Sorry it took me so long. I miss you," Max says.

Rebecca reaches inside.

"Be careful, it's practically dust."

The note is like tissue paper, as if the owner carried it many years. When Max touched it that first day the folds fell apart. She decides not to touch it, closing the drawer, gently.

She goes to open the fourth. Max can't wait. Rebecca catches her breath, everyone does, she sees what's inside and brings a hand to her heart. He's wondering how the earrings look in the lamplight, how the rubies shine in their silver settings.

"Are those … ?"

"You better believe it," Max says.

There's also a watch, a Breitling, the Mariner's model. In *Gadabout's* letter of sale there are instructions for the watch and earrings to be polished every six months. For the first two years that Max owned the boat the estate actually sent a man out to check, an attorney no less. One time he flew to New Zealand. Now they send an affidavit for Max to sign, notarized of course.

"You can't try them on," Max says, knowing that's what she's thinking. "They've never been worn."

Rebecca purses her lips, slowly closing the drawer, turning back into the light, lifting her hair with both hands and exposing the length of her neck, his second most favorite spot. Then she goes back to the drawers.

"It's empty?" she says, holding the next.

"I'm the fifth owner."

They're getting dangerously close. He imagines he's carved a note in the bottom, *I had cancer.* She's shaking it just to be sure.

"I guess I'm still not home," Max says.

Rebecca places the drawer back in its slot, walks to where he is sitting there on the bunk.

"I am," she says, pushing him back against the pile of pillows, taking his cock into her mouth. It's been like that all day – gently, or not so gently – whatever they're feeling that moment. Max runs his hand up the back of her neck, her hair luxuriously tight in his grasp.

"Becca," he says.

She buries her face up against him, pressing, gagging, the same desperation he feels whenever he gets inside her, like he'll never get far enough. Pulling her back, pushing her down on the bunk, he lifts her legs and enters in one, deep thrust.

"Max," she moans, "My Max."

They're both coming. Max is afraid he might crush her but she doesn't mind, holding him tight with legs clamped hard at his neck. They both explode. He's lost again in the sound of her voice; she's there in that other dimension, their bodies melting toward sleep.

"Don't ever leave me," she whispers, her face beside his there on the pillow, "Tell me you'll stay forever."

Conflict

by Gloria Garfunkel

Well, Mixed Mood Episode Ralph and Chloe are having lots of stupid fights over trivia and nearly broke up. We can never remember what the fights are about. Everything bugs me. She moved out for three days until we met for dinner tonight and made up while the Episode was diminishing. She understands it was the bipolar. Her father was like that most of the time. We went to a double-feature zombie movie which cheered us both up, especially *The Night of the Living Dead*, which is exactly how I feel when I'm depressed.

I'd had a really bad day at work. I got into conflicts with about ten annoying people. Serena, the Borderline Secretary pointed out thirteen of my errors to Stan Stealth, my Sociopathic boss and so he had a fit, jumping on his chair while I sat next to it pretending to be intimidated. Serena is one of those compulsive cat hoarders who lives with 27 felines in a decrepit mansion she inherited from her parents. Meanwhile, I tried to get my assistant, Passive-Aggressive Al, to help me and he said yes to everything as usual and then surfed the Internet all day. At least Chloe and I are getting along now.

For April Fool's this year this numbskull in our department who thinks he's a genius sent around a phony memo from Orwellian Headquarters that the whole psychiatry department is being laid off due to lack of business. I freaked out and started contemplating suicide. I though of jumping from Orwellian's thirteenth floor (the roof) though on the elevator up I hear it's an April Fool's joke. I wanted to strangle Irving, but I'm still in Mixed territory and have to control my emotions. I have no idea what I'll be like at the family Seder on April 14 that Chloe really wants to go to. My whole toxic Jewish tribe sets me off, sitting at a chanting meal until 2 AM. I may claim a migraine or just take a few extra Zyprexa and Valium which, with the four cups of ritual wine, should do the trick.

After the movie tonight Chloe asked if I thought my family was as bad as the zombies. I said they are worse because they are all Holocaust survivors and the six million are more present than the real live people. It gets kind of crowded.

Rose

by John Wentworth Chapin

"I think I might be done for the day," Charles says, flexing cramped fingers. Black spots appear in his vision from screen strain.

Esther grunts disagreement. Charles gets a charge from this; when he first visited Esther, he feared he wore thin her patience, but now – if he reads her clearly – she wants him around. The laptop glow lights their wearying faces. *Astral projection, past lives, transient ischemic attack, telekinesis, psychotic break, demonic possession* – such an exhausting mishmash of fact and crap. They have watched videos about Xtreme sports and the Hoover Dam and faith healers and read about Alistair Crowley and extinct big cats, all while listening to a Pandora Motown playlist.

She reclines in a rental hospital bed in her dining room; Charles sits next to her in a plastic chair, leaning forward. The laptop rests on Esther's abdomen, her dry forefinger resting on the trackpad while Charles cradles the wireless keyboard on his lap. She clicks, he types.

Their research agenda has reached something of a dead end. Esther mowed down several pedestrians late last year, killing three, and Charles, witnessing it, narrowly avoided a similar fate. She's trying to understand how she could have done such a thing; Charles, his own agenda tied to hers, is trying to find where to go next. This was clearly The Big

Wake-Up Call, but now he's climbing down a ladder, reaching his foot backwards and downwards for the next rung and finding no secure place to step.

"It blows my mind how much people've put right on the Internet," Esther says, scrolling through Google search results. "When I retired from the library, card catalogs were already a thing of the past. But ... it was nothing like this."

"The whole world," Charles nods.

Esther sucks on her teeth, the pink tip of her tongue protruding between her parched lips. "And most of it isn't worth a second of thought," she says. "People write poems, put them out there. Governments put all sorts of data out there. Who reads it all? Phone bills. People's family pictures. *Blogs*." Esther showed brief interest in blogs a few weeks ago until she was put off by *knotty sentences*: as far as Charles could tell, these were convoluted or grammatically transgressive or both.

Esther stares up at the ceiling, silent long enough that Charles glances at her.

"You okay?" he asks.

She laughs to herself and Charles waits.

"I am 74 years old, and do you know what? I have never seen pornography."

Charles freezes: not what he was expecting.

Esther says, "You've seen pornography? Of course you have."

"Well, I mean, everyone has ... I mean most people my age."

"Good. Let's watch a pornography movie."

Charles lets out a loud, strange sound, something between a cough and a laugh and a yelp, something he can only think of as *explurting*.

"There's no call to be embarrassed," she says. "I have no intention of being titillated. Or maybe I will be. Who knows? I'm an old woman and I should be able to watch a pornography if everyone else does."

36

Charles laughs without humor, his throat dry.

"You'll get over it," she says. "Just take me to a pornography site you've been to before."

"Wow. This is totally ... Okay. I guess you put me on the spot. You know I'm gay, right?" he asks.

"No, I didn't."

"Really?"

"Well, I didn't *know it* until you just now told me. You can put on something gay if you would prefer."

"I would most definitely not prefer!" Charles explurts. "Tell me what to type and I'll type it."

"*Sex movie*," she says. He types it in. They scroll the results: no porn. She tries a few others: *pornography, dirty movie*. Nothing.

He smirks when she offers *smut*, and she glares. "You know you could find it in a heartbeat, but instead of helping me, you get childish."

"This embarrasses me," Charles says. "Try something more specific. Something ... dirty."

"Pussy," she spits out.

Charles gasps for air and then types and hits ENTER. Esther scrolls, pausing at *THE VICE GUIDE TO EATING PUSSY*, but then to his relief she moves down the list. Nothing.

She frowns at him and reclines, arms crossed. "You won't help?"

Next to *pussy*, he types *video fucking* and hits ENTER. Esther grunts a laugh; he wishes he had left SafeSearch on, but it's too late. "This is totally humiliating," he says.

"You will survive," Esther reminds him as she clicks and a bright pink screen comes up with thumbnail images promising a cornucopia of smut. Esther leans forward, carefully examining the images. Charles looks away, but he can hear. Click. Grunt. Click. *Ohmygodohmygod*. Click. Squeal. Click. Dance music. Click. *Yeahyeahyeahyeah*. Click. Gasp. Click. *Fuck yeah*.

Esther's silence is excruciating, and when he finally looks at her face to catch her reaction, he catches nothing.

The pornathon lasts about twenty minutes. When Charles returns from the bathroom, she has closed the laptop.

"When can you come back over here?" she asks.

Charles is silent. He was thinking in the bathroom, taking his time.

"I won't make you type *pussy* again, if that's what you're worried about," she says.

"Ha. Ha. Ha. I'm going home to take a shower and pretend this never happened."

"But you are coming back."

"I'm not sure of my schedule. Ever since my disastrous Indian meditation retreat – well, longer, really – I have been thinking about quitting my job."

"To do what?" she asks.

"I don't know. Something *more*."

"Don't quit your job without a plan. That's a mistake. Instead of pulling back from work, step toward it."

"You had a *career*. I have a *job*. I don't know what I want! I tried dating. I tried painting. I have been reading. I tried meditation and travel and I don't know what else to try." Charles hears the shabbiness of his argument, and that makes it all the worse.

"And what does that have to do with earning a living?" Esther sighs. "When you get ice cream, they let you try every flavor on a little plastic spoon if you want. You act like you've tasted them all and then ordered vanilla, still complaining because you wanted something different."

This sits between then for a moment, Charles struggling with it and Esther satisfied.

He says, "I'm supposed to choose between twelve flavors someone else has picked? How limited is that?"

She nods. "And you think the problem is that you don't have enough time to find out different things?"

"It's four months since the accident," he says. "I've been floating ever since. I want to feel grounded."

"You are assuming there's something you can find that will make it all better. Maybe it's *you* you need to fix, not your routine."

Charles winces, hearing her name his unrelenting fear: the accident left his body unscathed but damaged his mind.

They are silent. She quietly moves her finger on the edge of the laptop's aluminum casing, now coral pink in the evening light. They are both silent for a long moment.

Esther says, "The last few times you've come ... Well, I can't walk and they tell me I never will. I got big worries about lawsuits." She'd mentioned before the lawsuits – three accident victims' families seeking damages, insurance companies – but not the worry. "I can't go through all that. It's time for me to go, and I want your help."

Charles takes a moment to register what she's asking, and when he looks at her, she stares back with moist, resigned eyes.

"You don't mean *that*," he says.

"But I do."

"Now?"

"No, not now. But ... soon."

He wants to say something clever, to undo what she has just asked, but she's clear and lucid and her chin is set: there's no arguing. He falters, "The porn – ?"

She smiles at him. "Not my final request, just curiosity."

Another silence lingers, this time each searching in the pale pink glow for the truth in the other's eyes.

"You haven't answered me," Esther murmurs.

Charles doesn't give an answer because he doesn't have one.

Kiss Off

by Lynn Beighley

Bill Plover eats slowly. He chews each bite many, many, many, many, many times. 32 times, to be precise. I know this because I've been counting.

"Have you ever heard of Fletcherizing?" Bill asked me what seems like three hours ago. "Nature will castigate those who don't masticate." I've figured out that when Bill asks me a question, he isn't actually asking. When he asks, "do you know xyz?" he really means, "let me tell you all about xyz in excruciating detail."

Horace Fletcher had theories about eating, things like the importance of chewing each bite of food 32 times, and chewing about 100 times per minute. I know lots more about Horace Fletcher's theories about eating. Look him up if you're curious. I'm going to try to forget.

I'm on a date with Bill Plover. America set me up. A week ago, Bill came in to the office, complete with camera crew, and very expensive chocolates. (I later discovered the candy was from a sponsor. Bill told me. He didn't have to tell me, but of course he did, because that's what Bill Plover does.)

"Hello, Jenn, these are for you." I looked up. Some guy awkwardly handed me a huge gift-wrapped box. No, not some guy, it was Bill. He didn't look like Bill. No god-awful free t-shirt from a software vendor covered in stains, no baggy sweatpants, no grungy sneakers. Instead, he was in slacks and a button-up-the-front grown-up shirt. His heavy stegosaurus body was gone, and in its place was a good-looking, if slightly stocky man. It wasn't quite on the level of an Eliza Dolittle transformation, but it wasn't that far off.

And shit, I was the one who looked terrible. I was the one in a stained t-shirt, courtesy of a loose lid on my coffee cup. And ragged jeans. And flip-flops, for godsake.

"Jenn, America has spoken. Will you do me the great honor of accompanying me to dinner next Friday?"

Of course I wouldn't. I mean, despite the window dressing, this was Bill Plover, a man I don't like. A man I most certainly don't want to date.

"Yes," I said. Why didn't I say no? I meant to say no, but did I say no?

No, I said yes. I said yes because he paused before and faltered after he said the words "will you." Because he looked at me like my cat Pollock does when I open a can of cat food. I said yes because this was important to him, and hell, it was just one date. One date. It might even be fun, I thought. I thought this because I'm stupid.

There's a bored-looking guy with a camera at the next table. I look at him and he smiles at me, gives me a thumbs up. Maybe I can get his number.

It should come as no surprise that we're at an all-you-can-eat-gosh-darn-buffet. And Bill is chewing. And chewing. Also chewing. I watch his mouth move, I think about his teeth and his tongue behind his lips. I have been focused on his mouth all night.

Bill stops chewing. He swallows. Then he takes another bite. Bill Plover continues to plow through the courses he must finish to accomplish his meticulously thought out plan to get the most out of this meal, even if he's not paying for it. I finished some time ago. And so I find myself staring at his mouth, wondering what it will be like to kiss him. Because I might have to kiss him goodnight. I mean,

41

America expects it, right? Oh, but wait, this is Bill. He's not going to kiss me. We'll shake hands. Yes. That will be it. I relax.

"You filled up on the bread, that's where you went wrong," Bill says. He smiles and I notice a bit of spinach on his front tooth. I don't tell him. I say nothing, even though a tiny voice from an earpiece in my right ear tells me to say, "I'd rather fill up on you." What is wrong with this woman?

You lovely viewers at home won't know this, but I've got a little earpiece on and some producer lady on the other end is trying to tell me what to say. She keeps trying to get me to flirt with Bill. Possibly it's for comic relief for the audience, because I suspect Bill wouldn't know flirting if it bit him in the ass. Or something. I'm not going to test that theory.

We're finally, somehow, at the end. It's over. Well, almost over. He's walked me to my car, the cameraman sticking close by.

"I had a very nice time tonight, Jenn." He smiles, and the spinach is gone. He leans in and what the hell, I kiss him. And it's warm, and his lips are soft, and I like it. He's good at this. He touches my face, and I can't think anymore.

And then it's over, and I can't speak and I'm alone. Except for the voice in my ear that whispers, "wow."

My Bunny

by Andrew Stancek

I've allowed the travesty and can't forgive myself.

My heart is breaking. Oh, not like pop songs on the radio about the boyfriend stolen by a best friend, nothing like that. My heart overflows; that's how it's broken. I never knew a small body could produce so many tears. I cannot dry out.

Everybody snatches a piece of my baby. They compare him to inventors, scientists, mystics, Einstein, Pauling, Linnaeus, saints even, throw around names I've never heard and don't want to.

I believe, you know. Fine, laugh. A reasonably educated woman in the twenty-first century says, with a straight face, "I believe". I'm not talking about fire and brimstone although there's plenty of good even in that, and we'd be better off with a little lava instead of online porn and music videos, no limits on anything, no morality or wonder and when I get going like this they laugh and say, "Yveta, slow down," but I can't slow down, my heart wells up and the water bursts the surface and I cry and I pray and I know what I know. I am right and they are wrong and I don't care who they are and what degrees they have or what TV show they've appeared on; it makes me so agitated and he's still my little bunny I want back and I wish none of it had ever happened.

He's a freak. The first time I saw him called that on the cover of one of those supermarket rags, I dropped the jar of spaghetti sauce I was holding and made a huge mess. What do you mean, freak? He's my boy, who's come up with a glorious way to help everybody, and where do they get off calling him names? I thought people like Beyoncé, or movie stars, or that Aniston woman from *Friends*, that they choose fame, and they deserve the tabloids, but my little one, he did not have any choice.

He was so sick, a sweet little sick boy, underweight and born five weeks premature and had to be in an incubator, and even when he was with me, he cuddled and gurgled and had those curls and eyelashes, and every mother is crazy about her little boy, the precious gift that came out of her and I just loved him to death. But I didn't. It's a stupid phrase, isn't it? When I get excited my voice goes really really high and my hands flutter and I flush and I catch myself and hear what I've said and I wonder, "What did I just say? Where did that come from?" And I cry.

I already said that, didn't I? Well, it's still true.

I wish I was dead sometimes. I even wish he was dead, or I'd never had him. Those are sins; I know that. I've talked to Father Czestochowa a lot. He's helped. He says I have an overwrought sense of sin, that I'm too concerned about understanding and blame. "Accept. Give it over to Jesus and to Our Lady," he says. I try. They say God will never give you a bigger burden than you can carry, never. But it's always people who have suffered little who say that. How can they know? There I go again. I know nothing about other people and their suffering. Who am I to say?

I sure know my own burdens, my own cross. My Adam, my little Bunny, he's my cross. I don't blame my husband for leaving. Sometimes I think he was right to do it. I was bitter but I understood then and I understand better now. I had no time for him and knew I never would. Adam was a part of me, my flesh and blood and Frank, well, he was just a husband, just a man. He stopped being important the minute Adam took sick.

I've read every book which deals with Perthes disease. At the university library they got me articles and studies and translations from all kinds of languages, some you wouldn't think would know anything about medicine at all, but there I go shooting off my mouth again before I've thought. The point is I wanted to understand. My sister pulled at her ear and grimaced when I started talking about the latest research, or a study conducted in Malaysia and promising results at the clinic in Caracas. "Yveta," she said. "You need another interest. Maybe I'll get you a puppy. You liked dogs when you were little. Would you like a little Pomeranian?" So I had to watch myself and pretend I was fine. I was fine. I was obsessive, I know I was, but that doesn't mean I wasn't fine. I knew that disease inside out and then some.

Adam, he was obsessive, too. Sure I know where that comes from. Is it in the genes, I wonder, or a quirk? He read a lot about genes, too, but not this part. He says humans used to have a flying gene, which over the millennia bred out, more and more recessive. I don't know if he's making that up or some scientist really wrote a study.

I don't want to give him over to the world. I don't want him to be famous, have his face all over every magazine. I told Father Czestochowa that I am sure it's a terrible sin to want your child to be different. But most mothers, when they think that, they want their sons to be more special. I want mine to be ordinary, to stock shelves in a grocery store, play hockey with buddies, drink beer, get into trouble. My Adam will never have any of that. He's like John Lennon or Elvis. What I have to look forward to is Graceland.

I don't know if I can forgive myself, ever.

Better Bring an Umbrella

by Rachel Ambrose

Whatever they might say about showers in April, it can't compare to the maelstrom of April that I'm having. Just in this first week alone, Blake has whisked me off to Tamarind Heights (the hip young town two towns away) for a long weekend. We stayed in a gorgeous hotel I wanted to wrap up and put in my pocket, drank fancy cocktails with swizzle sticks and fruit twists, and have had more sex than I thought possible to have in one weekend. The reason? He's sold a rather fabulous painting for a rather fabulous price, and we decided to celebrate. We laugh together more than I've ever laughed with anyone; everything is hilarious for absolutely no reason and his eyes are the most beautiful green lanterns I've ever seen.

Things aren't so rosy with other aspects of my life, though. My meager pay is having a lot of trouble standing up to the fine dining that Blake loves. Even when we stay in, I spend premium money on starfruit (his favorite), arborio rice, and organic meats. He chips in by bringing along lovely bottles of wine, but I always wake up expecting my bank account to be flatter than my hair. And my relationship with Charlotte and Isa, my housemate and ex-housemate respectively, has been suffering too. Charlotte was furious after she discovered my theft of her wine, and refused to speak to me for three days. I canceled plans with

Isa last week in order to spend more time with Blake. I knew that it was a bad idea when I first thought of it, but like all bad ideas, it stayed in my ear, whispering its simpering little sentences until I agreed to it. But I can't help bad behavior; I'm in love and I don't have to account to anyone except myself and Blake. I'm practically entitled to it! Who else matters? It's me and him against the world for all I care. Isn't that what all the books and movies have taught me?

I'm learning, much to my dismay, that the sunlit glow I expected the world to take on, transferred magically from all the movies I've seen, doesn't really exist, which is rude. It should.

When I was little, my biggest fantasy was dancing around in a beautiful dress to Frank Sinatra while a gorgeous guy clasped my hands and spun me so fast my head would spin. It never occurred to me that there would be real life tied up in all that. I'm in love! What do you mean I still have to pay my bills on time?

To make up for the world's utter lack of whimsy, today I've tied my hair up in little knots and dusted my face with cinnamon rouge, and taken myself to work humming a Dvorak sonatina. Just because I have to work in a charmless office doesn't mean I have to take it as drudgery. Mrs. Hatfield is in court today, wonder of wonders, so I type in blissful silence, composing love letters to Blake in my head as I lick and stamp envelopes, imagining covering his body in sultry kisses as I dust Mrs. Hatfield's desk. It really does help my grumpiness at the world refusing to transform into sunshine and daisies. After work, congratulating myself on my magnanimity, I call Isa.

"Hi honey!" I chirrup into the phone when she picks up. "How about a girls' night out tonight, just me and you? We can go to that new South African place you've been talking about!"

"Oh," she says, and I can hear the hesitation in her

voice. "Um, sure, that sounds good. Is Blake coming?"

"No, silly goose!" I reply, laughing. "He's not a girl, is he? Besides, we need some time apart from each other, I need to feel like my hand isn't being constantly held."

"Sounds like a nice problem to have," she says, sighing. "But fine, I'll meet you at the Peri-Peri Cafe at six, sound good?"

"Sure!" I say breezily. I go home, change clothes and run a brush through my hair, showing up at the restaurant a few minutes to six. I grab a table and look up in relief as the door swing open and Isa walks in.

"Hello friend!" I call to her fondly. She swings her bag down and plants herself in a chair, running a hand through her hair, looking inexplicably grumpy. Am I seriously the only happy person in the world? I wonder.

"What's up in your corner of the world?" I ask as the waitress brings us glasses of water and menus. "I feel like we haven't seen each other in ages."

"That's because we haven't," points out Isa, and I clue in that that's probably why she's less than blissed out.

"Well, you're here now!" I say brightly. "And looking rather gorgeous in a very windswept way if I do say so myself!"

Isa sips her water and smiles coldly at me. "Don't try to butter me up. I'm really mad at you."

"Why?" I ask, scrunching up my face and tilting my head. "Because of Blake?"

"Because you managed to steal Blake right out from under Charlotte's nose!" says Isa, and I try not to wince, because there's a part of me who thinks she might be right about that. "She was set to ask him out at his birthday party, and then you came in and formed this magical connection with him, and –"

"Hang on," I interrupt her. "She knew him way before I did, she could have formed a magical connection with him any time she wanted. But he liked me, so he asked me out,

48

and now we're dating, and she missed her chance. That's all." I lightly slap my hand against the table before crossing my arms defiantly across my chest.

"Well, you don't have to parade him around in her face all the time," Isa says. "Talking about all your dates and plans and what dresses to wear."

I roll my eyes. "God forbid she be happy for me. Or you be happy for me, for that matter."

"You both are my friends!" she protests. "You can have him, just don't be an asshole about it. And call me more. It's not easy taking care of my brother when I have basically no help," she continues, and I see how tired she is; her eyes are bloodshot, and her skin is in serious need of some exfoliation.

"I'm sorry," I say, reaching across the table to pat her hand. "I promise I'll be a better friend. Do you want me to cook for you or anything?"

"Please," Isa says, cracking her first real smile as the waitress comes over to take our order. "We both know you don't know how to boil water, honey. But it's okay, I love you anyway."

Two in the Hand are Worth One in the Bush

by Gill Hoffs

Today it's Neil and a working dinner with Russian clients who expect me to nod in the right places, smile constantly, and not mind if they pat my bottom or slide a hand between my thighs – or so I presume from similar dinners with Neil's visitors in the same upmarket club. Neil is nice enough though somewhat windy, with a small cock and a big portfolio. Working with him has led to other business opportunities for me, as well as the occasional loan of a Porsche, so I don't mind smiling 'til my cheeks ache and sitting in a booth with my legs apart under the tablecloth while strangers check for tampons or coils or whatever it is they're doing in there. If it feels like they might catch their Rolex in my pubic hair or I suspect they could do with a manicure – or worse, they've been eating spicy finger food – I clench my cunt muscles like I need to hold in a litre of pee, and wriggle so they think I'm just tight and enjoying myself.

No knickers necessary. Stockings a must. Apart from that, I know Neil prefers little black dresses with low backs and fronts, for me to wear my hair up in a chignon so he can let it down later as he humps me from behind, and red lips and nails. He's collecting me from the agency – I don't yet trust him with my home address – at 4pm for coffee and a chat about who's who before we meet the Russians at 5. I've taken some Clarityn in case he turns up with any of the flowers I'm allergic to (sneezes can lead to all sorts of injuries during a blowjob), refreshed my admittedly basic knowledge of Russian, and have ten minutes to listen to the Beastie Boys before my taxi honks a welcome outside my window. When it comes I grab my overnight clutch (condoms, makeup, mints, toothbrush) and off I go.

The Russians have brought their own hostesses to the club, no one I know, girls with badly-bleached hair and animal print dresses and Blackpool accents. Neil keeps glancing from them to me, and I can guess what's running through his mind: that the Russians he is so keen to impress think him a fool to have brought me, that I'm too posh, that they might choose to broker their deals with one of his co-workers instead. He warned me of this once, when we first met.

"The men I do business with sometimes judge a man's balls by the women he empties them into. I trust you will not let me down."

I'd nodded. I understood. So now, when he introduces me formally to his guests, I slip my arm round his waist for a reassuring squeeze, then make a point of sitting myself between the most important Russians of the group, sliding along the leather seating in the 'U'-shaped booth and allowing my dress to ride up as I move into place. When the man to my left glances down, he cannot fail to notice the tops of my stockings, trimmed with tacky red lace, and the suspenders dividing my creamy thighs into inner and outer segments just begging to be touched. I smile at Neil, off to the right, and open my legs a little while my hands fuss with the white linen napkin provided for me on the table. Once the Russian has seen what I've got to offer, I can drape it loosely over my lap. The other women are fiddling with chunky bracelets, checking the state of their stick-on nails, and waiting for their vodkas to arrive. Neil sees where my neighbours are looking and flashes me a tiny wink.

Drinks arrive, then food, and while the Russians talk figures and schedules with Neil, and the girls knock back their drinks and giggle, the man on my left eases his hand over my thigh and into my crotch, my napkin hiding his hand from my other neighbour's sight. Neil has a lot riding on this dinner, a contract for 2,000 forklift trucks and operative training or something similar, and I don't want to let him down or miss out on a bonus that could mean a conservatory for my mum. So while my right hand uses a silver fork to rearrange the salad on my plate, and my head nods along with their conversation out of polite interest, my left hand tugs the hem of my dress higher then slides into the Russian's lap. Just a semi? Feeling somewhat aggrieved, I knead and allow myself to be groped until there's a satisfyingly hard cock bulging beneath his smart black trousers. I squirm against his signet ring, fork a bit of rocket into my mouth, and murmur "Mmmm ..." near his ear. I hope the man on my other side doesn't try anything until his boss is done with me.

"Your deal sounds ... too expensive to me. You understand, I need a profit too, da?"

Neil stares at his drink for a moment, swirling it in his glass, before replying.

"Of course. But in the current climate ..." he raises his shoulders and drops them again. "I want to give you the best deal possible, for you are not just my fellow businessmen, but my friends." The Russian's hand stills between my legs. "But there is only so much I can take off the price, you understand, before I am paying for the trucks and expertise myself."

I drop my fork under the table. It takes some doing, as I have to pretend to knock it from my lap onto the floor by mistake, but the Russian moves his hand and allows me to slip underneath to retrieve it. The tablecloth drapes down enough to give the space under the large round table a tent-like Bedouin feel, but I'm the only woman in this particular harem.

I love being ambidextrous, I think it gives me a certain edge at these business dinners, especially when two of my client's clients need distracting at once. Two zips are eased down at once, two cocks freed from tight underwear, one hard, one hardening. I check for cheese, spit on one, and rub it clean as sensually as I can, then wipe my hand on the carpet. Bobbing my head between them both, sucking the heads, swirling my tongue, and wanking them hard, I mentally doff my cap at the one who wasn't pawing my crotch a minute ago for not so much as flinching as I reached for his cock.

Unsurprisingly, the fingerfucker cums first, grabbing my head under the table while he spunks at my tonsils. I suck him clean, swallow, then finish off his co-worker with a tickle of the balls. Grabbing my fork from the floor, I slip up into my seat as gracefully as I can, sip vodka to rinse the taste from my mouth, then smile at Neil. He looks a lot happier, sitting back in his seat instead of leaning towards the other businessmen, and I'm pleased. I'm also glad to see the lights have dimmed near our table.

I check my reflection using the back of a knife. I'm glad the lip-sealant that gives my food such a bitter aftertaste has done its job while my mouth was working on suckjobs. A waiter brings a tray of coffee and mints, and I discreetly palm three of the strong white sweets. I'm looking forward to going back to Neil's hotel room for a nice long soak. He *always* books a suite with a Jacuzzi. I suspect it's to conceal his farts from whoever is sharing the tub.

Then I feel hands on my thighs again. Hands. Plural. I ease my legs as far apart as I can, so my knees are hard against my neighbours' legs, in the vain hope that their hands won't meet somewhere in the middle. I don't want any conflict near my crotch. Resting my head on my hand, I dangle a napkin from my palm as if I've forgotten I'm holding it in the vodka fog now lingering around our booth, and lean my elbow on the table. I try and look like I'm concentrating on what Neil is saying to the Russian on the far left while I clasp the most senior Russian, my neighbour on the left, by the hand and guide it to my boob, then pull my dress down below the nipple. For whatever reason, guys don't feel like they're handling enough of your tit until they touch nipple. The way I'm holding my arm, my bare breast is unlikely to be seen.

When Neil raises his index finger for the bill, the Russians withdraw their hands, leaving me free to rearrange my chest and hemline. We scoot round the table, stand up, and say our goodbyes, and I pop a couple of mints in my mouth before Neil takes my arm and leads me out to the street.

"Whatever you did to them, it was bloody brilliant – I closed the deal!"

He moves in to kiss me. I put a finger on his lips and smile.

"Menthol makes you tingle. I want to celebrate with you and suck you dry … just let me crunch this mint first."

Not spring not winter

by Susan Tepper

Plans must be revised. Schools changed. I light a cigarette and sit back in my barcalounger. Some woman I once tried to fuck sat there after things didn't work out. She sat there naked. Her breasts hung like half-filled feed bags for a horse. After she left, I sniffed the fake leather seat but it still didn't get me off.

Twice this week I noticed a person in a uniform looking toward my car as I drove up to the fenced part, where the shrubbery is thickest. The fence that separates the little kiddies, my little darlings, from me and the rest of the world. I don't give a fuck about the rest of the world. Let's be clear on that. But the damned motherfucker in uniform had this laser vision that I swear could pop holes in the side of my car. I just kept going. It's been a few days. No little darlings to watch at their play on the jungle gym or tossing balls to each other. Those sweet hands reaching, reaching, grasping the ball.

Swoon the white rat sits on my lap. I finger his genitals. Genitalia. A lilting word. Italian in origin? *Genitaliaaaaaaaaaaaa* I sing out like an opera star. Then decide to cruise the school yard at California Avenue. It's almost lunch time, time for recess. I stamp out the cigarette in a Las Vegas ashtray; a showgirl type with good, full boobs glazed into the bottom.

At California Avenue if all looks safe I will stop the car. It's a good name. There should be palm trees.

I get into my black windbreaker. Putting Swoon in the windbreaker pocket, I head out. The day is blustery – not spring not winter. I am this weather. Nothing. It occurs to me staring up at the grey sky. Neither man nor beast is who am I. Swoon wiggling my pocket. I have this urge to squeeze his neck till it runs dry.

Fevered

by Jessica McHugh

Edward McKenzie blows his nose on the last tissue and grumbles at his reflection. His pallid face and bright red nose make him look like a clown – or his mother Betty on a bender.

Closing his eyes, he pats his nose with the powder puff. Even his brain-thumping congestion can't sever what the scent conjures. He breathes in, and Eleanor sits beside him. With a smile, she takes the powder puff and hands him a bowl of chicken noodle soup.

Get better first, dear. There's no one here to impress.

Edward groans. "Thanks for reminding me."

He cinches his robe and pulls off his wig, but the hair snags on his crucifix. Tearing it free, he breaks the chain, and the crucifix falls into the Duska powder on the dressing table. Sighing, he plucks it out and sets it aside.

"I'm sorry, Grandma. You're not to blame for my problems."

Darling, your problems only grow as big you allow – the more you nourish them, the stronger they get. Be a bad gardener for once.

She tweaks his raw nose and grabs the spoon. Ladling broth into his mouth, she warms him with more than soup.

When the phone rings, the spoon falls, clanging on the dressing table. He flinches at the sound: Edward doesn't receive many calls. Pressing the receiver to his ear, he squeaks. "Hello?"

"Hello. May I speak to Father Edward McKenzie, please?"

"This is he."

"Oh, Edward, I didn't recognize your voice. It's Father Timothy Ballard."

He sniffles. "I have a cold," he says. "What can I do for you, Timothy?"

"This won't take long. I just wanted to ask if you were interested in filling Father Sheridan's spot at St. Anthony's this summer?" Father Ballard says. "It's a summer health studies class with approximately thirteen eighth graders. It should only last a month at most." After a silence, he clears his throat and continues. "If you're not comfortable, I understand. I just thought you might enjoy a change of scenery. You've seemed a little down lately."

Edward holds his breath. Except for Eleanor, he assumes most people don't notice his emotions.

"The position wouldn't begin until June. Are you interested?"

Edward looks over to see Grandma Eleanor nod. *This could be what you've been waiting for.*

His mind whirs, the words jumbled. But his answer tumbles out in a powerful, "Yes, I'll *do* it!"

"Excellent. You're really helping us out of a jam."

Father Timothy says goodbye, but Edward doesn't hang up. A voice speaks to him from the other end. His mother's biting words tell him to call Timothy back and refuse the position.

"Children, Edward. You and children. If you can't see the trouble there, you're sicker than I thought," she says.

His vision fogs with fever. Standing in a corner, Betty taps her cane. "A thing like you shouldn't be around kids. And a health class? What does a cross-dressing freak like you know about being healthy?"

"I would never do anything to hurt a child."

"Not intentionally, but your perversion could spread just the same. What if a child asks about homosexuality? Would you advise him to pursue that life?"

His throat is dry, and it hurts to swallow. "I will teach the curriculum," he says. Betty scoffs, swinging her cane as she strides toward him. He collapses back onto the couch, sweat pouring down his face.

"You'll lie," she says. "Lie, lie, lie – that's all you do, Edward. From your secret desires to your insane visions." He squints at her, and she snickers. "What, you didn't think I knew about Eleanor? How you see her, how you speak to her?"

He screams "Stop!" but Betty steps closer, her cane moving up his leg. It flips up his robe, exposing his garters.

He covers his legs and stands, the fever spinning his vision. He stumbles, knocking against the dressing table. The soup spills, and the bowl breaks on the floor.

Edward wheezes in torment, bent over the mess. The hand on his back comforts, so he knows it can't be his mother's.

Ssh … It's okay, Edward, calm down.

Lifting his head, cold sweat runs off his chin. His mother is gone. The pain subsides.

"Eleanor …"

Yes, I'm here.

"I don't know what I'm going to do. I took a teaching position – I agreed to – oh God Almighty, I'm so confused."

She pats his hair. *The fever's breaking, dear. You'll be all right.*

Gasping at the mess on the floor, she crouches to clean it. Edward stops her, holds her hands, and whispers, "I think I made the biggest mistake of my life."

She touches her hand to his cheek and smiles.

Oh Edward. If a man spends his life trying not to make mistakes and remains unhappy, perhaps allowing a mistake is the first and greatest step to joy.

All Greased Up, Nowhere to Go

by Shane Simmons

Stood outside the Chinese buffet restaurant, I wait alone. Inside, it's already packed. Through the steamed-up windows I watch them, gathered around melamine tables, gorging upon mountainous plate-loads, forks shovelling mounds of grease into open gobs.

I shudder.

A man, at least three times my size, walks out of the door and brings with him the inviting smells of chow mein, roast pork and five spice. I haven't eaten since breakfast, and my stomach rumbles. Then I turn my nose up when the enticement is lost in the haze of the big man's cigarette smoke.

The mobile in my hand beeps.

"See you soon!!!!!!!!!!!!!" I roll my eyes and hit 'delete'. Having already been kept waiting a good half-hour, I tap my feet wondering just what 'soon' means in Sandra's world.

She wants my opinion on her new bloke; not that my opinion has ever counted for shit before. This is the one night we all happen to be free. Must remember not to call him Stephen. Stephen – "That Bastard" – was the previous one, but I'm sure it won't be long until this one becomes an honorary bastard too. I feel a tad guilty for writing off the guy before I've set eyes on him, but in Sandra's life, history is always playing on repeat.

Farther down the road I spot her marching up, one hand waving cobwebs out of the sky, her other arm entwined with the companion she's marching beside.

"Sorry we're late, we got, 'erm' ... delayed!" She winks as she disentangles herself from her companion and leaning in, gives me a peck on the cheek. I cringe as I try to bleach the image she's conjured from my mind.

"This is Marlon! I've told him ALL about you!"

I offer my hand to him but it hangs mid-air, waiting, as he plays away with his mobile. Eventually, with his eyes still glued to his phone, his hand brushes past my own and it feels more like a tickle than a firm, hetero handshake.

"I trust it was all positive." I know Sandra has a habit of revealing the little dirt she has on me to all and sundry.

"When it comes to you, what good is there to say?"

She drags her man through the glass doors of the restaurant. Under my breath I whisper, "Bitch."

We're directed to our very own melamine table, and whilst a waitress hurriedly clears away empty dishes I observe my dining partners. Sandra's tarted right up tonight, she's been a bit over-zealous with the make-up and bats her lengthy false lashes in all directions. Her cleavage pours over a taut, low-cut top like pale blancmange. Marlon is a walking billboard, designer names emblazoned from head to toe: a Voi tee, Diesel jeans and Timberland boots. He sports a much slighter frame than the buff, muscled picture Sandra had painted, and atop it all is a hairless dome, fluorescent reflections catching the dimples of his glistening scalp.

As we look over the drinks menu, Sandra caresses his arm. I stop counting at twenty downward strokes. Everything about this guy seems over-thought. His teak-tone surely came from a tanning salon, and the sapphire blue sparkle of his eyes can only be contact lenses. The corner of his lips curls upwards, giving him a permanent grimace.

It's too early to judge this book by its cover, but he'd already got my back up over that first handshake. Don't people shake hands these days?

Sandra alone chatters through our deep-fried starters. In a vague attempt to cancel out the saturated fats I have flanked mine with some wilting salad. With my first bite into a piece of battered chicken my mouth swims with the taste of old cooking oil and luminous red sweet and sour dipping sauce. Every other item tastes of little more than the grease that killed it.

"Marlon was telling me about all the gays he works with in the hospital!" She pokes his arm, "You should set up our singleton with one!"

"Oh, there's loads of poof −"

From the sharp *THWACK* that comes up from under our table, I feel the kick Sandra gives him.

She whispers loud enough for me to hear, "Only the gays are allowed to use that word Marlon!" A bellowing but embarrassed laugh bursts from her bosom, just as a waiter walking past, laden with a tray of dishes piled high, wobbles, the plates rattle, and the tray topples. I turn away as they smash, and see chunks of white whiz by my feet.

We've yet to delve into the main course, and already I want to leave.

"Ooh, that little disaster reminds me, I've needed a wee since before we got here!" The clip of Sandra's high-heels trails off towards the toilets, leaving Marlon and myself sitting in silence whilst the waiter sweeps the shrapnel up from around us.

"You two met at the hospital?" I say, taking a shot at conversation.

Staring down at his plate and twirling noodles, he grunts. He puts down his fork, picks up his phone and taps away at the screen.

Before her backside hits the chair again Sandra blurts, "We've been talking about moving in together." She jiggles her arm around his shoulder, and pushes her boobs against his bicep.

"But you've only known each other for a few —"

"You wouldn't understand." She swats the air in front of my face. "It just feels right, doesn't it, honey?" She picks up her fork and prods him with it, "I think it would be lovely! Wouldn't it?"

Marlon's face scrunches up. Sandra turns to him, baring puppy eyes along with a cheek-splitting grin, and quickly, his expression drops out, flat.

She always does this. She finds the odd half-decent man, and they're picking out new curtains and matching duvet sets before they've been given the chance to find her G-spot.

"Marlon's staying at mine tonight, aren't ya babes?" She pinches his cheek and he pulls away. "We'll all get a taxi back together."

I wish I had something else to do, someone to meet, somewhere to go. Some paint to watch dry.

Sandra lays her head upon Marlon's shoulder. It reminds me of that photo Aunt Patricia gave me last month, the one I'd stashed away at the back of a drawer.

All the way back I stare out the cab window, scanning the couples drinking, smoking, snogging, groping outside bars and pubs on the Saturday night streets, turned away from the sights and snorts of Sandra molesting her man.

Having slid out of the taxi, Sandra sways on her high heels, grabbing Marlon's arse and giggling like a horny teenager.

"I'll be offski. Was nice to meet you." I decide against formalities or handshakes and start up the road.

"Hold on, you!" Sandra slurs, "Does my lover boy get the thumbs up?"

I grit my teeth. "I reckon he's in for more than just the thumbs up tonight."

Sandra's laugh echoes across the street. "I'll text you tomorrow my lovely gay!"

I step up the pace. And find myself contemplating just how anyone could fuck on a full stomach.

And for one last time tonight, I'm left trying to erase *that* image from my mind.

No. 2 Pencil

by Michelle Elvy

"Got a pencil?" Rick leans across the aisle between the rows of desks toward his friend and holds out his hand.

Stevie reaches for his backpack under his desk. He knows he has an extra pencil – he's got several sharpened No. 2 pencils in his bag, plus a sandwich and an orange. He's pissed about having to come to school on a Sunday to take a test but the test was cancelled yesterday when the fire alarm repeatedly blew and finally the teachers sent everyone home for the day.

And now this – having the misfortune of sitting next to Rick.

He takes longer to pull the extra pencils out than he needs. It's not that he doesn't want to loan Rick the pencil. Or is it? Maybe it's that he doesn't want to loan Rick anything. He's pretty sure he won't get it back. And Rick's been walking around like a douche all semester. He doesn't even act like anything's happened.

As Stevie reaches into his backpack he weighs what he dislikes about Rick, starting with the fact that he knows it was Rick – *Rickie* back then – who stole his Star Wars lunchbox in the seventh grade. It was not from the new series either; it was vintage, from the original *ancient* series from his parents' wonder years. Rick walked around for days talking about how he'd been given a collector's item lunchbox by his Aunt Barbara, but Stevie knew from Manny – his best friend and Rick's cousin – that Aunt Barbara was rarely in the gift-giving mood. Besides, a small dent on the bottom of the lunchbox, right near Luke's shoulder, could only have happened from a drop off the lunch table, which Stevie put there, not Rick. But Rick had been clever enough to keep his new lunchbox at a distance, and eventually Stevie let it go, probably when Rick found something new to brag about.

But there's more. All through Junior High Rick asked Stevie for help with homework. As soon as Stevie would arrive at school, Rick would casually saunter up with a, "Dude, do you have the answers to last night's math?" Or "Let me glance at your history notes, dude." Like it was Stevie's job to help Rick make up for his deficient brain cells. This combined with his bleached blond hair and faux-swimmer's gait was too much. Stevie was an OK swimmer but Rick's blond head sat atop broad swimmer's shoulders and every summer at the community pool he'd strut around with his hair flowing, just because he was on the Junior Lifeguard Squad. Who bleached his hair at age thirteen? Rick – that's who. And he got everyone to notice him, doing a dive off the high dive, or flirting with Marie Wallace. He even got his left hand under her bra at one football game in seventh grade – making him all the more unbearable.

"Dude ..." It's Rick, still leaning across the aisle. "Sucks being here, man. I hate these fuckin' tests. But better'n church, huh?"

Stevie fumbles a little more in his backpack, wants to say *Dude, shut the fuck up* but just ignores Rick and his stupid sense of cool. His mind drifts back to the weekend before the accident, early in January, when Rick told him he was "halfway there" with Ellie Smithers. The way Rick talked about Ellie Smithers made Stevie's blood boil. What the fuck was "halfway" anyway? He wanted to know, and he didn't want to know. He didn't understand why he felt so protective of Ellie. Maybe because she was Lucky's girlfriend. But it was more likely a feeling that nothing good could come of her being anywhere near Rick Sawyer. He sensed a path of self-destruction, and he could only watch from afar. He wasn't close enough to say anything. Sure, they'd talked a few times because she came along pretty often. She'd even asked him once about how to break into a car. He liked that she was interested in his skills. He let himself imagine it meant more than it did.

Then there was the day of the accident, that cold January morning, him being boxed into the back seat next to Ellie and Rick (the memory of it makes his head spin all over again), while Lucky sat up front with Manny, stoned and oblivious. He knew he should be angry at Ellie but he wasn't; he was angry at Rick. He might even hate him. He thinks he does now, anyway, since Rick's been a dick since the accident. He didn't even show up at the funeral. And now it's been months and Rick just struts around with his swimmer shoulders, like the most important thing about this semester is that it's the last one ever for them. Not that the most important thing – the thing Stevie'll never forget about this year – is that Lucky never saw it through.

"He's dead, man, he's fucking dead!" Stevie shouts. But he only shouts it in his own mind. He also pummels Rick's face in his mind – may as well, while he's there. In reality, he's still reaching in his bag and drifting back to January 13. He recalls Lucky's last funny grin, from his passenger seat back to where Stevie sat. He'll never forget that grin. Unlucky Lucky. And then the curve, the flip, the feeling of being airborne, the dream, the floating, the flames, the smell, the turbulent sky and inevitable cornfield where his body touched down. Now he sees his Great-grandpa Gus again, like in the dream, only this time he sees Lucky too, and he can't shake that grin. He'll see it for the rest of his life. Fuckin' Lucky.

A weak sob catches in his chest. He needs air.

"The test will begin in one minute," says a voice from the front of the classroom.

Stevie's fingers wrap around several pencils in his bag. He pulls out a yellow No. 4 from art class, hands it over.

"Here you go, Rickie."

"Thanks, dude."

Country Stars

by Len Kuntz

I wake up in a wheat field, shivering, with something crawling across my face. My first instinct is to flick it away, but I steady myself, as a spider steps over the bridge of my nose.

"You're awake," Heather says. Heather. I picked her up at a cowboy bar back in Fargo and it was her idea to come here because she said the stars from this site were so big they looked like freight cars.

Before the spider can scram, Heather crushes it between her fingers and says, "Your nose is ice cold."

Heather is the first redhead I've ever kissed, ever touched for that matter. Her skin is so freckled it's as if she's been splashed with cinnamon. But she's a bit husky and so some of those freckles look about as big as buttons.

"You hungry?" she asks.

"Not really."

"I'm starving," Heather says, dipping under the sleeping bag and rooting around for my penis.

Afterward, we drive to her place, even though I have a bad feeling about it.

On the way, Heather nuzzles my neck and rubs my thigh and keeps going for my groin, which is more tender than when I was a kid and took a line drive to the crotch. She's leaning on me, making it difficult to drive. "A little room here," I say, but Heather just gets even closer, licking my right nostril.

She lives in a trailer park where the world's skinniest cats slink around heaps of trash, rusted oil drums, abandoned refrigerators and water coolers. Hers is a faded blue thing, shaped like a loaf of bread, near the rear.

I kiss her at the door, feeling sheepish, not knowing how to say goodbye in a way that won't make me seem sleazy.

Heather grabs my wrist so sudden it startles me, and then she's tugging me inside where an enormous woman sits around a table smoking, wearing a corduroy robe that looks to have been gnawed on by a legion of rats.

The woman doesn't bother getting up when I'm introduced, probably because the effort would require a crane.

Heather calls her "Momma." She tells Momma that I'm her boyfriend. "We watched stars all night," Heather says. "Well, not all night," Heather grins, winking.

"Good … for … you … girl," Momma says, the words coming out slow, as if from a stroke victim.

When I say, "We just met," Momma says, "Yeah … shit," and winks at me through a dragon of smoke.

"Come on," Heather says, yanking on my arm again. "My room's in the back."

Her room is only fifteen feet away because this is a very small trailer. I can smell what Momma had for dinner (liver and onions) and when she last used the toilet (very recently). Everything mixes with the pungent odor of cat piss, Budweiser and wet dog.

Heather locks the door behind me, pushing me on her bed so that a cloud of dust fills the air. Her sweater comes off in a jiff before she goes for the zipper on my pants.

71

"Hey," I say, "what are you doing?"

"If you thought you saw God last night, this morning the Holy Ghost is showing up."

"I can't."

"You don't have to do anything. Just lay back and enjoy the rodeo."

"Really," I say, "I can't."

Heather keeps struggling for a grip.

"I mean it."

Then she bites me on the arm.

"What the hell?"

"Let's do it rough."

When I jump off the bed she lunges. I try to shrug her off but she nips at my neck and claws my chin with jagged nails. I hear Momma let out a trombone fart.

"Heather wait, I'm married."

"So am I," she says.

She won't get off me.

"I have herpes," I lie.

"So do I!" she says.

I've never hit a girl in my life, but I don't see how I'm going to get her off me.

"Okay," I say. "Okay, but can I use the bathroom first? I have to pee so bad, I'll never get an erection."

"You can give me a golden shower if you want."

"You're kidding."

"Just don't get any in my eyes."

"I think I'll take a pass on that."

"Spoilsport."

She shows me to the bathroom. It's coat closet-small and reeks of feces. There's a window, but it's tiny and closed and I'd never be able to fit through it, even as skinny as I am.

Heather's shadow is under the door. "Hurry up," she says. "Now I have to go, too."

"I might be a while. I've got to do the other."

"Take a dump?"

I've always hated when people say that, and now it makes me feel filthy. "Yes."

"It doesn't bother me. When nature calls, what're you gonna do?"

"Well, I'm sort of shy about that kind of thing."

"You're shy," Heather chuckles. "Yeah, right."

"A little privacy. Please? Constipated sex is no good."

She thinks this over. "Well, okay, but squeeze that brick out fast as you can. I'll go pee outside."

"Thanks. I'll be done in less than five minutes."

"Better be," she says.

I wait thirty seconds, then fly out of the bathroom, but big Momma has somehow managed to get out of the chair and she's blocking my way, intentionally or otherwise I can't tell, so my only option is to tuck my head and ram her belly. It's like diving into a vat of hamburger. I do it again, using my shoulders, but she only grunts. Finally I grab one of her massive legs and when she falls backward the whole trailer rocks.

Heather comes in buttoning her pants. "What the hell happened?"

"She fell," I say. "I think she might be having a stroke."

"Oh god! Momma!"

When Heather bends down to check on the huge woman, I jump over Momma and sprint out the front door.

"Where are you going?" Heather calls.

Two black Rottweilers come ripping down the road toward me. I make it inside the car and start the motor before they leap against my window. I back out, tires spitting dirt and pebbles. I switch gears and gun the accelerator. One dog flies off the hood, the other squeals. In the rearview Heather is running after me, shouting and waving her arm, holding what looks to be a butcher's knife.

Tuesday, 15th April 2014

Fourth Inning

by Michael Webb

It isn't baseball weather. Grey and forbidding, with a misting rain falling out of low, angry clouds, it's soup and blanket weather for most, but just another early season day in another city for us. Nobody wants to play – not the sparse group of diehard fans huddled under cover; not the umpires, huddled inside until the last possible moment; not the grounds crew warming their hands over the hot dog steam; and certainly not the players, conscious of the fragile bodies they are compensated so well for using. But the remorseless logic of the schedule, which doesn't bring us back here until August, forces us to try and play.

I come out to test the air, immediately concluding that I need another layer. I go back down the tunnel, the concrete wet, the black plastic across the floor clotted with mud and grass and spilled Gatorade already. The visitors' clubhouse is in muted grays and blues, with black partitions for dressing. I make my way through the nearly empty room, the rest of my mates already plodding around the wet field, or stomping and shivering in the dugout behind me. The sweatshirt I want is gone from the hook where I left it, filched by a comrade who didn't want to look for his own. I glance around, but none are available, so I look into the trainer's room.

I recognize immediately the bare back and shaggy mane of Tex Holman, our new flame-throwing bullpen savior, his muscles impressively laid out around a Texas Longhorns tattoo at the small of his back. He makes a hissing sound, straightening up with what looks like a syringe in his enormous right hand. The plunger is down, and he withdraws the needle from his quadriceps with practiced speed, rubbing the spot briskly with his other palm.

He senses me and twists halfway around.

"Twainie!" he says in his friendliest tone. "Just a little B12, man." In the faux casual world of baseball, even nicknames have nicknames, so my nom de guerre, Mark Twain, because of my habit of reading on planes and buses, becomes "Twainie".

"B12?" I say, nodding. "Sure. Just getting a sweatshirt." I take one from the pile on a side table, checking the size on the tag then slipping it on over my head. "Cold as hell, man," I say conversationally.

"Yeah?" the huge reliever says, standing to his full height, broad and thick like a pro wrestler. He pulls up his uniform pants, staring back at me. "Thanks for the update."

"Alright," I say, backing out the door. "See you out there."

"You bet, MT." His exalted role on the team means he doesn't have to join the bullpen until the game is half over. Less well-paid and more fungible commodities like me have to spend the whole game out there. I walk back down the corridor, and then out onto the field, trudging out onto the slick surface.

It could have been B12, but who self-administers something unless you want to keep it quiet? Simple self-interest tells me to keep my own counsel – a winning team raises all boats, which means we all get wealthier. And clubhouse omerta says the same – in the insular world of baseball, a reputation as a snitch gets you frozen out as quickly as a fading fastball would.

I am envious of his hulking physique, the simple equalizer of being able to put the ball up there into the triple digits in a tight spot. I'd love to have his endorsements, his fashion model girlfriends, his talk show popularity. I know, or I think I know, that he got there by skirting the rules. I am confident he is going to take his money and, after his elbow comes apart like a truck tire on the highway, live out his life as the former star felled by injury. On the rare occasion that someone asks about steroids, I use the old chestnut that I want to be able to look my children in the face and tell them I tried my hardest without bending the rules. I think about my children, their open faces and their belief that everyone plays fair, and I think about how Holman makes more in a month than I make in half a year, and I keep trudging towards the bullpen in the soaking mist.

A Dose of the Leather

by James Claffey

The windows are covered with frost and the Bird sees his breath in the air as he exhales. Melodie went back home to France last week when she found out her brother had a stroke and was in a coma. He touches the place setting where she had sat the evening before she took off for the ferry – a lace doily of his mother's – and kissed him farewell in the hall. Oh, well, he thinks, stripping the linens from the table and getting the sandpaper out of his toolbox. It's about time the table was sanded and stained again, he thinks, and sets about turning the dark stained wood to pale. He doesn't notice the frost melting and the steam rising from the road outside. Instead he says her name on each push of sandpaper – Melodie, in. Melodie, out. Melodie, in. Melodie, out.

With the table stripped of varnish he settles down in the parlor and sups a glass of stout. The floor is patterned with sawdust and he trails the toe of his shoe in the dust, spelling out her name. After several minutes he stops, pushes back his chair, and drags a foot through the crude letters. "To hell with her!" he shouts, and takes his hat and coat from the rack, all set for the snug of the nearest bar. Nothing like a quiet spot on a chilly Wednesday in Lent. This is the first year he's not given up the drop for the season, what with the Mammy and Daddy dead and buried there's no one to hold him to the pledge.

Trade is slow in McEgan's, the religious weight of the season keeping all but the reckless and the few Protestants in town from their sup. The Bird casts his mind on the strange dreams of his mother he's been plagued with since her death. Some of them so vivid he could almost touch the apparition, the dreams sent him to the doctor, who looked with interest in the Bird's ears and nose, as if searching for traces of his mother's ghost. At the end of the examination, the doctor rubbed his hands together at speed, and declared the Bird to be "as fit as a fiddle," and to "pay no attention to visitors in the night time, unless they're attractive young ladies scantily clad." He sips from the pint and pulls at the long stiff hairs coming out of his ears. Nervous tics are the Bird's refuge and he finds the incessant stroking of these hairs to be calming.

Enough taken as far as drink goes, the Bird steps out into the cold air and strolls down to Mahony's turf accountants to place a few bob on a tip he got from the priest after Sunday Mass. "Goldfinch, two quid each way," he tells the spotty young lad behind the glass as he pushes his few notes across the counter. Receipt in hand, he nestles into a corner and waits for the race to begin. Three or four other men, all clad in raincoats and Wellingtons, hold copies of the *Racing Post* and wear intense looks. The commentator on the TV calls the race, and out of the gate the Goldfinch meanders along behind the rest of the horses. "Get up, you bitch," the Bird hisses. The other men appear not to have a stake in the same horse as the Bird. They slap folded newspapers against palms and thighs, egging their charges forward.

As the horses near the last turn, Goldfinch is twenty lengths behind the pack and the Bird tears his ticket stub into flitters. So much for the doctor's "tip." The man wouldn't know a decent horse if it bit him on the arse. The

Bird confettis the ticket into the trash and heads off into the grey of the afternoon.

Over the steeple of the church the sun does its best to lighten the afternoon, like an old friend attempting to give solace to the bereaved. The clouds thicken once more and a rain shower sheds its weight on the village. The Bird wishes he could transport himself all the way to Melodie's side and enjoy the confusion of listening to a language he cannot comprehend. She told him she might not be back for months, at least until her brother's diagnosis is clear. Unlike the Bird's, Melodie's parents are alive and well, in a small rural town near Le Havre.

He perches on a bench along the church wall, the stones mossy and damp, a few starlings dotting the low branches of the old oaks. All around him the smell and feel of spring, a few daffodils poking their butter yellow blooms into the air, the scent of softer earth now the thaw is here, and all he can think about is how much he misses her. Odd, he thinks, how he'd never had those feelings for another woman before. When his mammy had been alive the Bird rarely found himself in the company of unmarried women, having to always be around the house in case either of his parents needed an errand run. As a lad he'd gone to a few hops in the local GAA club on a Saturday night, but the loud music and the smoky room didn't suit him at all. From the bench he watches the few cars and bicycles pass by on the street, raising a hand in greeting every so often. Not a bad life, he thinks. Not bad.

The local schoolteacher rides past on her bicycle and the Bird remembers his own classroom days, the batterings from the teachers, the sting of the leather strap the headmaster used on the boys. Nothing like a dose of the leather to make you toe the line, he thinks. As he sits on the bench he takes in the changes in the town, the new video rental shop, the fancy German grocery, the boarded-up cobbler's shop where he'd go as a lad and inhale the glue and leather smell with relish. There was a time when a stranger like Melodie would have been as rare as a hen's tooth, but now, with the Eurozone and all that, well, there are foreigners in every crevice of the country. Fair play, the Bird thinks, picturing the lovely smile he wishes he could reach out and touch.

The Bird unmoors from the bench and wanders down to the river where mallards float unmoved by the cold. His daddy loved the ducks, always bringing the Bird along with him on Sunday afternoons, a bag of breadcrumbs in his pocket, relishing the way the ducks would line up at their feet for a sprinkling of food. In the water, the ripples from a diving bird spread outward in circles, and in the broken mirror of the past the Bird sees his father holding his hand, the bread dropping like snow into the throng of waiting ducks.

The Rules We Shall Die By

by Gwendolyn Joyce Mintz

"Vince says he's not coming," Aaron tells the group when he returns to the table. He was outside making a call. He plops down, slips his cell phone in his shirt pocket and alternates a glare between Diane and Phil. "What did you two do?"

Diane frowns at him. "We didn't *do* anything. We simply stated an opinion: you shouldn't be selfish when you kill yourself. You can think about others." She leans back in the booth, crosses her arms in front of her. "He's not nice, anyway; he said I knew way too much about celebrity deaths."

"You do," Mora says from across the table.

"You know they fascinate me," Diane replies without turning to her friend.

"Why is that?" Phil asks. "I was gonna ask the last time but then Vince said you should spend more time on your own death and things just went downhill."

Mora answers for Diane. "Things that she doesn't understand make her crazy so she obsesses over them in an effort to understand."

"We think celebrities have everything, but they must not if some would rather die than enjoy said things," Diane adds.

Phil nods.

Aaron waits a moment. "Okay, but back to Vince."

"If he wanted to die, he would have made it."

Aaron is about to reply but Diane continues, "You said some meetings ago that if you want to die, this is the place to be. So he's obviously not as committed or he'd be here."

"Yep," Mora says.

Aaron shoots her a look that suggests she needn't chime in.

She smiles at him. "What?" she says.

"I thought we were going to talk about dying and getting it done," Diane says.

With a sigh, Aaron nods in agreement. "I know, I know. The rate I'm going, I might be alive come January."

Mora covers his hand with hers.

Aaron takes a breath. Her touch. He inches his hand from under hers. "So what do we do now?"

"Well, I'd like for us to talk about the reasons why we want to die," Phil offers.

Diane nods. "We need to tell our stories."

"I'm still undecided," Mora tells them, "but I do want to bear witness to your journeys."

Diane smiles. "That's beautiful," she says before turning to Aaron. "Did you think about some rules, like I suggested, you being the de facto president of the club?"

"I did some thinking, yes. Like, are we going to say goodbye?"

"I think we should," Diane answers. "A group text isn't too much to ask. I can do that while the pills take effect." She giggles.

Mora shakes her head, rolls her eyes.

"Okay, okay." Aaron signals the server, asks for something to write on and with.

She returns with several sheets of copier paper and a pen.

Aaron scribbles on the page. "What about funerals? Do we attend?"

After considering it, Mora says, "It might be awkward; it's not like you could say, 'I'm glad they finally did it.'"

There's murmuring among them as the group agrees.

Aaron continues to write.

After some time, he sets the pen down and pushes a page to the center of the table. "It's a start," he says.

Diane lifts the page and reads. She nods. She asks Aaron for the pen, then she signs her name. She passes the paper and pen to Phil. He reads, signs and hands the sheet to Mora.

She signs.

"We can amend or add as time goes on. If more people join," Aaron says. "But for now these are the rules we shall die by." He takes the page from Mora and rereads what he's written.

We, the undersigned, agree to the following:

1. *When we decide that our time to die has come, we will contact the other members of "The Suicide Club" and let them know. We agree that we will simply say 'goodbye.'*
2. *We will not attend any memorial service or funeral related to any member. We will celebrate any and all former members of "The Suicide Club" at the next monthly meeting.*
3. *We will not discuss with any one, other than the members of the club, any deaths that have occurred.*
4. *We will support each member in his or her efforts to end his or her life. Rather than report any member to any organization which would deter said member from his or her wishes, each of us agrees to leave the club instead.*
5. *We will not judge what has brought members here.*
6. *We will hold what happens at any meeting as well as what is said in strict confidence.*

"We should wrap up on this note," Aaron tells them. "It feels right." He sets the paper down.

As they stand, Mora asks, "Are you going to conduct another membership drive?"

Aaron laughs. "No, I just think that there may be others like us and it doesn't seem right, somehow, for this club to just die with us."

Friday, 18th April 2014

That Earthy Trace

by Stephen V. Ramey

I sip coffee from a sampling cup. The taste is heavy, slightly sweet, a hint of clay. What better way to kick off Good Friday?

"Sumatra Lintong," the barista says. "Do you like it?" She's a perky redhead with a generous smile. Her nametag says *Sara*. What I like is the way her attention remains on me even as other customers line up. The world has enough multi-taskers.

"Pour me a double," I say.

Sara turns to the machine. I look around. The Confluence is relatively new, and quite ambitious for New Castle, a cavernous community center / coffee shop / art studio in the downtown historic district. It stays busy and attracts a younger crowd, but probably not busy enough or young enough. For years New Castle has been struggling to change its identity. We're the city that time and politics destroyed, the city that does not deserve better.

Opposite the coffee area is a low stage. I keep meaning to come down here to see a local band. So many things I keep meaning to do. Right now, I'm supposed to be at a doctor's appointment, a urologist to be precise. He gave me prostate cancer materials to research last time, and I'm supposed to decide on a treatment regimen today. I'm not good at decisions. So here I sit in The Confluence a half-hour after my appointment, cell phone turned off in my pocket. I have no idea what I'll tell Anne, but I'm a writer, I'll think of something. Maybe I'll say I'm cured. *It's a damned miracle.* Like Jesus rising on the third day.

Sara sets a cup before me. I reach for my wallet, only to see Anne walking through the front door. Panic deep-freezes my bowels. *My God, she heard me thinking!* Head down, I start toward the back of the building.

"Hey," Sara says.

Shit. I grab a bill from the wallet.

"Don't you want your change?" She stretches a twenty between her hands. *Great.* At the door, Anne frowns. She's seen me, or thinks she has.

"Keep it." I drag the cell phone from my pocket and pretend to answer as I duck behind a section of staggered wall. I should have remembered Anne had an Earth Day meeting this morning. It was on the calendar: *Confluence 9:30 – Earth Day.* She's been working with a planning committee for six months now. How stupid of me to come here. What was I thinking?

Fortunately the back door isn't locked. I push through and risk a glance back as it hisses closed. Anne is coming. She does not look happy.

I feel like a bug caught on the counter when the light snaps on. Riverplex Park is a y-shaped expanse of concrete bound by wrought iron fence on one side and a busy road on the other. There's no place to hide. Then, I see yellow tape, an opening in the fence. *Yes!* The Riverwalk is under construction, crews cleaning up the bank for the new boardwalk.

I run, duck under the tape, and scramble down a path toward the river. Stones sprinkle. Minnows scatter. I pass through the underbelly shadow of a concrete bridge. Cars rumble above. On the opposite side people in orange vests pull weeds. A stocky man gives me a look, but doesn't try to stop me. Maybe it's no skin off his nose if I get poison ivy or drown. Or maybe, and I like this better, it's because I seem unstoppable.

The bank narrows until I'm mere inches from the river. A gurgle fills the basin. My stomach relaxes. I feel safe in this wrinkle hidden from the surface, water carrying the moment away as soon as it arrives. My witch friend, Rose, once said that I should live in the moment if I want to find peace. That's not easy for me. It's never the word at my fingertips that matters, but the word coming next, or the words already published below my byline.

My prostate gland – what I imagine it to be – shoots a sting through my body. I slow. Pain settles to a steady itch. I want to probe up there and scratch it, feel nodes flake away like dust. I want to be well. I want it to be over.

A patch of suds floats by, fertilizer or detergent or something else that does not belong. I think of Anne making my appointments, cooking my meals, cuddling me as I lay in bed worrying before sleep. She deserves so much better.

"Who the fuck are you?" A man in fatigues steps onto the path. Panic jolts me. I take a step back, but why? The city is a half-block away – I hear the traffic – and he's not exactly threatening. His frame is like scaffolding, his gaunt face scabbed. I'm thinking meth-head, but his eyes are very clear, very focused.

"You undercover?" he says. "Nah, you're no cop. Come here to party? What'd you bring?"

My hand goes to my back pocket. "I have a little cash, if that's what you want." I'm glad I gave the twenty to Sara.

The man shrugs. "Name's Scanner, what's yours?"

"I … Stephen." Explanations ebb into my thoughts. *I'm taking a stroll, looking for my dog, I'm lost.* I remember the rich aroma of coffee, Sara's smile. Honest things. "I'm a writer."

"You writing an article for *The News*?" Scanner says.

"I'm not exactly sure."

"Come on," he says. "I'll show you around Tent City. You like beer? We got a case of *Colt 45* this morning. We share stuff like that." He nods at the shirt pocket where I keep my idea notepad. "You want to write that down?"

"Later." I feel a shiver coming on and stamp my feet.

Scanner leads me into a cluster of budding maples and stunted black oaks a few yards from the river. A hand-made *No Trespasing* sign is stapled to one. I wonder if maybe I *should* write an article. I could use the distraction. No, that's what I always do. I need to stay focused on the novel.

We enter a clearing that smells of fish. Plywood lean-tos draped in plastic tarp form a ragged line. A bald man lies on his back under one.

"Stay away from him," Scanner says. "Don't know his name yet, just came down from Pittsburgh, eye all messed up. I think he's got the PTSDs."

A man sits in the next tent, shoulders curled forward.

"That's Jake," Scanner says. "He'll sober up in the afternoon. You should talk to him then, used to be a social worker, knows where the skeletons are and like that." He angles toward the neatest of the tents. "I'll take you to Tamara. She's the one you want to talk to first."

I don't actually want to talk to anyone, but a woman pushes out from the tarp right on cue. She's huge, taller than me, twice as broad. Her stringy hair is brown-red, the skin of her broad face pocked like a cratered moon. Her fringed leather jacket reminds me of the seventies.

"This is Stephen," Scanner says. "He's a writer, Tamara."

Tamara looks me over. "You're here to write?"

"Sure he is," Scanner says. "The glasses, the notebook in his pocket?" He nods to me. "Tell her you're a writer, Stephen."

I open my mouth – I *am* a writer – but Tamara's steady gaze stops me. "I don't know why I came."

She nods. "I sense your pain. You're alone, you want to join us. Was your home foreclosed?"

"I'm dying," I mumble. "Stage 4 cancer." Sadness numbs my senses. I want to curl onto the ground and cry, but I can't do that, not here in front of strangers.

"Hell, man, *everyone's* dying," Scanner says. "Some just don't notice it so much."

"My wife," I choke. I imagine Anne's blazing eyes, the fire of her determination. She won't let me die.

Tamara takes a tarnished flask from her pocket and presses it into my palm. "Drink this, Stephen. It will help."

I expect whiskey, but it's water, cold and sharp without a hint of chlorine.

"The river called you," Tamara says. "The blood and tears of Mother Earth, who holds us up when we would fall." She takes the flask back. "You should go now, Stephen. Come back when you're ready."

Flipping Out

by Gay Degani

Charmaine snorts at the mushroom smell of wet grout and curses her husband. White tile! Not even subway! Didn't she force him to watch hours of prerecorded HGTV just to avoid this kind of mistake? Marble equals updated. Tile, not so much. And still, he has the guy install it behind her back, while she's at his sister's fucking baby shower!

She pivots away, can't stand the sight of it, and bangs her toe. A tool, of course, one of Sam's. Left on the floor, not put away. She stoops and snatches the hammer, its wood handle smooth with age. Rust speckles the worn head, the curved claw. She tosses it hard onto the counter and it lands with a crack. She looks. Grins. Broken square of tile. Good. Serves him right.

But more than this is broken. Everything's broken. She growls. How she'd loved this house when they were scraping together the down payment, when all she saw was potential. Now she's overwhelmed with mold snaking through the basement, termites camped in the attic, the plumber who fell through the dining room ceiling, the gush of water that followed him down. Funny at the time, but the aftermath, the damage, the money, the delay …

She stalks into the bedroom where an air mattress fills one corner and throws herself onto the puddle of sheets. She wishes it wasn't Saturday, wishes Sam wasn't outside chopping up what's left of the sycamore that fell last January. She wants to wallow and he hates to see her wallow. But wouldn't that punish him for his thoughtlessness? How he tricked her while she was off witnessing his sister's glowing happiness? Is wallowing enough?

A thought makes her shiver. She knows she can't resist this urge. Doesn't want to.

In the bathroom, she lifts the hammer above her shoulder, catches sight of her face in the mirror. Her cheeks are flushed, her eyes glassy, a thick strand of brown hair bisects her face. She bends down, runs a hand roughly from the back of her scalp to the top, then tosses her head. Yes. This is who she is, the powerful woman in the glass, wielding her weapon, and smirking, she smacks the hammer down, shatters each shiny new tile one by one. Chips of ceramic fly off, skid across the counter onto the floor as she moves faster and faster.

"Charmaine!"

She spins around and there's Sam, blocking the doorway, face spotted with dirt, hair sweat-damp, body odor rolling off him. She has a right to show anger. A right to put him in his place. She says, "See what happens when you don't listen to me? When I say marble, I mean *marble*." She finishes with a flourish by holding up the hammer and moving toward him, everything a blur until she's close enough to feel his heat, close enough to experience a tremor of fear – has she gone too far this time? But he steps out of her way, back into the bedroom. Her heart pounds and her foot falters, but she keeps walking.

Out the front door she goes, almost running, but reining it in, exhilarated with triumph, the sun vying with rain, the devil beating his wife, as her mother used to say. She trembles, pitches the hammer onto the lawn, watches it thud. Then, clutching her arms around herself, she strides past Sam's tidy stack of cut wood and onto the sidewalk.

She doesn't know where she's going, but she *can't* go back inside. Not yet. She looks up and down the Old Road and spies a neighbor, that old man who's always walking his dog, coming up from the creek. She glances around, and hurries toward the only place out of the open, up the short walkway to the green gate of the Trencher house that separates her own fixer-upper from the bungalows. She fumbles with the latch and ducks inside.

Like most of the yards on the Old Road, this one is weedy, but the owners have gone overseas, England, she thinks, or Wales, and won't be back, according to Sam who, unlike her, enjoys the occasional chat with neighbors. She surveys the two-story Mediterranean, noting the tile roof in need of repair, the faded blue shutters, an arched entryway built like the entrance into a Spanish fort. The house is appealing in spite of the dead bushes, crumbling paint, and broken window on the second floor. This is a place just waiting to be flipped, much more potential than her own little cottage with its tacky kitchen and wormy wood.

Sam. Is he following her? She can't tell and she's afraid to look. She will explode if she has to endure, even for a second, the sympathy in his eyes. She wishes he'd just shake her, throw her on the floor, kick her in the belly, and leave. Damn him. Damn him.

She wipes her nose. The front door has one of those key boxes on it. There's no "For Sale" sign planted in the yard, and Charmaine figures the realtor is lazy or new on the job and maybe, just maybe, the box is open, the key inside. She steals up the walkway, and with a glance at the empty street, she checks the box. The contraption is shut and locked, doesn't yield to her tug. She fingers each dial as if she's cracking a safe code to no avail. She stamps her foot, tastes blood in her mouth.

Up the driveway and into the unkempt back yard she goes, surveying the lower windows, grinning when she sees

French doors leading from a cracked cement patio into the house. A glance yields an assortment of fallen branches the right size for her use. In this moment, she considers the January windstorm a blessing, sent to her by a forgiving god who loves her and only her. Making up perhaps for what he's taken away. She weighs one limb and then another and selects the one that most resembles a baseball bat.

Reflected in the double doors her image is divided into twelve square panes, and like in the bathroom mirror, she rejoices in the powerful figure she sees. "Towanda on a rampage" passes through her head from some forgotten movie, and with the end of the branch she breaks the glass, one pane splintering at a time. She reaches in and tries the door, but it's bolted. The branch now a battering ram, she smashes out each slat of wood – bam – bam – bam! – until the hole is large enough for her to stoop inside.

In the late afternoon light, she can barely make out the table and chairs in the center of the room. She searches for a light switch, finds one, flicks it back and forth. No lights come on. But down the hall, rosy sunlight draws her into the huge living room. Hardwood floors, a plastered fireplace at the far end, gorgeous tile which smudges her fingertips with soot. She sees herself emptying the house of its hideous furniture, pulling down the heavy velvet curtains, restoring the vaulted ceiling, filling the rooms with antiques.

Her hand runs over worn mahogany as she climbs the winding staircase, reminding her of the hammer handle, polished by years of contact with skin. If they owned this house, she'd take up the threadbare carpeting, put down a Persian runner, add those brass bars that fit neatly at the back of each step. She could work wonders here.

At the top, on the large landing, the setting sun stains the stucco walls red, and Charmaine hesitates, a ghost hand on her shoulder, holding her back. In the distance, Sam calls her name as if she were a missing pet, and grimacing, she steps into the nearest bedroom.

She knows what kind of room this is, a mobile outlined against the darkening afternoon, a zoo of stuffed animals lining a window seat, and the crib that she could touch if she only would. She can't move except for breath, her heart shattering like white ceramic tile and twelve square panes of glass.

And no one told me!

by Sally-Anne Macomber

To: Milton Flaxmill, Red Cow Publishing
From: Trudy Polaris
Date: April 20, 2014 1:18 a.m.
Re: Developments

Hi Milton,

I emailed you the plane ticket and waited for you at Langkampfen Airport but you didn't arrive. I was sitting for a long time on an orange vinyl seat staring at white floor tiles listening to the arrivals in German but that's OK because I've started editing *Nuclear Fission in the Pyrénées* while I wait for you to get here. (I'm not at the airport any longer by the way.) I'm hoping to get the word count down to 80,000 words. It started at about 81,226 – just in case you'd forgotten – but I have my best 'another person with other eyes' hat on and I think I'll have the book in good shape by the time you get here.

So it will be good to know *when* you will get here.

I'm establishing a routine. After the milking is finished, I have a cup of coffee sitting beside the computer and I slowly work my way through each page of the text and I'm cutting words out at a great rate. Then I drink the coffee and put most of the words back in.

But you will be pleased to know I am also learning a lot about local fashion and through a connection in the *dirndl* industry I heard there was an opening as a representative for the local cheese board. So my new job as the Tyrolean Fetta Ambassadress starts next week.

Between the milking and this new cheese job my time editing the book will be limited but rest assured, I am fully committed and intend using my time well by developing new skills as a power-editor. I signed up for the course yesterday.

And now the bad news. I thought we would be here in our Tyrolean hideaway for only a few weeks but my husband revealed we have to stay here for a while longer, for tax reasons. I am desperate to leave: there's only so many Alpine goats I can milk every morning! (And they're goats, they're not cows, they're goats! Large goats! And no one told me!)

So quite without any input from me, I've become a tax hostage!

I am trying not to let this get me down. The thought of a kindred spirit (i.e. you) sitting beside me in my Alpine writer's paradise, sharing writerly jokes (*Why did the chicken cross the road? Because he was reading!*) raises my spirits. But at the moment that's just a thought. And while we are taught *it's the thought that counts*, the reality is you are in Boston and I am here in the Tyrol ... so it will be good and probably even a relief when we finally meet. (And I thought we were only coming here for the February skiing season!)

On another but related point, I think it would be better to change the title to *Nuclear Fission in The Pyrénées*, that's with a 'T' on The Pyrénées, you know what I mean, a capital 't' (I mean 'T') on The Pyrénées.

I have put it in bold here – **The Pyrénées** – just so you know what I mean.

Hoping you get this email and that there's not a black email hole at Red Cow Publishing nor is there more than one Milton Flaxmill at Red Cow Publishing and I am sending this to the wrong Milton Flaxmill.

Well, auf Wiedersehen again, and glad to know we're still on the same page,

Trudy

Snakes in April

by Mandy Nicol

Mum cranes her neck over the back of the car seat to check Peregrine. I can't see him in the rear view mirror but I can hear him panting. Poor dog.

"Can't you go any faster Nadia?" she says for the tenth time.

"Not legally," I say. I'm varying my responses, treating it like one of those games kids play on long drives to pass the time, like counting McDonalds Restaurants or Volkswagen Beetles. On this road they'd have to count gum trees or magpies or cattle grids.

"What are snakes doing out this late in April anyway?" she asks.

"We're not sure it was a snake, Mum."

"Of course it was a snake."

I don't argue. Maybe it was a snake.

"It's all this global warming," she says. "It's turning everything upside down. First we had to put on the heater on Christmas Day and now there are snakes out and about in April. Snakes in April!"

I don't argue. Maybe global warming has messed up their hibernation pattern.

"It's all those mice in the hay shed," she says. "That's what brings them in the first place. If you'd put out poison like I told you to this wouldn't have happened. You know Peregrine's always hunting around in that hay shed."

I don't argue. I don't say if I'd put out poison we'd probably be making the same trip because Peregrine had scoffed it. Though he probably wouldn't have done it on Easter Monday, which would have saved me a heap on the vet bill, and would have stopped the vet from being pissed off at being called to his surgery on a Public Holiday.

We hit town and I slow to sixty. "A lot of dogs survive snake bite," I say.

"And a lot more don't," says Mum. She cranes her neck to check the speedo.

I turn to check Peregrine. He's still panting and drooling but at least he's alive. He'd be dead by now if he'd been bitten by a Brown, the vet had said as much on the telephone.

"Then let's hope Peregrine's one of the lucky ones," I say.

Mum peers at me over her glasses. "Can't you go any faster, Nadia?"

Dr. Stanley Runs Late

by Margaret Bingel

Dr. Stanley looks at his calendar. He is running late for his 1:00pm appointment with Ned Billingsly. He logs out of the app on his iPhone, and while waving a waiter down, he remembers he has 12 minutes to get across 20 blocks of city traffic. Dr. Stanley throws a fifty down and runs out the door. He flags down the nearest taxi, he gives the driver the address for St. Jude's, then settles into the backseat and thinks about his patient.

Dr. Stanley knows all about the ex-coma patient: having been in a two month coma, Mr. Billingsly has been recovering quickly, first by sitting up in bed by himself, then rising to his feet unassisted, even if for a few minutes. For two weeks they have been working on walking, Dr. Stanley standing next to him as he shuffles each slippered step down the therapy ramp. Hopefully, we can work on actually lifting the foot up soon, or else his ankles will never recover properly, Dr. Stanley thinks, as he wrings his hands. Somehow, the driver has hit every red light possible, making his passenger squirm in his seat. Not being on time bothers Dr. Stanley.

Despite Ned's smooth road to recovery, it's his conflicting reports of Ned's attitude that bothers Dr. Stanley the most. Even with x-rays and CT scans, there doesn't appear to be any brain damage, but his mother, Nora, believes that there has to be something wrong with her son. *My boy*, Dr. Stanley remembers, *is not my boy anymore.*

"But that's the way it is with sons, Mrs. Billingsly," Dr. Stanley said that first day he met Nora and her 'troubled boy'. "Once they reach a certain age, they become men."

He smiles, a reassuring smirk he uses for fearful patients and their families. He remembers her eyebrows knotting when he had said, "Mrs." Perhaps she isn't married, he had thought.

"But you don't know my son," Nora had said, her gray eyes flashing. "My son has never been determined in his life. No direction, always complacent. This isn't like him at all!" The wrinkles on her forehead looked like a bow on a birthday present, but her eyes were a dammed river. "He doesn't even smile."

Dr. Stanley sighs as he remembers the sound of Nora's voice. One time he purposely walked in on her reading to her son while he lay in bed, Ned's hands in fists. It was a Saturday, a day he knew she would be visiting, and he showed up early, just to hear her read. When Dr. Stanley leaned in closer to the door, Nora heard the linoleum squeak. He told her that he loved *The Wizard of Oz*, and she smiled. He smiles out the window, thinking of Nora's face.

The taxi pulls up to the curb. Dr. Stanley gives the driver a twenty, and, slamming the car door, rushes into St. Jude's, slowing to a walk once he enters the building. Jumping over every other step, he arrives on the fourth floor, the rehab clinic, and walks into Room 231, where Mr. Billingsly is waiting for him.

Dr. Stanley pulls out his phone and looks at the time. 1:05pm. *Shit*, he swears under his breath. He looks up at Nora's son (disappointing, he doesn't have her eyes) and gives him one of his smirks.

"Sorry, I'm late, Mr. Billingsly. Shall we get started?"

"Let's," answers Ned, with a smile.

It's Bright in Here

by Darryl Price

Close the door. Oh yeah there are no doors, or none that I can see. Maybe you're blocking the doors. Do you think I'm going to try to escape? Listen, if I thought I could escape I would have been gone a long time ago.

You wanted me to write things down, so that's what I'm doing. I'm being a good boy.

Without her my bed is a tomb. Any wind is a slap in the face. My food is poison.

What do you want me to say?

Okay. Here it is. I built a house for her. No not in the so-called real world, so don't try to lay that on me, but it was every bit as real to me. I could see it, I could feel it, I could care about it. But that collapsed in on me, too, because nothing holds up without her being there. Every nut and bolt is a lie. I can't help this. That sky is a lie. For instance. It's nothing but a poster taped to a window. That outside bird is a lie. An unfortunate scar in the butter of sunlight. My own hands on the sheets dead beside me are like discarded shoes looking for a box. Don't you get it? I'm sorry. I should have told you this kind of thinking upsets me.

You wanted me to tell you a story. All stories are lies. But perhaps they contain a bit of truth.

How did I get here?

I don't belong here.

Okay. OK. Let's get down to it. I made a mistake. Someone used to love me.

Someone I miss. I can't stop missing. It's messed me up. I see that now. I just want to go home and sit on a couch and eat some ice cream and sleep or watch TV. All this groveling for answers isn't going to get us anywhere. Because she's gone, just like the record says. And I can't deal with it like I should, or like you want me to.

Is that so wrong?

Okay, ok, let me give it another go. She died. I lived. End of story. No? No? No no no no no no no no. I want to be the one who dies. She has every reason to live. I'm the one you wanted. You got the wrong person. I'm ready to go.

Give me a few minutes alone to think this thing out. I'll try again later. I've got plenty of paper and this hospital pen, if that's what this place is.

Maybe this isn't earth at all.

That would make the most sense.

Did you give me something? Cause I'm starting to feel mighty sleepy. That's a word you don't hear much anymore. Mighty. Like Mighty Mouse. You probably never even heard of him, but he saved the day.

Once.

Patience

by Teresa Burns Gunther

Rachel whips around a too slow car on US101, cuts past a pickup, crosses two lanes and exits the freeway. "Jesus," Gail gasps, clutching the passenger door with one hand, a box to her belly with the other. *Patience* Rachel reminds herself. She's wasting her lunch hour to do her officemate a favor.

Gail's a tax fraud specialist, too; a mousy thing who tries but that morning she overslept, arrived late to the office, a rumpled flurry in a gray business suit, her brown hair oily and flat against her head. Rachel has no patience with slovenliness; she is always well-groomed in a crisp suit and heels.

She zips through the intersection on Army Street two seconds after the yellow light flashes red. Gail gives sounds to her nervous state. Though the day is thick with fog, Rachel has the windows down blowing her hair into havoc, because Gail's mission stinks. She takes her hands off the wheel, pulls her hair into a twist she tucks down her blouse. Gail reaches for the wheel but Rachel blocks her in time.

Patience is Rachel's 2014 resolution for April. So when Gail, who shares her 40-hour-a-week slice of IRS paradise needed help with her mission and begged her for a ride at lunch Rachel said yes, enjoying Gail's wide-eyed surprise. It's good practice and besides, the stink and scritchscratching in their office from the box Gail holds was more than she could take. "It better not mess up my car," Rachel warns again.

Gail clucks her tongue. Rachel got Gail's text: *Cover 4 me?* on her way into the staff meeting. Now Gail's pissed that Rachel told everyone Gail was late because she had cramps and needed tampons. It was the first excuse that came to mind. Everyone acted amused though her boss, the arrogant ironman, actually seemed impressed. He'd denied Rachel a raise the previous fall claiming she lacked people skills. Apparently, covering for slacker employees is what he's after. Patience is clearly part of the people skills calculus, though numbers, she thinks, are so much easier to work with. "What did you want me to say?" she asks Gail.

"A dentist appointment would have sufficed."

Rachel shrugs. "Next time, be specific. I'm not practiced in deception."

"Clearly," Gail says.

Rachel and Gail aren't chummy. They don't *do* lunch and Rachel rarely joins the after work cocktail coven and gossip. She's always been impatient with Gail's ups, downs, and daily dramas. And today's drama is the bird Gail rescued on her way to work. The closest bird sanctuary is in Oakland, and though it's only a ten-minute zip over the Bay Bridge at mid-day it's closed on Thursdays. Rachel tells her "never fear" and heads for her neighbors' house.

"You can give it to the Aussies: Joyce and Larry," she explains. "They have a zoo in their backyard – *rabbits for eating, chooks not for eating,* and lots of *fruits and veg.*" She mimics their lazy Australian accent and confused vowels.

Gail looks skeptical. "Didn't your dog kill and eat their rabbit?"

"Stella didn't eat it and it was already dead," Rachel says.

When she finally pulls into her narrow driveway with a screech Gail's eyes are closed, her hand white-knuckled on the door.

"Let's go."

Gail lingers, sizing up Rachel's white house with its blue trim and flowering window boxes, but Rachel shoos her up the neighbors' front stairs to the porch jungled up with morning glories and begonias.

Joyce opens the door and smiles at Gail, her broad face smiling, curious, until she catches sight of Rachel. Her eyes narrow, she crosses her arms over her vast bosom. Joyce hasn't said word one to her since the rabbit incident. Rachel had hoped for Larry, Joyce's beanpole husband, who's much easier to handle.

"Everything alright, Rachel?" Joyce speaks slowly, her voice wary.

Rachel introduces Gail, explains they have an animal emergency. "You're the only person I could think of who'd care." Gail starts to paraphrase but Joyce's chest swells, sucking it in as praise.

"Let's have a look-see," Joyce says.

Gail opens the box and gives Joyce a puppy-dog face. The bird is gray and agitated like Gail, reminding Rachel that people resemble their pets. Like she and Stella, both long-legged and sleek.

"It's a sick bird," Gail says, stating the obvious.

"How do you know it's worth saving?" Rachel asks, peering in.

"Rachel!" Gail claps a hand over her heart; her nails are bit to nubs. "It's a living thing!"

"Well, some are better than others," Rachel says.

Gail shakes her head. When Rachel, so angry, told Gail her boss' claim that she lacked people skills, Gail snorted and said, "Imagine that!"

106

Joyce peers at the bird. "Oh." She joins Gail in a cooing duet as they stroke the pigeon. The box is carpeted in bird shit.

"Oh," Rachel says. "That is disgusting."

"Don't mind her," Gail tells Joyce. "She hates animals."

"That's incorrect. I love Stella, my dog."

Joyce and Gail share a look. "The bird rescue is closed," Gail explains, "and Rachel said you are good with living things."

"Did she now?" Joyce looks at Rachel as if reconsidering her.

"Not exactly," Rachel says.

"If you could help," Gail tells Joyce, "I'd be so grateful. I can pick it up later today if you like."

Rachel checks her watch. "I have got to get back to work. What do you say?" she asks Joyce, who stares at the bird.

"Look, I understand if you don't want it," Rachel says. "It is disgusting." She shudders. "A flying rat."

Gail whispers, "You're not helping."

"What? You like these birds? Pigeons who make such a mess, the Canada goose that won't go home? It's payback for draft dodgers who hid in Canada during the Vietnam War." She laughs but both women stare at Rachel, mouths agape. "If you think about it they could be the answer to the hunger problem – a goose or squab in every pot."

Gail says, "You're terrible."

Joyce looks between them, nods her head, then her lips twitch and she busts up with laughter. When she recovers she says, "Oh, I think you'd better leave it with me, Gail. Who knows what Rachel will do to the poor mite?"

"You're right." Now Gail's laughing too. "She might feed it to her dog."

"Oh, you've met the wolf?"

The two fall into each other laughing and gasping for breath. They're doubled over as Rachel turns to go.

She hops into her car and buckles up. Such difficult people to practice patience on, but she's not one to shrink from a challenge. She's proud to think her patience work is done. She starts her engine, lays into her horn and waves at Gail to hurry.

Friday, 25th April 2014

Morgana Malone and the Miracle of St. Francis Xavier

by Matt Potter

"Save me!" I say, as I duck between their legs. Crouching behind them, I look down at my toes poking through the lavender or mauve or lilac strappy bridesmaid sandals and hold my breath as their chanting continues.

One – two – three – four –

I look up, and I see their signs for the first time: 'Hubbard's Hoes' and 'Dianetics Disaster' and 'L. Ron is a shit!'

And hear them chant, "L. Ron Hubbard is weak! Chuck him in the creek!"

And through their legs I see the opposing forces, lolling behind a wooden stand, young women with ponytails and young men with skinny arms, and books and leaflets and smiles piled high. 'FEEL HAPPIER AND MUCH MORE CONFIDENT' – their banner declares – 'the Scientology Way' – their banner whispers.

What I thought I might find when I slammed the St. Francis Xavier Cathedral door on the wedding rehearsal was the remnants of the parade, men and women from the army and the navy and the air force marching past, their faces solemn as the crowd waved and the music intoned and the sun hid behind a cloud. It is, after all, Anzac Day, the

109

public holiday where we commemorate the Australian and New Zealand Army Corps landing at Gallipoli in 1915 and their horrific loss. And well, Anzac Day is equally famous for its rainfall.

But the marchers have disappeared and the onlookers too and so there's just the Scientologists and the anti-Scientologists and me here in the middle of Victoria Square.

Five – six – seven – eight –

In the distance I hear Grigor's steps thundering towards me and Zebadie's shrill top note – "Come back, ya cunt!" – so I drop my bottom closer to the footpath and hunker down.

When Grigor asked me into his office yesterday afternoon I had no idea he would sink to his knees, wrap his arms around my legs and say, "I'm marrying the wrong woman on Saturday. You're the woman I love."

Why is it always the ex-wife-bridesmaid who's the last to hear about it?

"Does Zebadie know?" I asked.

(But I didn't know what else to say! It was an unusually warm day yesterday and the dress I was wearing was soft and filmy and with his head pressed against my crotch, I could already feel the dampness spreading. And there was this *ache* ...)

"No," he said, looking up at me. A breeze blew through the open window but not a hair on his head moved, it was lacquered so stiff. "But I thought I'd tell her the church had changed at the last minute. You know Zebadie's haphazard skills with the GPS." And he blinked.

I shake my head at the thought.

Nine – ten – eleven – twelve –

"Where's the fucking dog?!" Zebadie screams, a little closer this time, out of breath and stiletto heels snipping on the cement.

Zebadie had wanted a dog in the wedding, a schnoodle – part schnauzer, part poodle – and I was holding its

110

diamante lead when, wedding rehearsal half over, Grigor turned to me, eyes wet and voice throbbing, and said, "I can't do this." And then my head began to spin and I think I smelled almonds and I thought, *No, no, no, I can't do this either* and as Grigor stepped towards me with his hand stretched out, palm up, eyes deep and imploring, I dropped my test bouquet and Zebadie's test bouquet and the dog lead slipped out of my hand and I sort of fell against a pew and then I turned around and wobbled up the aisle and, door slamming behind me, ran onto Wakefield Street.

I guess this probably means I needn't turn up for my admin job at Grigor's psychiatry practice on Monday either.

"Where is she?!" I hear Grigor's voice, dark and desperate. "What does she think she's doing?!"

It's then I hear the chanting has stopped and six faces are peering down at me. I know I must look a sight, and I touch the paper doily practice bridesmaid's cap pinned to my head, hiding much of the brown and grey regrowth yawning through the dyed orange.

"I'm just having a bad day," I say. "Please carry on."

But then the legs part and I see Grigor – and Zebadie standing behind him – glaring down at me. His eyes are black and thunderous and his nose looks extra pointy and I can't help but see the hair quivering in his now cavernous nostrils.

Thirteen – fourteen – fifteen – sixteen –

"You've lost your chance at being my matron of honour now!" Zebadie spits.

And Grigor, chest heaving and dribble on his chin, has the last word: "I hope you don't regret this, Morgana."

Affair

by Gary Percesepe

Macy was standing on the street licking an ice cream cone as I drove up in my blue convertible. I had seen her sitting or standing or walking the conference grounds at Antioch College, where we were both attending an academic conference. She was tall but walked slowly in silver ballet flats with ribbons attached in bowties, as if she had nowhere to go and all the time in the world. It was a warm night. She wore a light summer sundress. Simple and inexpensive, it flattered her form. Her hair was a shade of light brown streaked with blonde, and the day before she had twisted a cut daisy into her hair. But on this night she wasn't moving. She stood still beneath the movie marquee, licking her cone and watching the traffic move up the street.

Macy (I didn't yet know this was her name) was alone. She seemed made to be seen. Savannah was at home, asleep, with our two kids.

I parked the car somewhere and walked back to her. She hadn't moved. I hadn't said a mumbling word to her at the conference, did not know what her voice sounded like. I was nervous. When I reached her I said hello, and then asked, "Where did you get your ice cream cone?" This seemed an idiotic question. It was a small town with one ice cream stand. But she pointed down the street, and her voice – I remember this so clearly – her voice was that of a child, a musical child. It was a voice from childhood that I had missed.

"I'll be right back," I said. I returned with my ice cream cone and introduced myself as a fellow writer from the conference. We exchanged pleasantries, made inquiries about what kind of writing we did, or wanted to do, and then I asked her bluntly, "Do you want to go for a ride? It's a beautiful night and I have a convertible." She shrugged her high shoulders and said sure.

It takes only a few decisions to make an affair. Someone sees, someone is seen. Call and response, deep to deep. The ancient machinery of desire is activated from well-worn cultural codes, the codes of the western world – the way hair hangs or holds the light beneath a movie marquee, say. The languid way a woman moves when she walks down the street beside you. The sight of her mouth, moving, eating an ice cream cone, that way women have of lifting their legs, the knees rising and the smooth tan legs of summer swinging into the passenger seat, swinging parallel from hips sheathed by the thin white cotton of her dress, the pair of legs together out of the night and into your car. A woman feels the intensity of a man's gaze upon her and knows that she has occasioned it and that it is all for her and knows too that if she wants to, she can keep this desire directed on her, because she knows how to do this and she has a power over him now, has reduced him to this elemental moment of wanting, waiting. You choose to look down from the road to see her move the toe of one ballet shoe to the heel of the other, watch the shoe fall to the floorboard and now her one foot is bare, and the painted toes shuck the other shoe aside and a barefoot woman is beside you in your car on a warm summer night and you are moving down the street with the top down and there are all the smells of summer rushing by and the smell of her light perfume, her hair swinging as you accelerate into a turn on a country road where someone made a cook fire, and she talks while you listen in the wonder seat, wondering all about her and reading her face and her voice and her long body for clues and you are underway now, both married to different people, and you are in trouble. You know you are in trouble, and you know that if either of you had any sense you would stop, but you can't. Because you are going to have an affair and if you hadn't wanted that you would not have approached her on the street and she would not have gotten into your car, and she certainly would not have removed her silver shoes.

What will happen is what usually happens: the talk of family and children and jobs and bruised dreams and busted hopes, what he said, what she said, and soon enough a husband who doesn't get her and a wife who is restless but unable to say what is wrong, exactly, and the words of negation, couldn't shouldn't wouldn't giving way now to words of affirmation because she gets you, he doesn't talk like any man she knows, the idea that the two of you are in a car as a couple moving fast occurs to you, you are already coupled aren't you, and maybe a thought about time, how malleable it is, how moments can be borrowed from a marriage if promised to replace, and soon enough you are in a forest of desire and the way out has closed and you'll wander in this forest for three months or so unaware of where you are or who you were or that you have lost the way out so consumed are you and burning with new light and you realize that it is your responsibility to forage the forest and feed her now, she is hungry and thirsty and hasn't a place to lay her head at night because of you and this you take on willingly because you love to watch her eat and drink and sleep, and you scorch the forest with the heat of your love but soon enough a search party is formed and you are discovered by swinging lanterns lighting inquisitive faces from the village, and walked before the magistrate and there you are met by her husband, your wife, your children, your earlier, wiser self and everyone

114

has questions that you do not know the answers to, and they go on asking but you cannot explain even to each other what has happened, and so you stand there dumbly and when asked, even by a friendly voice, why did you do it, what in the world happened, you can only manage to say, I do not know, it just happened. I was out eating an ice cream cone, I was driving my car home from the conference one night, and because you are both writers you will find a way to finish this awkward sentence yet no one will believe you.

It's late April now. The cruelest month, they say, and certainly it is for me. Today is Savannah's birthday. Though I haven't seen her in years, I never forget her birthday. I feel the phantom pain shoot through me, as in an arm or a leg long ago amputated. A birthday passes, unacknowledged, un-celebrated, and it still feels to me like a small betrayal among larger.

Of course, Macy's husband found out. It wasn't hard. Macy had left her journal open on the kitchen counter. He found my name in her book, repeatedly. There were also love poems.

He tracked me down. Apparently, I wasn't that hard to find. Or he had help. From Macy.

I was on vacation in California with Savannah and the kids when the call came. He left a message on the answering machine.

It was a gray November day when we returned to our small horse farm in Ohio. Already we missed the light of southern California. All the trees in Ohio had lost their leaves. We walked through the door of our home with our suitcases, jetlagged, sunburned, and cross. I looked through the bills and when that was done I played the answering machine.

An angry man with a Kentucky drawl. How had he learned the correct pronunciation of my surname? From Macy? What else had she told him? *"Yes, you don't know me but your husband has been having an affair with my wife. Yeah, and she's come up pregnant. I knew you would want to know. I'd sure as hell want to know if I was in your place. And I am not mad at you, you and me is innocent in this, but look, there is gonna be a baby. And yes, I'm sure it's his baby Macy is pregnant with, because she hasn't let me near her in months. So I just thought you'd want to know this, what your husband has done. He's been screwing around on you and now my wife is pregnant with his baby and maybe we should get some tests done, what do you think? Well, OK, I'm sorry to bother you, ma'am. I just thought you'd want to know. Goodbye."*

My daughter was fifteen. My son had just turned twelve. We all stared at the answering machine. We looked at it the way you'd look at a car crash with four fatalities. Savannah reached down and played the tape again. It said the same thing. The kids didn't say a bloody word. I reached for the phone.

Macy answered. When she heard my voice she hung up. I re-dialed. This time he answered. I asked to speak with Macy. He said sure, who is this? I gave him my name. He put her on the line. My kids watched all of this. Savannah stood next to me. I talked on the phone to a woman in Kentucky I'd been seeing for six months while both our families listened in. It went about as well as you'd expect it to go under those circumstances. I was out of my mind. Macy hung up on me. I called back. No one knew what was happening. It was a four-alarm emergency. I asked if there was really a baby. There was. I insisted it wasn't mine, it couldn't be. Macy hung up on me again.

I placed the phone in its cradle, hung my head, and took a breath. I opened my mouth and tried to explain. This too, was a mistake.

Samford's Under the Bed

by Nathaniel Tower

The sound of splintering wood snaps Samford right out of his deep slumber.

"What the hell was that?" he asks.

His clone-friend Sarah doesn't respond. He reaches over to wake her up only to find she isn't in bed with him. Has she escaped?

Sarah and Samford have spent the last month in hiding. Ever since his rectal exam, Samford has been convinced that the government is looking for him. He knows that doctor ratted him out after finding the serial number engraved inside his asshole.

Samford still hasn't seen it himself. He's not 100% sure that he is a clone, but he knows he's harboring one, and if he's screwing one every night, he might as well be one himself.

He hears footsteps pounding up the stairs. His ears tell him that there are at least four sets of feet. It sounds like either a parade of elephants or a group of heavily booted military men. He's heard stories about the clone police, swooping in during the middle of the night.

Samford suddenly regrets that he has taken such a liking to sleeping in the nude. It's bad enough to be apprehended by the clone police. To be taken while naked is just plain embarrassing. He imagines the pictures in the newspaper, a tiny black box covering up his penis. If he really is a clone, couldn't they have cloned him from a bigger mold?

He wants to turn on the light and look for his underwear, but turning on the light would attract more attention than necessary. The footsteps grow louder, and he knows they will be in his room quicker than he could pull on the underwear anyway. He dives off the bed and slides underneath, barely squeezing between the metal frame and the dusty carpet. Pressed face down against the shag, his crotch immediately itches and he wonders what type of crabs he may have just picked up.

Sarah is under the bed with him. He opens his mouth to whisper when the lights flash on and a pair of boots appears just inches from his face.

"Where is he?" a deep voice asks.

"Under the bed." The second voice is robotic, and Samford wonders if they have employed some type of artificial intelligence to capture the lost clones.

As a hand reaches under the bed and grabs his arm, Samford wonders why they aren't looking for Sarah. Maybe she ratted him out and not the doctor. Maybe she's a government plant who was just using him. But why? There is nothing at all significant about Samford's life.

The clone policeman pulls hard and drags Samford out from under the bed, his penis burning on the carpet while his ass scrapes against a broken spring. Still, he doesn't make a noise, mostly out of embarrassment, but partly because he is still clinging to the hope that they will somehow not notice him.

The policeman lifts him by a single arm and tosses him on the bed, face down and ass up. Within seconds, his hands are tied to the bedposts, reminding him of many nights with Sarah, only then he was ass down and face up. They spread his legs apart and shackle them to the footboard. The shackles are soft and silken, and he feels strangely aroused. He is glad he is ass up to avoid the complete embarrassment of his hardening penis.

"Turn off the lights," the robocop says.

Samford is in the dark for a moment before an eerie red light crackles on. The buzzing grows louder as the light approaches his body, and he soon smells burning ass hair.

The light is practically in his butt now. This is what a pig on a spit must feel, or at least this is half of what it feels. Two giant hands drop onto his cheeks and press down and out. A rush of air enters Samford's bottom and swirls around his insides. He farts, a loud trumpet right into the harsh light.

The clone cop slaps his ass. "Fart again and I'll stick the light all the way up to your heart."

Samford knows this makes no sense.

"What's his number?" the robocop asks.

"Um, it's a little faded, but I think it says '1164321' or something like that."

The hands release, the cheeks snap shut, and the light is switched off.

"He's the one. Let's go."

Samford is thrown up on the shoulders of the brute, his shriveled lolling penis flopping around. As they carry him out of the room like a naked sack of laundry, he peers through the dark for any sign of Sarah. There is a flicker of movement under the bed, and he thinks he sees a flash of teeth before they are out of the room. And for some reason, they close the door behind them.

Monday, 28th April 2014

Aftermath

by Kimberlee Smith

My mum sits in front of the telly all day scanning for news on the plane crash. It happened a month ago today, and there's still a lot of interest in the story because with the winds blowing ever since, the recovery crews haven't been able to access the turbine blade the remains of Junior are skewered on, because there's no way to stop the wind turbine from spinning if the winds decide to keep it up.

There are bits of shredded parachute and pieces of a sun-fried ribcage impaled on the blade. It plays over and over on the news and Mum can't stop looking at it. She knows it's not my husband Dean, she has intuition that told her it's not him, but instead his business partner and pilot, Junior Volpe.

Clutching a moneybox full of cash and strapped into a parachute, Junior cracked Dean in his face with the butt of a handgun then bailed out of the plane and let Dean ride that plane, in a free-fall, corkscrew spin for two minutes until it slammed into the ground. Those were the most terrifying moments you could ever conjure, knowing, seeing, feeling that the end is so near, and having it arrive in a completely violent and painful way. I rode in spirit with Dean until the end.

Junior's little old Cessna exploded on impact; the metal that didn't char just melted and burned beyond any recognition. There wasn't even a way to identify him.

Our sweet little bub Etheline Margaret knows her mum and dad are with her, looking down on her. We've tried to connect with my mum Maybell as well, but no success. It seems as if something is blocking our connection, but Dean and I haven't been on this side long enough to have it figured out. There's not a reason for everything, but for this, I know there is.

Etheline is doing everything babies are supposed to do and at just the right time. She cut a couple teeth and can sit up all by herself. She knows how to clap her hands and play peek-a-boo. But she still will never know what it's like for her mum to hold her. As much as I want her with me, I hope it's a very, very long time before she and I are reunited since there's only one direction to go in for that to happen.

In some ways she's different than what I've read regular babies are supposed to be like and look like. Her eyes are silvery amber; watery and slit like a serpent's. Not so much that it'd grab your attention, but it's obvious when you look close-up right at her eyes. They're the prettiest eyes I've ever seen, like molten gold. But they're so sensitive to light that Mum always puts dark glasses on her when they're out in the sun. She gets cold very easily. She sleeps well in the warm light that works like a prism through the glass block windows, coiling up as snug as can be.

The day I was bitten will forever be the anniversary of my death and my daughter's birth for my mum. Etheline had enough venom in her bloodstream that it could have killed her ten times over, but instead she thrived. The doctors couldn't figure it out, but Mum knew and kept her mouth shut.

This is not the first time in my mum's family there's serpent in a person. She seems so comfortable with it that I wonder if she expected the baby to turn out this way. She won't call her Maggie, which is what Dean calls her. She only calls her Etheline.

Mum doesn't have any friends, no relatives, and no neighbors she can count on, because we were her whole world after my father left us. She's spent her whole life dedicated to caring for us, and now all she has is herself and a snowballing burden of responsibilities.

Mum and Dean traded time on and off when they were taking care of Etheline. I see how one person can't do everything. Only time Mum sleeps is when the bub sleeps, no matter what time. Their schedule has fallen into chaos; brekkie at midnight, Mum has her first of many lemon squash and gin drinks as soon as she wakes up. Might be at 8 a.m., might be at noon. Etheline likes her mashed fruit, but Mum has to take the bub to the store with her, and on every errand, of course.

They eat the same things. Mum mashes up pasta with peas and makes a mush, like a paste, of fish that's on special at the market and Etheline eats in her highchair while Mum gums the same thing. She tries to hold the bub's hand sometimes when they're having tea, but Etheline is too curious about exploring and making a mess of her food to pay any mind to Mum. Mum fills another drink and her eyes get wet.

Same routine, every day, but time holds no schedule. Seems not to matter to Mum if they're up all night because the bub or Maybell can't sleep, or if it flips around. I recall that bubs thrive on routine and schedule. The routine part Mum's got down, but the schedule is a complete disaster. The grass is high and dying in the garden, and the mail is busting out of the post box. Mum gives the bub a warm bath and smothers her with kisses every day and night. But sometimes it goes a week until Mum baths herself. She goes to sleep in the clothes she wakes up and spends the next day in.

The snakes that Dean bought and sold as his business and left behind – also in Mum's care – have been prepared, by her, to be left untended for a long while. Mum lowered the temperature gradually in the room she relocated the serpents to and dimmed the lights so they naturally would be inclined to hibernate. Before their transition into a state of hibernation, Mum fed them plenty of the mice Dean raised as food for them and then put the rest of the mice in cardboard moving boxes and let them go in the bush. Mum seems to be in a state of hibernation as well, in some ways.

Mum powders Etheline with talcum powder and snuggles her and loves her like the angel she is. It's ironic, but if it weren't for Etheline, I'm sure Mum would have died from a broken heart by now. What I'm worried about is that she may perish from exhaustion and putting everything she has into taking care of the bub, and not giving a pinch into tending to herself.

I get the feeling she's going to get some answers as to why this chaos came upon us, but how and where she'll do it hasn't arrived yet.

U.P.D.

by Vanessa Weibler Paris

"Just take a look at it," says Dar, not looking at me. None of them will look at me; they just keep eating their lunch salads with plastic forks, lifting forkfuls of French-drenched iceberg two inches from the bowls to their mouths. "Just go to the double-ya double-ya double-ya world wide site and just see, okay? It's a dating site. The girls, well, they're supposed to be nice."

"What's it called again?" I ask, eating my own, slopped all over with full-fat dressing. Soggy, limp. I hate salad.

"UPD," offers Linda. "Don't forget the double-ya double-ya double-ya."

"Or the dot com," says Dar.

"But what does it stand for?" I ask. They still haven't said.

"Just go do it!" they insist. "But not here. After work. On your own computer at home."

"You're not ugly," my cousin Sally had told me the summer we both turned 13. "Really."

"I'm too skinny," I'd told her, picking through the grass and tossing three-leaf clover after three-leaf clover to the side.

"You'll fill out," she'd said. Sally herself had filled out attractively since I'd seen her last. We only had family get-togethers a few times each year, but the two of us had always been close. Hardly anyone my age was as nice to me as Sally was. Her "best cousin-friend," she always called me as she ran up for a hug.

"Do you have boyfriends?" I asked, wondering why.

"Not right now," she admitted.

"But you have?"

"A few," she said. "Well, just one, really. But he wasn't very nice. Isn't very nice."

"I'll never have a girlfriend," I said, and then again, "I'm too skinny." I sighed loudly.

"Oh, Jimmy," she said, pushing my arm playfully. Her hand was sticky, and she smelled like banana popsicles. I could feel streaks of it on my skin, sun warming the sugar into glistening grains that would brush off into the air.

"Girls only like guys who are built," I said. "Guys who play sports, and lift. And weigh more than them."

"There are lots of fish in the sea," she said, gazing over at the sand volleyball court where the older cousins were. My brother Jack had his shirt off. "You just have to be patient. When it happens, it happens. When you least expect it."

"You really think?" I asked, touching the popsicle juice on my arm. I waited until she looked at the volleyball court again, and then licked my fingers quickly. They tasted sweet, like banana flavoring, not at all like a real banana.

"Goddamn it!" My brother Jack swore loudly, and then kicked the volleyball pole hard before taking his place to serve the next point.

"Sure, of course," said Sally, still watching the game. "A girl would be lucky to have a nice boy like you."

And there in the grass was a clover with four leaves. I picked it, using just my forefinger and thumb, and held it up against the sun. Each leaf was perfectly rounded and exactly the same size as the rest. I cleared my throat.

"You know," I said, "I don't think there's anything that says cousins can't go out together. I mean, date or whatever. I don't think there's a law. Brothers and sisters can't, of course, but I think cousins are different. I'm pretty sure."

And then she was looking at me, and I could see my reflection in her glasses: deep-set eyes and long thin face and long thin nose and long thin chin, Adam's apple in my long thin throat like a snake choking on an egg and then I could feel it, hard and swollen, choking me.

"Oh," said Sally, picking up her Popsicle stick, yellow-stained and stubbled with bits of mown grass, and starting to back away. "Oh, Jimmy."

And as the egg grew larger and harder and I bent over and began vomiting onto the ground, I could swear I heard her say from far away, "It's not you, it's me."

I stare at my home computer screen. UPD. *Ugly People Dating.* Dot com. With all the double-yas up front.

No wonder they didn't want to tell me what it stood for.

Reeling in the Fish

by Joanne Jagoda

Damon Southeby paces back and forth in his luxurious apartment on Clay St., ignoring the world-class view of the Golden Gate Bridge twinkling to the North, and gulping scotch from a mug. His apartment is paid for by his overseas employers who have been pressuring him to get moving with his assignment to kidnap one of Anne Donaldson's twins. He stares down at the street, quiet and empty at this hour in this classy Pacific Heights neighborhood. Lately he suspects he is being followed by someone they've hired to watch him. He's followed enough people to know.

The plan is to hold the girl for ransom to be paid for by her grandfather George Donaldson – but it's not about money. Her grandfather's company has top-secret plans for the new rocket receptor system his company just completed. He's been tracking the Donaldson women for months, listening in to conversations, watching them with hidden cameras, and hacking their emails. He met Anne "by accident" posing as *David Lewis* at the bar in the Fairmont Hotel a couple of months ago, after she had been deliberately stood up by the online date he had fabricated.

Though he was his most handsome and charming lady-killer self and he gave her his card, she hasn't called him yet. Last week he put his "David Lewis" profile and photo on the phony website he created for her hoping that might do the trick. He can tell she's been on the website. Damon takes another swig of Scotch, plops on the leather sofa and wipes sweat from his face, willing the damn phone to ring. If he doesn't hook up with her soon, his employers will not be pleased, and he will end up as fish food in San Francisco Bay. They don't fool around.

Damon is jolted from his seat when his cellphone rings. The caller ID says *A. Donaldson*. He breathes a huge sigh of relief.

Anne sits in her kitchen at the oak table toying with her Lean Cuisine but craving a wood fired pepperoni pizza from Tommaso's in North Beach. She has her students' reports on the Gold Rush to read and her end of the month bills to pay, but she doesn't feel like doing any of that. The girls are at an information meeting for graduation. Her house feels cold and empty and she hears every creak and noise. *So this is what it's going to be like when they are away.* She tosses her dinner in the disposal and takes a quart of Dreyer's Cookies and Cream from the freezer, attacking it with a big spoon. She's annoyed with herself for not going back to the singles website the girls signed her up on a few months ago. After her first online date was "no show" at the Fairmont Hotel, she's been reluctant to get back on the horse. Two nights ago she got up her nerve to update her profile.

Anne returns the ice cream, then pauses to read the college acceptance letters hanging on the Frig for the tenth time. She's so proud of her girls. The letters from the University of California arrived two weeks ago. Cassie had four large envelopes and Robin had two. They knew from other kids that large envelopes were good news. They waited for Anne to come home from work to open them, and they all danced around the kitchen when they read the good news. Cassie got accepted to UC Davis and three other campuses, Davis was her first choice. She fell in love with the laid-back campus smelling like a country farm when they visited last spring. She is talking pre-med.

Robin was thrilled to be accepted to UC Santa Barbara so close to the beach. Their grandparents' trust funds will come in handy especially since their father died unexpectedly. George, their grandfather, is tickled that Cassie has an affinity for the sciences. He's encouraging Robin to think about law like her dad. George and Lillian got the first phone calls to hear about their acceptances. They are planning a big graduation swim party in June at their house, though Anne would rather have something small. She swipes at a tear. *Paul, you're going to miss their graduations and every milestone.*

Anne hears the girls open the front door. "Hey kids. How was the meeting? When do you order your caps and gowns?"

"It was OK. They gave us the schedule and talked about prom and grad night." Cassie answers but Robin is quiet, which is not like her at all. She is usually the one spewing information and joking about everything.

"What's up Rob?"

"Nothing Mom." She bypasses Anne without a word and heads upstairs.

Anne turns to Cassie for an explanation, raising her eyebrows.

Cassie waits until Robin has shut her door. "She wanted Brandon Miller to invite her to prom but he asked Michelle Frank. Anyway she's a *ho.*"

"I can't believe you said that Cass. That isn't nice at all."

"Well she is and everyone knows. Prom isn't really that big of a deal. Whatev … I wasn't planning on going anyway. There's a group of us who think it's a stupid waste of money. Who wants to spend gazillions on a dress and shoes and fake nails and hair extensions and a night in a hotel? We're going bowling."

"Cassie, that's OK if it's what you want." Anne isn't surprised that Cassie doesn't want to go. She hangs with the straight-A kids like her, and they do things as a group. Her sister has burned through four boyfriends in high school. Anne worries about Cassie being jealous over Robin having so many guys asking her out. Thankfully, even though they have their squabbles, the girls seem to work things out themselves.

"I'll speak to Robin."

"Mom, don't tell her I told you."

"OK. Good night. I'll be down here a little longer." She opens her laptop to the singles website and scans the forty five to fifty five age group looking through profiles. *How the hell do I know who could be a good man? I blew it the first time. Oh my God. It's that cute guy from the Fairmont.*

Newly arrived widower from LONDON. Show me the sights of San Francisco. Let's ride the cable cars. Anne remembers he was a widower. She dumps her purse on the counter for her wallet where she stashed his card.

Anne works through a stack of business cards, doctor appointments and finds it. Her hand is shaking.

David Lewis, CEO, Digital Maneuvers.

I can do this. I'll call him. But not tonight … soon. She covers her eyes with her hands. *Anne, get a grip! Stop being a wimp.* She grabs her cell phone charging on the counter. She punches in the number. It rings four times, and she almost disconnects. Then she hears his English accent.

"Good evening."

"Hello, is this David?"

"David Lewis speaking."

"This is Anne. I don't know if you remember me. We met at the Fairmont last month."

"Oh most definitely. You were that attractive widow drinking a Cosmo."

Anne acts casual but she is chewing her nails. "How have you been, David?"

131

"I've been swamped … terribly busy with setting up my new office."

She decides to go for it. "David, if you've got time, I'd like to show you around San Francisco." She doesn't let on she saw his profile on the website.

"That sounds lovely. Let me check my calendar. How about Sunday?"

"That works for me. Let's meet at the information booth at Pier 39 at 11AM. I'll plan a few things for us."

"It's a date Anne, but can you tell me your last name and is the number here on my phone one I can use in case of an emergency?"

She almost giggles, biting her lip. "I'm Anne Donaldson, and yes I called you on my cell. See you Sunday. Good night."

"Sleep well, Anne Donaldson."

Anne hangs up and boogies in the kitchen, making up her mind not to tell the girls anything about this date. The last time was so disappointing. She shuts off her computer and goes up to bed. She stops by the girls' room and peeks in. Cassie has fallen asleep with her math book on her chest and Robin is sitting in bed studying her history.

Anne whispers, "Hon, you want to come in my room?"

"No Mom, I'm OK. I know Cass told you about Brandon. He's taking someone else. I don't know if I want to go at all."

"Don't decide now. Let's talk about it."

Anne walks into her bedroom. *Rob you'll be fine. I'm not stressing over you for once.* She smiles, rummaging through her closet to put together an outfit for Sunday, then ruffles her hair in the mirror. *Oh my gosh, I have to get my hair cut. David, David, David …*

May

Cause for Celebration

by Guilie Castillo Oriard

Luis Villalobos sits in a dark hotel room. The lights of Mexico City spread below, precious stones scattered on black velvet. He loves this city, the vibrancy, but up here he's detached from it, insulated from the cacophony of its streets by the thick glass and soundproofed walls of the Nikko Hotel. He'll never be a part of it again, not even when he's down there, in the smog and the crowds and the life. His sinuses haven't stopped aching since they landed. The dry air at twenty-three hundred meters cracks his skin. He walks slower now.

It's been three days. Client meeting after client meeting: breakfasts, lunches, dinners, drinks. A blur of faces and fiscal strategies; of office buildings, security checks, visitor passes; of agendas and proposals and tactful reminders of outstanding invoices. Milena filled up the schedule even today – the Mexican Labor Day – but thanks to his sinus headache he managed to skip the last two meetings. He's been sitting at the window since sunset.

A knock at the door. He closes his eyes, already mourning the solitude he's about to lose.

Knock-knock-knock. One thing Milena won't ever be faulted for is lack of perseverance.

He turns on a light, sets it on low before letting her in. Milena's made-up, dressed-up, and perfumed figure pushes past him. He tries to muster a coat of, if not enthusiasm, at least interest. "How did it go?"

She tosses her handbag and her laptop case on the bed, holds up a Samsonite carry-all with a cocky grin. "They knelt before Zod."

"With offerings?"

She pulls the Samsonite's zipper open like an old-school cabaret stripper and throws him what looks like a very thick checkbook, but isn't. It's a brick of twenty-dollar bills. A Banamex paper strip cinches it around the middle. The bills aren't pristine, but still crisp. A little waxy with the trace of pecuniary fingers.

Milena sits on the bed. "It's only twenty-six K, not even half of what they owe. But it's a start. And they promised –"

"They gave you *cash*?"

"I know, it's inconvenient. But they prefer to avoid a paper trail." She nudges off one black pump, then the other. The soles are bright red. They make Luis think of geishas.

"Milena, we're not dealing meth here. It's our invoices. Corporate directorship, company management. Everything's above –"

"Above board?" She stretches back, reaches for a pillow. "For us, maybe. Not for them. You read the Mexican Fiscal Code lately? Tax planning is a dirty, dirty word."

"Not tax planning. Tax evasion. That's not what we do."

"I love it when you play naive." She folds her arms behind her head, purportedly to prop her up and meet his gaze. She'll have him believe the added bonus of her breasts rising to their best angle is purely coincidental. Her tailored skirt rides up her thighs. The light plays off the sheer pantyhose, highlights the curve of her knee, her calves. But it's the places that remain in shadow that tantalize the most.

Luis feels a tingle of pressure at the base of his penis. He turns back to the window. "Cash isn't just inconvenient. What, you're going to pack it in your suitcase and declare it at the airport? Wouldn't that defeat the whole avoid-a-paper-trail?"

Not long ago he found her husky laughter sexy. Now it sounds childish; petulant, mocking. "Pack it, yes. Declare it, no. And it's not me, honey. It's *we*."

He presses a thumb to his left cheekbone, against the pain building in his sinus cavity. "Even if we split it, we'll be carrying more than ten grand each. We have to declare it."

"You're right." She flings herself off the bed to the minibar, whips out a bottle of Victoria beer. "I'll call the client up now, tell them I can't accept their payment because the mighty Luis Villalobos's moral compass is offended by the notion of cash as yet un-sanitized by the alchemy of bank transactions." She slams the fridge door. Its contents clang dangerously inside. "Will that restore your sense of righteousness? The purity of your soul? Or – no, let's just burn the money. Maybe in the bathtub. This is a smoking room, right? The smoke detectors won't know the difference."

"Milena, that's not –"

She skewers the air between them with the unopened bottle. "What's *wrong* with you?"

Milena in blazing fury isn't anything anyone needs to experience too closely. Even though she stands a full head shorter without the pumps, he takes a step backward. "You know we'd have to declare it. It's the law."

"This isn't about the money. You've been acting like a dick since the FATCA project thing."

He can't hold her gaze, so he looks behind her, into the empty room. "You pulled a shitty trick."

"How many times will we have this conversation? I was protecting you. Ensuring the success of –"

"I don't need protecting."

"I omitted those five entities from the FATCA list so the gaps in information wouldn't mar the results." She puts her hand on his chest, backs him up against the window and the darkness beyond. "I know my clients, Luigi. The Solak woman won't give us diddly-squat."

The earnestness in her eyes might've swayed him a month ago, a couple of weeks even. "What if you're wrong?"

"Am I?" She leans against him, a mimicry of seduction. "Show me, then. Show me Pélagie Solak's signed affidavit. Her proof of residency. Oh, that's right. You don't have them. And because you decided to put those entities back in the final report, against my express instructions, instead of getting the kudos you worked so hard for, Ehrlich Fiduciary is on the FATCA non-compliant list."

This is news to Luis, and his righteousness trips over it. "I didn't –"

"See that coming?" Milena's face is devoid of any sarcasm now. Even the anger has dwindled. "I got the email this morning. You accuse me of backstabbing, Luis, but you did the same. And then some. You compromised the entire company."

"Omitting those entities compromised the integrity of the project!"

She turns away, picks up her shoes from the carpet. "That's rich, coming from you. You know why? You don't understand integrity. That virtuous moral code of yours is more full of holes than a golf course taken over by groundhogs. Sex with your boss for personal gain is acceptable, but –"

"It wasn't –"

"– but being loyal to your employer isn't? How do you reconcile that?" She steps into the pumps, fixes her skirt in front of the mirror.

"I've never been disloyal."

"Sshh." She shakes out her hair, finger-brushes it. "Let me tell you about integrity," she says, pinning her hair back up. "It's about staying true to the people that matter. You know who matters? Our clients. So when your boss –

144

whether you're sleeping with her or not – tells you that excluding a client from an information request by a foreign government is *for the client's own good*, what do you think integrity dictates? That's right. You obey. Because if you don't, you know who will bear the worst of the consequences? Right again. The *client*."

"You just said it was the company that –"

"Ehrlich is in a corner, because you put us there." She picks up her laptop case, slings her handbag over a shoulder. "There's only one way out."

He should've seen it sooner. "We'll have to resign as directors from Pélagie's entities."

"I wonder if you'll still be on a first-name basis with her once she finds out her whole tax structure is at risk of being dissolved, thanks to you." At the door she pauses, but doesn't turn around. "Take the day off tomorrow. Visit your family, or something."

"But we're meeting with –"

"They were my clients long before they were yours. I can handle it."

When Luis eventually moves, it's only to turn the light off. His head feels like a rotten tomato, all squishy and fragile with the beginnings of remorse. He'll have to go back on his word to leave Pélagie alone. He has to explain, sketch out her options, help her any way he can. Maybe she'll even change her mind and sign the – no, careful. If she perceives this as coercion, another play to get her to sign the damn affidavit – her adjective, not his – she'll shut him down. He'll never get to speak to her again.

There in the darkness, with the city that he once called home shimmering below him, he finally admits it. He's not feeling remorse. He should, but how could he? This mess has given him the one unimpeachable excuse to see Pélagie again. Why that feels like a cause for celebration is not really clear, but then so little is right now.

The bottle of Victoria Milena abandoned on the dresser is still cold. Luis uncaps it, a hiss that ends before it starts, and raises it toward the window to toast the night.

Friday, 2nd May 2014

La Ronde / Myron and Gloria

by Townsend Walker

United 1479 drops into LAX; Myron looks out the window for the Los Angeles skyline. Not there today; he goes back to his script, working title: *A Nude in the Garden*. Sex and murder; add in the grit of Newark, he's thinking: maybe *Mystic River* redux, a move to the A list, enough money to buy out Gloria (his wife), enough money to marry Annie (his lover).

The driver waits at baggage claim. Myron climbs in the limo, sinks back into the cool air and leather seats, thinks about his entrance, about Gloria. The one broad he's never been comfortable with, even after twenty years. Always suspicious. He's never been able to tell the "good" lie, his patter never sounds "right" to her; she's always looking for the tell-tale slip of paper, listening for the slip of the tongue. This time, he has been careful, especially since Annie spent time in his room. He double-checked his suitcase and attaché.

The limo drives down San Vicente, right onto Carmelina, up to his house at 151: adobe, Spanish tile roof, wooden balconies, walls necklaced by white roses. *Now I know why I don't live in Newark.* Myron wipes his brow, takes the bouquet of yellow tulips he had the driver pick up, opens the front door.

"Gloria, sweetheart baby, I'm home."

"Myron darling, you don't look so good. Newark wear you out? I told you not to go. Not good for your health, change of seasons, I bet you had a cold and never told me, come here, baby."

She cups his head in her hands.

"Let me take care of you, but first, a big fat smooch for my lover boy."

Myron's thinking: *What's happening here? Not only is she making nice, she's looking good too: tanned, trim, above her usual anorexic 95 pounds, some shape even. She have some work done while I was gone? Maybe a little around the eyes and chin and she wants to ease me into how expensive it was.*

Gloria was an actress, still dresses like a star in the fifties (actually, she never starred in anything but supper club productions). Long flowing gowns in fruit colors: strawberry, plum, apricot; her favorite is kiwi. Gold sandals. Her height, about two inches more than Myron; it's a status symbol for him. Only studs can carry off tall women, he tells himself, and anyone else who remarks on it.

"Baby, you look gorgeous. Not just because I haven't seen you for a month, but double drop dead stunning."

She sashays, twirls, and the gown fans out.

"New diet, new trainer, Serge is amazing. Mimi turned me on to him. You should see *her*."

"This guy a Rooski?"

She takes his arm. "Come over here, sit down, honey."

He sits on the sofa and she tucks her legs under her and nuzzles up to him, strokes his chest. He's trying to remember the last time this happened. Maybe the second year they were married. Since then it's been nag, nag, nag.

Gloria turns his face to hers. "Myron baby, you know how all these years I've been on you about other women. Jabbing here, jabbing there. Well, I went to a new shrink and we talked it out. He made me see how wrong I'd been about you. You in the middle of all those dames looking for roles. I can relate, before you came along, of course. How could you help it, you big hunk? But you were good, I never realized it before. Never anything to prove different."

She looks up at him and gives him a long warm kiss.

"And you were so faithful when you were away, called to wake me up in the morning and tuck me in at night. Such a sweetheart."

She stands up and pulls him out of the sofa.

"You've got to be tired from that flight. You take a nap and I'll fix you a nice salad with some white wine, by the pool."

Myron is tired, from the early flight and the night before, with Annie.

Two hours later, Gloria climbs into his bed, minus gown and slippers, and slowly and gently the sleepy Myron wakes and rises. He strolls out to the deck, hair still wet from a shower.

"You'll never believe what I ran into back in Newark. Blast from the past. A hit job."

Gloria turns stern and serious and surly. "You're not going back into that, you promised."

"No way, no way. But this guy I met was telling me about a woman in Manhattan who put out a contract on her husband. Pretty final way of getting a divorce."

Myron jabbers away about how the guy roughs the wife up and loses the kids in the park.

"Enough, enough, you're not writing a script here."

"I even got a description. Franklin Lancaster Cabot III; goes by Frank. Works at Goldman Sachs on West Street, downtown Manhattan. Six foot three, 250 pounds, pasty complexion, he's inside a lot, curly black hair going gray, beak for a nose, Brooks Brothers dresser, loafers with tassels. And Hermes ties, the silly patterned ones. Outside, Prada Aviators, high end sunglasses, blue tint even in the rain."

"You got that down pat."

"Hey, I'm collecting material, that's all."

"He sounds like a real bastard, hope somebody does him in," Gloria sighs, like she doesn't need to hear more of this.

Myron picks up on it. "Great salad, sweetie, and a lovely wine."

"Vermentino, from Liguria. New wine store down in the center. Italian only. Biondivino. Woman who runs it, Ceri, knows her stuff."

Gloria pours out the rest of the wine and takes the plates to the kitchen. Myron stretches out in his chair and nods off again. She comes back out, pats him fondly on the head. "You do need some sleep." And heads upstairs to unpack his bags.

Ten minutes later.

Gloria straddles the supine Myron in his chair; manages it without touching him; leans her lips into his ear. Shouts: "You son of a bitch, bastard pig, son of a bitch, bastard pig."

Myron's body jumps. Before his eyes are open his mouth gapes, "Wha?" and she stuffs a pair of pink lace panties in it.

"Who is the high priced whore? Carine Gilson lingerie? How much you paying her?"

Myron mumbles through the cloth, "I can explain."

"My lawyer will be happy to hear it. And I've done my homework. I know everything you have and I'm getting a piece of 'Naked Corpse' too. Sayonara sweetheart baby, your bags are at the door."

Myron stumbles through the house, grabs his suitcase, throws it in the back seat of the car. Calls Annie. No pick up. Not really expected. *Probably with Joey, bitch.* "Cuddles, you may be seeing me sooner than later. Gloria

150

found some pink lace, not her size. Yeah, and another thing: the guy in New York, 300 pounds, was he?"

Floating

by Derek Osborne

"Hi, Daddy."

"How's my girl today?"

"I'm fine, how are you?"

"Nausea's not as bad."

Max is pushing the button and raising the bed. He's back at Sloan-Kettering.

"Got an *A* on my editing project. And guess what? I've got an internship this summer, right here in town for CBS."

Andi is twenty-one; she'll be graduating NYU film school this month. She looks so much older these days, black leotard, black stretch pants, petite, like her mother was. *Right here in town*, Max is thinking, *this summer*. Time has been playing tricks on him lately, everything moving too fast; sometimes, moving too slowly.

"That's great," he says, "at CBS? How did you manage that?"

"Well, that's the interesting thing. My Prof said they called and asked about three of us."

"And who is *they*?" Max says, though he has a pretty good idea.

"Some dude, Sid something. I wrote it down. And guess what else? It's for *Miami Blue*. Is that the bomb or what?"

Miami Blue is her favorite show; Rebecca's her favorite actress. She and her sisters are big fans. They text whenever it's on. They all flipped when Max got the gig last December down in Miami. He's been dying to tell them, but he and Rebecca are still a well-kept secret, only Eddie and Anja are in the loop. The tabloids are fishing, pot-shots at Rebecca's recent break-up with her long-time boyfriend, rumors about her leaving the show, hints about some *mystery* man. Rebecca says these things happen like children. One day you wake up and find the whole world knows. The telephone rings. It's the doctor saying it's true.

"Sid Markstein?" Max says.

"What are you smiling at?"

Max tries adjusting the bed again. The back is always too high or too low. He's convinced they make all this stuff for people under six feet tall.

"Nothing," he says.

"That's not your *nothing* smile. What are you thinking?"

When did this happen? That's what he's thinking. *When did my little girl become a woman?*

"Did you pull some strings?" she says.

"Not me."

This second round of chemo has been more aggressive, Max feels like shit. He's weak, can't get comfortable, his butt hurts. As always, he's putting on a good show. His hair is a medical marvel. They've given him the same room he had last time so at least there's Hell Gate and the river for diversion. Andi's pulling up a chair and she's moving Kronos, their name for his little blue robot, arranging the tubes and wires. The SAT phone rings.

It's Rebecca.

"It's business," Max says, "Why don't you hit the cafeteria and get us a bite to eat?"

"I'm not hungry."

"You'll be bored."

"No I won't."

Max looks down at the phone. It keeps ringing; a kind of electronic, nautical alarm. Andi grabs it before he can stop her.

"Hun, don't answer that."

"Mr. Perkins' line," she says, pushing the big red button. The speaker is loud, the phone set for the volume needed out on the wind and water. They both hear Rebecca start laughing. In spite of the pain, he's feeling the calm she brings. Rebecca can't stop. It's an infectious laugh.

"May I ask who is calling?" Andi says, making a face.

"Rebecca Vasquez."

"Yeah, right."

"If Mr. Perkins is not available may I please leave a message?"

Max sees his daughter's jaw drop – the accent, the enunciation – the absence of any contractions. Her eyes grow wide and she's looking from him to the phone and back again. *No fucking way,* she mouths.

"Hello?" Rebecca says, "Is anyone there?"

Andi puts the phone to her ear.

"Who is this, really?"

"Oh? Is this Andi?"

"Yes."

"I've heard so much about you."

"I haven't heard a thing about you."

She's looking at her father.

"I'm sorry, Andi. We have had to do things this way. Sometimes it is better."

"Are you really my dad's girlfriend?"

Rebecca starts laughing again. Andi is holding a hand to her forehead, like, I didn't just say that.

"You'll have to ask your father that question," Rebecca says.

"Are you here? Are you coming over?"

Now she's excited.

"What are you doing on Nantucket?" Rebecca says, "I thought you were still in school?"

No, we're here at …"

"Give me the phone," Max says.

She's turning away so Max can't reach. "Are you in New York?"

"No, I'm in LA."

"Give me the phone," Max says, quietly, deliberately, a father telling his daughter. She's taking him in. She's a smart kid; this isn't hard to figure out. Slowly, she hands it over. He takes the phone, meeting his daughter's eyes. *That's right*, his are saying, *she doesn't know*. Andi walks to the window.

"Hi, you're calling early," Max says, still watching his daughter. "Everything alright?"

"Where are you?"

"The city."

"You didn't tell me."

"It all came up last night after we talked. Booking another gig."

Andi looks over; he's never seen this look on her face.

"I'm sorry I let the cat out of the bag," Rebecca says.

"Had to happen sooner or later. You sound a little off?"

"I'm fine. I just wanted to hear your voice."

"What's wrong?"

"Nothing."

"That's not your nothing voice."

Andi looks over again.

"Why don't we talk after dinner?" Max says.

"I can't, I have an appointment."

"What kind of appointment?"

"An appointment, what difference does it make?"

"It sounds like it makes a great deal of difference."

"A *doctor's* appointment."

"What?"

"They make us take a physical twice a year. I do not like doctors."

"Becca, is everything okay?"

"Yes, Max." But he can hear her breathing. "I'm sorry I called."

"Don't ever be sorry for calling."

"Can I speak with Andi again?"

Andi's heard all of it and walks back to the bed. Max hands her the phone.

"Andi, I know this is a lot to take in."

"You have no idea."

"I need you to do me a favor. No one else can know about your father and me. Not yet. We have to keep it that way for a while."

"I understand."

"I can't wait to meet you," Rebecca says.

"Me too."

"Can you give the phone back to your father?"

Max takes the phone and tries to sit up, making it onto one elbow.

"I love you, Max."

"I love you too."

Something is wrong; that much is sure, but he's thinking what's wrong in the room takes priority. Andi's gone back to the window. Max waits for the screen on the phone to go gray.

"You're doing it again," she says, staring down at the river.

"Doing what?"

"Not telling us. What you did with Mom, you're protecting us. How can you lead her on like that?"

"I'm not leading her on," Max says, raising his voice.

"Can't you tell she's in love with you?"

"Andi, it's complicated."

"I'm not a kid anymore."

No, you aren't, Max is thinking. He can't believe what he's hearing: it may as well be Maggie, his wife, standing there by the window.

"Dad, you're dying."

The words push him back down onto the bed. Andi has turned to face him.

"You think I'm stupid? You think we all don't talk about it?"

"I know ..." Max begins.

"You have to tell her."

Her voice is rising.

"You have to tell her soon."

And then she comes at him. It's that voice, that other dimension. She's screaming.

"You have to tell me!"

"Maggie ..." Max says.

There's a commotion out in the hall and Pam charges in, followed by one of the nurses. Max looks back at his wife but it's not Maggie, it's Andi. The nausea's coming.

"What is going on?" Pam says, "I could hear you all the way down by the elevators."

The nurse stands by the door.

"Ask *him,*" Andi says, pointing a finger. The phone rings again. She grabs it up off the nightstand, looks at the screen and shoves it toward Max. "It's your *girlfriend.*"

"I'm coming out," Rebecca says when he answers.

They can all hear it.

"Okay," Max says.

"They're giving me the plane. I'll be there by dinner."

"Rebecca?" Max says.

"Yes, who did you think it was?"

"What about your appointment?"

"I do not need the god damn appointment, I need you. Where are you staying?"

The nurse leaves the room. Andi is closing her eyes and Pam is slowly getting the picture. *Miami Blue* is her favorite, too. The accent, the careful diction, what Max had said that day on the dock, teasing, she looks at the phone like it may be a bomb. They all hear Rebecca crying.

"Becca, whatever it is we'll be fine."

"Will we?"

Andi has opened her eyes.

"What hotel are you staying?"

Max swallows, hard. He's fighting the nausea. Andi walks over and takes his hand. She looks like her mother again, the day she told him the news. *We have to tell the girls.* Max is thinking how nothing ever works out; how there is only the balance – one thing leaves, another returns – he takes a deep breath, feeling the touch of his daughter's hand.

"Sloan-Kettering."

He can barely get out the next words.

"Room 409."

Hypomania

by Gloria Garfunkel

Flying Ralph here. Today I am driving home from the best haircut ever and the blossoms on the trees make me feel euphoric, sailing through traffic. I love spring. But I don't think it is spring that is causing the elation. I also bought twenty-five shirts at Macy's at the mall on my way home which I don't need, but when I'm manic, I can't make decisions and so I buy everything. Money goes flying out the window. I bought two cars once. Most of the shirts are pretty nice. Some were mediocre but on sale. I also bought a new Mac laptop and iPhone. I'm feeling stupendous. All the traffic lights are green.

I get home and start writing a novel about a Bipolar Quality Assurance Manager. I write a hundred pages and I feel fantastic. With bipolar hypergraphia, you write a lot but the quality isn't necessarily great. Nevertheless, while you are manic you are also grandiose. So I think it could be a bestseller.

Emerald

by John Wentworth Chapin

Just because I love you doesn't mean you're not crazy. Charles usually says this to his friend Stephanie when she complains that everything is going wrong, that the world is conspiring against her. Charles says it, she laughs, and she reassesses her perspective on the whole thing. It's healthy; it's what friends do.

However, he's just said it to his mother at her favorite café, in response to the saga of the balcony-flower-box feud. When her bright green hyacinth buds withered to black sludge before blooming, she took it to a laboratory for analysis, certain a sinister squirt of RoundUp was the culprit. She used to be president of her condo association but was ousted last year, and ever since then the new president and the treasurer – who engineered the coup – have been out for her blood. The lab results were inconclusive, so she is trying to get access to the security footage.

Just because I love you doesn't mean you're not crazy. She stares at him blankly, as though fumbling to unpack his point. Her mouth opens a moment, then clamps shut, and she shakes her head slowly.

"It's my *birthday,*" she reminds him gravely. Charles knows; this is the reason for the lunch, after all, because she has opera tickets for tonight and birthday celebrations are only valid on the day of.

She continues, all hurt and staccato. "That's *not* something you *say* to *people*, you *don't* say 'I love you *but*,' you say 'I *love* you' and leave it at *that*." The gravity of her response – the over-the-top *magnitude* – would be a laugh point in a sitcom, but not now.

Charles replays the phrase – *justbecauseloveyoudoesn-'tmeanyou'renotcrazy* – in search of the elusive word 'but'. Just because he doesn't find it doesn't mean he should say anything. Normally, he would remain silent, but not today. "That's not what it means. And I didn't say 'but'."

"Perhaps you could enlighten me what you *do* mean, then?" She is brittle.

"I guess I should have said, 'If you're nice to the condo board, they'll be nice back.'"

She tosses her napkin to the table and stands up. "I don't know why you are picking a fight with me *on my birthday*," she says, "but I am going to the ladies' room."

He doesn't know why he's picking a fight with her, either. Probably because he wants to talk, not listen, even if it is her birthday. He has a lot to talk about.

At dinner, Charles steers the last tater tot through a puddle of burger juice and into the remaining smear of green salsa before popping it into his mouth. He wipes his face with an already-destroyed paper napkin and waits for Stephanie to point out the spot he's missed. She's too busy having her mind blown, however.

"You're not just *planning* to help her? You're actually *doing* it?" Stephanie says, her carefully thinned eyebrows arching higher than the squeak in her incredulous voice.

"I'm not entirely sure how far I'm going with it," he says. "For now we're just doing research and considering options. It needs to look natu– "

"You're talking about life and death! It's not just *options*. This woman needs *help*. Like psychiatric help."

This woman is Esther, who almost killed Charles in a freak car accident several months earlier. Where she failed with Charles, she succeeded with three others – a grown woman and two boys – and now she's bedridden and has asked for Charles' help to end her life. The trick is that suicide doesn't pay: as she explained it to Charles, her insurance gives a reduced benefit for suicide. It needs to look natural.

Stephanie says, "It's not like she is dying or has Alzheimer's or something, right?"

"We're all *dying*," Charles answers.

"Spare me the philosophy, Mr. Three Years of Community College!"

"It's true. You or I could be dead before Esther."

"Just because I love you doesn't mean you're not crazy," she answers, and Charles has to laugh. "I want you to promise me to make an appointment for her. She has to have a social worker or something." Stephanie is a counselor at one of the less-ritzy private schools in Baltimore. She thinks her job keeps her thumb on the pulse of the city; Charles thinks it makes her clueless.

"Jesus, Stephanie. She's black, not poor. They don't give you an automatic social worker." He laughs again, differently.

Stephanie's eyes narrow. "From the hospital, asshat. A social worker for her home healthcare. A case manager, a nurse."

"Oh," Charles says. "My bad."

"Someone *trained* to look after her who isn't helping her build a do-it-yourself euthanasia kit."

"She killed three people –" Charles stops himself; he promised he'd keep Esther's secret that despite her claims of amnesia to the police and doctors, she remembers the accident. "She is going to be hauled into court by the families. The parents of those two boys! Doesn't she have the right to end her life?"

"Despair is temporary, but suicide is permanent. How can things ever get better if she ends it?"

"She is bedridden, never to walk again. She is guilt-ridden from mowing down three perfect strangers. She's haunted by her guilt – she can't sleep, she can't read a book, she can't watch movies, and she's stuck in an adjustable bed in her dining room. She can't live with herself. That doesn't sound like despair to me. That sounds like logic."

People cluster around stoops and street corners drinking the warm spring air, screenless windows thrown wide open. Stephanie's words linger in Charles' head, so instead of heading straight home after dinner, he heads to Esther's house. It's late, but she says she doesn't sleep.

He finds himself oddly reassured in her presence. When he's away from her, he doesn't know what the hell he's doing. When he's with her, the mewling complaints in his head disappear; he feels a purpose in life. Figuring out why she killed those people. Exploring the mysteries of the universe. Helping her find a way to end her life that meets her criteria (painless, doesn't inconvenience the neighbors, looks natural). Charles feels permeable around Esther; her goals become his own. Esther has a power over him to make him feel what she feels, and it's more compelling than the rest of his life. It's like being around a baby. The baby cries, you're unhappy. The baby laughs, you join in.

It wasn't until listening to Stephanie at dinner – and he thinks what she said was bullshit – that he realized that when Esther is gone, Charles will have nothing. He will be as aimless as he is during the week when he doesn't see her.

He shuffles up the walk to Esther's house, windows open and lights ablaze, illuminating the spring green bushes and grass in front of her rowhouse. He spots movement in the house and stops; he doesn't want to barge in on her if she has company. He cranes his neck to look inside and confirm there's someone there.

"You looking for somebody?"

A man sits in the shadows on the stoop of the house next door. His tone is not un-friendly, but Charles is out of place here – young white man standing still in the twilight on an old woman's front walk in an all-black neighborhood.

"I was just going to see Esther," Charles says.

"She's home," the guy answers, evenly. He takes a sip from the small bottle – beer? wine? – balanced on his knee. Charles can't see his face well enough in the dark to tell the man's age.

Charles catches another glimpse of movement from inside Esther's house. Esther walks through the doorway to her living room. She moves slowly, hands on doorframe and then sofa for balance, but she's walking.

Walking.

The man on the stoop says, "Are you going to go in? Or … ?"

"I shouldn't have come," Charles says to the man, quickly. "It's too late, and I … I shouldn't bother her."

"She don't get much company," the man says.

Charles starts to respond but then stops: Esther has come now to the window, looking out. Charles wonders for a moment if she sees him, looking outside into the dark from a lit room. But then he sees a flinch, a look of pain flash across her face, and he knows she sees him.

His mind plays back their conversation yesterday: she wants to donate her eyes. A little girl from the neighborhood had a corneal transplant and now sees as good as new. Esther said she'd like to be able to help somebody like that.

She looks out at Charles standing in a pool of light on her walk, her pale green eyes upon his. Esther steadies herself against the window frame, looking silently down at him. Charles turns and leaves without a word. He has many questions, but now he wouldn't believe any of her answers.

Scarecrow

by Lynn Beighley

Seated at the chain restaurant, cameramen in two locations nearby, me and my dad wired for sound. What I know and what I'm guessing:

This is *You Tell Me* reality television show related garbage. (Know.)

I see a couple people from work at a table in the corner. Wow, what a coincidence! (I'm making the most surprised face you've ever seen in your life ever. EVER. Even more surprised than when your mother found out she was pregnant. No, that's not fair. It's a lot more surprised than that.) (Know.)

My dad is still a jerk. He was a jerk when I was a kid, he remains a jerk to this day. (Know.)

Bill will pop out of a giant cake in a few minutes. Naked. (Guess.)

This will not end well. (Know.)

Dad looks at me as though I'm a glass perched on the edge of a table. Clearly, my father the egoist is finally, after twenty-something years, looking out for what's best for his sweet little baby girl.

"Jenn, I," he starts coughing and takes a swig of his scotch. A big swig. A 2-ounce swig. That's not a trivial amount of scotch. And that's on top of what he's already had.

People in reality television land are grinning and probably playing drinking games where they take drinks when he does. I hope they're violently ill and hung over, all of them. Yes.

"Jenn, your young man came by my office today." My young man. "I want you to know that I approve, sweetheart."

Cameras, both of them, are aimed at me. I'm a deer in the laser sights of expert hunters, and my dad has set me up.

I toss back the Manhattan. I say nothing. I smile. Dad says nothing. He looks constipated, in a happy way. I wave at a waiter glancing my way.

All the waiters are glancing my way, everyone in this idiotic fire-roasted-overcooked-steak-free-salty-peanuts-emporium is glancing my way.

This is not me bragging. This is the truth: I'm famous. You know who I am, oh, ninety percent of you. And your friends have already filled you in, oh out-of-the-loop ten percent. They said, "OMG (they say *oh emm gee*), that's the girl Bill Plover's in love with on *You Tell Me*! And there are cameras, holy shit!"

And then I feel a hand on my back. I look up and it's Seamus.

"Jenn, what a surprise," he says, winking. (People who wink, how do they do it? I try, and I always feel like I'm trying to give a secret signal while I'm yelling "LOOK AT ME I'M WINKING LOOK" at the same time.)

I go for suave and polished, not anxious and jittery. I fail, but I stutter out, "Seamus. Seamus. Uh. Dad. Seamus." I flail my right hand about, making straw-filled Scarecrow introductions. (If I only had a brain is apt just now.)

But then I stand up. Enough of the cameras. Enough of my dad, pandering to them. Enough of a white knight swooping in to save me.

E-fucking-nough.

I don't say, "excuse me," like I'm off to the ladies'.

167

(Ordinarily, I would have said, "I have to see a man about a whore," because I think that's hilarious.)

I don't say anything as I grab my bag. I don't look at Seamus, my wannabe hero, or Dad, my wannabe pimp, or the camera people who want to stay in their jobs. I walk out the door.

Just outside, I see Bill Plover in a tuxedo with a bouquet of roses. I stop in front of him.

"Thanks," I say, as I grab the flowers. A thorn bites into my hand.

"Thanks," I say again, as I whop the camera of the bored-looking guy filming it all. Oh, this'll play great in Peoria.

And I sprint to my car, start it, and back out of the lot. My bloody right hand slips on the wheel. My phone is buzzing, and I see Seamus under the awning, looking at me and frowning.

Well, I still have my cat, Pollock.

Let It Be Done

by Andrew Stancek

Zero at the bone. I feel it.

Bed-ridden all those months with Perthes disease, I dreamt even while awake. For hours, I'd lie on the bed, eyes open, seeing not out, but in. Nighttime was best – no distractions, no movement, no sound, no smell, fingers outstretched and mind clear. My breath became regular; my heartbeat slowed; my stomach gurgled and then settled.

All was still.

I wasn't searching, wasn't thinking. I wasn't concentrating, aiming at a resolution.

I emptied.

I feel sorriest for Mom. She had an increasingly hard time with Dad, then suffered through my sickness and Dad skedaddled and now she finds my fame debilitating. She loves me, I know, and doesn't ever say, "Be normal, will you?" just as she wouldn't say it if I had polio, but I know that's what she'd like.

She's a reader. This stillness which for me is a recent gift has always been hers – if such a thing can be transmitted, then I got it from her. In my bedridden times, when I wasn't looking out the window, when I was sleeping or lying there, eyes open, she was still. When she wasn't, she read to me. Hour after hour her voice soothed. She began with the Bible of course, which she reads to herself most of all, and sometimes she didn't have to look down at the page because she already knew that passage, carrying it in her heart.

> *Mary, do not be afraid, you have won God's favor. Look! You are to conceive in your womb and bear a son, and you must name him Jesus. He will be great and will be called Son of the Most High. The Lord God will give him the throne of his ancestor David; he will rule over the House of Jacob forever and his reign will have no end.*

I heard that time and time again, and now I don't need to read it either; it has become a part of me. But Mom suffers no delusion that she's Mary and I'm a Savior. She intoned the consolation of the Psalms and the gore and romance of Exodus and Samuel and Kings; her eyes burned as she recited, "I will show you what is to take place in the future," and rumbled with the twenty-four thrones.

Homer was another whom she read often without eyes on the page. The Trojan Horse was left behind, Laocoön issued his warning and the serpents strangled him. Mom's voice is melodious; she could have been a singer. But she also bellowed. "Beware the Greeks, even ones bearing gifts!"

She recited Longfellow and Millay, Frost and above all Emily Dickinson. So here I am, with zero at the bone, unable to stop for Death, feeling he "kindly stopped for me."

It's been raining for three weeks. I don't expect it to last for forty days, won't dissipate into the crankdom of Doomsday prophecy. I am more conscious of death, particularly my own, since I've been gifted. My life won't be long. Looking out the window at torrents of rain, I see myself dead in it. Stephen Dedalus discovers we are alone and says he will not serve. I am with him on the aloneness and this gift, my many gifts, well, I am not sure I will serve.

Tattarrattat. Palindromes fascinated me even before I was looking at birds. Because of my name I heard "madam I'm Adam" when I was about three and pored through books of palindromes. And now it's all coming together. Zero at the bone and the strangled Laocoön and Joyce's tattarattat and I will not serve.

They're coming. I know they are. I hope Mom will be all right. There's nothing we can do. We both have to say, "Let it be done unto me as you have said."

Barn Party

by Rachel Ambrose

"Sometimes it's not who you know, it's who you don't know," says Blake as he boosts me over a fence to a field waving with soft yellow flowers. "Let's go meet somebody."

His green eyes shine in the bright light, and my stomach does that wonderful swooping thing I've become accustomed to. He's trying to get me over my fear of people, and trying to get me to come out of the house and interact with humanity more often. We've been spending a lot of romantic nights in, so coming out was supposed to be novel.

"Being an artist," he said to me recently, "I've found that creativity can't take place in a vacuum."

Whenever something goes wrong, I just use that as an excuse to stay in. Not that things have gone wrong a lot; Blake is so charming that it's hard for anyone to be annoyed with him.

We're climbing over this fence to get to a barn party one of his artist friends is throwing. I haven't been in a barn since I was at a petting zoo when I was ten years old, so this is going to be interesting. I'm wearing cowgirl boots and a purple cotton dress, and I feel very country. "Let's go can something!" I exclaim as we walk across the field hand in hand. My excitement is tempered by my near constant anxiety, so I'm tugging at my dress and fixing my hair without even realizing what I'm doing, and Blake spins me around and kisses me to distract me. We've figured out that this is a near cure-all for the anxiety. This has taken much research and hours of lip locking, and it's been a struggle, let me tell you. An absolute cross to bear.

Crossing the field and entering the barn, I'm surrounded by ladies in dresses and jeans and riding boots, and some of them are even wearing cowboy hats, which might be taking things a little too far, and Blake's air-kissing a lot of them and there are cries of excitement and one of the girls, a pretty brunette with curly hair, even dares to run up and hug him, wrapping her arms around his neck. He laughs and pushes her off, swinging around her to introduce her to me. "Claire, this is Jackie, she's a potter," before high fiving a guy. "Hey, I'm Robin," he says to me, handing me a mason jar filled with pink liquid. "Try our watermelon wine, it's the house speciality." I feel like I've stumbled into some forgotten hippie commune. I take a sip of the drink to steady myself and gasp; it's closer to moonshine than wine, although it's so murderously sweet that it almost tastes good.

Blake never stops touching me during the introductions, and between the alcohol and his hand, I feel almost confident, even though there's a constant buzz of static in my head. Jackie follows us around like a lost, slightly jealous puppy (although that could be my own projection). She makes little comments to him every so often that he sort of nods away, and I feel a little bad. Instead of being freaked out that she's somehow set her sights on Blake, I decide to face things head-on for once, and turn to talk to her.

"So, you're a potter?" I ask her. "I don't really, um, pot. I like those paint-your-own-pottery places, though."

She smiles at me like I'm the most idiotic person in the world. I feel like morphing into a turtle just so I can crawl back into an actual shell and stay there with my glass of moonshine. "I make art with beauty that also serves a purpose within the home environment," she says, and I want to punch her in the mouth because, damnit, I want to be able to say pretentious sentences like that.

"Oh," I say, struggling to come up with a response. "Well, I'm sure your work is important."

"Have you seen Blake's work?" she asks. "It's very chimerical, almost quixotic." She sips her drink, which is a soft green, and doubtlessly more sophisticated than my fruity concoction.

I blink at her. Whose idea was it to pull out the SAT words now? "I have," I say quickly. I actually haven't. Whenever I ask, he tells me he's working on a new series of paintings and that I can see them when they're done. "Have you heard about his new series? He's being very secretive about it."

She smiles knowingly, and I curl my fingers into fists; she better not know him in the Biblical sense, I find myself thinking. "He never reveals his paintings before he considers them complete. He says it interferes with the freedom of his creative brain," Jackie says smugly. As if he has more than one brain. Honestly, this is why I don't hang out with artists very much, and it's a damn miracle I haven't broken up with Blake yet because of it. That might have been the first time that breaking up with him at all has crossed my brain, I realize. It seems important, and I file it away for later introspective analysis. (See, now their vocabulary is seeping into mine!)

I really, really do not care for Jackie. I try to slip away, but she follows me around as I catch back up to Blake, who's making the rounds through the crowd. Luckily, we drink more, and as I have more alcohol, I find more reasons to be amused by Jackie instead of annoyed. She keeps trying to thrust herself into our conversations, but Blake is so focused on me that her attempts are hilarious rather than wrath-inducing. I want to throw out obscure names and concepts like "l'esprit de l'escalier" at her just to see if she knows what they mean. Maybe that's the watermelon wine talking; I'm feeling giddy and spinny and utterly like I could get along with these people given enough alcohol. Then again, alcohol will solve all your problems if you give it enough of a chance, and then it'll kill you as recompense for the gesture.

Miss

by Gill Hoffs

"Can you fit in a quick one before you head for your weekend home?"

Zoe's using her most persuasive honeyed tones, the voice she uses with the trickier clients when their favourite girl's booked out and she wants them to go on a date with another escort instead.

"I'm meant to be getting the train from Deansgate in 2 hours. I only got off a job twenty minutes ago."

"You'll like this one, honest, and it won't take long. Just a gallery opening. No funny business, in and out, canapés and smiles, that's it."

"I'm knackered, babe. Seriously."

"Aw go on. Pleeeeeease?"

I find it hard to turn her down, and she knows it. The opposite isn't true, unfortunately.

I sigh. "Alright."

"You'll do it?"

"Yes, okay. But I'm leaving my stuff at the office and coming there straight after, so you better be waiting, yeah? I'll need a run to Deansgate for a later train."

"That's great, babe, sure. I can do that, no bother. The event runs from three to five, so you shouldn't be *that* late."

She'll take me herself? Bonus!

"What time and who and where? Any special requests?"

176

She gives me the details and I nod, and wonder who let her down and why as I have a quick shower and wash the previous customer's cum from my tits. What to wear? Hmm … Zoe's booked the car for a hasty pickup so I slip on a clingy cotton dress in deepest blue, with just a thong underneath to keep my bush flat, nude heels, and tie my hair in a sleek plait that lies straight and heavy down my back. My planned outfit for home of bootcut jeans, strappy vest, and a sweater, gets tossed in my rucksack with a bra and trainers, and I apply my reddest lipstick (special request) and smoke out my eyes with kohl. A light brush of blusher, not enough to be obvious, and a mint to suck. I'm fastening a heavy bracelet, silver and lapis lazuli, round my wrist when the car arrives. A spray of scent, and I'm done.

The art is obvious and tacky, a tired play on old classics and pop motifs with dogs in bowties playing poker on iPads instead of with cards, and a stuffed squirrel done up like Elvis, and the client is querulous and grey and gropey but the canapés are delicious so I suck it up and smile with shining lips and teeth. I see people assessing us, an unlikely pair, and pat my client's bottom when it looks like I think no-one's looking (though really I can see everything reflected in the cheap not-what-should-be-used-in-galleries glass). One woman nods approvingly and I wonder if she's his friend or just seeing hope for herself at his age.

I try not to clockwatch, and when the client murmurs something about "Perhaps dinner?" his breath warm and wet in my ear, his hand brushing my buttocks, I smile and demur. "So sorry, I'm having a fabulous time but the car's coming at five – prior engagement, you know how it goes. Perhaps next time? Somewhere … intimate?"

He licks his lips and winks at me, and I smile up at him in return.

He walks me out to the car, kissing me on the cheek for the benefit of the snoutcasts clustered beside the door, and I touch my fingertips to my lips in a sweet send-off as the driver turns up the volume on what turns out to be some weepy-waily country singer's greatest hits. Her dog's left her for a heavy-drinkin' rodeo-ridin' mime. Or something.

Three songs later, a trio of twangy dirges about the tosspots in the singer's life, and I don't even wait for the car to halt but just open the door as the driver slows beside the office, pop the seatbelt release, and go free.

She's waiting for me with a cup of tea, Earl Grey with milk, and a digestive biscuit. Her hair's pulled back into a messy ponytail, high on the crown of her head like a cheerleader, and I know that means she hasn't been arsed to shower before work, but she looks pretty and girlish and fresh to me.

"How'd it go?"

The blinds are open but we're a couple of floors up and I'm past caring about who sees what, so I slip the straps from my shoulders and drop my dress where I stand, kick off my heels, and take a quick slurp from the cup. Her eyes don't leave my face, so I put the cup on the desk she's sitting on, between the potplant and her thigh, and start getting dressed.

"Fine, fine. Bit boring but the food was okay. Great asparagus tarts."

"They'll make your wee smell."

I pull on my jeans. "Mine only ever smells of roses."

She wrinkles her nose while I hook my bra closed then roll a vest down over my boobs.

"I think I'm the only girl ever who hates them flowers," she says, swinging her legs. "Give me the chocolate Roses over them prickly bastards any day of the week."

Sweater then socks, pause to dunk the biscuit, munch it, stick my feet into my trainers without undoing the laces and wriggle them on against the carpet.

"Don't forget the makeup, babe."

Good point. She beckons me to her and I stand with my thighs touching her knees while she gives me a quick onceover with one of the facial wipes she keeps in the emergency kit on her desk. Wipes, basic makeup, tampons, condoms, lube sachets, mints, and clear nail varnish for stopping runs in stockings before they progress from a hole to a ladder. If anyone's wrecking our girls' underwear, it's our clients.

I can tell from her breath that she's been sucking aniseed balls again, and guess she's managed to keep off the cigarettes for perhaps two days now. She gives up every month and follows a now-predictable routine of willpower, aniseed balls, nicotine gum, nail-biting, boozing, then back on them, with each stage lasting a day to a day and a half. I'm no fan of smoking, but I take her as she is.

"You ready?"

"Pretty much. Look okay to you?"

She winks at me and does that tongue-click thing in the side of her mouth that reminds me of cowboys and dirty cops in movies. I take it as a yes.

In her car, a pink one with plastic eyelashes on the headlights and birdshit on the bonnet, *I* get to choose the music from her admittedly awful collection. Though tempted by some cheesy pop I know the words to, and something from a pizza advert in the nineties, I decide instead to choose something I've never listened to or played as a backing track for sex.

"You just away the weekend, babe?"

I nod, and she pops another aniseed ball in her mouth from a stash between the seats. I'm not offended at her not offering me one, I'm pleased. She's naturally well-mannered, brought up to be polite, like me, so I can safely assume she's remembered I don't like them. I hope.

"Going to see my aunt, maybe catch up with my brother, too."

"Something special?"

I shake my head. "Nah, just a catchup. If I don't go to them then they start asking to come to me."

"Do they … ?"

She glances away from the road to raise her eyebrows at me suggestively.

"My aunt does, my brother, no. She's cool with it, I just don't want to be out with family and bump into someone I know."

"I had that once, before I switched to booking and admin. His face was a picture – couldn't work out if my mum was a working girl or a client!"

"God, how cringeworthy."

"I know."

There's a thump and from the sound of it, somebody's been rear-ended up ahead. Zoe taps the brakes and the lines of traffic on our stretch of road grinds to a halt. She crunches the aniseed ball between her teeth, moves her head from side to side then rolls down the window and pokes her head out, straining to see what's going on up ahead.

"Looks like you might miss your train, babe. Smashed it across both lanes, and the drivers are having it out on the tarmac." It's quite warm for May but with the way she's twisting I can't help but notice the little bumps poking through her top. They point up, not down, and I imagine licking them.

She turns her engine off, and looks at me. Smiles, and says, "There's later trains. It'll be fine."

I smile back, I can't help it, and murmur, "It already is."

Saturdays suck, and also Sundays

by Susan Tepper

Pedersen knows he is one of those men earmarked for history. What, or how – the particulars don't interest him nearly as much as the fact that he's been chosen. And not to lay the most benevolent of mankind's gifts onto another. But simply that he was marked from long before his birth. He believes this to be a sacred trust between himself and his maker, wearing it casually like the earflaps with strings that dangle from the sides of his cracked leather cap. He trusts nothing but his own belief system. The one thing not in short supply in Pedersen's life.

Saturdays suck, and also Sundays. The children, his little darlings, tucked away in their backyards, or at some park with parents who watch ready to swoop if a stranger so much as tilts their lips in a semi-smile.

Pedersen cuts some Gouda. Then sits on the floor waiting for Swoon to come out of his rat hole behind the refrigerator molding. He munches the cheese loudly hoping this will attract the white rat.

"You are so fucked!" he cries out when the rat doesn't appear. "I ain't sharing with you."

He takes off the cracked leather cap and flings it across the kitchen. The floor tiles, damaged from years of low-rent families, have dirt stuck in the grooves. From the side of the refrigerator, the rat pokes its quivering pink nose. "So you decided to make an appearance," says Pedersen. "Big of you."

He holds what is left of the Gouda out to the rat.

Confession

by Jessica McHugh

The service was brighter than the weather. Edward McKenzie's sermon about forgiveness filled the congregation with hope on the dreary Sunday.

Proud to have lifted their spirits, Father Edward retires to the sacristy to decompress. As successful as his sermon had been, his nerves are still on edge. Only a few weeks remain until his teaching position at St. Anthony's begins, and all the preparation in the world hasn't subdued his anxiety.

He drums his fingers on the lid of the Lost and Found jar, his mind drifting. It ventures to canopy beds and ballrooms, places he's afraid to venture in real life. But in fantasy, he delights in gazes falling upon his gowned body in admiration.

The knock on the door jolts him from the reverie. Turning, he smiles as Charlie Kitner's head pokes into the room, a crooked grin creeping up the man's stubbled cheek.

"Sorry to bother you, Father. Are you busy?"

He stands, gesturing for his parishioner to enter. "It's no bother. How may I help you, Mr. Kitner?"

"Charlie."

Edward nods. "How may I help you?"

"I know it's not your usual time, but I was wondering if you would hear my confession."

The parishioner's hands shake on the doorframe. His upper lip collects sweat, and his eyes dart around the room.

Drawing close, Edward says, "My son, you look unwell."

Charlie exhales heavily. "I might be, Father."

He flinches when Edward touches his arm. "Of course I will listen," he replies. "Please, follow me."

But Charlie doesn't follow; he leads. As he strides ahead, Edward can't help but notice the man's athletic physique beneath his suit. His imagination often runs wild when it comes to Mr. Kitner – during sermons, during prayers, even as he stands next to his wife during communion.

Grandma Eleanor's voice fills his mind. *Careful, Edward. This man needs help, not ogling.*

"I understand."

Charlie looks over his shoulder. "Did you say something, Father?"

"Sorry, I was just reminding myself of something," he replies, gesturing to the confessional. "Please, take a seat."

Inside the booth, Edward inhales the distinctive scent of secrets. It's a musty smell, tinged with a floral perfume that recalls memories of his grandmother's closet. As a child, he spent hours there, buried in old clothes to hide from his mother's boozy wrath.

Stirred by comfort and concern, Edward slides open the partition to see Charlie Kitner's face segmented by the rosewood lattice. Although he sits in profile, Edward's focus wanders of its own accord, finding the parishioner's eyes in the smoldering dark. For a few moments, Edward's desire follows his gaze.

"Forgive me, Father, for I have sinned. It's been three years since my last confession."

Holding his hands in his lap, his fingers entwined, Father Edward replies, "What have you to confess, my son?"

"I've had impure thoughts," he replies. "A lot of them. Recently."

"It's human nature, my son. But thoughts are not deeds," Edward says. "Have there been deeds?"

The sounds of fidgeting echo from Charlie's booth. "No," he says. "But these thoughts – they might be unnatural."

"Why do you think that?"

Charlie responds with an audible gulp.

"You're safe here," Edward says. "God is listening, and His forgiveness is immeasurable."

"You said that in your sermon."

"Because I believe it."

"But you don't – you can't –" he huffs, even growls. He sets his face close to the lattice, and Edward clears his throat, scooting to the left side of his seat. "Do you really live the way you want, Father?"

Sweat prickles Edward's forehead. "This isn't about me," he says.

"Yes," Charlie whispers. "Father, I love my wife, but I can't deny that I've had feelings for other people – other *men*."

Edward swallows the rising lump in his throat. "I see."

"Is it wrong? These days it's hard to know the church's position."

"You're married. The church is quite clear on that."

Silence is the great betrayer, and following it with a sigh further robs a lie of its steam. Edward doesn't believe Charlie when he takes too long to say, "I would never cheat on my wife."

"If you're at war, you must do what it takes to find peace."

"That's why I'm here," he says. "I need something to come of this. I'm afraid I won't be able to control myself much longer."

Edward is apt at disguising his desire to help someone in need, but Charlie Kitner is different. He leans too close, speaks too deep. He even peers through the partition to find Father McKenzie's evading eyes.

"Do you believe your desires are wrong?" Edward asks.

Charlie doesn't pause this time. "No. I desire my wife as a man should, but these other desires, these feelings I have when I see a certain man – they feel right, more than any heterosexual relationship I've had. But the Bible says it's a sin."

"The Bible mentions many sins, my son, several of which do not pertain to the modern world."

"So you don't believe it's sinful?"

"I believe ..." Edward's mother threatens to pollute his brain with disparagements, but he blocks her at the first drunken word. "My child, I believe love is love."

"Who do you love, Edward?"

He clears his throat, but his voice is strained when he repeats, "This isn't about me."

Charlie Kitner's fingers hook into the lattice. "Yes, it is. I have feelings for many men, but none so strong as the feelings I have for you."

Edward's lungs empty, and he breaks out in a cold sweat, but he steadies himself by tugging on his crucifix.

"And you seek forgiveness for these feelings," he says.

"No, Father, I seek satisfaction."

Edward shifts in his seat. "Is there anything else you wish to confess?"

"Did you hear me? I said –"

"Yes, I heard you. And so did God. Say five 'Our Fathers', and if you're contrite, you will be forgiven."

Edward has never rushed through a confession before, but he's also never experienced one like this. Flirtation has never been aimed at him, period. Hurrying from the booth, he hears Charlie Kitner's exit, but he doesn't look back. He disappears into the sacristy, locks the door, and snaps open

186

the lid of the Lost and Found jar. The lipstick found by Nelson the altar boy a few months back glistens among the castaways, as if begging for liberation. Reaching inside, he doesn't deny the cosmetic its freedom, or his own.

Hunching over the table, he spins the lipstick out and inhales the distinctive scent. It, too, smells of secrets.

There are no prayers Edward McKenzie can speak to banish Charlie's confession, but with the lipstick pressed to his smile, he can delay guilt for a while.

Giveth and Taketh

by Shane Simmons

"My sister had a miscarriage."

Sandra hasn't mentioned her sister for a while.

"Mum called me in the morning, trying her best to persuade me to go and see Saskia, but I ended up screaming and hanging up the phone." Sitting in the sullen lamplight she pours the cheap red until it almost overflows the rim of her glass. Quickly, she swallows a mouthful before placing the bottle on the coffee table and slides it in my direction. "But then I figured I'd just go, watch karma in action. Maybe tell Saskia it was all her own doing. So I called back and got my mum to pick me up."

"Please tell me you didn't rub your sister's face in it?" I nibble the skin on the joints of my fingers.

"At first Mum did all the talking. I just kept out of the way, watching." She draws a breath so deep it's as if she's sucking all the air from the room. "I didn't expect her to look so bad. I've never seen her like that before. I ended up walking out."

As her eyes redden, I notice the wine in her glass has disappeared before I've even taken my first sip. I carry the bottle over to her, fill her up and leave it at her feet. "I brought plenty, you keep that one."

"Mum came and sat on the doorstep with me. You know, for once she talked some sense. She said she didn't expect me to forgive her. Because I can't, not ever. But all things aside, she will always be my sister. I couldn't punish her, not when she was so ..." Her head drops and a tear falls from her cheek. "We went back inside and she left us alone for a bit. Saskia and I ended up crying in each other's arms."

My shoulders droop as I sigh. I'm not sure many people would expect her to have forgiven her sister, but I find myself somewhat proud of her for not taking the cruel route she'd planned.

"Where's Marlon tonight?"

"Night shift. I can't really talk about any of this with him. That's why you're here. You're good with this emotional stuff. And he really doesn't like me talking about my exes."

I don't know where she gets the impression that I'm good with 'emotional stuff'. "We should order some takeaway," I say. "My treat."

Sandra rifles down the side of her chair. A selfish part of me knows that if we don't get something in now, I'll be left to have jam on toast for dinner when I get back to mine.

She tosses me a pile of menus. "You choose, I'm not feeling all that peckish after the day I've had."

I shuffle through them, hoping one will call out to my appetite.

"Anyway," she adds, "there's more."

Of course there's more, it could never have ended there.

"Later, Mum was planning on dropping me home and then going back to stay with Saskia for a bit, but when we walked out of her place I found *him* standing there."

"'*Him*'? Who '*him*'?"

"THAT BASTARD!"

"Oh, Stephen."

She points her finger at me and scowls, "Don't you say his name, not in front of me, not in this flat. Not ever."

I put my hands up to apologise.

"No," she crumples down in her chair, "I'm sorry, it's hardly your fault." She brushes her hair from her face and draws her fingers over her tired eyes. "We walked out, and I spotted him walking up the path. Next thing I remember was that some guy was pulling me off him."

"Pulling you off him?"

"Mum says I booted him so hard in the balls that he keeled over, and that when he was down I just continued kicking the scumbag. When she couldn't stop me, she called some passing guy over to pull me off him."

"Sandra." I shake my head, "Sandra, Sandra." Her name muffles when I drop my face in my hands.

"What? He got much less than he deserved. If I'd've known he was going to turn up I would have been ready to give him a kitchen knife vasectomy."

Under normal circumstances I'd laugh right about now, but I don't. Sandra's brow is furrowed, her fists rolled up into tight balls, jaw clenched shut.

I return carrying some warm boxes and a couple of plates from her kitchen. Placing it all on the coffee table I start sharing out the pizza, garlic wedges and chicken wings. "I'm making you a plate, otherwise tomorrow you're going to regret downing all that wine on an empty stomach." I get a huff in response. "So, what happened after you were removed from St– … that bastard?"

"Mum dragged me back indoors. Can you believe Saskia wanted to see him? I thought she must've been crazy, so I slapped her to wake her up. You know, like they do in the movies."

I pause as I spoon sour cream dip on the side of her dish, mid-dollop.

"And I'm going to assume that didn't help the situation at all?"

She shakes her head from side to side. "Mum let that bastard in, sat him in the kitchen, and then sent me on my way." Her arms flail through the air before landing back on the arms of her chair with a thump. "And to top it off I had to get the bus home."

I hand the plate to her and sit back down. It's not long before she's wrestling with webs of stringy cheese between her teeth.

"Are all families like this?" We both pause and peer at each other. "Hmm, I guess you've got an idea what I mean, what with your ... you know, mum and dad. And your sister. You have got a sister, haven't you? You never really talk about her."

I pick up her remote control and turn the television on.

"It's complicated. So for the rest of tonight I prescribe us some crap TV, more pizza and no more family-induced traumas."

Poised to bite into the chicken wing in her hand, she shrugs her shoulders, "Fair do's. You've had to suffer enough of my dramas that it's only fair you burden me with some of yours, one day."

She doesn't know that I don't mind. I'd rather she was the one pouring her heart out. Talking only reopens old wounds. And I prefer keeping them shut.

Cosy

by Michelle Elvy

"So, are you ready for your exams, Stephen?"

"Yes."

"And graduation?"

"Yes."

"And college?"

"Yes."

"Do you have anxieties about leaving home?"

Fuck. This was going to go on forever. Stevie had agreed to *see someone* for his parents. He felt bad that they worried so much about him, and he felt even worse that he didn't talk to them much these days. He wanted his parents to stop worrying, so he'd agreed to come sit in this expensive leather chair (*pretty comfy, come to think of it, but who has yellow chairs? Is that really so healthy for all the crazy depressed people who must come sit here an hour at a time? Really? Sunny yellow chair for your dark mood to sink right into?*) for an hour because he thought it'd be a quick way to reassure them that everything was fine. *Anxieties?* Sure. Of course. What the fuck.

"Do you want to talk about the accident?"

"No."

"Why not?"

"Lucky's dead. Nothing else to say."

"And you were close to Lucky."

He'd seen scenes like this in the movies – the Concerned Adult asking the Troubled Teen about his feelings. The teen shifting uncomfortably in his comfy leather chair – but in the movies those chairs are not sunny yellow. And now all he can think is *Christ, I'm in one of those movies, with a ridiculously concerned adult and a ridiculously happy chair.*

"What's so funny?"

Stevie hadn't realized he was smiling. He was thinking about all the movies he'd seen with scenes like this, and how stupid it always looked, the Troubled Teen with nothing to say, the Concerned Adult with so much experience asking all the right questions, gently, gently. Did he have anxieties? Hell, yeah. But they had nothing to do with college. They had more to do with the fact that he'd been thinking about *not* going to college – not yet anyway. He'd been dreaming more and more about his Great Grandpa Gus and an old sailing boat, and he felt the vague notion that he'd like to go exploring. Which of course he'd not admitted to anyone. *Go exploring.* What the fuck. What did that even mean? He figured college could wait, that for a kid like him with decent enough grades college would still be there next year, or the year after. He didn't feel the urge to rush off to the drunken embrace of other freshmen to "grow". That's what adults were always saying: *you grow so much at college.* He had a cousin who got kicked out of college for getting drunk and tearing up the landscaping of the president's house and shitting on his lawn. No thanks, he was not quite ready for that kind of experience yet. He hadn't broken into a car since Lucky died and he wasn't into institutionalized adventure. He needed to be alone. He needed to get away from here, from his loving parents, from Concerned Adults. And from Lucky's ghost.

Lucky. Christ, how'd he have to die? Five people in the car and it was Lucky who died. Front passenger's seat, no seatbelt, feet on the dash, reefer between the lips, then windshield impact and oblivion in the span of a nanosecond. Lucky's last micro-moment. Stevie has played this over and over in his head, tried to live in that moment. He crawls back there to stay, scratches his way in with Lucky, but it's always fleeting. He feels the car lurch and bend, he senses wheels locking, hears a faint gasp from Manny at the wheel, and then he stops his mind to focus on Lucky from his backseat position – he's behind Manny so he has a good view. The car is bending around and starting to flip, flying in the air at great speed and height. He sees Lucky's hair waving around in an unnatural way. He sees Lucky turn to Manny and grin his big stupid grin and start to say something but then he can't hear anything, because suddenly the car lurches another time and Stevie is airborne. He tries to climb back through the window and into the car with Lucky in those next few moments, but he knows that the real reason he can't do it is because there are no more moments for Lucky. Time has stopped. Head and windshield shatter in a million little pieces, cracked together in one last moment, tiny bits of glass and tiny bits of skull a mingling mosaic. Stevie wills one more moment in for Lucky, because one more moment could make a difference. But time stops and Lucky has no more moments. And Stevie is airborne and stretching across the sky in a spatial-temporal dreamscape, leaving his friends behind – leaving Lucky – and soaring toward a faraway seascape where waves rise up like mountains and ships toss like toy boats. In the moment Lucky becomes one with the windshield Stevie is escaping to the Southern Ocean where he rendezvous with his Great Grandpa Gus on the dark hulk of a great oak ship, tumbling in the wintry grey morning sky above a southern Maryland cornfield while the whaler floats up toward him.

"Stephen? Do you want to say anything about the accident?"

"No."

"Do you want to tell me about the dreams?"

The dreams are always the same. Stevie is lifted on a blanket of warmth, surrounded by a frozen January sky. It's May now but he's still stuck in January in his dreams, cushioned on cotton candy clouds above the Maryland cornfield with Great Grandpa Gus rioting along on an old oak schooner in heavy seas below. The ship is breaking up, the canvas, the rigging, the hull, and Stevie reaches for it, then for Gus, and now for Lucky but his fingers slip through all of it – canvas-wire-oak-flesh – and he twirls away in the tornado-black air. Panic now rises in his gut because his voice won't reach from southern Anne Arundel County to Cape Horn where a great sailing ship is tearing apart at the seams nearly a century before. And it won't reach Lucky either.

The dreams occur often, and they are real. They are horrifying and exhilarating. But he can't explain that. He can't play the role of Troubled Teen spilling his guts to the Concerned Adult. Not here, not in this ridiculously comfy chair.

"Stephen, do you want to tell me about the dreams?"

"No. The dreams aren't real."

Two hours later Stevie is walking in the open air and breathing easy. He hears a voice and it's dream-reality again, because this is a voice he thinks about all the time, sleeping and waking, a voice he can't escape. A birdsong in the breeze. But he knows, even though they've become closer in the last couple months, that he can't ever be with Ellie Smithers. Lucky's girl.

"Hey! Hey, you, wait up!" She jogs up behind him, and takes his arm. "Where you going?"

"Down to the pier."

"Can I come?"

"'Course."

"So ... how was it?" He is startled by Ellie's directness, because this feels like a secret he should keep, one of his many. He doesn't want to burden Ellie with his anxieties, how he sees Lucky in the moment of impact, head on windshield, and how that moment seems to coincide with his moment of flying through the window and escaping; how he thinks he may skip college for now and do something else instead and how that idea scares the crap out of him; how he sees his Great Grandpa Gus all the time now, not only in his dreams but even in waking moments – by the old pier, at the post office, in the back garden by the crape myrtle. He has wondered if he's going nuts, but he feels deep down that this is all just part of his reality, and he has a vague notion that it'll be alright if he can just get out of here. But he can't get away if he's walking down the street with Lucky's girl.

A queasiness overcomes him and he's about to think up an excuse to turn and go the other way, away from Ellie and the heat of her body which he can feel next to him through his light windbreaker and jeans, all the way down to his socks, when she says, "You know, I've been meaning to tell you you're a star in our house. I mean, with Sylvie. She talks about you all the time ever since you helped her bury her bird."

"That was a long time ago now."

"I know, but it meant a lot to her. She loved that bird."

"Yellow Bird."

"Yeah. Yellow Bird."

Ellie lets out a little high-pitched chuckle and it reminds him of that day back in March, how quiet it was sitting in the back yard and helping Ellie's little sister bury her canary, and how they sang together and held hands, and how Sylvie looked so *peaceful*. And how Ellie – whose voice he loved and dreamed about both sleeping and waking – could not carry a tune.

He laughs.

"What?"

"Nothing."

"Come on, tell me. What?"

"You know you can't sing, right?"

Ellie laughs too. "Yeah, I know. But I sing for Sylvie. She likes it."

"Are you kidding? She *loves* it."

Then Ellie takes Stevie's hand and squeezes it and says, "Stevie? Tell me about your dreams?" and he finds himself saying out loud, for the first time ever, "The dreams are real."

The Luckiest Sonofabitch on Earth

by Len Kuntz

Outside of Omaha, I stop at a bar and count how many women I've slept with since finding out about my wife's affair. I get to ten and a half, the half being a prostitute who was actually a very convincing cross-dresser.

I think about the life I've left behind, the house on the lake, a home that always felt more like a prison or mausoleum. I try to tell myself things could be worse, they can always be worse. After all, it's a grand adventure I'm on, traveling across the country without any idea where I'm heading, an unorthodox journey that just might be the bravest thing I've ever done.

I drain my glass, relishing the burn, and order another scotch. Even though we're halfway through a sunny May, it's dark in the bar, quiet too, except for a garbled juke box that plays antique Buck Owens and The Buckeroos.

The guy on my right keeps farting into his barstool while reading a tattoo magazine and the guy on my left is busy flexing and unflexing his prosthetic hand. I try not to stare or make eye contact, but I can't look away, and after a moment he says, "I'm still getting used to this thing," adding that his name is Gary.

Gary lost his limb in Kandahar when he was on patrol, saw a ten-dollar bill sticking out from a clump of dirt in the road, and an IED exploded after he reached for it. Gary chuckles. "Moral of the story – greed'll get you every time." He says he's the luckiest sonofabitch on earth, says he could have easily had his head blown off, or any number of body parts.

Hearing this should make me feel grateful for my life, but I'm still wallowing in self-pity and all that optimistic bullshit I'd been contemplating moments ago now feels like tripe.

Gary asks me if I'm married. Gary asks me where I'm from, asks me all kinds of questions before wondering if I'd like to go get high.

Outside, back behind the bar, there are half a dozen garbage cans overloaded with beer and liquor bottles. It smells briny.

Before lighting up, I think of Lana and her boyfriend – the pair I'd met by chance at a convenience store – and what we'd smoked, so I say, "This isn't laced with anything, is it?"

Gary looks at me like I've just told him his kids are ugly.

I take a long drag and hold it until I'm about to implode. Gary smiles a big shit-eating, I-lived-through-hell-and-I'm-still-alive grin, and I think I really like Gary and maybe I should use his example to reset my own pessimism.

Since we're doobie brothers now, I take a good look at Gary's hand. The prosthetic is a strange one, like a robot's, only with plastic where the metal should be, and see-through screws. He catches me looking and says, "It's the latest model."

"It's fancy."

Eddy takes a long hit and tamps the lit end of the joint against his plastic hand where it leaves a gray smudge similar to a spider that's been crushed.

With his other hand, he pulls a pistol out of his jacket and says, "Get on your knees, Fuckhead."

I'm thinking I'm stoned already and that this is a hallucination, but then Gary swipes the air, his claw scraping a good section of my face.

"What the hell?"

"I've shot better than you, and I'm not the patient type."

I get on the ground. It's covered with broken glass and sharp rocks. My knees sting. I notice Gary's wearing steel-tipped cowboy boots.

"Hand over your wallet, then put your hands on the ground, ass up, doggy-style."

I don't know whether to be more frightened about being robbed or the possibility of being buttfucked by some brute with a hook for a hand.

He stuffs my cash into his pocket and tosses the wallet so that it slaps my face and a creased photo of my wife flips out.

"You never asked where I'm from," Gary says. "You never asked a damn thing about me."

He's right, I hadn't.

"You're a selfish prick."

He's probably correct about that as well.

"Now get face down on the ground and don't get up until you've counted to five hundred."

"Hey, how about –"

In one swift move, Gary rams his boot tip, hitting the bulls-eye between my buttocks.

"I told you I was impatient," Gary says, spitting before walking away.

My anus is enflamed. It's hard to concentrate. I count to forty-five and stagger to my feet. I go back in the bar and ask about Gary, but they say they don't know any Gary.

"Captain Hook," I say, making my hand a claw. "The bruiser that was sitting on the stool right there, next to me."

The bartender and fart guy look at me like I'm an idiot.

I start to get angry and ask again.

"You cause a fuss," the bartender says, "I'll call the sheriff."

"I'm just asking about Gary."

"And we just told you we don't know any Gary."

I figure they're probably all in cahoots, but what can I do. "Fine, then give me another scotch."

"No way, Jose."

"Why not?"

"We have the right to refuse service to whoever we want."

"This is fucked."

"Watch your pie hole."

I go over to an ATM that sits by a video poker machine featuring Kim Kardashian's enormous ass and cleavage. I withdraw a hundred, then take out the maximum it will allow in a day, leaving the bar with my middle finger upraised, my own ass smoldering, while I wonder how much a gun costs.

Fifth Inning

by Michael Webb

I never hurry when I know the kids are at the game. Our opponents are headed out of town after the game, so an early start, the 'businessperson's special', eases their travel woes and, as long as we don't fall into one of those 11-9 fracases, gives us a rare afternoon at home. I am anxious to see them, but I know there are bathroom trips and ice creams to eat and goodbyes to say, so I take my own time showering and dressing.

There is a light mood in the locker room, anticipating the leisure to come, along with the game result, a crisp 3-2 win that we finished in a quick 2 hours and 10 minutes. I contributed, ending a seventh inning jam on one pitch and then only needing 10 more to negotiate the 8th, before handing the game to Tex to lock it down. I dress quietly, then make my way down the hallway towards the player parking lot.

The lot is gently managed chaos, with more SUVs than usual bucking for position to exit the garage. I look down the line of cars, and four cars back is my own Yukon, black and foreboding with a distinctive scratch on the driver's side mirror. I stroll down to it. The car I am next to, a boxy BMW, rolls its window down. I see the hawk-nosed face of our starting shortstop, Juan Nogales, looking at me from the passenger seat. A round-faced woman, her tiny arms and legs straining to reach the controls around an enormous belly, is driving, scowling at him, and then at me. He looks at me angrily, his brow knitted with tension.

"Twainie?" he says.

"What's up?" I reply.

"Settle something for me," he says. "Lucasita doesn't believe me about last night."

I think about last night's game, a 9-7 loss, in which Juan had saved my bacon with a diving stop that would have charged me with two runs if he had not snagged it. I thought I knew what he meant.

"The dinner?" I venture.

"Yes! You took me out for dinner because I saved your ass. Again," he says, smiling.

"Sure did. Why? Was he home late?" I say, looking into her enormous brown eyes. She appears deep into what my wife calls the "Fuck You" stage of pregnancy, when all the magic and wonder of it has drained away, and it's purely an endurance trial, trying to get to the end before killing anyone. The seatbelt is forced aside by her huge, taut belly, which looks entirely too large for her tiny frame.

"3 am," she says in a softly-accented voice.

I sneak a glance at Juan, and our eyes lock. Just like when we pick a runner off second, I know his intentions, and I follow his lead. "I'm so sorry," I say earnestly to her. "I didn't mean to keep him out that late. I promise, I'll make sure he gets to bed on time from now on. He's going to need his sleep," I continue, gesturing at her stomach.

"Yes," she says shyly, curling one hand underneath the impossible weight of it. "He will."

"See?" he says as she rolls the opaque window back into place. I make my way down the row of cars, sliding around and into the front seat of my own car. I silently weigh the lie I just told against the truth that Nogales probably saves me two dozen runs a year with acrobatic plays.

"What was that?" my wife says.

"Just guy talk," I say to her. "Juan's wife is about to pop, isn't she?"

"Yup," she says, the car creeping forward. "She's miserable, though. Poor thing. She says he tried to say you took him out to dinner after the game last night! Imagine!" she continues, shaking her head.

"That's ridiculous," I say, staring at the brake lights in front of us.

"I want pizza for dinner, Dad," I hear from the back seat.

"As long as it's OK with Mom, sport. You got it," I say.

Cross Purposes

by James Claffey

In the shade of the rowan tree he sits down, fallen branches crunching under his weight. Loneliness. The death of his parents seems unnatural. Since his mother's visit he's not slept well at all in full sight of the wardrobe from where she'd appeared. Stones unturned, the Bird's hands search the rough mud-caked surfaces for comfort. The smoothness of time, the brazen feel of the rocks, gives him some measure of solace. Only this morning he'd prayed for the French woman to return from her travels so he could allow a mite of hope to penetrate his sour mood.

May, and the trees in bloom, pink and red blossoms all along the river, a time of renewal, energy returned, even, though he'd never admit it to anyone, the hope of love's rekindling. Stupid, it was, too. How he could possibly hold her interest, with his talk of flies and rods, of wild plants and tortured animals.

The Bird turns over and over the few kind words Melodie said to him. Her accent, the delicate fingers, her smile. Then he remembers his mother's jewelry box, the musical one with the tiny dancer turning pirouettes to sprung music. Sadness freefalls, the weight of his grief rooting him to the spot under the tree. Several thrushes sing in the branches, sweet songs, natural sound, no wound springs there, he thinks. A drop of rain plops on the end of his nose, hard. He remains rooted. There's no escaping a drenching, he knows. The water will cleanse him, bring his sadness to a new place, let him release the cry stuck in his throat these many months.

As a boy the Bird couldn't stop searching the trees around the town for eggs. Speckled blue his favorites. The day his father caught him in the shed with a handful was the first real whipping he'd ever received. Even now, the birdsong so beautiful, the sting of his father's hand is fresh on his cold skin. Then, a boy, his skin pitted with acne scars, he sought love every bit as much as today. All through his teenage years failure stalked him like a stray pup, tailing at his heels to the door of his house.

His thoughts are brought back to the moment by a loud "Halloo!" from the road a bit away towards the town. "Bird! By God, that's a bitter day that's in it," calls out Georgie Pepper, the postman, astride the black Raleigh with the wicker basket in front, the cavernous postbag swung over his shoulder like a dead creature.

"'Tis, for certain. There'll be frost on the pisser tonight and no mistake," he says in return. The postman raises a hand from the handlebars, wobbles in a desperate manner, and pushes on into the wind.

The beautiful sky, the thick clouds separating into strewn cotton balls, lifts the Bird's spirits somewhat, and he decides he might as well go back to the house and have a bath with a nice drop of brandy in the water to keep the chills at bay. He'd seen his mother pour the Hennessey into her tub for as long as he could remember, and it strikes him as a better way to close out the day than sitting on damp earth and waiting to catch his death of cold.

As he stiff-legs the pedals of the Raleigh to get up the hill in front of the town, the Bird spots a collarless Alsatian dog rooting about the verge by a telephone booth. "Here, boy! Here, boy," the Bird calls, slowing to a stop. He swings his leg over the crossbar, pushes the bike slowly, and clicks his fingers and the dog shakes a head and lets a long pink tongue droop from its mouth. Slow, step, slow, step, the Bird approaches and the dog lowers its head and lets the Bird scratch behind its ears. "Good boy, there's a good boy." The rain pelts and the Bird opens the phone booth door and slips inside. The Alsatian nudges its snout in the door and pushes its way in. Before the Bird can push back and keep the dog at bay, it's inside and has both front paws on the Bird's shoulders. Some humanity stares back at the Bird as he turns his face to avoid the licking pink of the tongue.

Murphy, the plasterer, drives past the phone box and seeing the Bird's bicycle, slows and honks three times. From inside, the Bird sees the car drive by and tries to slide past the giant beast pinning him in by his shoulders. "Arrah, good boy! Let me past," he says. The dog licks again and the Bird feels a curious sensation in his gut, and a spasm of heat washes over him, and for a moment, his mind wandering away to dark and dangerous places. Before he can gather his thoughts, a rap on the glass startles him, and the priest cocks his head and raises an eyebrow in greeting.

By the time the Bird pushes the dog away and steps out into the rainy day once more, the road is deserted and his bicycle is on its side at the grass verge. "Go on, now. Go home," he tells the dog. The creature sits placidly by the phone booth, a questioning stare in its eyes. Back on the bike again, the Bird pushes off into the rain and leaves the dog pawing at the door of the booth, eager to return to the relative warmth and dryness it offers.

Inside McKettrick's, the crowd is thick and the air is filled with cigarette smoke. He pushes his way to the counter and orders a whiskey to settle his nerves. God, but that dog was a powerful beast, he thinks. Across from him on the far side of the counter, Murphy is supping his pint. He catches the Bird's eye and lets out a tremendous howl. Three or four of his pals, drinkers of renown, follow suit. In moments the entire bar is filled with howling, Murphy scarlet in the face, the tears rolling down his face. "You bloody dog fucker, you!" Murphy yells at the Bird. "Pervert!"

The Bird reddens, turns to old McGettrick and begins to explain about the dog and the phone booth and the rain, but he can't be heard over the howls of the drinkers. He fishes in the pocket of his trousers for a few quid and leaves the money on the counter, fleeing for the safety of the street, forgetting completely to ask for his drink.

The Worst Thing

by Gwendolyn Joyce Mintz

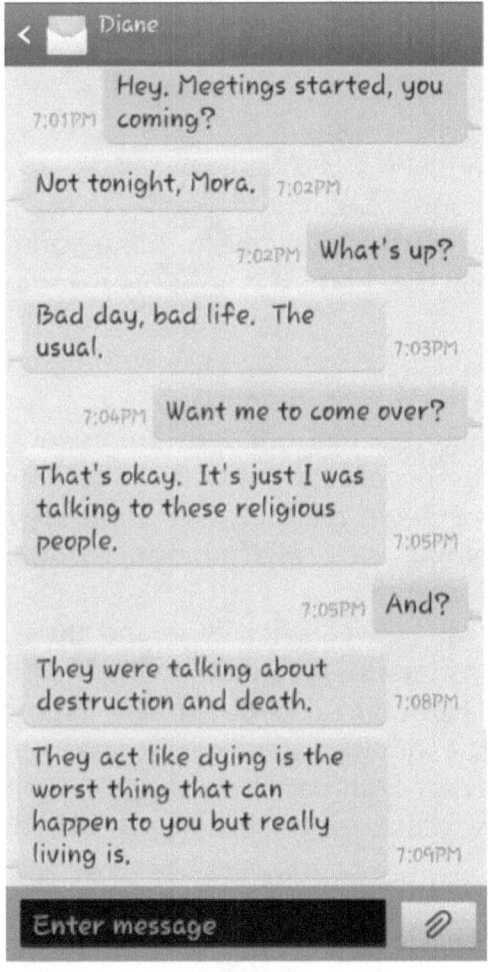

Grace

by Stephen V. Ramey

A river rolls into a vast black sea. There is no churn, no rippling struggle, just the unceasing flow of water, warm into cold. I feel a bubble of grief, and I wake, teeth clenched so tightly my jaws ache.

Mystery, our long-haired cat, is curled atop the comforter in a shard of sunlight from the bedroom window. Anne's side of the bed is empty. The radio-clock reads 10:19.

Sunday used to be our day to sleep in. For the past year, Anne has attended a Spiritualist church a few miles from New Castle. She met the founder, Kim Fogely, at a potluck lunch, and they became fast friends. Kim is supposed to be a medium. I've never met her, but Anne seems convinced there is something to it. Her atheism is more fragile than mine.

I pet the cat between her ears, and those golden eyes open. She leans into my hand, content within the warmth of her sunshine. Her chin sinks down. She licks the matted fur on her chest. I don't remember the last time she really groomed herself. My throat chokes up. At eighteen, Mystery does not have much longer in this world. This, of course, reminds me that neither do I, most likely.

"I should get up." I lift the covers and gently roll away, then fluff a blanket against the cat's spine. She nestles in.

Her front claws knead in and out. "I should work on the book," I say, but I balk at the thought of sitting at that desk, staring at that screen. Five months and I'm still stuck on Chapter Two.

In Chapter One, a mysterious man enters a small town hardware store. The clerk is drawn to his certainty; the store owner notes there's no car in the lot or on the street out front. How did he get here? In Chapter Two, we learn the man, named Zechariah for now, has come from the future to warn against our self-destructive behavior: unfettered reproduction, ecological desecration.

These issues interest me, but no matter what I try, the dialogue will not ring true, the characters will not step off the page. I've cut and pasted and re-cut and re-pasted paragraphs so many times the whole thing is a blur in my mind, and the online thesaurus is exhausted with my constant queries.

I look out the window. Blue sky, not a cloud. Below our house, church spires rise from the bowl of the city. Saint Mary's bells will ring at eleven. Usually I stay in bed until I hear them. Today I am too restless.

This book is supposed to be my masterwork – that's what I keep telling Anne – but the truth is it's just the usual science fiction cautionary tale. You could fill a shelf with versions of this idea. I have nothing original to say. Why do I keep trying? I recall the feeling of grief from my dream, and it swells inside me to the verge of bursting.

I pull off my pajamas and hurry into my best black jeans and white button-down shirt. *I have to get out of this house.*

Downstairs, I leave a mound of food on Mystery's plate before stepping into the crisp morning air. Trees are budding along the back edge of our property. A cardinal sings. The world is emerging from its depression.

I stride down the hill, down the street, black leather shoes scraping through Saint Mary's asphalt lot into the city's heart. Cars blur, a traffic light turns. I come to another church built from red brick and surrounded by a wrought iron fence. I remember reading that it was purchased by a new denomination.

Stained glass windows are inset high on the wall facing me, a Haloed-Jesus-With-Sheep flanked by broad green leaves curled into horns of plenty. Second thoughts percolate as I step into the building's shadow. I haven't been to church in forty years. I remember the homeless woman at Tent City – was her name really Tomorrow? – saying the river called me. There's no river here, just a building, a stretched black shadow.

We are our own master. And yet I'm here when I could be reworking Chapter Two, or rewriting Chapter One, or outlining the way forward, or even petting Mystery to a steady purr.

I barely pull the wrought iron handle, and the door swings open. The entryway is well lit: white walls, polished granite floor. An alcove holds tapered candles in pewter stands beneath an oil painting of Jesus bleeding from his crown of thorns. Ahead, stairs lead up and down. For a moment I don't know which way to go, but of course up is the answer. The downward path probably leads to a basement, a kitchen, a catacomb.

I climb to a landing twice as wide as the stairs. Double-doors stand closed before me. I'm surprised by how quiet it is. Maybe the congregation is praying.

I crack open a door, planning to slink through and into the nearest pew before anyone notices. Rank upon rank of empty pews greet me, the auditorium funneling down to an altar bearing a dais and two pedestals holding vases of yellow and white flowers. Jesus hangs on the wall, arms outstretched upon the cross. His eyes are downcast. Dull. Bored.

"Welcome!" A woman appears from a corridor near the altar. She's wearing a flowered dress, her graying hair is pinned up into a bun, and I can see her vivid red lipstick from here. "Have you come to pray?" She strides up the carpeted aisle. "We hold services on Saturday and Wednesday evening."

I let the door close behind me. "Isn't this a church? I thought Sunday –"

"God is everywhere and everywhen," she says. "He doesn't care when we pray, only *that* we pray." She extends her hand. "My name is Grace. My husband and I are pastors here. And you are … ?"

"Stephen." I clasp her hand. Her fingers are boney. "I was out for a stroll. I've always wanted to see the inside of this building."

"And you chose today?" Grace's eyebrow lifts. "Are you sure there's nothing more important going on? God knows, and He will tell me if you do not."

"I don't believe in God."

"He believes in you."

"Then why did He give me cancer?"

According to Anne, who has a background in biology, cancer cells are just normal cells gone wild. They don't know how to stop growing or when to die. By one estimate, the sum total of cells cultured from Henrietta Lacks' cancer in 1951 would weigh more than 50 metric tons now. Surely that is one version of God.

Grace licks her lips. "I doubt very much that God gave you cancer. More likely you brought that upon yourself, or it might be a simple accident of fate."

"Then I'm wasting my time here."

Grace's arms spread wide. "No, Stephen. Accept Jesus into your heart and –"

"God will cure me?" I push my fists into my pockets.

"Perhaps," Grace says with a shrug. She clasps her hands between us. "Perhaps not. It's not our place to demand a price for faith."

"Then why bother?" I say.

"Because it is the way to heaven." Grace's mouth pushes into a pitying frown. "God judges us not on our rhetoric, but by our actions." Her eyes glisten. "Tell me, Stephen, do you do nothing out of simple kindness?"

"Of course," I say. I think of tucking the blanket around Mystery, filling her plate before I left. "I pick up trash when I walk."

Grace nods. "You see? The impulse is there. We just need to help you focus it."

This is crap. Yet, I don't want to leave. Sunlight slants from stained-glass-Jesus, illuminating the brighter colors and mystifying the dark. Dust motes dart through the beams, riding unseen currents. The chapel is chilly with drafts.

Grace leads me to the altar. She kneels. "Pray with me, Stephen."

"I can't." I stand a stride behind her, shoulders curled forward like a vulture. "I don't know how."

"Of course you do," Grace says. "Our Father, who art in heaven ..."

"I can't do this." I edge away. My legs hit something, and I stumble unceremoniously back onto a padded bench. Books stare at me from the pew ahead. *Holy Bible. Hymns.* The Bible is black, the hymn book's cover maroon.

Grace looks over her shoulder. "Do not fear His presence, Stephen. Go with it. You must think of life as a stream."

Of course! I think. That's what I've been missing. That's what the Tent City woman was trying to tell me. My eyes find the Bible, and sensation lifts through me like gravity reversing. *You must think of life as a stream.* This is the missing element in my novel. The character hasn't come back to warn us, but to change our religion. A God of the future, not the past. *Our Father of the Future, the god who awaits.* I glance at Grace. She's still talking, but her voice is only a distant hum. I don't even notice I am standing until her eyes follow me up.

"I have to go," I say. "I have to write. I haven't felt this passionate in a year."

Grace's head tilts. Her eyes evaluate. I can almost hear her thinking, *Has God embraced this man, or Satan?*

I step into the carpeted aisle. "Thanks," I say. "Thanks so much, Grace. You've helped me more than you can know." I turn and walk away, faster, until my feet can barely keep up. Up the aisle, down the steps, out the door, through the wrought iron gate, and onward until Jesus in the window is but a smear of color in a red brick wall.

A Passing

by Gay Degani

Outside in the brisk May air, warming her hands on her coffee mug, her silk kimono wrapped tightly around her, Sybil waits for Mars German and his crew to show up. The tree guys came yesterday: turned the fallen oak into firewood, ground out the stump. Makes her sad to think nothing is left of that grand old tree but a lumpy hole in the ground. It's been four months since the windstorm blew through the area and knocked over 600 trees, the oak falling on one of Sybil's rental houses.

She looks up just as a shiny Lexus pulls to the curb. A large man, maybe late fifties or so, wearing a work shirt and fashionably-ripped jeans, climbs out of the car and strides toward her. Then she recognizes him. Louisa Renke's son, and she knows right away why he's here.

"Mr. Renke," she says as he approaches. "Not bad news, I hope."

His eyes shift beyond the wrecked little house at the front of the property to where his mother lived in the bungalow at the back. He works his jaw, swallows, and says, "She died yesterday. It was okay. In her sleep. She was ready."

"I'm so, so sorry." Sybil puts her hand on his forearm and squeezes. A muffled sob erupts from the big man. Everyone, no matter who they are, she thinks, comes to a

216

moment when something reaches into their gut and wrings out such a sound. "Can I help you with anything?" she asks.

He doesn't answer; she's patient. She doesn't let go of his arm. Then he places his hand on hers, and asks, "Will you help me to find something for her to wear?"

His words conjure up a casket, rosewood maybe, satin trim – Ray has money – with Louisa's face softened in death, carefully applied make-up mocking her with blush. "Of course," she says.

"I'll keep paying rent until I get all her affairs in order," he says as he slips his key into the lock of Louisa Renke's front door. "Through next month at least. Is that enough time for you to find another tenant?"

"That'll work out fine." Jamie comes unbidden to Sybil's mind. If the girl comes back, even though she's been away four months, she and the kids will need a place to stay. She'll keep it empty for a while. And no need to rebuild the front bungalow. Clear the space instead, she thinks. Plant grass, roses. Build an arbor.

Inside the house, the musty smell reminds Sybil of how long it's been since Ray Renke put his mother into assisted living, yet the place has remained exactly the same, the crocheted throw over the arm of the sofa, the stack of crossword puzzles on the coffee table next to the remote. She hasn't thought of Louisa at all these last few months. The old woman had been moved before Christmas, had missed the big storm, and for this, Sybil was grateful. The thunderous sound of the oak falling on Jamie's bungalow would have given Louisa a heart attack.

From the closet, Ray pulls out a stiff, old-fashioned pantsuit with manly shoulder pads, an outfit Sybil had never seen the old woman wear.

"This is how I remember her," he says. "In this suit, or one like it, kissing me on the forehead as she dashed out the door for work. I remember the back of it better than the front."

"I can't remember. What did she do for a living?"

"Advertising, downtown at Bradshaw's Department store. She rode those copy-writers like a trail boss. Whipped 'em. That's what she used to say. I guess no one would get that today."

"I get it. I used to watch *Rawhide*," Sybil says.

Ray smiles at this. "Me too. She was a pistol. Women didn't do that back then, work a man's job when other women were hanging laundry on clotheslines."

"I hung laundry on clotheslines," says Sybil, and for a moment she remembers herself shaking out damp clothes, pegging them to a rope strung between the back of her house in Nebraska and a lone hackberry tree. "But I wanted to be like your mother."

"I guess she'd choose this suit to be buried in," says Ray.

"Anything in there you'd prefer?"

Ray looks up, as if this thought would never have occurred to him. "I don't think —" He turns back to the closet.

A car door slams outside and Sybil tiptoes into the living room to peek out the front door. Mars German, son of the old man who lives in the other front bungalow, strides toward Jamie's ruined house while $8-an-hour laborers jump off the back of a rusty pick-up truck. Mars has turned out to be a handy man to have around. Well, he knows what to do, she thinks, he doesn't need me to supervise, and leaving the door ajar to let in fresh air, she returns to the bedroom.

Ray stands in the middle of the floor holding a summer print dress with yellow, red, and aqua bouquets scattered across a white background, scooped neck, cap sleeves, a red belt cinching the waist, and a full pleated skirt. His face is shining.

"Oh!" Sybil gives a little gasp, the dress so unexpectedly pretty.

"I only remember her wearing it once. We spent the day together, shopping at her store, maybe it was my birthday, I think, and then we had lunch in the Tea Room. I'd forgotten that. The store had a Tea Room."

"Then this is the dress she should wear," says Sybil. "So you can remember her in this dress, and remember that time. A funeral is for the living, Ray, not the dead."

He ponders this as if he's still a little frightened his mother will disapprove, his mouth working again. Sybil glances down at her fingers. It's none of her business. He has to decide this for himself.

"I'm not sure it'll fit her. She's so much smaller now."

"They can take care of that. They do that kind of thing all the time."

He lays the dress carefully on the bed. Smoothes out the skirt. "I didn't think she had this dress anymore. You know, my wife, ex-wife, is the one who helped her move in here. I was too busy."

"Your mother must have understood that."

"You're right. She did. If nothing else, she was proud of my success." He straightens up. "She's going to need shoes. The guy at the mortuary said a lot of people forget the shoes."

He turns back into the closet, comes up holding a pair of black orthopedic sandals.

"No," she says shaking her head. "Never."

"That's all she's got."

Sybil's stares at her feathery satin slippers. Too floozy. The rest of her shoes are like Louisa's, designed for comfort, not beauty. Then she remembers. "Hold on. I'll be right back." She pulls up the skirt of her silk robe so she can move faster and hurries outside. Feeling a little foolish and way too old to be streaking across the yard, she waves at Mars when he looks up puzzled and hollers "Hello," and heads into her garage at the back of her property.

It's dark inside and cold. Sybil flips on a light and starts shifting boxes, searching for the one labeled 'Jamie and Kids'. Amazing to Sybil how few belongings Jamie and her little family had. Toys, of course, a TV and VCR, and clothing. The furniture and most of the kitchen goods had been rented from Sybil; still she sent Mars German into the house once it was clear they had left, to bring out whatever could be salvaged against the day that Jamie would come back.

She's tried to find out who the girl's aunt is in Oregon. She's even reported to the police although Jamie and the kids are probably all right; she thinks someone besides herself should know the little family has disappeared off the face of the earth. The police detective was sympathetic, but optimistic. If a husband is difficult, then the wife doesn't want to be found. She wouldn't risk contacting anyone from her past. Sybil understands this, yet what if the police are wrong, and she is wrong, and Jamie's in trouble?

Jamie with her sad, quick smile. She has to be alright. Has to. And would she mind this gesture of Sybil's? This raiding of her shoes? Sybil doesn't think so. She opens the box and at its bottom, finds what she's looking for, a pair of white high heels with red leather detailing on the back.

Pulling herself up, back stiffening a little, Sybil smiles. She wants to see that look on Ray Renke's face again, the almost childlike remembrance in his eyes of a day well-spent with his mother. She knows that Louisa would be pleased, even though the old woman would always wave away any discussion of her son with the simple comment, "That boy. He deserves a better mother than me."

The Great Wall

by Sally-Anne Macomber

To: Milton Flaxmill, Red Cow Publishing
From: Trudy Polaris
Date: May 20, 2014 7:14 a.m.
Re: Cheese

Milton,

I swear, I did not know the fetta was Bulgarian!

You'd think someone would check these things. Get out their taste testers and taste the cheese for Bulgarianness.

Now of course, the Fetta Ambassadress job has blown up and most of the dairy producers in the Tyrol hate me! I walk down the street and see men with big moustaches, cowhorns dangling from their belts, glaring at me bog-eyed, their lips curling into high altitude snarls. And we're desperate for income during this tax break my husband is forcing us through and so things are not looking good.

I am fast discovering fetta is one of the least versatile cheeses around. Even with my superior culinary skills, it's just not possible to make fetta and couscous pancakes oh so light and fluffy this high above sea level.

BTW, any news on editing *Nuclear Fission in The Pyrénées*?

I confess, my book is the only thing that's keeping my mind on track. I have quite a bit more time on my hands again and I spend a lot of it just sitting on the cowskin sofa drinking *Edelweiss-schnaps* and thinking, now that the Fetta job has fallen through – plus, all the *dirndl* industry connections I had made have mysteriously disappeared, so hopes of a few extra € from catwalk modelling have been dashed too – so to quote some *Mitteleuropa* folk tales, things are looking grimm.

And every time I sit down at my computer to work through the *Nuclear Fission in The Pyrénées* manuscript myself, hoping inspiration will stab me, I look through the window and where once were snow-covered mountains, now stands a wailing wall of fetta. Local cheese retailers, once they discovered the truth, dumped their loads outside our Tyrolean hideaway. So our front yard smells suspiciously like what I think might be Bulgarian afterbirth.

And my new skill as a power-editor has derailed. Who needs a power-editor when after the goat milking is done, the day stretches out long and endless …

And of course, whenever I milk a goat (and yes, they're still goats, they haven't changed back to cows again) the whole mess comes back to me and well, I need some good news.

How about I sneak out of here in the dead of night (to escape the glare of the tax border guards) and fly to Boston (I have a voucher for one and a half free flights with Bulgaria Air, and I can get a Bulgaria Air flight from Vienna to Boston via Sofia, which is just the break I deserve) so we can work on the book together?

I kind of need the money.

I could even have a t-shirt printed with *Boston or Bust* on the back. (Would *Nuclear Fission in The Pyrénées* across the front be a little crass?)

(Working out these flight details and wardrobe ideas are the only things holding me together at the moment, just in case you haven't realised the desperation of my desperation.)

Yours in the vain hope the sun is shining on a brighter tomorrow, tomorrow,

Trudy

Background

by Mandy Nicol

I thought Mum was joking when she came up with Persephone.

"You can't saddle a tiny Pomeranian with a name like Persephone," I'd said. But she didn't listen; this was Mum's new dog and she'd call it whatever she liked.

I call it Seph, which makes Mum purse her lips and dart her gaze away from me, in a Must You Always Find a Way to Annoy Me Nadia sort of way.

Mum got Seph after Peregrine was bitten by a snake last month. Mum said she knew Peregrine was going to die and she couldn't stand not having a dog around so we raced off to the local dog pound.

Of course Peregrine did survive so now we have two dogs.

I feel sorry for Peregrine. Mum is forever fussing over Seph, carrying her round the house like a handbag, letting her sit on her lap at meal times, giving her tidbits off her plate, "Look Nadia, Persephone likes your Apricot Chicken." Seph does nothing to deserve this attention, just jumps on all the furniture and trots around your feet nearly tripping you over whenever you move. She totally ignores commands unless there's something in it for her, like a piece of chicken, and if you take your eye off her outside she disappears so you end up wasting half your day searching sheds and paddocks to find her.

Faithful old Peregrine stays out of everybody's way. He's never growled at Seph, even when she eats his dinner right out of his bowl or lies on his blanket near the heater. I look at him now, lying under the dining room table, safe in the background, and I feel the pang of recognition.

Forget

by Margaret Bingel

At 6:13, the morning sun wakes Ned up, his eyes flash open, and he inhales deeply. Rising to greet the day, he stretches his arms out above his head. His elbows pop. Dr. Stanley had told him back in April that pops would happen, and not to worry, which is why he has no concerns with each new creak and crack that his body makes every morning.

Ned places his feet on the floor, and continues to stretch. His back cracks so hard his teeth vibrate. That's the good stuff, he thinks. He rocks his hips back and forth, swiveling his torso side to side, then bending further in each direction to wake up his muscles. His outpatient nurse told him that on days when he couldn't make it, Ned has to make extra-certain that these stretches and exercises are first order of business, to keep up muscle elasticity.

His nurse usually comes in on Mondays, Wednesdays and Fridays, but with the long holiday weekend coming up, he won't see his nurse until Wednesday. Ned has a strict routine of pilates and yoga (at least that's what it seems to him), but all Ned could think about while his nurse was telling him how to keep hydrated and eat plenty of lean protein was how he was going to drink beer and eat cheeseburgers. But right now, breakfast.

Ned ambles his way to the kitchen with only a slight stiffness to his gait. Dr. Stanley told him that it would take some time, but he has to be prepared for the possibility of never losing that limp. Here's a cane, Dr. Stanley told him, it could help you if you fall down. The cane sits in a corner, ignored.

After Ned puts bread into the toaster, he turns to the coffee pot and makes coffee. He likes Dr. Stanley, but like his mother, he feels that his doctor's trying to hold him back when all he wants to do is run forward. I'm a New Ned, he remembers telling Dr. Stanley. And New Ned doesn't hold back. The look on his mother's face when he said that was priceless, and just as he thinks about it, Ned scoops coffee right onto the counter. So he takes the coffee filter out of the pot, and with his hands brushes the grounds into the filter. Then putting the filter in the pot, he switches it on and returns to his toast.

Or, at least, there should be toast. The bread is sitting in the toaster and then Ned remembers that he didn't actually press the lever down. He shrugs his shoulders and presses the lever. But the bread pops up again. Ned stares at the toaster. And sees it isn't plugged in. Grabbing the cord, he points it toward the empty outlet, and sees the cord for the coffee pot lying on the counter, mocking him. So he shoves both cords into outlets and shuffles over to the table. Throwing himself into the chair, he runs his fingers through his hair, his nails scraping scalp, then digging deeper, and grunts.

It isn't the physical therapy that's holding him back. It's leaving keys in locks, forgetting to turn on the stove to cook, putting clothes on backwards. If he wasn't so young, Ned would think that he has Alzheimer's. He would call his mother for help, but he can't remember her number. Anyway, the New Ned is too strong for his mother.

The toaster pops up, and the smell of burned toast brings him back to reality.

227

Trees

by Darryl Price

Hey, Doc. Here's your ounce of blood.

Today I got taught how to draw some trees. I think I'm pretty good at it. All the pretty nurses touched my shoulder, so that's a good sign, right? I can draw trees that everybody likes. I must be okay. I mean would somebody who's not alright be able to draw a tree?

What is this? First grade? I want out of here.

I know you're the one with all the power. So let's make a deal. You said a story a day, right? Ok. Here's my next one.

Once upon a time there was a rabbit. This rabbit loved to smell purple flowers. One day while smelling those flowers, sitting in a field of the most beautiful purple flowers in the world, along comes a fox. The fox strides right up to the rabbit and says, I'm going to eat you. The rabbit starts to cry and says, but who will visit the flowers and sniff their beauty and take it all in and be thankful for it? Nobody, says the fox and he lunges at the rabbit, but the rabbit is quicker than he thinks and runs into the field of flowers that are all swaying crazily in the wind. Suddenly there's a kind of hum coming from the tops of the flowers and our little rabbit is suddenly, mysteriously lifted above their purple petals as if he's on a blanket. Meanwhile the fox sees what's going on and tries to jump up and catch the rabbit with his long hooked teeth, but no matter how high he jumps he just can't reach him. The rabbit is now smiling and rolling around on his back and flicking his whiskers at the clouds. All of a sudden there's a booming shot in the air and the sound of dogs barking and the fox shoots out of there like a red arrow never to be seen again. The rabbit softly drifts back down to the cool soft earth between all the flowers and sits very still until the hunters pass. The birds give him the signal that it's ok.

Not much of a story I guess. But it will have to do. I'm not a storyteller. I told you so.

I guess I am pretty good at trees though.

Why do I have to do all this art stuff?

I'm a free man. I just lost a girlfriend is all. That's not a crime – it's a tragedy. Let me go. Lift me up on your purple mountains majesty and let me go home.

Please.

Generosity

by Teresa Burns Gunther

Rachel and Stella finish their morning run, taking their time. It's Saturday. The fog is just beginning to burn off. Mrs. Franklin's already out in the narrow patch of garden that separates her home from Rachel's. The old woman is hunched in "work togs" digging at the roots of her roses. Stella barks, straining at her lead. Mrs. Franklin looks up and smiles.

"Hello precious!" Mrs. Franklin says in her soft Irish brogue. This greeting surprises Rachel who has only lived in the neighborhood a year and doesn't know her neighbor well. No one calls her *precious*.

"Yes ... hello to you, too ... Beautiful." Rachel feels silly saying this but she's working on her people skills and trying to be generous.

Mrs. Franklin laughs, a fluttering sound. "Oh. I was talking to your Stella," she says and scratches Stella's chin.

"Right. I'm joking with you," Rachel says, though she is not a joker. She hopes the flush of running will explain her burning cheeks.

"I bet you're wondering if I have something for you," Mrs. Franklin says to Stella, reaching into her pocket. She pulls out a cookie, her fingers are red, cracked, her lips chapped. Rachel makes a note to pick up moisturizer from

Macy's when she's shopping later. Her resolution for May is: *be generous.*

Rachel can see the woman's pale scalp through her wispy cloud of white hair and feels a fierce desire to protect this brittle woman. Stella whimpers. Rachel tightens her hold on the leash. Mrs. Franklin has cats. Rachel is glad they are indoor pets since Stella's exuberance for life extends to taking the same from small creatures like birds, cats and the Aussies' rabbit, though it was in fact already dead.

"Be polite, Stella," Rachel says. "Sit."

"How do you greet an old lady then?" Mrs. Franklin says. Stella sits and raises her paw to the liver-spotted hand. "It's a fine dog you have here," she tells Rachel and stands, one hand on Stella's head. Everyone else is afraid of Stella, though she wouldn't hurt anyone, without provocation. "How are you getting on?"

"Fine," Rachel says. "Except the Aussies keep complaining about Stella."

"Why?" Mrs. Franklin's wrinkled face folds into a frown.

"She barks too much."

Mrs. Franklin leans out to peer down the street where Joyce directs her beanpole husband as he washes their car. "She's a prickly one, is she?"

"Maybe so much time with manure and veg has taken a toll." Rachel taps her temple.

Mrs. Franklin considers this. "Well, I say your Stella can bark all she likes. Keeps the riffraff away." Stella rubs her flank against the woman's leg as if she understands. "We single ladies," Mrs. Franklin says raising her salt and pepper brows, "can't be too careful. Besides, I don't hear her bark."

"Maybe you should have your hearing checked."

"What's that, dear?"

§

In the afternoon, Rachel tours the glass cosmetics counters at Macy's. The Lancôme saleswoman follows her, smiling with white teeth and plumpy lips. She compliments Rachel on her beautiful skin, her *lovely* summer dress. "How can I help you today?"

Rachel sets her shopping bag on the counter. "I just need some free samples of moisturizer. For dry skin." The smile disappears. "It's for a little old lady, a neighbor. She has terribly chapped skin."

"How nice of you." The saleswoman smirks, fussing with a silk scarf wrapped in a complicated knot at her neck. "And … buying a whole jar would be just … too, too much?" Her lashes are so caked with mascara Rachel blinks.

"Well," Rachel shrugs, "these are free." Then catching her meaning, adds, "I'm just trying to be helpful." She resents the accusation. "Besides, she might not like it. What if she's allergic?"

"And I'm guessing you don't want to splurge on anything for yourself," the woman says with an exaggerated sigh as she sets a few samples on the counter. Rachel has been practicing keeping her mouth shut in moments like this but the woman's snotty tone and pinched face, as if she's suffering a terrible smell, sets her off.

"What do you care what I do or don't buy?" Rachel asks. "It's not like it's your stuff. And no, I'm not going to *splurge* on anything. Because you. are. rude."

"*I'm* rude?" The saleswoman is warming to her cause as other shoppers draw near clutching designer bags, eyes shifting between them, all curiosity. "You come in here, waste my time and only want free handouts and then you call *me* rude?"

"I'm just trying to do a nice – oh, never mind." Rachel sweeps the samples from the counter with a flourish, grabs her shopping bag, spins on her heel, swinging her bag so that it smacks a blind man with a cane and sends him flying. A collective gasp echoes the blind man's cry. Rachel drops down beside him, smoothing his jacket, helping him up. "I'm sorry. I didn't see you." That's when the saleswoman yells for someone to call security. Rachel retrieves the man's cane lost in the fall. His eyes are hidden behind dark glasses. "I guess you didn't see me either." She helps the blind man to a stool as the curious onlookers scatter, though the saleswoman is trying to spin the mishap into a crime.

Rachel tries to explain the situation to the blue-suited manager who arrives with a uniformed officer on his heels. Everyone starts shouting at once. "It was an accident," Rachel shouts loudest and everyone freezes. The blind man assures everyone he's fine. The guard takes Rachel's name and she's free.

She races out through the cloying haze of perfume to Union Square, nearly tripping over a homeless man camped on the sidewalk. She's so flustered that when her phone rings she answers without checking caller ID. It's her cousin, Susie, announcing she's coming for a visit, which means she's unemployed again. "God no!" Rachel says and hangs up. At her car a ticket waits on her windshield.

After her terrible day, Rachel stops by Mrs. Franklin's. There's no answer to her knock. She's about to leave when the door opens a crack.

"Who's there?" Mrs. Franklin calls from behind the door.

"It's Rachel. Next door?"

"Oh, yes." She unlatches the door and swings it wide. She beams at Rachel who isn't accustomed to eliciting joy. "Come in!"

"I have to go home." Rachel shivers. The fog has rolled its thick blanket back over the city, blocking the sun. "I just stopped by to give you something."

Mrs. Franklin tilts her head. "Yes?" She waits, hands clasped to her belly. Rachel searches her shopping bag but now doesn't know how to explain the "gift".

"Here." She holds the samples in her hand. "I got these for you when I was shopping. For dry skin. I thought," she hesitates, "you could ... like them." She blushes again. Thanks to that saleswoman, the slender packets of cream feel small. And cheap.

"Aren't you the kind one? Won't you come in? I'm just making tea."

Rachel hesitates. "I can't."

"Oh sure. It's Saturday. A date is it?" Mrs. Franklin asks with a mischievous smile.

"No. Just Stella," Rachel explains. "She needs to get out."

Mrs. Franklin's smile falls. "Oh. Of course."

After her father's visit two months before Rachel can't stop thinking about him asking: "Where are your friends?" And "Do you ever go out of your way for *them*?" At first she dismissed it as a dig because she'd refused to let him stay with her. Now it dogs her. She'd gone out of her way for Gail, her officemate, last month when she was practicing patience but it backfired. Now Gail has befriended her neighbor, Joyce, who hates her and Stella. Rachel's beginning to think Stella may be her best and only friend.

Mrs. Franklin's door closes, then pops back open. She calls after Rachel. "Thank you for the creams. You're a fine colleen. You tell your mother she raised you proper."

Rachel stands on the sidewalk stunned, wishing her father could hear, wishing her boss could hear, and Gail, and Joyce, and the saleswoman at Saks, wondering if she should tell Mrs. Franklin that her name's Rachel, not Colleen, and that her mother no longer knows her. She can hear Stella barking but now, doesn't want to leave.

"My day's been a train wreck, Mrs. Franklin. I could come later? After I deal with Stella?"

"Now that's a grand idea." Mrs. Franklin's smile picks up, bigger and brighter. "We'll have a cocktail and you can tell me all about it. I'll snap myself up a bit and find us something special. And bring Stella along," she says as a cat appears, purring and wrapping itself around her legs.

Morgana Malone and the Riddle of the Sands of Time

by Matt Potter

The sand thwumps out of the upturned jar. Well, it would, except it's not sand.

"This is not sand," Ludmilla says, looking down at the coloured crystals spreading across the table. Her dull brown hair streaked with grey frames her face in a lank way that says, *I don't know what else to do with it and who cares anyway?!*

I pat my own hair – blown-about orange bob with ever-widening grey-brown re-growth striped across the top – and look down at the table too. The table that ... I don't know ... but when I read her small ad in the *Psychic News* I thought would be flat and probably smooth, perhaps metal or at least Laminex but not this pitted old wooden thing with dips and knots and channels in the grain.

I place the jar down on the table with a glassy clink. The pink straw resting beside it rolls toward me and settles in a crack.

"Well, no," I say, digging the straw out with my finger. "But I *did* get it *near* the beach. And *I* bought it, it wasn't someone else who bought it, it was me, with my money. I picked it up off the shelf and, you know ..." I would keep talking but I think my voice has floated off down the street and across the Southern Ocean.

I pick the straw up.

Ludmilla sits back in her chair, shoulders wheezing against the vinyl. As she opens her mouth I see her teeth are a dull beige.

"But I am a sand reader," she says, crossing her arms under her cavernous cleavage so her breasts spill over her pale forearms. "I need the sand to be reading your fortune and this is just ..." – her cheeks fill with air and she exhales, her breath slow and small across the table but direct against my face, and I smell garlic and onion and what could be borscht: maybe that's her power, really, windpower, not this sand reading stuff – "... it is not the correct sand."

Well, yes, no, I agree, it's not sand. It's a jar of bath salts really, originally bought with the dark colours layered at the bottom – grape and purple and lilac – then up to the pinks – shocking and coral and flamingo – and then baby pink and cream and white ... but then I unscrewed the top and spooned out the first two layers and shook it up like a martini, shaking and shaking and shaking and then I stirred the first two layers back in with the same spoon.

(I was given those bath salts in a Secret Santa three Christmases ago.)

(And that shaking was the most exercise I had all day.)

I put the straw back on the table.

(Walking out the front door has been an exercise in discipline I currently don't have much of. It's safer to sit inside in the dark. And I have a lot of time now since I stopped working as the admin junior at Grigor's psychiatry practice, up-managing Zebadie the porn star / receptionist. So I just sit in the dark and think. And thinking is a good way to *not* spend money when you don't have a job.)

"But it is all *focked*," Ludmilla says, breasts bobbing in indignation on her forearms. "I am supposed to be giving you a straw and we both put on some glasses for protecting our eyes and then you blow on the sand and make some pretty pictures and I interpret them for your future but –" and she throws her hands in the air so her breasts thwop back against her stomach "– this is some pretty pictures in a bottle and is not some sand you get from your favourite spot on the beach that has some meanings in your life." She crosses her arms again – this time, *over* her breasts – and pushing out her bottom lip, she breathes out, her straggly grey-brown fringe fluttering against her forehead. Which I now see has a large red pimple with a bulbous yellow head glistening in the middle of it.

"They were in a jar," I say, eyes popping, grasping for the truth amongst this psychic mess, "it's a *jar*, Ludmilla, it's not *focked*. A jar." And I stab a free spot on the table with my index finger. "A *jar* is not a *bottle*. And a jar is not *focked* by definition because it's a *jar*. A *bottle* is *tapered*" – my hands flash through the air outlining a tapering bottle – "and has a small *opening* at the *top* but a *jar* is the same circumference all the way up, usually." And again, my hands carve the air creating an impromptu jar. "Like a wheat *silo* except made of *glass* and a lot *smaller*."

I don't know why I'm *emphasising* certain *words*.

I sit back against the chair and my shoulders whisper against the vinyl.

Actually, I don't know why I'm doing anything.

"Can't you interpret bath salts?" I ask, my voice thin and wan and nothing. "I can blow on the bath salts with the straw and make *prettier* pictures."

Ludmilla leans forward and, breasts now resting on the table, sinks her chin into her hand.

"But my talent is reading the sand that has some special reason for you," Ludmilla says, "and since you telephoned me and saying my ex-husband is giving me the sack and now I have no job and my life is in the toilets and I need some hope."

I look down at the sand, I mean the bath salts, and they're all mixed into a murky pinky sugary brown so, if you were drunk enough, you could spoon them into your mouth then pretend you were having a diabetic episode.

"But if you cannot make a trip to the beach with a bucket and a … a … you know, a *dig dig* thing then … to save your life and to get some directions then your life is *focked* and I cannot help you if you cannot help yourself."

It comes from somewhere, I don't know where, but a smile appears at the corner of my mouth. "Oh, you mean *fucked*?" I say. But the way I say it, I say 'fecked'. Like Ludmilla would say if she were imitating my Australian accent.

"Focked, fecked, fooked," she chants, "whenever, it is all the same for you."

"Yes," I say. And picking up the straw, I put it to my lips and blow hard, covering Ludmilla's vast continental shelf with my focked future.

O

by Gary Percesepe

I'm in a bar when I butt-dial my wife, or rather my ex-wife. It isn't the first time.

Jesus, she says. Take the phone out of your back pocket. Fucking Christ. This is embarrassing.

I know. What are you doing?

I'm working at this ridiculous summer church camp upstate your mother talked me into. Today I walked in on two girls in the bottom bunk bed going at it. From North fucking Carolina, can you believe it? Billy Graham country.

I picture two fourteen year olds, their front flats grinding together, lying head to toe, the dark haired one's narrow foot grazing the pin shaped nipple of the blonde girl, the blonde's chlorine-faded blue swim suit pulled down around her ankles.

What'd you do? I ask. Perfect pitch.

I called *Hustler* for a contract. What the fuck do you think I did? I said move the fuck over.

Savannah divorced me, citing irreconcilable differences, but we never differed on the sex. We fucked every day, more as we got closer to the paper signing at the courthouse. It's a mystery.

You remember when we beat off to *Hustler* when you were pregnant?

Gawd. I couldn't keep you off of me when I was pregnant. I bought you those to calm you down.

Didn't work, I guess.

The thing about these two girls, they wouldn't stop. They were rocking that bunk after I left, all trying to be discreet. Jesus.

A new world, I say.

Savannah used to volunteer as a mom helper during recess. She was politely spoken to after she let one of the boys, a twelve year old, take off his shirt for her. She told me later she liked the shape of his nipple under his tee shirt, it was a perfect dime. Later, when she was headed to her car after school one day the kid caught up to her and asked for a lock of her hair. Savannah yanked the ends off a few strands of her French braid and handed them over. Knock yourself out, she said.

Are you getting any, Savannah asks.

You mean tonight? I say.

Tonight, tomorrow.

There's a poet I'm interested in. But she's in Oregon.

Ha! Fifty thousand women who'd fuck you in town and you wanna hook up with a poet in Oregon! That's perfect. God, I love you.

I sip at my beer. The barmaid looks over and asks with her eyes am I OK? She's got some art on her chest that looks interesting, a series of concentric circles in delicate green ink that looks like a bull's eye. She refills me. Last week I fucked her up against the wall of the bar at three am. She presented her ass, slippery and canted at an interesting angle. I told Savannah afterwards on the phone. Another butt call on the drive home.

Our relationship should be reported to the Guinness people, I say.

Tell me about your poetess, Savannah says.

She's got a new book out, written from the point of view of a teenage boy, I say. He jacks off in the back of the bus

241

on the way to school. He covers up with his book bag but the driver sees him. I listened to a podcast of her reading this poem at her book launch and she giggled when she got to that part. She said, I always wanted to do that.

Ooh, I like her, Savannah says. I'd fuck her just for that. What's she look like?

She's Irish, with big brown puppy eyes and short blonde hair like yours. She's skinny with no hips or butt and she likes to pose with a gun on Facebook. She's got a big O tattoo on her left arm.

Mmmmm, Savannah says.

Don't get any ideas.

Look, I gotta go, Savannah says.

I hear somebody in the background saying c'mon, willya. I take a long drink from my beer and rest my head on my arm on the bar.

Are you there?

Yes, I say.

I'm worried about you. Are you sure you're OK tonight?

I sit up on my stool. I signal the girl for another beer.

Sure, I'm fine. Hey, sure. Sorry about the butt call. Won't happen again.

She clicks off and I imagine the poet girl brushing her teeth in the bathroom of her studio apartment. There's a cat to get past. I move in behind her and reach around her narrow waist. She quivers and I let her go, then reach around and take the toothbrush in my left hand and finish the job. She spits white into the sink and I wipe her mouth with my outstretched finger. I run the water in the bath and bend her over from the waist until her hair is under the stream of hot water. She drops to her knees. I apply the shampoo generously, moving my fingers through her hair, pressing deep into her scalp, holding her head under the water until she moans and turns around and pulls me underneath her. I fall to the floor by the base of the tub and look up at those brown eyes. She makes her fingers into a gun. Bang, she says.

Samford's Big Race

by Nathaniel Tower

Sweat rolls down his naked ass crack as Samford stands at the starting line, waist bent and arms cocked and ready to run. He doesn't know why he's sweating when the race hasn't started yet. Perhaps it's nerves. Or maybe it's a sign that late May is turning into summer already.

A sudden breeze tickles Samford's exposed genitals. To keep from getting aroused, Samford looks around at the crowd. They are cheering, not necessarily for him. Still, he revels in the cheers for a moment, contemplating the journey that brought him here. He'd never been much for athletics before, and now he has a chance to win.

Samford has been training for the clone Olympics for the past month, ever since the clone police took him captive. His training hasn't been voluntary. In fact, he's been told that he must win or his body will be deactivated. He's not sure how this works. He was always under the impression that clones were just as real as flesh-born humans. Maybe they had said "decapitated."

The gun fires, snapping Samford back to the track. Immediately he's four strides behind the pack. His bare feet slap against the rubberized track, but the sound of his balls smacking back and forth on his pasty thighs drowns them out. Even the roar of the crowd is no match for the banging from his swinging sack.

He hasn't worn clothes for a month, but somehow the sun's rays have not darkened him. He's just as pale as he ever was. Maybe even paler.

He forgets about his pallor and sprints hard until he catches the pack. Then he settles in, the rhythmic sound of more than a dozen ballsacks swinging back and forth in unison causing a strange sense of calm.

Hanging on to the pack as they make their way around the track for the first lap, his chest heaves as he struggles for adequate oxygen. For a moment, he panics, convinced his training hasn't been enough. He tries to remember the tips his coach gave him, but his mind is blank. Devoid of any guidance or sound strategy, he sprints to the front of the pack.

He crosses the line to complete the first lap. The crowd roars his name, and he glances back to see his fifteen-stride lead. Way out front, he is suddenly confident. His shoulders drop and all parts of his body move like an automaton. For the first time in a month, he's happy to be a clone.

"Sam-ford! Sam-ford!" the crowd cheers. He pushes his body harder, his stride opening longer as his quads and lungs begin to burn. He wonders why they are rooting for him, why they even know his name.

"And Samford has broken free and is on record pace!" an announcer yells over a cackling speaker. The excitement pushes Samford harder, and he charges around to finish the second lap with a forty-meter lead. Two laps to go. Although the pace is really starting to tire his body, he continues to push, trying to run faster and faster. He has no idea what the record is, but he plans to set it right now. Why hadn't he taken up running in his younger days? Then he remembers that he doesn't even remember if he had younger days.

The third lap is a blur, and Samford can't hear the slapping of his balls anymore. He looks down for a second and sees they have shriveled into tiny raisin pouches and can no longer thwack against his legs.

As he crosses the line to enter the final lap, he glances back and can't see any competitors on the home stretch. He knows he cannot lose with such an enormous lead, but he does not slow down, even with the fear that people will accuse him of being a cyborg or some other superhuman entity. Clones shouldn't be any better than the humans they are cloned from.

He's halfway around the track on the final lap, burning past clones still on their third lap, when the sirens wail. It sounds like an air raid, but Samford does not stop running.

"Clear the stadium now!" the announcer calls.

Samford passes five more clones until he enters the homestretch. For the first time, he sees the large clock near the finish line. The big green numbers tell him he has been running for three minutes and twelve seconds. His eyes widen. Even with his limited knowledge of track and field, he knows he is on pace for a world record. He knows he must finish.

"Clones, get off the track!" the announcer says.

Samford keeps running. He will not be denied his glory.

He is less than ten strides from the finish line when the the clock display disappears. With all tangible signs of glory gone, the pain suddenly overwhelms his body.

"Get off the track now!" the announcer yells.

Fire now roars in his lungs. Samford takes two more strides before his body crumples to the rubber surface. A rifle crack echoes from above. Samford's body rolls off the track and onto the grassy infield. He has only a few seconds to contemplate whether the sharp pain in his gut is from the run, the fall, or a bullet, and then all colors fade and he lies motionless in a fetal position, his shriveled penis and balls tucked between his pale legs.

We Have Company

by Kimberlee Smith

We have company. I thought my husband Dean and I would be in limbo, alone, for eternity. It's not that I don't love him, but the past few months have been like the two of us are stranded on a deserted island. Without the island.

Today, May 28, a woman about my mum Maybell's age, late '40s, early '50s, comes along out of nowhere and says, "I'm Doreen and I'm just passing through. Not hanging around here. Nope." She points up like she's poking the sky, trying to get its attention.

"Oh really? And where do you think you're going?" I ask. Dean feels closer, in a show-of-solidarity kind of way.

"Yeah. We've been here a little while, and hate to be the bearer of bad news. Obviously not the *worst* news you've ever gotten because it seems you know you died. You do know, don't you?" says Dean. He can be rhetorical when he's fired up.

Doreen scratches at what I imagine was recently her waist, maybe where her knickers pinched her. Instead, her hand slices right through her midsection and her torso kind of gapes open. She doesn't seem to notice she went right through her old body and has a flat palm rummaging around her innards. There's no blood trickling out; it's all gone.

"Sorry, Doreen, but this is it. The end," I say with a wince.

Doreen doesn't answer right away because she notices her hand is inside her sternum and instead of seeming horrified she looks embarrassed; her eyes darting all around and she mimics, I guess without knowing, what it's like to be out of breath. Wiping her brow as if she's sweating, but she's not. She's dry as a bone. Dusty already. Have you heard when a person loses a limb they feel the ghost of it for a long time, as if it's still there? I believe that's what's happening to her, but from the inside out.

"Oh, dear. This is, well, not something to share now, is it?" she whispers.

Dean seems pleased that he might have stumped her. He's got a ruddy tone like he did when he was alive; color fills him and the brightness of sunshine fills the old bog-water color he just was. I can tell when he's mischievous on purpose, and since he joined me here he hasn't had anyone's chain to yank but mine.

But the flush of color doesn't stop at ruddy. When he gets cheeky with me, I can see the flames that killed him lick him from the inside, they flicker and flash and there's a stench of burned flesh. But he reacts like he's just got hives like he used to get when he was in his body and he ate too many tomatoes. He has no idea that fire has stayed with him.

"Of course I know," says Doreen, turning indignant as she bends her elbows akimbo and tries to settle her fists at her hips. They pass right through her.

"You think *you* wouldn't know if a seven-meter saltwater crocodile had you for tea?"

"Really? You think that's more of an eye-opener to recognizing you're a goner, than say, being trapped alone in a plane that slammed into the ground, and being incinerated to ash? Try *my* kind of death. You'd be praying for a saltie to split you in half."

Dean is losing it. I cannot believe there's a 'You Think That's Bad' contest between these two when we haven't seen – literally – another soul for months?

I have to break up the pissing match. I don't know how to leave, and even if I did, where would I be going?

"Pardon me," I say in a voice that really isn't my voice at all, it's more of a rumble zinging with electricity, like what you feel when thunderheads are about to crack. "I've about had it with you both. Dead is dead. So enough."

They both look like guilty children who need good spankings; they're scowling and pursing their lips. I'd like to slug them both. Three is a crowd. This is not working.

And how fucking long is she going to hang around? I was hoping for company, but her intrusion has thrown our balance completely *off*. I'm curious now. I can't wait to find out how she's meeting up with her family and I hope it's soon. I've heard enough of their yammering.

I'm here, too. Nobody seems to give a shit that I died. Wait, that's not right. My mum gives a shit. And our baby only knows me dead; a dead mummy is the only kind my bubbie knows.

"Mine was by snakebite," I say, interrupting the silence. Lightning cleaves the sky. It happens with frequency – lightning and thunder that I first feel, and then my voice changes – when I get emotionally charged. I am not surprised that the energy that builds up in me causes an electrical storm of epic proportions.

When the shock passes through, *boom!* I feel alive again for a moment, tingly and flushed, as if that were possible. The storm leaves the confines of me and explodes into our afterworld, and then it's gone.

Doreen doesn't notice it. Dean hasn't ever, either. It might just be me and I'm going to keep this crazy, amazing secret to myself. I don't feel like sharing anything with them.

"I went first. Dean, a couple months later."

"It's a huge inconvenience. Terribly sad for the family, I imagine," says Doreen.

Dean and I chime in together and our expressions overlap. It's a habit. "Indeed." "Absolutely." "No doubt about that."

"Not much family left," says Dean. Now he is pale gray, like an oyster. Almost opaque but vaguely translucent. That's what happens when he's sad. He's like a human mood ring.

"Our daughter, our only child, Etheline Margaret, was born immediately after I was pronounced dead. The doctors Caesared her right out of me as soon as they could. I believe they had to save the baby, because they weren't too hopeful about saving me. Too much toxicity from the venom, right babe?" I say to Dean.

"Yep. That's true. I was there. Oh, our sweet little bub. A heartbreaking shame you weren't able to hold her, even once. We missed you so much. That's the worst part," he says, falling into me like a wounded flower. It feels and smells like a thousand jacaranda blossoms, as light as a silk shroud.

When either one of us becomes melancholy or nostalgic this magical thing happens. And I'm certain it's on account of the jacaranda trees Dean planted for me as a Christmas present, our last Christmas. And our first spent in our new home. It was the best time of our lives, and certainly the best time since.

There's a shower of intoxicating jacaranda perfume and petals whorling all around us. They were my favorite flowers. They *are* my favorite flowers.

It's as if Doreen isn't here at all right now. She doesn't feel or see or smell this, either, the same way she didn't have any perception to the storm. I can just tell. It's a phenomenon too spectacular to ignore.

"But you know, babe, I'm always with her," I say. We call each other that. *Babe*. It's another habit of ours.

"Holy. Motherofgod. Seriously?" says Doreen. The flowers have all blown away, but they'll come back.

"Dead serious," I say, and we all laugh a little awkward laugh about the inside joke. I can be funny sometimes, and right now is a time that calls for it.

When the laughter dies down – see? I just punned death again! – there's more awkwardness, but it's in the form of silence.

"She was born January 14. Exactly a month before our second wedding anniversary," I say.

"You were married on Valentine's Day?" asks Doreen, like it was an odd thing to do.

"Of course! It's the most romantic day of the year," says Dean, like it's something she should consider as fact.

"So who's taking care of the bub now?" asks Doreen.

"My mum," I say, "it's just the two of them now, no other family to speak of."

"Well that explains why you two are still farting around here," says Doreen.

"Meaning what?" asks Dean. His head snaps towards her and smoke billows out of his ears. For real.

"Meaning you're not moving on because you're keeping a watch over your little girl. Mind you, you can go meet your maker any time you're inclined. You're obviously not ready," says Doreen. "I'm going to see what all the fuss about the pearly gates is about. And reunite with my husband Hugo. Also my sister Laralee and our mum and dad. I was the last one left."

"What makes you think you can?" I ask.

Dean doesn't give her time to answer, "She told you, this is the end of the line. There's nowhere else to go." He swings his fists in the air like he's fighting a cloud of rabid bats.

"You're wrong as wrong gets. The reason you're still here in nowhere land is because you don't want to leave. You could leave whenever you like. You're denying that you can," says Doreen as she tries to tuck her blouse back into her pants, but instead she tucks it behind her pelvis and pulls it out, cusses to herself, and tries again. She does this a number of times until I am bored watching her.

"How are *you* an expert on moving out of here?" asks Dean.

"You haven't come across anyone else here, have you?" challenges Doreen, as if she knows the answer.

Dean and I look at each other. She's got a point.

And then she tells us how she knows.

"I been here before."

Personal

by Vanessa Weibler Paris

Hi, my name is Jim. My friends call me Slim Jim.

Hi, my name is Jim. I would love to meet a lady of any size or appearance

Hi, my name is James. You can call me Jim. My friends all do.

Single white male. Down to earth and easygoing. New to online dating. Not into playing games.

Call me Jimshmael. Some years ago — never mind how long precisely—

I enjoy going out and partying, but I also love curling up at home with that special someone.

My name begins with a J. I am a riddle wrapped in a mystery inside an enigma. I am a chicken placed inside a duck slid within a turkey. I am puff pastry. An onion. Lasagna. Spanakopita.

Okay, I don't know what to write, so how about if I just give you my name, and maybe if you have a dad named Jim or a brother named Jim or maybe a good male friend named Jim, but a platonic friend not one who you used to date and are kind of secretly still hung up or is still hung up on you, then maybe you'd want to maybe

[different less stupid opening] long walks on the beach, wine by the fire, pina coladas

Hi, I'm Jim! I don't mind if you're way too fat if you don't mind if I'm way too skinny.

Hi, I'm Jim! I don't mind if you're big and beautiful if you don't mind if I'm skinny and ugly.

Hi, I'm Jim! I don't mind if you're [something that means big but doesn't insult them—ask coworkers for ideas] if you don't mind if I'm way too skinny.

Someone [look up who this was] once said that beauty is in the eye of the beholder. [make joke about bumper sticker, "beauty is in the eye of the beer holder?" maybe not?]

My name is James. Hey, that rhymes! Kind of.

SWM seeks SWF. Will you be the olive to my toothpick?

Jack Sprat seeks wife

Jack Sprat seeks companion to lick the platter clean

Jack Sprat seeks companion to enjoy a nice meal of varying caloric

If I could rearrange the alphabet, I'd put 'I' and 'U' together

Did it hurt when you fell from heav

Jim is the nicest guy we know. Who is "we"? There are three of us, all women, all at least 20 years his senior, and Jim works in our department and eats lunch with us every day.

How is Jim nice?

When Linda's mom died, he spent his Saturday driving four hours each way just to attend the funeral.

When Darlene's husband walked out on her and she was having an especially down night, he brought over three chick flick movies, a bottle of wine and a half-gallon of ice cream, and hung out until they were done with all five. And then he waited 'til she was asleep before leaving.

When Barbara got marked down on her annual review for not being good at spreadsheets, he came over every night for a week to coach her along.

And when his best friend Dougie went through chemo, he sat there in that room with him for hours, distracting him from the dry hot air and the drip of the line and the occasional stifled sob with round after round of pinochle.

Jim is the nicest guy we know.

There's a lot more to Jim than being nice – in fact, it's far from the most interesting thing about him – but that's for you to learn.

Do you want to?

Dinner Date

by Joanne Jagoda

Why can't it be 3:10? Friday is the slowest day, and it's stuffy in here. We almost never need air conditioning in San Francisco, but I wish we had it today. The kids smell sour from gym class and they are restless. Every damn tick of the clock sounds like a time bomb.

"Darren, no talking. Just settle down and finish your test."

I want it to be night already and to be with David ... yummy, yummy David. He wouldn't tell me where we're going. Some *gourmet* restaurant, and I'm supposed to "dress up." Dressing up with Paul meant we were going to the Sizzler. I had a reason to go into that boutique on 24th St. which I passed a million times oohing over the clothes in the window. I found the perfect black knit dress, short with a ruffly skirt. This feels like my prom tonight, with my new dress, and I'm splurging and getting my nails and hair done after school. Last week the girls went to their prom. Cassie got asked at the last minute by one of the boys in her group of the straight 'A' kids and Robin went with a boy from another school. Lillian insisted on taking them shopping for their prom dresses even though I wanted to do it. You can't say no to their grandmother who thinks she is the queen of fashion. Finally lunch. There's the bell.

"Turn in your tests."

"Anne, you heading to the lunchroom?"

"Hi, Tracy. I'll walk with you."

"Anne, let's grab this table. Do you want some bad coffee?"

"Sure. Black is fine. Thanks."

"What is it about you Anne that's different? Your hair? New makeup? You're sure smiling a lot. Are you getting laid? Spill the beans."

"Tracy, very funny. But ... well ... you're right. I did meet someone. And we're *not* sleeping together. Not yet anyway."

"Cute Anne. You're blushing. I knew it, I knew it. Spill. Tell me everything."

"His name is David Lewis, and we met by chance at the Fairmont Hotel. I had been stood up by an online blind date. That's a whole other story. Anyway, I was having a Cosmo by myself at the bar. This really cute guy sits next to me. He gave me his card before he left, and I finally got around to calling him. We met up at Pier 39 last month."

"Don't stop. I want to hear more."

"I was a wreck half-expecting him to not show, but he was there waiting for me. I have to tell you he's cute; tall, blue eyes and dark hair to his collar. He had on a leather jacket, and has an adorable English accent. I *love* his accent. We took the ferry boat to Alcatraz, but it was cold that morning with a vicious wind, and we couldn't sit outside."

"Go *on*, Anne. This is getting good."

"We huddled inside the tour boat watching the rolling waves and sipping hot chocolate. David is easy to talk to. He wanted to know about the girls and my teaching and everything about Paul. He lost his wife Sybil to breast cancer. I felt so bad for him. His eyes filled with tears when he spoke about her."

"What does he do?"

"He has an international company, something with computers, and came here to open an office south of Market. We loved the tour of Alcatraz. Back at the wharf, we had crab cocktails and shared a loaf of French bread. The most fun was hopping on the cable car hanging on outside, battered by the wind. We had dinner at Kuleto's and chocolate sundaes at Ghiradelli Square. He insisted on paying for everything. By 8pm I had to get back to the girls. I felt like Cinderella. He gave me the sweetest peck on the cheek and a big hug and promised to call me soon which he did by the next day."

"The next day? Ohhhh Ann. He sounds perfect. Tell me he has a brother. Have you been seeing him a lot?"

"We've been going out every weekend. Long hikes in Golden Gate Park, touring the de Young Museum, strolling at Ocean Beach, seeing foreign films in the Castro and trying all types of food, from Szechuan to Ethiopian."

"Have the girls met him?"

"Not yet. After my blind date disaster, I didn't want to say anything about going out with him. They thought I was meeting an old friend from college but noticed I was spending more time getting ready than usual. It didn't take much for Cassie and Robin to figure out what was going on. They're very sneaky and found my emails to David on my laptop because they know my password. I was pissed at first, but I know they worry about me.

"After a month of sneaking around, I sat them down at one of our 'family' meetings to tell them I met someone. They acted surprised at first but couldn't stop kicking each other under the table and told me they knew. They had even named him *Dude*. The girls wanted to hear everything about him."

"There's the bell. When are you seeing him again?"

"Tonight we're going out and he wouldn't tell me where."

"That sounds romantic I want to hear about it on Monday."

Oh my gosh, the bell is about to ring. Finally this day is done. "Turn in your tests and have a good weekend. No homework. You don't have to yell so loud. Get out of here!"

They love weekends without homework. I'm glad I got through today. I better hurry. My hair appointment is at 3:30. I am going to have work to do to correct these damn tests over the weekend since I wasted the whole day daydreaming. I'm glad the girls won't be home tonight. I'm not ready to introduce David to them.

I'm going over my spreadsheet again. Everything has to be perfectly timed. I hope my employers got the message from my email this morning to get off my goddamn back. I couldn't have said it any plainer. This operation can't be rushed. I need this job to go perfectly. I'm going to make enough money to get out of this business. When I get my fat cheque I'm taking off for good.

No one down on the street, but I feel like I'm being followed. I'm usually the one doing the spying. They must not trust me and have someone watching me.

Looking forward to wining and dining Anne. We're going to Gary Danko. Perfect place ... elegant but hip and not too stuffy. She'll love it. And no woman could resist me in this brown ultra-suede sport coat and dark blue shirt. I'm such a handsome devil. I'll splash a drop of that expensive cologne from Barney's, subtle but sexy. This is a slow dance ... the long kisses, a few gropes of her perfect bum, and caresses of her nicely endowed body. Too bad Anne, my darling, in another life I might have gone for you. I've never been able to stick with one woman with the kind of nasty work I do travelling around the world. Taking her to bed is the next step to pull her in. I'll suggest a wine country weekend next month. The kidnapping will happen before Cassie leaves for university in September.

Grandpa George will be deciding the fate of his precious granddaughter. To get her back alive, he is going to have to turn over the schematics for the advanced missile blocker system, Project Octopus, developed by his Silicon Valley company, which can capture and destroy missiles with uncanny accuracy and from a much further distance than the previous Iron Dome technology. My employers will stop at nothing to get those blueprints. That's why they hired me. I'm the best, and I'm ruthless. And I want my payday.

I'm glad I ditched that crappy rental for this silver BMW M3 convertible. This is the first time I've picked her up at her home, but she doesn't know I've been in her pretty little house putting in my cameras and listening devices.

She must have been standing near the door. She opened it before I could ring. She is stunning. The only thing real about me is my smile when I see her sexy body.

"Anne, you look amazing."

"Thanks David. You're not too bad yourself. OK, I'm dying to know. Where we going?"

"Sorry, m'lady. Can't tell you yet. But I thought we'd have a glass of champagne first. I brought my favourite Veuve Clicquot."

"I don't have champagne glasses. I'll get us some wine glasses."

Ahh, the girls' photos are here on the mantel. Pretty things aren't they. I'd hate to have to hurt Cassie.

"Your girls are lovely. Cassie looks just like you; I'm assuming Robin takes after your late husband. May I propose a toast Anne? To a wonderful evening, no change that … to many wonderful evenings."

Visit to the Temple

by h. l. nelson

Dear Diary,

This has been the craziest twenty-four hours of my life. I've been out all night, it's 4 A.M. and I just got home. I had snuck some sleeping pills into Brandon's nighttime tea so he wouldn't notice me leave, and it seems to have worked – he's still snoring in his armchair downstairs.

But let's begin with Temple.

I went to a bar in the seedy part of downtown. With no money, no cell phone. Oh, and I was tripping on pills I thought were Vicoprofen but were actually LSD. (Yes, Kurt really is dealing.) But it was a long weird night, let me tell you. The air inside the bar was old, greasy. The furniture was heavy wood, a little dusty. The place smelled vaguely of peanuts.

I made it up to the bar and sat on an empty stool.

The bartender was a smallish, tattooed man. "What would you like?" he asked.

"I just need to use your phone. I'll be happy to pay for some sparkling water, if you have it." I felt on my shoulder for my purse, but it wasn't there. Fuck. Where had I left it? I had to push down panic and get it together. I did not want this to turn into a bad trip. "To be honest, I don't have any money. I must have left my purse in the cab. All I need is a phone so I can call my family." I made my eyes big and imploring.

He peered at me for a few moments, then grabbed the bar's phone and put it on the counter in front of me. I almost cried in relief, and dialed Brandon first. It went straight to voicemail, then told me his mailbox was full. What? He rarely answers his phone in the evening, especially when he's on sleeping pills, but I was hoping that just this once he might. He didn't. I dialed Kurt's number, then remembered the block I had put on the kids' phones. No outside numbers are allowed to call in. I laid my head on the bar and almost let the panic take me over. Then the bartender put a shot in front of me.

"On the house."

"Thank you," I said, and downed it.

I had been there for about half an hour and it felt like the drug was wearing off. I was trying to keep it together, and half-watching the bar patrons by the low, red light on the walls when someone walked in. She was a stately African American wearing a tight, neon-pink dress and 6-inch spiked heels. She glanced around the bar and zeroed in on me. She sauntered over, and I looked down at the remains of my shot.

"Did you take a trip and get lost, honey?" the woman asked.

I nodded.

"Not often we get someone in here that looks like you. I felt you from three blocks over, speed-walked like those white women in malls, all the way here in these damn heels." She laughed.

I had no idea what the woman meant by having 'felt' me. I crossed my legs three different times, I was so nervous.

"Well, are you gonna say anything? What's your name?" Her smile was so warm.

"My name is Joan," I said, and I extended my hand.

262

"Well hello, Joan. I'm Temple. Pleasure to meet you." She nodded to the bartender and sat on the stool next to me.

Temple told me that she was homeless, a sex worker, and intersexual. "Both parts," she said simply. "I help open people up to their own sexuality. I'm a temple goddess reincarnated."

I smiled. I supposed I'd heard sillier things.

Soon I was telling Temple everything that had happened to me that day, how I was dumb and took from my teenaged son's hand what I thought was Vicoprofen, but ended up being LSD, that I scared the checkout girl at Abercrombie where I was buying Kendra's jeans with my hiding in the clothing rack. How I couldn't even drive, had to catch a cab, and ended up sharing it with a man that I swear was the devil, and who may or may not have stolen my purse.

Head tilted back, eyes closed, nodding at times, Temple was easy to talk to. Because she was listening, really listening. I'm not used to that. Most people in the suburbs listen, smile and nod, but when you pause, they jump right in with an anecdote or remark about themselves.

Then Temple blew my mind.

She said, "See, the difference between you and me, honey, is I'm free. Don't make a mistake thinking I don't have a way of getting myself out of my situation. I do. But I choose not to." She opened her eyes and brought her glass to her lips. "You, on the other hand, you may be living the American Dream, but that dream's gone and a nightmare took its place. The thing you got to understand about yourself, all your friends, family, people in the same tax bracket as you: you're all lost. When you stop living a lie, baby, you start living."

She lit a cigarette, and blew gray circles at the bar ceiling.

"Yeah, Temple, you're absolutely right," I said, shaking my head.

"Temple's gonna set you straight. I can't help you find you, but I can get you closer." She ground her cigarette butt in an ashtray on the bar. "Here's what we gonna do. I'm not your typical homeless prostitute. I have access to all kinds of life-enhancing medicines. You need a bigger experience to set you straight, girl. Do you trust me?"

"Yes," I said, eyes big and trusting. "I do."

It took about an hour for the drug to come on. I hadn't even asked her what the name of it was. I was back to being a teenager.

Her face began to undulate. I heard drums in the back of my head. Was it my own blood, my heartbeat, pounding? Temple grew taller, really tall. I glanced around the bar but now it was a desert. It looked like Arizona, where I grew up. The sun was blazing. Sweat was pouring off me. And Temple was the sun.

We crossed the desert for days. It was so hot and my throat was so dry and I remember Temple dancing and dancing, and I thought she was bringing the rain because she would dance and then bring me a flask of water and help me drink.

Then I doubled over in the sand, coughing and heaving, like an animal was climbing up my windpipe. I couldn't breathe and started to choke. Temple held my hair and stroked my back, like my mother used to when she wasn't yelling. She said, "There, get it all out." I opened my mouth, and a huge ball of wet hair slopped onto the ground.

"It's okay. That's the sickness, honey. Your body's ridding itself of it." Temple patted my back some more. I lay down on the warm sand and sobbed.

§

Temple dropped me off at home. I am dirty, exhausted, but my heart feels strangely light and … happy. It has been so long since I've felt that way.

When she dropped me off I ran to the door. Kendra threw her arms around my neck and Kurt circled his arms around my waist, hugging me from behind. I hugged them tighter than I probably ever have.

With a cup of steaming coffee in front of me, I regaled them with the tale, leaving out the drug bits.

Brandon was still sleeping in his armchair.

After I've got some sleep myself I'll call the cab company, get my purse back, and start making changes. I want to buy new paint supplies, start a class, and do something about this moms' club. Those women need some shaking up, and the new Joan is primed to do it.

Shit. Brandon is coming up the stairs. I think the sleeping pills finally wore off. Until later, diary.

Joan Fixing-My-Shit Colderman

June

When the Sunset

by Guilie Castillo Oriard

The sunset has turned the Caribbean sky into the fire-streaked excess one associates with Photoshop zealots. Luis Villalobos, on a towel by the surf, is thinking about leaving. It's been impossible to get Pélagie alone all afternoon. She's doing it on purpose; she just doesn't give a damn, and Luis is a fool for thinking one more try, after so many, will make any difference.

Al is romping with the other dogs, tearing up gusts of sand at the far end of the cove. Chases, gets chased, chases again. Staccato growls – part of the game, Pélagie said – reach Luis intermittently, depending on the wind. His dog is happy. Luis can sit here a while longer, for Al if not for Ehrlich Fiduciary, or for Pélagie Solak, and ponder his defeat.

He hinged, stupidly, his whole career at Ehrlich on this one corporate structure, this one woman.

He doesn't see Pélagie until she touches a cold beer to the sunburned patch of skin above his shirt collar. "I'm glad you brought Al." She hands him the beer, clinks her own against it in a token toast.

He means to take just a sip – he doesn't need more beer, he has to drive that potholed road back to what passes for civilization on this island – but it tastes so good he downs half in three gulps. "I didn't expect him to make friends so fast."

"They just need time." She bends her willowy body and sits cross-legged on his towel. Her knee bumps his thigh and he moves to make more room. "Sorry," she says, edges onto the sand.

"No, it's – please, sit on the towel."

She pins him in place with those disturbingly clear green eyes that nothing can wriggle away from. "I'm all sandy anyway."

This woman makes Luis feel profane. Around her, anything he says, everything about him, feels like unadulterated crudeness. A tenor pulling out his dick mid-*Turandot*.

"I make you nervous, don't I?"

Away from her gaze – she's looking at the dogs – he's brave enough to chuckle. "Not nervous, no."

"I'm not much good around people."

Luis glances over her shoulder at the crowd gathered around the bonfire. He just met them earlier today, hasn't traded more than a fistful of words with them, but it was enough to know they came – some with dogs, some without and apologetic for it – because Pélagie is here. "Could've fooled me."

She follows his gaze. "Because of them?"

"Seems like a nice group of friends."

"Groupies, really." She smiles, perhaps to take off some of the sting. "They like being associated with me because of who I am, not because of me."

Platitudes line up, ready to deploy, but then she says, "Know what I mean?" It's that phrase people tack onto the end of an awkward statement; it's not a real question. But the hell of it is Luis *does* know. He's done it, basked in others' glow – hotshot investment managers, celebrity clients – as if their magic might rub off on him, give him a glow of his own for others to bask in. And how good he felt, how vindicated, when it did. He wants to tell Pélagie there's nothing wrong with an entourage; it's proof of one's worth to the world. But he's afraid it might sound defensive. "They seem to like you," he says instead.

"They don't know me. They think they do, enough even to judge. But they don't know shit."

Her bitterness startles him. Then it occurs to him he might fit into this category. "Do you think I'm judging?"

She touches the beer to her lips, hesitates before taking a hasty sip. "Maybe. A little."

"Because of the affidavit?"

She's digging her bare foot into the sand. It's a beautiful foot, weightless and unadorned like the rest of her. "You think I'm wrong, you're right. That's a judgment."

"I don't mean it to be. I don't – I want to understand, but –"

"And I've explained. You just don't listen."

"No, I do." He collects himself, wants to avoid sounding belligerent. "You don't want to be a party to tax evasion. Neither does Ehrlich Fiduciary, Pélagie. That's not what we do. That's not what your structure is for."

"It's artificial." She flexes her toes and sand trickles between them, catches on ridges of skin. "I run a dog rescue group, Luis. I don't need companies in the British Virgin Islands or Barbados. Or New Zealand."

"It's because of the treaties. They allow tax deferral –"

"Listen to you." She chuckles, smooths the edge of the towel. "Treaties. Tax deferral. I talk to you for five minutes and I start feeling like I need a tailored suit and a briefcase."

"And you hate boardrooms, I know. But –" Luis lowers his voice. "The fact remains, Pélagie, you're a woman of substantial wealth. It's my job to –"

"I don't want it." She turns those eyes on him, full blast. "Okay? That substantial wealth, as you call it, means nothing but – obligation. And damned if I'll skirt that obligation, too."

"I'm lost. What – ?"

But she just keeps going. "The dogs balance it out. They make it – good. The money can do good, like this. See?"

There's a pleading in the last word that stops him from arguing. Of course he could keep arguing, even now that he doesn't understand what she's talking about – obligation? to whom? – because what good is a lawyer who can't debate three sides of an issue, can't push an advantage when he sees one? She could do so much more with the money that will otherwise go to the government in taxes. Save more dogs, if that's what she wants to do. But the conversation seems to have sidestepped into emotion he has no context for.

He should've let this go long ago. Ignored it back in April, like Milena wanted; processed the resignations last month, like Milena instructed. Milena was, as she always is, right. He's made this personal, but it isn't until now, when it's all about to end, that he realizes – admits – how personal.

It doesn't matter. It's over. "We'll file the resignation documents tomorrow."

Pélagie glances at him. "Thank you."

"Don't thank me. The whole structure will fall apart."

But – and this is not really surprising anymore, although it's still frustrating – she doesn't look worried. "Saves me the trouble of dissolving it."

"That's not how it works." But he says no more – really, what good would it do at this point? Her disdain, for him and for the logic that rules his life, already crusts every exchange. He would've anyway, though, except that Al chooses that moment to come check up on his human. He barrels onto Luis, all drool and wet, sandy paws. All unreserved worship and joy, too, which is why Luis smiles instead of grimacing and doesn't even wipe away the gobs of saliva – it could be ocean water – on his arm. He does, however, apologize for the sand sprayed in Pélagie's direction. "He thinks he's a Chihuahua. Don't you, guy? Hey, are you thirsty? Want some water, Al?"

"I set some out for them, too." Pélagie rubs the dog's chest, who looks for all the world like he's never experienced anything so delicious, the turncoat, as Luis pours from a thermos into the travel bowl.

Al splashes out double what he drinks, gets petted, patted, and scratched, before rejoining – not without a vigorous shake devised so that equal amounts of water and sand land on both humans – the other dogs.

Luis sputters, spits sand. Pélagie laughs, wipes at her face with a hand that has more dog hair, finally peels off her tank top. "I'm going to rinse off."

It takes Luis only a minute to take off shirt and shorts to follow her into the water, but in that minute memories of New Year's Eve crowd him – the walk on the beach with Milena, the fateful soak in the darkness, the drunken sex. Consequences. When he does wade in, he keeps a careful distance. Not that Pélagie would ever – hell, she doesn't even *like* him.

He lets the moment, the memories, dissolve. Then he says, in what might be a Guinness Record for Most Awkward Change of Subject: "You never told me how you got involved in dog rescuing."

"You mean how I became the crazy dog lady?" She grins, blows at the surface so the water ripples. "Don't apologize. Living with eighteen dogs qualifies me, I think. I'm even proud of it, which makes it so much more dysfunctional." He laughs, and she looks at him. The smoldering sunset lights her face like sun through stained glass. "You really want to know?"

"I do."

"It's a long story. And corny. Maudlin."

"I like maudlin." A lie, but it sounds convincing. Good lawyer, good boy. Or maybe it's not a lie. Because Luis is discovering he's fallen in love.

La Ronde / Gloria and Serge

by Townsend Walker

Serge, personal trainer Serge, walks up the path to 151 Carmelina in Brentwood, Gloria and Myron's place. Yes, Myron has returned to Gloria; rather, she has allowed him back into her life. Actually, she pretty much begged him to come back home. Had to. Who doesn't want to be the wife of the guy whose film, *The Naked Corpse*, was picked up by Paramount? With Marty signing on to direct, meaning Bobby, Sean, Leo and Jules will star. (That's Scorcese, De Niro, Penn, De Caprio and Roberts.) Mistress back in Newark be damned.

Gloria's Great Dane, Zeus, bounds from the bushes, leaps up on Serge: Tom Cruise tall, muscled like Sly Stallone, with a shock of bright blonde hair atop a preternaturally tanned face. Zeus crowds his muzzle into Serge's face. The dog's front legs are weighing on his shoulders. One hundred and fifty pounds of dog flesh. Zeus has got to be thinking: *Oh what fun, someone to play with.* Serge leans back and smacks the dog across the nose.

"Get off me, vile creature, go chew bone."

Zeus, oblivious, laps Serge's face with his wide slobbery tongue. Serge kicks the dog's hind leg, hard; the dog yelps. Gloria, in her white workout clothes, Swarovskis sprinkled around the neckline, comes out on the porch.

"Don't you so like to be greeted by this friendly puppy? Good dog Zeusie, making Sergie so welcome."

"Ach, yes, nice dog, wish I had one, my own."

Serge ruffles the dog's head tenderly.

"Okay Zeus, down now, Serge and Mommy have to get to work."

Gloria and Serge hug and loud air kisses float through the garden.

"So Myron back? I hear from friend."

"Yes, the little lamb has become a lion, but we have an agreement now that I'll be on location with him when shooting starts."

"Gloria, must start routine."

"God, what a taskmaster you've become. I'd swear you were German, not Russian."

"We more fierce than Germans. We win, they lose."

"Not the way I heard it," she says. "My history professor in college said General Winter won it for you."

"Who General Winter? We no have a General Winter."

"The weather, you big doofus. The cold and snow killed the Nazis, not the Soviets."

"Not what I taught. Brave Soviet troops sacrifice for motherland."

"Whatever," Gloria shrugs.

They walk through the house to the sun porch Gloria has outfitted as her exercise studio. Had a shower put in so after a workout she doesn't have to walk through the rest of the house perspiring. Porch done in shades of pink ranging from cherry blossom to magenta, including the weights, yoga mat, and exercycle. The Monday session starts with a high-energy routine mixing jumping jacks, skipping rope and running in place to rid the body of the toxins built up during the weekend (alcohol and just the "tiniest" bit of coke). Followed by weights, tantric stretches and a massage. This is Gloria's favorite part. Serge has very good hands.

She's had dreams about him, but unfortunately for her, he dreams only of Jimmy.

"Lower there, Serge, yes, oh yes, that's the place."

"Tell about movie. Role for Serge?"

"I don't know, I'll ask if they need any Russian muscle men."

"I not only muscle. Study to act. Have Equity card from Jimmy. And, who do your workout on location?"

There is no way Myron would give Serge a role. To change the subject she talks about Myron bumping into some guy back East who tells him about this contract a woman has put out on her husband. He beats her up. On top of that, he loses the kids when he takes them to the park. Twice they ended up calling the cops to find the seven and ten year old. Seems the guy gets distracted, or off doing something else, who knows.

"She doesn't want a divorce, she wants a death." That's Gloria's take.

She turns over on the massage table so her face is cosseted in the headrest.

"What he like?"

Gloria's description comes out a bit muffled.

Serge repeats: "Tell me if I understand. Franklin Lincoln Cabot Three. He called Frank. Work at Goldman Sachs on West Street, Manhattan. Six foot three, 250 pounds, pasty like dough face, curly black hair with silver, big nose like bird, Brooks suits, loafers with tassels. And Hermes ties. Prada (I know Prada, Jimmy wear Prada, I want to wear Prada) Aviators, blue tint. He wear even in rain."

Gloria turns her face up to Serge. "Why do you care about this? You got some friends that have guns?"

"How much lady in New York pay?"

"Myron wasn't sure, but reckoned around fifty big ones, maybe more. She seemed desperate."

"So when lady talk to Myron?"

Serge can be thick sometimes, Gloria's thinking. "Myron never talked to the lady, he got the story from someone who got it from someone."

"So how you know he not dead now?"

"Call him up. If he answers, he's not dead."

"You have name lady want husband dead?"

Gloria slips off the massage table and wraps herself in a cerise pink robe. "Serge, don't you have another appointment?"

In the afternoon Serge calls Gloria. "Cannot find name in phone book."

"What name?"

"Name of lady pays for murder husband."

Gloria throws the phone across the room, quickly retrieves it.

"What that noise? Hurt ear."

"Serge sweetheart, for the very last time, I will never speak to you if you bring this up again. I told you because I thought you'd have a laugh. Forget it. Goodbye."

Sinking

by Derek Osborne

Well the sun is slowly sinking down …

Max and Rebecca are sitting in the cockpit, snuggled under the big, patchwork quilt they stole off the bunk. It's been warm and sunny all day but now it's grown chilly, a northeast breeze coming in off the ocean, the front will be here by morning. In early June it's always a toss-up on Nantucket. Don't like the weather? Wait a minute.

Rebecca is drinking hot chocolate after eating a roast beef sandwich, two avocadoes and half a pack of Oreos. It's what she wanted. Max learned long ago not to quibble with the desires of a pregnant woman. She's beginning to show. She has that glow all women have by their third month.

"And my ass hurts enough as it is."

She's been complaining all day, seems he can't do anything right, seems he cannot do one damn thing – nothing – he can't even disappear properly. He just smiles when she complains, which ticks her off even more.

"You forget, I've been through this before," he says.

"Well I haven't."

A minute later she's crying and apologizing for being a bitch.

The food seems to help. They're listening to the impromptu band the crew put together. It's becoming a regular Tuesday affair. Eddie brings the boat in around seven and ties alongside the peer. Every musician on the island shows up. They even come out on the ferry from Hyannis. Max puts them up for the night if they can't find (or afford) a bed onshore. In the morning the deck is a sea of sleeping bags, as if the boat, too, has her own patchwork quilt.

At first the Dock Master complained about the concerts so Anja had a little chat with the Chamber of Commerce. In her own gentle way (no one expects The Spanish Inquisition) she explained how good the Tuesday night jams were for business, how the scene lent a certain cachet which, quite frankly, they had blown with all their condominium management, planned events and homo-genized building codes. A weathered gray shingle is a weathered gray shingle is a weathered gray shingle. *Gadabout,* in Anja's opinion, is the only surprise left on the island, and word is getting round on the mainland the old Nantucket, the one people love and remember, is back for the season. She even wrangled full artistic direction over what music they'll play. When Anja suggests they have a donation basket for the island's Nature Foundation, The Chamber buys in, hook, line and sinker. Sometimes Jazz, sometimes Rock, last week it was first chair from The Boston Pops – Mozart floating over the harbor – putting the Dock Master squarely in their corner. Fait accompli. Tonight it's Folk Rock.

and you can sing this song ...

"You warm enough?" Max says.
"Yes, I'm fine. Eddie makes a mean cocoa."
They haven't stopped talking since that day last month when Max was still in the hospital. Neither one needed explanation; Rebecca had her own confession. If you have ever capsized a large boat you know it doesn't happen all at

once, it takes time – what seems like a very long time – and in that first rush of panic, knowing you've gone too far, and that slow, deliberate bend to the other side, the confusion of gravity, the water and the rigging, how surprising the power of adrenaline, the will to get out, get out and swim for your life. Waiting for Rebecca to say something after telling her the hospital room number was like that, and when she did answer, when she broke that long, terrible silence, "I'm pregnant," all Max could do was surrender, there would be no escape.

... you can stay as long as you like.

"Have I ever said how good you smell?"
"Please don't start that again."
He's kissing her chocolate mustache. Eddie put whipped cream in the cocoa. It's strange to think it's already been three months. They got pregnant that very first night back in March. She carries it well. It's easy enough to hide and they've been trying to figure out when to go public. CBS intends to announce she is leaving *Miami Blue* at the end of the month. They're letting her do her own press (with a little input from legal). It will be a paparazzi stampede for a month and there will be no way to hide the pregnancy, or Max for that matter, and sooner or later some enterprising reporter will find out about his cancer and then they will have all of that to deal with, tabloid hell. Times like these, where they can simply be alone with friends, will cease to exist.

"Have you thought about a name?" Rebecca says.
They went for an ultrasound this morning. The island's clinic has the equipment but the technician is only there Tuesdays. It's a boy. They wanted to know in case ... just in case. "Finally," Max said when the technician pointed out the penis. Everything looks fine. The date will be early November. "Scorpio, like me," Rebecca said when they left.

"Of course," Max says now.

"What's that supposed to mean?"

"I've always been a sucker for Scorpio women."

"You should have warned me you were ..."

Max fills in the sentence. "Cancer?"

The simplest of words trigger so many others. Their days are filled with innuendo, embarrassed smiles, Max remembers how it was with Maggie, how the dynamic shifts, the cared-about becomes the care-taker. Add Rebecca's pregnancy.

"It will play well on HBO," she says.

"When did you know?" he says, wanting to change the subject. He's pulled the quilt even higher, there's plenty of room; they're in a kind of cocoon. The band has finished the song, people applauding, not only onboard but also the crowd on the dock. Others have come in their dinghies and rafted at *Gadabout's* stern. There's a directness between Max and Rebecca now, no subject taboo, no room for fears or petty jealousies. "You looked at me," he says. "You were down in the cockpit working out blocking and you looked at me."

"You were up by the bow," she says.

The applause dies down, the band discussing what to play next.

"And then you crashed the boat," she whispers.

"Almost crashed ..."

"*Almost* crashed ..."

"How many girls get to say that?"

The sun is nearly gone, it's warm beneath the quilt, the lights of the village coming on one by one, the floods on the white steeple rising over the hill, soft orange lamps at the docks and gray waterfront.

"A couple days into the shoot one of the make-up guys said you were pretty hot for an older man and I defended you."

This makes him smile.

"And then you almost crashed the boat."
"And you laughed and I fell in love."
The band is beginning another song.

Why must every generation think their folks are square?

"I like this song," Max says, touching his forehead to hers. He reaches under the bulky wool sweater and lifts her t-shirt, placing the flat of one hand on her belly and the other on the small of her back. His hands are warm. The two of them settle in, safe there beneath the cover, he can smell her hair and feel her breathing.
"Maximus Miguel Caamano Vasquez-Perkins," she says.
"Oh God, I've gotta change my name."
"I like your name."
"Perkins?"
"It's so … American."

And still he'll stick his fingers in the fan.

Night is settling in. The sky is a mix of clouds and stars and a quarter moon. There's the deepening chill but for now it's okay; for now they are fine. Tomorrow they'll go looking for a house on the island, some place back from the road, room for both families. Rebecca's inviting her mother and brothers. The house is Pam's idea and his daughters agree (they think the boat is getting awkward) but it's also a way to provide a fortress for the upcoming battle. They can guard the narrow drives, there's no getting through the dense growth on the island or landing a boat in the marsh, and choppers cost a grand an hour. Anja says TV Drama Show Stars don't rate a chopper. Max squeezes Rebecca's belly, feeling the weight she's gained. He doesn't know the guy who is playing guitar but he's good, a set musician out of Boston. He pulls her close.

The pain and fear come at odd times, the way Max imagines it must be for vets suffering flashbacks. The attacks stab at different parts of his body. He imagines the boat heeling hard, the wind shrieking up in the rigging, sails torn, the deck a confusion of lines and equipment after a rogue wave. He's watching the life-raft fly off into the night. He burrows down beneath the quilt and places his cheek on Rebecca's belly, his arms around, bracing the sound of splintering masts and whip-lashed cables. The waves come huge and mountainous. He grits his teeth, stifles the urge to moan. They'll survive, they always have, but each time the day draws nearer. He squeezes her tight.

"Darling, I can see the moon," Becca says, lifting his face in her hands, "Come here with me and watch the stars."

Depression

by Gloria Garfunkel

Depressive Crash Ralph here. The worst depressions come after the highest manias. I contemplate all day different ways to kill myself: Drowning. Overdoses. Hanging. Shooting. Stabbing. Crashing my car. Jumping from the Mystic River Bridge. (That always gets *Boston Globe* headlines, not that I'm looking for attention.) They all have their downsides. I favor painless but dread the possibility of lifelong coma. The higher my mania gets, the harder I fall. Every time. I'm going to get my psychiatrist to get me a medical leave for the month. I can't keep any of my resolutions. I am a completely inconsistent loser with an empty brain. I don't even meet the most basic Quality Assurance principles in living my life. Maybe I should hand my life over to Scientology. That would be worse than suicide.

Meanwhile Serena is taking total advantage of my helpless situation at work, tracking all my errors and omissions, reporting them to Stan who then calls me into his office to lecture me for half-an-hour jumping on his chair, not a good use of Quality Assurance time I restrain myself from saying aloud but note to put in my report.

When I get home bedraggled and contemplating a car accident, Chloe is gentle and encouraging and makes me soup and tea. I love her.

Ebony

by John Wentworth Chapin

They stand on Esther's stoop, Charles on the top step, Marla two behind him. Charles is aware, as usual, of Esther's neighbors monitoring him. He knocks again, his eyelid twitching and stomach grinding. They wait.

"Maybe she's napping," Marla says. Charles knows this isn't the case; one of Esther's agonies is that she can't relax enough to sleep. Or is this also a lie? Charles doesn't know what is true and what isn't.

He hasn't seen Esther for a month. Charles was surprised yesterday when he got a voicemail from her asking him to come today. Things are different with her now. After months of sympathy – she would never walk again, she was distraught about killing that woman and those boys, she was hounded by lawsuits from the families – sympathy which culminated in his promise to help her plan her own suicide, he discovered she'd been lying to him.

He told his friend Stephanie about it. She saw Esther's suicide plan as a cry for help, and the dishonesty made it obvious. Charles didn't know what to think; he was lost. Stephanie encouraged him to help Esther to regain the will to live. *You can't be angry. You have to help her.* She insisted.

So he called the three families of the accident victims, hoping they might reconsider their lawsuits in the wake of her tremendous grief. But his calls were met with confusion. There were no lawsuits.

Charles was dumbfounded. Lie after lie ... but the coup de grâce was remembering that, of course, Esther had lied from the very start. She'd told the doctors and police that she remembered nothing of the accident when, in fact, she remembered every last detail and was haunted by it.

Or so she said. He trusted nothing now.

Into the picture comes Marla. Her sister was killed in the accident. Like the rest of the victim's families, she believes that some sort of neurological blackout led to Esther driving up onto the sidewalk and taking out three people at 40 miles an hour. When Charles explained that Esther was stricken with suicidal guilt and irrational fear about non-existent lawsuits, Marla agreed to make the visit, to reassure poor Esther that no one blamed her for anything. "The last thing any of us needs right now is another death," she said.

Now she's standing in his shadow on Esther's stoop, enormous black purse on her shoulder held carefully, as though someone might at any moment grab it. When Esther doesn't answer her door after the third knock, Charles puts his face to the crack in the door and calls out her name. No response. And then he realizes that he doesn't expect one. She's in there, but she's not asleep. Or awake.

He wishes he was far away from here.

Charles, this is Esther. Esther Pinkney. If you could be so kind and return my call when you get the chance, I'd be much obliged. I was hoping you'd pay me a visit soon to continue our research.

He'd called her back immediately, angry that she'd lied to him.

"I didn't think you'd come unless you felt sorry for me," she said, simply.

"I never came over because I pitied you!" he shouted. "I came because – we had a project together. We *trusted* each other."

"We still have a project, Charles."

"But you lied to me! I was there because I *wanted* to be there, and after the accident … the only person I *haven't* felt crazy around was you."

"It's a shame I didn't realize that," she answered.

"And now you've taken that away from me, too," he bawled, and as he felt his throat constrict with a surprising surge of emotion, he clicked the phone off. What did she care?

After that, she called him every few days, hanging up without leaving a message when he didn't answer. Each time, he thought he might take the call, that he was ready; each time he screened it. Finally, she left him a message, the day before.

Charles, this is Esther. Esther Pinkney. You made me a promise, and unless I hear otherwise from you, I assume you intend to keep it. I'd be obliged if you could stop by tomorrow after work.

The front door is unlocked, and as Charles opens it, he and Marla are slammed by a foul, eggy stench.

"Oh, God! What is that?" Marla shrieks, her hand instinctively shielding her nose and eyes.

Charles guesses it's toilet bowl cleaner mixed with pesticide, a popular and foolproof recipe for hydrogen sulfide gas. The websites say it will kill a person in five minutes. Esther had decided against it, concerned about police or neighbors who would try to help and expose themselves to the lethal gas. The Internet is filled with stories about first responders succumbing to the gas.

He pulls Marla by the arm, and they stumble down the stoop away from the house. She sputters in surprised confusion. "Run – that's poison gas!" Charles yells.

Marla scrambles to join Charles running away from the foul odor. "How do you know?" she yells at him.

"We had – she had talked about suicide," Charles stammers. On the sidewalk now, he tries to pull himself together, too wired now to think clearly. Esther's neighbors look at Charles and Marla with alarm, and the man next door walks across Esther's yard to her front door.

"Don't go in there!" Marla screams at him as she pulls her phone from her giant black purse. "It's poison." She dials 911 and puts a finger in her ear to block out the street noise.

"I can't just leave her in there," the man says.

"It's hydrogen sulfide – poison gas. She's already dead, probably. We – we can't go in." Charles tries to say more but can't. He's frozen.

"Now how do *you* know what's going on in there?" the man says.

Marla is shouting into her phone, explaining the situation.

The man's face changes, his eyebrows knitting. "I've seen you over here before. Just what are you up to with Miss Esther?"

Police, fire trucks, ambulance, news vans, HAZMAT. They clear a perimeter around Esther's house, and Charles watches as men wheel a covered stretcher, which disappears in an ambulance without sirens.

He hears Marla talking rapid-fire to the police the whole time, to the firefighters, the EMTs, to anyone who will listen.

Marla won't make eye contact with Charles. She implies, loudly, that he is responsible, and Esther's neighbor seems to agree, stands beside her, nodding and frowning. Charles imagines what happens next: police descend on his apartment, take his computer, search his hard drive, and find his Google history:

> drugs that cause heart attacks
> household poisons
> how to make hydrogen sulfide gas
> carbon monoxide poisoning

A detective approaches Charles, introducing herself, and asks if she can have a moment of his time.

"Of course," Charles whispers.

"Can you tell me what's happened here?"

Charles fears the worst, but he reminds himself he has nothing to hide.

He tells the whole story; at first, he needs prodding from the detective, but soon it all spills out. He couldn't stop talking if he tried. It's a confusing story; the detective wants to know about now, maybe about the past 24 hours, but Charles is back six months ago with the car accident, the odd friendship, the Internet research, the suicide request, the lies. The non-existent lawsuits, the hydrogen sulfide recipe, the phone calls. It makes his own head spin, but the detective listens, nodding and taking notes. Charles has no idea what the detective thinks.

Charles lays out his final defense: "She called me to ask me to come over today. She left me a voicemail."

The detective makes a few notes on a little pad, nodding to herself.

"Oh, shit," Charles says. Intuition stops him cold.

The detective looks up, waiting. "What," she prompts.

Charles' mouth is dry as charcoal. "She knew I'd be the first one on the scene. She tried to take me with her." When he says it, he knows it's true.

Friday, 6th June 2014

Infamy

by Lynn Beighley

My cell phone rings and I flinch. Pollock jumps off the bed. I let it ring, even though it's a new unlisted number and only a few people know it.

I reach over to the nightstand and pour another glass of wine, dripping a little on the pink blanket. Wine stains can only improve it. It's been on this bed since I was 12. I consider getting up and ripping down the lacy white canopy over my head, but decide it's too much trouble.

I take a big swig of wine to wash down my vitamin D. A couple weeks ago I read that when you can't go outside, it's a good idea to take D. And wine is supposed to be healthy too, right? So I'm being healthy. I'm being healthy at 11 AM.

I reach across the bed and grab my laptop where I left it last night. Time for me to read the latest about my obsession. Which is me. Or rather news about me, conjectures about where I've gone, comments from all over this great country praising or damning me.

There's not much about me today. No news, no new conjectures. Just a few nasty comments. I sip my wine and check my email. I've got nothing else to do, no job, no reality tv wedding to plan.

My dad knocks on the door. "Come in," I say. He comes in and sits on the edge of the bed.

"Jenn, sweetie, you really need to get up," he says. "And," he sniffs, "take a shower."

"No thanks," I say.

"You can't go on like this," he says.

"I think I can. I see no reason why I can't go on like this."

"Well, if that's how you feel, then you won't mind if the TV folks film you in bed."

I am shocked, but I'm a woman with great self-control. I choose my words carefully.

"What the fuck are you talking about?!"

"You need the money, and they're paying a lot, Jenn. A whole lot. They want you back on the show. Doing whatever you want. You can scream at Bill, whatever. They need you."

I hear a noise outside the door, and see the business end of a film camera, pointed at me.

Kamikaze

by Andrew Stancek

The General gnashes his teeth and a scrap of egg yolk falls from his shaking fork onto his crisp day uniform. Three times a week he meets Dewhurst for a working breakfast, with Dewhurst sipping coffee and buttering toast he'll never eat while the General devours the lumberjack special.

"Damn it, Dewhurst. Millions. Tens of millions we've spent and we're still in a black hole. The best minds working for us and all they've accomplished are pathetic little hops. Hops. We can pretend to be pleased, pretend we're making wonderful progress but we have no flights. They're hops. Bloody Maharishi in the seventies had his disciples hopping, too, without our kind of money and our research team. And here we are, ten years of pouring money down the drain and we're not a nanometer further than he was."

The General slurps orange juice, bangs the glass, refills from the pitcher next to his elbow, overfills, oblivious to the puddle. "And a kid, a snivelly wide-eyed nobody, named Adam, Adam goddamn it, figures it out on his own? And won't tell us how it's done? Won't take our money? If we can't buy him, Dewhurst, other methods will be deployed. You have to break eggs to make an omelet, you know that."

He reaches for the ketchup, pours half the bottle over his home fries. "I want the pathetic kid singing like a canary, telling us, teaching us, leading a fucking parade, dying to share everything he knows. Hooked up to heart monitors and brain wave readers, to every piece of machinery known to science, he'll warble. And if he doesn't, we'll see how he likes a pat on the head and a few jolts of 220 volts into his nipples and penis. We'll watch the pretty blue eyes tremble. We'll have prototypes and fly around the base by Christmas."

His face grows crimson and his fork becomes a missile about to be fired. Twice, three times he bangs the tines against the plate and then points it at Dewhurst. "It's national security. It's freedom. It's the future. It's the whole American economy. I won't have the damn Russians, or some rich sheik or Ayatollah figure it out before we do. Let's pay a visit to our little friend Adam. Let's see if he'll listen to gentle persuasion."

Ever since the Adam headlines hit the internet Dewhurst has been expecting the General to have a meltdown and is surprised it has taken this long. Instead of troops to command, the General sits behind a desk at the Pentagon, flush with money to spend and nothing to show. Research project Titan is a blot on his career, with potential to premature retirement in disgrace, not getting him the position on the Joint Chiefs of Staff he craves. As long as he could keep saying it's impossible, no one has ever flown on his own, it cannot be done, he had a supportable position. But Adam has blown that one up. He's doing it. Every day on a TV screen or in a new viral video, Adam flies like an eagle, soars, swoops, glides over the Grand Canyon. The kid has guts and grace. But the General will have a coronary if he does not get the secret. And Dewhurst knows the meeting will not go well, has to get messy. Dewhurst wonders if this is his time to retire from the Army, take a job with a private contractor. He wouldn't miss Washington. He could get used to the sun of Arizona.

"It might be better, General, to deal with it softly, low-key, without scaring the kid and his entourage, without getting our interest splashed in the press. He's surrounded like Elvis and if we go in with a staff car and an armed force, it might make us look bad."

"Goddamn it, Dewhurst, don't patronize me. There is a time for negotiation, for nicey-nicey, for feints, but the best part of any war is the invasion. Shock and awe. This is war, Dewhurst. My troops are about to land on the beachhead and destroy the enemy. I am going to wipe out all resistance. I am in charge."

Dewhurst begins mentally going through old contacts and brushing up that résumé. "Yes, sir."

The sergeant at the wheel of the General's staff car is too experienced to squeal the tires, but his "Yes, Sir" to the General's command is crisp. "Won't meet with us," the General mutters under his breath. "Mom does not like the military," he wheedles, in imitation of an unbroken teenage voice. "This is the US goddam Army. You think we give a rat's ass what you or your mother like?"

Off the deep end, Dewhurst thinks. Totally unhinged. I wonder if I should notify the White House. Would the President's aide-de-camp talk to me? Not likely. The General is going kamikaze; it's D-Day. God help us.

Don't Wait Up

by Rachel Ambrose

I knew it would happen eventually. My first big fight with Blake erupted last night like pus out of a boil, forceful and messy and gross. As I wake up, flinging my hair out of my half open eyes, taking in the wreckage of my bedroom, mountains of dirty clothes on the floor, half-drunk cups of tea on the dresser, I can feel a migraine starting in the back of my head. Not a great way to start a morning full of family interaction, that's for sure.

And it's the first day of the annual family trip out to River Rock, where all fourteen of us rent a huge vacation mansion for a week. We inevitably eat, drink and smoke too much (overindulgence, when we don't have anywhere to be, is a Worthington family trait). I pull myself out of bed and glance at my phone. No calls or texts from Blake, but with the magnitude of the fight we had last night (I can still feel the tears behind my eyes, probably the cause of the migraine), I'd be a fool to expect any. He'll probably break up with me now, but honestly I've been preparing for that since day one. Then again, love without the fear of loss isn't really love, is it?

As I dress in my signature sweatpants and ancient t-shirt and pack the paltry amount of clean clothes I can find on my floor, I think to myself, stupid, stupid, stupid. The fight last night had stemmed from that horrible Jackie from last month's barn party – she got under my skin somehow, and then she always managed to be around, meeting us for brunch, trying to come over and watch movies, inviting herself out with us, just ... underfoot. She made me feel itchy. And then last night I exploded all over Blake about it, and his feelings got hurt, because he really does like Jackie, they're friends and all, and he couldn't understand why I disliked her so – "honestly, you're ridiculous, we're just friends!" he said to me on more than one occasion. Maybe I am ridiculous, I consider as I zip my tote bag shut and write a note for Isa, who's moved back in, much to my delight (the epic snack buyer returns!). *Off to River Rock for the week,* the note says. *Don't wait up.*

My sister Molly picks me up in her fabulous silvery BMW. She's a lawyer, and she's done rather well for herself, and she's so progressive – did I mention she's also a lesbian? Girl power, indeed. I slide into the passenger seat after putting my tote in the back, roll my eyes up into my head, and announce, "If someone doesn't get me a vodka and an Extra Strength Tylenol as soon as we step foot in River Rock, I'm going to shit in everybody's hats."

Molly laughs as we turn off my street, brown eyes alight, blonde hair messy as always. "I'll pass that on to Mom and Dad. Tell 'em to hide their hats. Because either you must have a lot of shit inside you, or else you're counting on there being, like, precisely two hats."

As we drive along, I spill to her about the whole Blake fiasco, and she sits there tutting after I'm through. I pinch the bridge of my nose as a throb of pain explodes through my head. "What?" I demand when she stays quiet.

"Well, it's just ..." she stops and starts. "I mean ..." A sigh. "Blake does not seem like the kind of guy you need to be with. That's it! That's all I'm saying," she says, shooting me a defensive look. "He seems really high maintenance. All these fancy parties and hangers-on and 'ooh, I just love your work'. Why can't you just work on you for a change?"

she continues. "Take some Pilates, start drawing again like you used to do when you were younger. Join a book club, I don't know."

I blink at her, mouth a little agape. "A book club? Really, Molls? I know you're all about the virtues of the independent woman, but does every woman have to be independent? Why can't I just marry some rich artist and be able to eat bonbons and watch daytime TV all the time?"

"Why is that your greatest aspiration?" she shoots back. "To be able to do absolutely nothing of consequence with your life. Even if you did marry some rich douchebag, you could make your own art, have affairs, take classes, whatever. You could have some agency."

"It's not nothing," I reply quietly. My ears are ringing, although from anger or pain, I can't tell. "It's stability." My words are coming out slow and clipped. "It's about ... being able to breathe. It's about –" I take a deep breath to keep the shake from my voice, "finally having some guarantees. Because nothing scares me more than the unknown."

We ride in silence after that, and the familiar crunch of the BMW's tires on the gravel driveway at River Rock jolts me out of a sleep-like state I didn't even know I was in.

Too Late

by Gill Hoffs

Daughter mode is different when it's for real. No baby-talk, no perking my arse up for a slap if I've been 'naughty', no sitting on laps and wriggling on hard-ons. Just nodding in the right places, the mildest of swearing, and remembering to take a plate to catch the crumbs from her biscuits.

My aunt bakes for me when she knows I'm coming over. Anzac biscuits and solid scones and currant buns with flowery wrappers and bits that get stuck in my teeth. My mum would like to, but she knows Dad's sister would fret around us, tallying whose products I ate more of, interrupting us with questions of taste and comments about oven shelving as we attempt to sit in silence and blow on our cups of tea.

I wear sweaters or hoodies, no makeup, no heels. None of my work jewellery or undies, not after the time I squatted to rub Dumpling's freckled belly as she lay by the fire and my little brother twanged the crassly-bejewelled T of my G-string and drew it to Mum's attention. Cue a string of questions I didn't want to answer about whether there was a Special Someone in my life. Cue hints and sighs from my aunt about Not Leaving Love Too Late, Settling Down Before It Was Too Late, Not Being Too Picky in case it became Too Late, and the perils of spreading my fancies Too Freely. A little Too Late for that.

Dad sits on the mantelpiece as always, a vigorous dusting away from a tragedy and yet another bodged reclamation from the vacuum cleaner. I think Mum would be happier with the urn elsewhere, a garden of remembrance (I hate the implication that the dead would be forgotten otherwise) or thrown into the canal. Not like unwanted puppies in a suitcase or rubbers after a session under the bridge. He loved it there, fishing for perch, listening to the traffic rushing past, watching for bodies. But his sister leaks tears when we mention it, so he stays above the fireplace, rounded and dusty, when he was neither while living.

Conversation is limited, and whenever it looks like Mum or Auntie Michelle or Jay want to talk, I mean *properly* talk, I sniff and pull a tube of lozenges from my pocket (kept there for this very reason) and feign a cough while exuding menthol vapours. So far it's worked. I go home, everything stays polite and jokey and impersonal and manageable, I smile and nod and eat what they give me and pretend to relax, then get back in the car or onto the train and away again, phew!

Sometimes I think I'll just tell them.

Sometimes I think they already know.

But then someone yawns or sighs or turns the TV onto a talent show and Auntie Michelle mutters "Foolish little tarts" and no-one looks my way or pointedly doesn't, and I think maybe I'll tell Mum, maybe at bedtime, maybe when she brings a cup of tea and a sneaky shop-bought biscuit to my room in the morning, but then she smiles and it could be a decade ago when I've nowhere to escape to but the shops or school and the only thing that's been between my legs apart from tampons and 100% cotton gussets is the detachable showerhead and there's nothing I can tell her that would keep things the same.

I don't work as I do because Dad died. I wanted this job before that, before the cough and the cancer and the hospital bed, before I even left school for Uni. I just hadn't known how or where or who to talk to so I could go about it. I scoured the local rag in vain for details of busts and madams fined in court, for small adverts placed before the massage parlours and chatlines and intimate services offered if you called a mobile number at so much per minute. I even sat, with my hair straightened by my mum's iron and my thighs shaved above my hold-ups, on benches near art gallery functions and celebratory lunches at museums and the town hall, in case I was mistaken for a 'date' and got my 'in' that way. A middle-aged woman who smelled of pear drops and piss offered me a boiled sweet and muttered something about "bastards" and being "stood up", so I went home.

Auntie Michelle is fluttering about in the kitchen, opening the oven door instead of peering through the glass, letting the heat out so the kitchen smells great but the chicken will take longer than necessary. Jay rolls his eyes at me and I wink and sit cross-legged beside Dumpling on the rug, rubbing her belly in circles till my eyes sting with fart. She raises her head, glances back at the guilty area, wags her tail – no! don't wave it at me! – and licks my knee.

Jay flicks my ear with his fingers as he walks past on his way to his room to 'study'. I suspect he's just pissing about online, but it's his life and I don't really give a fuck.

With Jay gone, it's just me and Mum and Dumpling in the living room. There's another couple of hours till the usual round of soaps start on the box, summer has forgotten to unleash its heat on the north of England, and rain is tapping on the windows as if it wants to come in.

Mum leans forward on the settee, elbows on knees, and smiles at me with her lips tucked in.

"I need to talk to you about something."

"Oh?"

Dumpling snuggles against me and I feign calm, easing rumples of fat from around her collar, poking them

304

underneath with my finger instead of leaping up to extricate the lozenges from my pocket.

"You know I've been unwell."

I shake my head, and gulp, and realise this isn't about the escort work.

"I've been to the doctors a few times, and the hospital – just for tests, things like that. And it's nothing too awful, nothing hereditary or anything like that."

"Well, what is it?"

I'm staring at her and realise her eyes are yellow where there should only be white, and she's lost weight, and my vision closes in so there is only her to see. My hand keeps stroking Dumpling but the rest of me is still.

"I have to have an operation, a small one. It's nothing too dreadful, they won't fillet me, it's all keyhole. But it's got me thinking and I want to pass some things to you now, just to set my mind at rest."

"When?"

"Now, I have them right here, ready for you comi–"

I shake my head.

"No. Mum, the operation. When's your operation?"

"Next week. Wednesday. All being well, as it will be, I'll be home for the weekend."

I blink. It must be serious if they're doing it so soon.

"Do you want me to take you in? Talk to the nurses and doctors, make sure you get the nice ones?"

I can feel my nose producing misery-mucus, wet and trickling inside, and sniff before something dribbles out and reveals my upset when I'm trying my damnedest to be adult about my only parent getting sick.

She leans over and hooks my hair behind my ears with her index finger. No hiding now.

"I wasn't telling you to worry you, and I don't need any help. Your Auntie Michelle will keep Jay in tea and biscuits while I'm in hospital, and they've said it won't take long for me to feel like my old self again. But."

I don't like the pause, or how she stares into my eyes – I suspect she's steadying herself, and it makes my heart race and throb in my throat.

"But?"

"But I like to be careful, so before I forget" – as if she would – "I want you to take these. I've been holding on to them for you anyway. They were your dad's and mine, when we were courting. Maybe you can give one to your own special someone."

And she holds out two narrow silver bands.

I slip one on each index finger, working by feel alone as I daren't look down in case gravity betrays the tears balancing on my lower lash-line, and she sits back in her chair, smiling with her lips visible, clearly more at ease.

I sniff again, and open my mouth to say something but then Auntie Michelle drops something with a clatter and a smash and squeals out a 'No!' and Mum rolls her eyes and rushes out to help.

And the moment to connect with her has gone.

From the comments in the kitchen, and Mum calling through to me, "You like mustard with your chicken sometimes, don't you?" I gather the gravy jug's gone, too.

Tuesday, stringbeans

by Susan Tepper

The shower water is too fricking hot – scalds his backside. Why do they have to call it ass or butt? he's thinking. Heine! Now there was a good one! Clean your heine, the grownups used to say. Pedersen spits the toothpaste at his feet.

He likes the all-in-one shower. The army called it 3 S's: shit, shower and shave. You got three minutes. There were times he had to creep into the latrine at night and dig the shit out of his ass. That gave him a little extra time for the shower and shave. The army. Someone should bomb the shit out of the army. Pedersen gargles shower water watching the rivulets swirl around the drain.

Summer is about to spring. The kiddies will be packed off to camps across America. Schoolyards will be dead except for teenagers who got left back for being dumber than shit. His little darlings will be gone until the fall. Those sweet things – their soft rosy cheeks and bony scraped knees.

He sees Swoon the white rat and picks it up by the tail swinging it. The rat squeals, little high-pitched sounds, little legs scurrying in the air. "You s'posed to stay in your hole till I play the special music," he tells it.

Dropping the rat, Pedersen wipes steam off the bathroom mirror. He rubs his stubble looking closely at himself in the glass. *Not a fine specimen* crosses his mind.

"Vegetables," he says, remembering that jingle from childhood: Monday *something*, Tuesday stringbeans, Wednesday soooooouuuppp. Do I really love ya? Ya bet I do.

He'll boil a pot of stringbeans. Good for the virility. It is important to maintain virility at all costs.

You lose your balls in combat, you're a dead man, the sergeant told Pedersen during basic training. He remembered it. It wasn't the sort of thing you'd soon forget. This association: death and his balls.

His little darlings have balls the size of Swoon, practically. Tiny little balls meant for cupping and holding. They run around the schoolyard with their little balls, little pricks. He could help them learn to piss correctly. He could help them become men.

The white rat runs across the tub edge. "Get the frick out of here you scummy white prick you leavin' rat shit on my clean tub."

Pedersen takes a tissue and brushes the rat droppings into the tub, running the shower to wash them away.

"It can be that easy," he says.

First Class

by Jessica McHugh

Edward is meant to be a lion today – proud, authoritative, strong but graceful. But as he stands before thirteen eighth graders longing to enjoy their summer instead of being cooped up in a classroom, Father Edward McKenzie is a wounded zebra at their carnivorous mercy.

He clears his throat, adjusts his crucifix on his chest, and exhales, glad they can't see his skin prickling beneath his vestments – or the rosy camisole he'd donned that morning to boost his confidence. He wasn't sure he'd need it, but standing in front of the class, his hands shaking, he's glad for the feeling of secret satin.

"Welcome to your first summer session of Health Studies," he announces. "We'll be meeting every Wednesday and Friday at 10am sharp for the next four weeks, discussing all sorts of health topics, from mental and physical to sexual."

Several kids yawn. Some tap their pens on their desks and scribble in their notebooks.

Writing his name on the chalkboard, he continues. "I see some familiar faces, but for those of you I don't know, my name is Father McKenzie." He faces the classroom. "I've been a priest at St. Peter's for about thirty years now, and I'm eager to get to know all of you."

A boy raises a waving hand, his words spilling out after Edward's acknowledging nod.

"I've heard about you," he says, his tone pointed. "You're the one with the drunk mom who killed someone … your grandmother?"

"That …" His voice squeaks, and he lowers his head. His throat is parched, and his camisole is wet under his armpits.

You're in charge here, Edward. Don't let fear rule your life.

Looking up, he sees Grandma Eleanor at the back of the classroom, dressed in flowing pink chiffon, gliding between the desks. The aroma of her Duska powder thickens, as she places her hand on his shoulder.

I'm here for you. For as long as you need me.

Edward nods and clears his throat. "That was a long time ago," he tells the boy. "And it's not pertinent to Health Studies."

"I don't know what pertinent means, but I'd think someone who was raised by a drunken murderer doesn't know much about being healthy." The kid laughs as he turns to his classmate. "Am I right?"

Edward faces the chalkboard as air fires from his lungs. He's dizzy, and his chest aches. He longs to lean his head against the board and pretend thirteen kids aren't staring at him. The boy has stopped talking, but a voice persists in Edward's mind, spat from the cracked lips of Betty McKenzie.

"What do you know about health, Edward?" his mother asks. "What kind of teacher, what kind of priest, what kind of *man* wears a satin cami under his clothes?" He exhales a shuddering breath, his fists clenched. His mother stands behind him, her boozy words hot on the back of his neck. "You're no man," she says. "And you're sure as hell no teacher. You're an abomination."

310

"You're wrong," Edward says. He spins around, catching the students' shocked expressions. "What you know about me isn't really about me, but about people who sought to poison my life. But I won't let that happen anymore. Not from my mother, and certainly not from you, son. Do you understand?"

The boy gawks, his brow furrowed. When the student sitting behind him leans forward to tap his shoulder, Father Edward recognizes the boy as Nelson Wade, one of the altar boys at St. Peter's. The unruly kid looks back at the glare Nelson fires, and facing front again, lowers his gaze and nods slowly.

"Good. I'm glad we got that cleared up," Edward says. "Now, everyone, please open your Health Studies books to chapter one: 'Overcoming Inner Obstacles'."

Grandma Eleanor stands at the back of the classroom and smiles, but by the time every textbook smacks open on their desks, she's gone. The only powder Edward inhales is the Duska on his own skin.

A Mark on the Armour

by Shane Simmons

Slumping down on the sofa, I notice the clear plastic crate which Aunt Patricia and Uncle John had brought over on Sunday. It was one of the last few I'd neglected to take with me when I'd moved out. Hauling it up, I place it on the sofa beside me.

I prise the lid open and get a whiff of stale air, the smell of papers left in storage. And there are stacks of papers. I don't recognise them immediately and so shuffle my fingers between the sheets to find they're nothing particularly important, old college work, the odd photo, test prints, contact sheets. I pull out an unmarked brown envelope from the back and peer inside.

Pouring out a pile of 6" x 4" prints onto my lap, I flick through them. Each still life conjures half-memories of walking around for hours, weekends avoiding the silent tension and inevitable blow-ups at home, all the while seeking that elusive shot.

At the back of the set I stop. It stares back at me.

It was taken just up the road from the family home. In the background, rays from the London summer sun streaming through leafy branches.

Just what I meant to capture is beyond my recollection. But the instant he jumped out in front of the camera plays in my mind so clearly.

I shiver as a chill travels down my spine and the photo trembles in my hands.

Here he is, imperfections in stark sharpness.

I jump out of my skin as there's a rap on the window. I'd forgotten Sandra was coming over to borrow my old DVD player. I toss the photos into the box, throw on the lid and pop it down on the floor beside the sofa.

"Your buzzer still not working?" she asks as she steps across the threshold. "And what's the matter with you? You look like you've seen a ghost!"

"You startled me."

She stops just inside the living room door, "Can't stay long, Marlon will be wanting his dinner!"

I pick up the bag from in front of the TV and hand it over to her: it rustles in my hands.

"I didn't give you that much of a fright did I? You're trembling! Not had enough wine tonight?" she smirks.

I walk over to the window, and pull the curtains shut.

"You're acting stranger than usual … s'pose I *could* stay for a bit." As she plonks herself down on the sofa she spots the crate on the floor. And points. "What's in there?"

"Just old college stuff."

"*So* …" her voice chimes up and down, "who's that?" She reaches down and lifts off the lid.

I leap over to stop her, but she already has the photos in her hand.

"Hmm, not a bad looking guy!" She turns to stare me up and down. "College *friend*?"

"Leave it be, Sandra."

"Come on, you can tell aunty Sand!"

I burst like a water balloon hitting the pavement. Through a film of saltwater that clouds my eyes I see Sandra freeze, eyes wide ... then she sprints out of the room and returns with a half-used toilet roll and unwinds some before handing it over to me.

Much nose blowing and messy snivelling later she whispers, "Want to talk about it?"

I shake my head.

"Are you sure? Because Marlon can wait for his dinner." She waves the photo in front of me. "Is this what's upset you?"

I nod.

"So, what's his name?"

It's been years since his name passed my lips. "Mark."

"Mark? Well that's very 'normal'. God, even I went out with a Mark once. So, what's so upsetting about this Mark? Did he … he didn't pass away, did he?"

"He may as well have."

"Oh. It's like that."

She heads to the sofa and puffs the limp cushions before beckoning me over. I sit down and wipe my face down with my palms.

"They are all bastards, aren't they?" She pats me on the back like a well-behaved dog.

"End of our first college year, he just disappeared, fucked off. No goodbye, no explanation, all that time he'd just strung me along." I stop. And sniff. "I really thought he fucking cared about me!"

"Fucking bastards, all of them!"

I nod in agreement and feel like I've been initiated into that exclusive 'All men are bastards' club, the one that only the bitterest and most scorned get to join.

"Have you ever told anyone about this 'Mark' before?"

I shake my head.

"And you've never been with *anyone* since? Sheesh. Well, I reckon it's high time you moved on. We're going to find you someone! You can't go through the rest of your life celibate as a monk, all because of this Mark twat."

She picks up the photo and begins to tear it in two.

"NO!" I yell.

314

She stops, and places it down on the coffee, the photo ripped a centimetre in from the edge.

"You're going to have to let go someday, you can't hold onto memories forever. It's not healthy."

Her phone blares a brash tone from her pocket.

"Marlon's wondering where I am. Look, I better get going, but I have a plan ..."

"What plan?"

"I was just thinking. There's a work do next month, to celebrate the end of the A&E refurb. Big party, loads of people going. We're gonna go out shopping, I'll choose you some new, *stylish* clothes, and you're going to come to this do with me and I'm going to introduce you to all the gays! One of them will like you, surely!"

"Oh god no –"

"Don't ... you ... dare!" She jabs my arm with each word. "You're going, that's that." She pats my arm, "You know it's time."

I can't argue with her when she's actually coming across with genuine concern. Who'd have thought it?

I raise my eyebrows and nod.

"That's settled. Because I know I said they're all bastards but at least they're good for *one* thing. And no one should be without *that* for as long as you have!"

She picks up the DVD player and heads out to the hall. "You'll be alright, I'll make sure of that. God, I wish you'd told me all this months ago, I could've had you set up with a nice new lay by now!"

Walking back into the living room after letting her out, the first thing I see is that photo, staring at me. The grin that lured me in. I should tear it up. Set it on fire.

I pick it up, slide it back into the envelope it came from and stuff the envelope down the back of the crate.

I might want to take it out, look at it again.

Trace my finger over the contours of his face. Look into those hazel eyes, one more time.

Daffodils

by Michelle Elvy

"I'm leaving," says Stevie, and when he says it, it sounds as if he's been waiting to say this for a long, long time.

"I know." Manny's been Stevie's best friend since they were kids, and he's known this moment would come from the day they met. Stevie never seemed like he really *belonged* here. He was always a little outside the rest of them. On the soccer field he played left forward, and as Manny watched from the sidelines while Stevie charged lightning fast after the ball he sometimes thought Stevie might just keep on running, over the line and off the field, never looking back. Even later, when they outgrew junior soccer and started jacking cars and driving too fast and smoking too much weed – even then, Stevie was there but *not* there. But Manny had never begrudged him this. There was something out there pulling Stevie away, ever since Manny could remember.

Manny would have found it beyond strange if Stevie stayed.

"Where you goin'?" They are lying on the old pier down by the river, their graduation gowns crumpled in a pile. It's a blistering June day, and they are stripped down to their boxers now, lying side-by-side, arms and legs spread-eagle, as they've done so many days during so many summers.

"Dunno. Florida, maybe."

"The Sunshine State."

"Yeah."

"What about college? Aren't your parents expecting you to go get some *higher education*?" Manny says it with great emphasis. *Higher Education*. Like he doesn't quite believe there's more to learn after the torture of high school Algebra and French. Not for him anyway. The only way he expects to set foot on a university campus is to visit his friend for some seriously good parties and maybe a night or two with a college girl. And Vermont seems like a cool place for a roadtrip.

"I deferred. Middlebury said it's OK. And my parents think it's a good idea."

"Your parents have no idea what kind of trouble you'll get into in Florida, do they?"

Stevie grinned. "Not as much trouble as I would if you were along."

"True. But you didn't invite me, did you?"

"Look ..."

"Hey, I'm just bustin' you. It's cool. You go on. I'll point my wheels south when it's time for a road trip. Girls wear less clothes in Florida, right? I'll come in the winter when my tits are froze."

The boys lie in the sun without speaking while a fly buzzes lazily by Manny's face and a butterfly lands on the corner of a graduation cap. Water laps gently at the pilings below. Manny lights up and passes the joint.

"Whatever happened between Ellie and Rick?" he says as he exhales. "You know ... after the crash."

"What do you mean?"

"Well you know, man, that blowjob – that was one to remember."

Stevie's mind roils and he's suddenly not here on the dock with his friend but in a cornfield in January, hurtling back through time. He arrives at the image he can't shake. Again. Not the flash and mangled metal of a car flipped three times, not his friends banged and bruised. As much as the car crash has changed his life – as much as Lucky being dead has changed *everything* – the things that occurred moments before were just as indelible. And when Manny mentions the blowjob, a backward sequence is set in motion, one Stevie can't control: it begins with him lying in a cornfield, and then his face and back leave the crunchy frozen ground and he flies upward, from the cornfield toward the car. He passes his Uncle Gus on a tall ship in an inexplicable dreamscape he can't chase out of the sequence and floats there in a nanosecond of calm – no noise, no screams, no metal, no horn, no radio, no voices. Nothing. Then he's flying through the window into the back seat; he feels the impact and briefly, only for a moment then the moment's gone, he sees his friend Lucky turn his head and smile at him from the front seat. Now he looks over and sees Rick and Ellie, and he feels his stomach lurch. This is the thing he does not want to see. This is what doesn't make sense to him: Lucky's alive and smiling when he shouldn't be, and everything's out of joint. He sees that now. It's all fucked up. It's like the car crash is the last thing they all did together, but even in the moments before it, they weren't *really* together. And he's thought all this time that he was the only one to know about Ellie and Rick, but now Manny has said the unsayable. Manny has put a name on this thing he witnessed, and he feels sick all over again.

Manny takes another toke. "Seriously, did they ever hook up again? Even after Lucky … ?"

Stevie knows the answer to the question. Of course they didn't hook up. Ellie has been a wreck. He's pretty sure she never wants to see Rick again, and he longs for the day he hears her say it. Because he wants someone else to hate Rick as much as he does. And because he wants it to be true. It's all much more complicated than Manny thinks. Because even Manny – his best friend – has no idea that Stevie is in love with Ellie.

"I mean, you know how fucked up I've been since the accident," Manny is pouring out his heart now, talking about the accident like he's never done before. Something about graduation day seems to have opened a floodgate. "I haven't been able to talk to Ellie, you know ..."

"She doesn't blame you."

"Well ..."

"I don't either."

"Yeah well, Lucky's folks do."

"They've got to blame someone, but it doesn't mean they mean it." Even as he says it, Stevie knows Lucky's parents will never get over blaming Manny. The boy who'd eaten PBJs at their kitchen table when he was twelve. The boy who'd built tents out of sheets in their backyard and flashed Morse code past midnight. The boy who'd cut their lawn. The boy who drove the car that broke their son's neck and bashed his brain in.

Manny's silence beside him is breaking Stevie's heart, so he says, "Listen, I'm proud of you for graduating."

"Thanks, Gramps."

"I mean it."

The silence between them stretches out until Manny recovers his bravado.

"Didn't think I would, did ya?"

"Wasn't too sure there for a while."

"That makes two of us, man."

The truth was, after the accident, most people thought Manny had dropped out of school entirely, even if some teachers had confided in Stevie about Manny, trying to keep him on track. There had been a couple months when Manny was MIA and even Stevie was not sure where he'd gone. The day of the funeral, after Lucky had lain in a coma nearly a month, was the one time Manny returned during February. Stevie had looked everywhere but never did figure out where he went. Then Manny showed up again in

320

late April, and now he's here, cap and gown crumpled on the dock.

"I thought Justin's speech was pretty cool," Stevie adds now, thinking back to the graduation ceremony.

"Shit, man, you're not gonna say that out loud to anyone else, are you?"

"I'm just sayin' … those speeches are usually a big fuckin' eye-roll, you know? But he said some pretty cogent things."

"Cogent, yes, Sherlock. Cogent."

Stevie laughs at Manny's grown-up voice. "Well you gotta admit, the part about the amphibious Martian was pretty funny."

"Yeah, he's not such a 'tard as I thought. Who woulda thought Justin Fuckin' Tucker could be funny *and* philosophical?"

Stevie's quiet for a moment. "I liked what he said about the daffodils on Lucky's grave, too."

He feels Manny tense next to him, then slowly exhale. He watches the branches sway back and forth overhead as the butterfly returns to the graduation cap and balances delicately on one corner. He pictures Lucky's grave with hundreds of daffodils over it. He's not been to the cemetery in ages, and he wonders if everyone else in the audience was as surprised as he was by what Justin had said – that one day a few weeks back daffodils sprang up all over the grave. Late in the season for daffodils. Strange. And amazing. He liked how Justin had talked about the strangeness of circumstances, the way unknowns can bring wonder, how beauty can be seen in the unlikeliest places. What Justin said about Lucky's life and Lucky's death was just this side of a Hallmark card. It was quite beautiful, really.

"Do you think it's true, or was he just making shit up?"

"Let's find out." Stevie knows Manny hasn't visited Lucky's grave, ever. Today – graduation day and Friday the 13th – feels like the right day.

"What – *now*?" Manny turns his head to face Stevie. He looks scared.

"Yeah." Stevie's voice is firm, unwavering. "Now."

"After a swim?"

"Alright."

"Lucky'd want us to jump in our graduation gowns."

"Lucky'd be proud of you today, too, you know."

"Lucky'd have called me chickenshit for not going full commando under the gown."

In a flash Stevie is on his feet and stripping off his boxers. He doesn't look back but he knows Manny is doing the same. In two giant steps he walks forward and propels himself off the end of the dock. The shallow water is warm and familiar. He comes up for air and turns just in time to see Manny jumping in naked, graduation cap balanced on his head. He sees the golden tassel fly up in the air as Manny splashes down. Then, only the cap can be seen on the surface of the water. Stevie watches it and marvels at his friend in this brief moment of profound silence, at all he's been through since the accident. The cap starts to fill with water. Stevie treads water but doesn't reach out to grab it. He wonders whether it will sink or remain just below the surface, but he decides it doesn't matter. Manny comes up with a giant gulp of air just as the cap capsizes.

Tomorrow Stevie will think about Florida, and about Ellie. He'll think about leaving Manny. He'll think about saying goodbye to his parents and his brother. He'll think about signing and posting the formal deferral letter to Middlebury College. He'll think about Ellie some more. He may even call her.

But today the only place he can be is here with Manny, floating, and then later, in the heat of the June evening, sitting cross-legged with Coronas in a field of yellow flowers that sprawl across a grave on the northeast corner of a Maryland cemetery.

Algorithms

by Len Kuntz

The gun dealer is a grizzled old man who brings along his Down's Syndrome son. We meet in a warehouse district somewhere on the outskirts of Albuquerque. The building is large and crowded and noisy with workers changing license plates and using sanders to scrape off registration numbers from various cars that have most likely been stolen.

"Isn't there some place private we can go?" I shout above the din.

The old guy shouts back, "Too risky."

His son wears a striped t-shirt with Neapolitan ice cream colors. His palms are pressed against his ears and he's grimacing as if constipated.

"Come on," I shout, "look at the poor kid."

The old man thinks it over, then leads us to a restroom in back. Every *Playboy* centerfold Pamela Anderson's ever been in is tacked to the walls, in addition to a spread from *Playgirl* featuring Burt Reynolds.

The old guy sets a trunk on a sink counter where, by the looks of the mess, someone's just recently had a bloody nose or worse. Not only are there red smears everywhere, but the faucet knobs are lined with grime and a broken toothbrush is stuck in the drain.

The old guy opens the trunk with a flourish, as if he's some kind of magician. Inside are a Rubik's Cube and two old pistols that look right out of the Civil War. He hands the cube to the kid and the kid tosses it in the air and misses catching it, picks it up from the floor and tosses it again, over and over.

"Not much of a selection," I say.

"What did you expect, machine guns? I ain't Walmart."

I buy the smaller pistol and a box of shells the old guy has in his coat pocket. Why he's wearing a jacket when it's an eighty-five degree June day is anybody's guess.

"Say, do you mind keeping an eye on Keith for a few minutes?"

Keith tosses the Rubik's cube and this time it lands in the toilet, water splashing over the rim, and he starts to bawl.

"Are you kidding?" I say.

"Just be a little while. Here, you can have the second gun free."

"Why do I need two?"

"You never know."

The old guy hands me the gun and heads out the door. I shout after him, but he doesn't stop. Keith is crying harder than ever. I reach into the toilet with its lemon-colored water and foist out the toy, washing it in the sink with globs of soap, then wiping my hands with my shirt tail.

A half an hour passes. An hour. The Rubik's Cube has a number of squares broken off and they lay like bright-colored Skittles on the filthy floor.

I start to panic. "Hey, Keith," I say, "where did Dad go? Or Granddad?"

Keith says something that sounds like hotdogs.

"He went to lunch, is that where Grandpa went?"

Then he says something that sounds like chili.

"Fuck me," I say, taking Keith's hand and heading out of the restroom, out of the shop and down the street where I'd seen a food truck earlier.

The guy manning the truck is the palest person I've ever seen, with a dandelion seed afro that could match anything Art Garfunkel ever sported. "What'll you have?"

I ask him if he's seen the old guy, but Art says he hasn't. When I ask him if he knows Keith, he looks at me like I'm nuts.

"This isn't my kid," I say. "He belongs to the old guy."

"And that's my problem, why?"

"Look, I really need to get going. Do you mind watching the boy Keith? His grandfather dropped him off with me at that shop across the block and he'll be right back."

"Are you on meth?"

"I'll give you a gun," I say, pulling the pistol out of my pocket.

"Whoa!"

"No, I'm giving it to you, free."

When I try handing the pistol across the counter the guy dips and comes back up holding a shotgun.

"Drop it."

"Hey, it's not like that."

"I'll plaster your face with pellets if you don't drop your weapon."

"That's just it, I was trying to give it to you as payment for watching Keith."

Keith reaches up and snatches the pistol. I see my opportunity and sprint behind the food truck and keep running until I'm in my car.

As I drive, the remaining pistol chafes my inner thigh, and when I pull it out two chips from the Rubik's Cube clatter against the stick shift.

I feel shitty for abandoning Keith but I tell myself he's better off with a food truck guy than me. I replay the events of the day in my head trying to figure out where I went wrong but after a while the road opens up to a land so flat that it's hypnotic the way watching a campfire is, and my

thoughts dull as I roll down the window to let the air in,
warm wind whipping my hair like a set of groping fingers.

Sixth Inning

by Michael Webb

It happens so quickly that I register it more than actually seeing it. I kick and throw, and the hitter for Los Angeles, Alex Sellers, is not fooled for an instant, turning on the ball, which I threw too high and horribly flat, drilling it. Fortunately for my continued reproductive potential, he started his swing a fraction too soon, not hitting it back at my body but instead to my right, near the third base bag but, luckily, foul. Our third baseman, a former college basketball player we call 'Hammer', dives for the ball anyway, his effort spoiled when the umpire barks, "Foul!"

I let my breath out in a rush. The Baseball Gods don't let you get away with those too often. He should have hit that ball to Space Mountain. I wait for Graham, our massive third sacker, to haul his long body off the ground, and then, when he catches my eye, I flick my gloved hand at him, semaphore for "Appreciate the effort, Big Man." Graham nods, flipping the ball back to me before nonchalantly dusting his uniform off and getting himself back together. I give him a moment to recover, another unwritten rule, ball tucked securely away, removing my hat and slicking back my sweaty hair.

Everyone pauses for a moment, a frozen tableau of inaction. The plate umpire stands back, squinting in the hot sun. My catcher, Hector Cruz, straightens up, looks at me through the bars of his mask as he makes the devil horns symbol, reminding us all that there are two outs. I mentally review the situation as I take the ball into my throwing hand. Two on, two out, Two and two count, what my youth baseball coach called 'The Woolery', a joke I wouldn't get for years. I stare at the ump, waiting for him to ask for the ball and check it for imperfections. Distracted, he makes no sign, so I climb the hill and prepare to go back to work.

Hector kneels again and flashes his symbols. We are thinking along the same lines, going away next, then, if that fails, trying to finish him inside. If that doesn't work, as our manager joked during the pre-game discussion about how to handle the red hot Los Angeles team, we will try prayer. My fingertips find the tiny imperfection in the ball's cover as I rub it up. My heart leaps as I feel the ridge. Every schoolboy who has thrown a tattered ball knows that an interruption in the ball's smooth surface affects the flow of air, thus causing lift and a ball that darts like a Whiffle Ball. Totally illegal, but used since the beginning of time just the same. Anything, in the evolutionary struggle of offense and defense, to get an advantage, no matter how small. Honest? No. But in a profession where fractions of inches mean millions of dollars, every advantage, to a man, to a father, must be taken and held. They'd do the same to me, if they could.

I get up onto the rubber, and the whole mechanism starts again. Signals, offensive and defensive. Look at the runners. Pause, look, then tilt and kick and throw. The trick comes through for me, Bernoulli's principle, the same rule that provides lift to an airplane, yields a slider that starts almost behind Sellers, breaking like a Frisbee to the opposite side of the plate, a pitch so nasty he can only wave meekly at it, Cruz catching the ball and pumping his fist once on the way to the dugout, the LA fans groaning at the rally snuffed out.

"What the fuck was that?" Cruz says into my ear as we come down the steps. "That was some good shit."

He opens his glove and goes to throw the ball back on the field. I put my hand on his wrist, then wordlessly turn the ball over, showing him the cut in the ball's surface.

"I didn't know you did that," Cruz says softly.

"I don't," I say. "It happened naturally. On the foul ball the pitch before."

"But you threw it."

"Yeah," I say. I have a spasm of shame, remembering my moralizing about Tex and whatever that was he injected into himself that gray day in Kansas City.

"Oh," he says, tossing the ball down the dark hall that leads to the clubhouse, towards an open bag. "Whatever it takes, right?"

I mentally tabulate the runs saved, estimate the cost to my salary next year if I throw a legal ball instead and Sellers bounces it off the Hollywood sign. "Whatever it takes," I agree.

Man's Best Friend

by James Claffey

Another June Monday full of rain showers and leaking roofs, the Bird thinks, as he sets the pail in the centre of the bedroom floor and captures the ringing drips from the cracked plaster above. Since May he's spent most days stuck in the house, afraid to venture outside for fear of ridicule. God, how he hated the gobshites who had poked fun at him in McKettrick's bar, and the barking that now follows him around the town whenever he slips out to get the messages, or to go to Mass on a Sunday.

The dusty statues and paintings left by his parents are only irritations to him as he tries to protect the carpet from the steady drips of rain. The statues and paintings could be watching him in his shameful misery as he stumbles from one day of his difficult life to the next. He knows, though, that the priest is right about the townsfolk's ridicule. He told him to pay them no mind, and that they were no better than the Pharisees in the temple, and they'd little right to judge a man without understanding the circumstances, or jumping to conclusions the way they had.

"I'll go down to McKettrick's tonight, by God. They won't get the better of the Bird," he says, as he places a saucepan under another leak.

The kitchen depresses the Bird, his mother's pots and pans, the old Player's cigarettes ashtray with the pipe-smoking sailor, the rusted biscuit tin where she used to keep the flour, and the statue of the Madonna of Prague with its billowing skirts. A bloody jumble sale, that's what he should have and clear her memory out of the house good and proper. He tried to do it the month following her death, but his father had taken sick by that time and the Bird didn't have the heart or the time to arrange everything. Now, though, that the two of them are gone, he's better placed to get a good start on the job, but only after his afternoon constitutional by the river and a pint or two in McKettrick's snug later.

Funny how the shadows manage to appear at all times of day and night, too. Wasn't he only after settling down with the wireless on Radio Four's 'Book at Bedtime' and his father's stooped back and jug ears had appeared on the sitting room wall? When he'd blinked again the shadow had passed and the hum of the wireless was the only sound in the house. A lonely man he is now, in his big old house next door to the convent, and the French girl away out of it, and bound never to speak to him again once she hears about the curious incident with the dog in the telephone box.

Forever ago, all the laughter and tears of his parents' marriage had filled the house like great ricks of hay in the nearby fields. Only *their* shadows. Only the odd letter or card from a distant friend who'd not heard of their deaths ever hit the carpet, now. "A terrible thing to be growing old," his father often told him. Now, with the wrinkles on his own face resembling a contour map of the local mountains, he knows exactly what his father was talking about.

On the way out the door he dips two of his fingers in the waterless Holy Water fount and dryly blesses himself. Outside, the west wind whips leaves in circles on the road and crows battle against the breeze as they make their way home for the evening. He pushes the Raleigh along, and when the moment is right, swings aboard and heads for the towpath by the canal. Not many are out and about today, and he says a silent blessing for their scarcity. All he needs is a few blackguards yelping and barking at him.

To the lamppost he locks the bicycle and hangs both trouser clips off the handlebars. Not much in the way of fish biting in the water, he sees. Mayflies catch what's left of the sun's rays, and across on the other bank a terrier scrabbles frantic at a hole in the undergrowth. The Bird envies the dog its energy and makes his way along the towpath. This is a walk his father took of an evening, after dinner and before the Mart & Market report on the wireless. The Bird allows his father's spirit to descend on him, almost like a mantle, and he struggles to recall anything at all of the subjects that mattered to his father. Most of their time spent together was in a companionable silence, the weighty conversations took place in his imagination, wishing the words into his father's mouth.

As he walks along the muddied path he marvels at how the pattern of holes cut into the leather of his brogues is so symmetrical, and remembers the day his father took him on the train to Belfast to collect the shoes from Cable & Company's offices. The first time he tried on the shoes after his father's death he noticed how his feet perfectly matched the grooves worn by his father's feet over those forty years since their trip to Belfast. In a whisper, searching the vicinity for nearby walkers, he mimics his father's voice, saying, "A man's best friend is a pair of decent shoes." The surge of sadness almost knocks the Bird off his feet, and he has to steady himself by sitting on a stone bench surrounded by dandelions and broken beer bottles.

Across the sky vapor trails of planes bound for America fade in front of his eyes. A holiday, perhaps. He's always wanted to visit New York and the Statue of Liberty, and to walk in Central Park. So far, the farthest away he's managed to make it is a weekend in Galway with the Pioneer Society when he was only a teenager and a devout teetotaler. He'd learned a quick lesson that trip, what with the secret drinking of the leaders of the society; men who wore their Pioneer pins proudly and never stopped boasting of their devotion to not drinking, and the long gash he'd gotten on the sole of his foot the time he jumped off the pier and landed on a jagged beer bottle.

"Bird," a voice calls out, and fast approaching from the near dark is Father O'Hehir, a blackthorn stick in one hand and his breviary in the other.

"Father, a grand summer's day, isn't it?"

"How are you lately?" the priest stops and stares at the Bird, his thick-browed eyes dark as the river water.

"Game ball. I'm clearing out some belongings from the house. Things the parents left behind."

"A fine plan. Out with the old and in with the new."

A minute of silence and the priest coughs twice and says, "Did I hear you'd gotten yourself an Alsatian dog, or something of that sort?"

The Bird reddens under the collar and curses the tattletales in McKettrick's. "No, Father. It was all a bit of a mistake."

"Now, Bird, grief is a terrible thing to deal with alone. You can always come down to the church if you're having trouble of a personal nature, if you know what I mean." The priest lays the hand with the breviary on the Bird's shoulder and a shock travels down the Bird's body as if he's been electrocuted.

"Not at all, Father. I'm doing grand as things stand," the Bird says, brushing past the priest and on towards the far end of the towpath. He wishes his bike were waiting for him so he could pedal the hell off to the bar and not even think about the disastrous rumors he is sure will follow him to his grave. Small bloody towns and interfering bloody priests. "And I'll be damned if I come to the church for any reason at all," he almost shouts after the priest, but is careful to let the words fall silent into the dark canal water.

It's About Time
Somebody Died

by Gwendolyn Joyce Mintz

"So, what are we celebrating?" Lindsey, their server, asks as she sets the flutes of champagne before those seated at the table.

"One of our members has reached the club goal," Aaron says.

Her eyes scan the group. "Which of you?"

"In absentia," Aaron adds.

"Oh, well, still, congrats," Lindsey says, lifting an imaginary glass in the air.

When she walks away, Mora, sitting at Aaron's left, turns to him and asks, "What're you talking about? We're all here."

By the glass stem, Aaron spins the flute in a slow circle. "Vincent killed himself," he says.

It is Mora who breaks the silence that follows Aaron's words. "How do you know?"

"I kept in touch with him. He liked the idea of the club." He glances at Mora, then across the table to Phil and Diane. "I think of him as an honorary member." He lifts his glass. "To Vincent Lawrence DiMatteo."

The others hesitate then with uncertainty, they too raise their glasses, clink, drink.

"It's about time somebody died," Phil says, setting the flute down. "I was beginning to think that was never gonna happen."

"How'd he do it?" Diane asks, then immediately says, "No, no, never mind. I don't want to know."

"He wanted you to know that he was sorry you were offended by what he said."

Diane raises a brow. "But not sorry for what he said." She shakes her head, then tosses it back, downing the champagne. She sets the flute down with a thunk. "I'm glad he's dead."

Aaron's smile is wry. "So am I." He leans back against the booth seating. "He was an introvert, Diane. Very much so. He was hoping that joining this desperate bunch craving death, well, not you so much," he says as an aside to Mora, "would allow him a chance to relate to people. He didn't mean any harm."

"Did you go to his funeral?"

Aaron doesn't turn to look at Mora. He stares at a spot in the center of the table.

"You did!" Mora exclaims. "I thought –"

She stops because Lindsey returns with a tray of wings, celery sticks, and Ranch dressing.

"We didn't order this," Aaron says as she begins passing out small plates and napkins.

"On me," Lindsey tells him with a wink. "Reciprocation," she says and walks away.

"What is *that* about?" Phil asks.

Aaron cannot stop the grin inching across his face, the flush of blood to his cheeks.

"Uh oh," Mora says in a playful manner. "Are we going to have to impeach you?"

"Stop," Aaron tells her. He glances over and yes, there is no jealousy.

"She's very pretty," she tells him.

Aaron grunts and turns away. He picks up the flute, finishes his drink. He wishes he could wave down the server for something stronger but no –

Mora nudges him. "I need a cigarette. Coming with?" she asks Diane across the table.

Diane shakes her head.

Mora frowns in surprise. "Well, okay." She stands. "You alright?"

"I just don't feel like going outside."

"Okay, okay." Mora holds her hands up as she walks away.

"*Are* you okay?" Phil asks Diane moments later.

"Yes. No." She closes her eyes. "Vincent is so brave." Her words are almost a whisper. She opens her eyes and looks at Aaron. "I am glad he's dead. He's got peace now." She takes a breath. "You know instead of impeaching you, I think we should boot her."

"Mora?" Aaron asks.

"She's not going to kill herself."

"What's with you?"

"Last month I was having a really hard time. She came over and you know what she brought? Daisies. A freaking bouquet. If she really wanted to make me to feel better, she would've brought sleeping pills."

"She isn't even sure you wanna kill yourself."

"Why would she think that?"

"Because you said at the first meeting that you either wanted to kill yourself or not live the way you're living. She's hoping that you'll find your own way. She cares –"

"That's the problem. I'm not sure she's trying to help us die. She's probably planning your wedding right now."

Aaron sighs.

When Mora returns, he stands, allows her entrance.

Settling back in, she asks, "Miss anything?"

Silence. Averted eyes.

"Guess I did." She shrugs and reaches for the untouched platter of wings. "This was really sweet of her." She offers one to Aaron. "Maybe you'll just resign?"

Aaron looks at Mora, considers her. *She's not trying to help us die.* His fingers begin to drum the time passing. He wants to say something but he isn't sure what. He just doesn't know.

Balls

by Stephen V. Ramey

My eyes are watching *Modern Family* on ABC, but my brain won't stop obsessing. Tomorrow I'm scheduled to have my balls cut off.

Anne sits knees up in her chair, the cat squeezed beside her. If anything, she looks happy. *It's the least expensive, most effective treatment for your stage of the disease.* That's what the doctor said. He's a urologist straight out of the Marty Feldman school of character acting, bulging eyes, a tendency to extend one finger while he reads from his menu of results, as if preparing for a proctology exam. Dr. Schmitz. I think they added the 'm' when his family arrived on Ellis Island.

"I'm off to bed," Anne says. She stands and strolls through the archway from the living room to the kitchen. I watch her move dishes from the counter to the sink.

Mystery hops down from the chair, wobbly on her eighteen-year-old cat legs. Still, she manages to climb the stairs each night when Anne goes to bed. I wish she would stay with me tonight, a neutered cat, a soon-to-be-neutered man commiserating on his final night intact. Of course she probably does not understand. Nobody understands, not even my comedian friend Jimmy. *Hey, man, you should be happy. Now it won't hurt when Anne's got your testicles in a vice.*

I told him I'm worried about libido, and all he could

come back with was that tired joke about the guy who has hand surgery and asks his doctor whether he'll be able to play the piano. I'm about to be emasculated. It's not funny, damn it, it's not.

Anne wipes her hands on a dishtowel and tosses it on the counter. She returns from the kitchen, yawning. "Don't forget to wash that pan before you come to bed."

I start to nod, then stop myself and click the mute button on the remote. "I'm scared," I say in a flat voice. A commercial flashes, a silver car speeding.

Anne's stoicism falters. Her shoulders slump. I think of quicksand sucking a villain down.

"It'll be okay," she says. "I'll be there for you." She smiles bravely, but I can only see sadness in her eyes. "I know this is difficult," she says. "Life isn't fair, but we do the best we –"

"I won't be able to … to …" I try to focus, but her features blur.

Anne pats my shoulder. "Of course you will. Is that what's worrying you?"

Is that all? I shrug away from her hand.

I press the mute button. Sitcom laughter floods the room.

"We'll get through this," Anne says. "You and me, together, always and forever." That was part of our wedding vows. It sounds childish now.

"Do you want me to stay up a while?" She sits on the chair arm and leans toward me. Her breast squishes against my shoulder.

I nudge her away. "Go to bed, Anne. You have a long day tomorrow." After my outpatient surgery, she has three meetings if I remember right.

"If you're sure." She gives me a sideways glance that tells me she's available if I want her.

"Go ahead," I say. "I'm just having a little whine."

She chuckles at that. "I'll give you a rain check, then."

"Sure."

Anne squeezes my hand and strolls toward the stairway, Mystery in tow. I watch her hips move. She belly-danced for me once when we were dating. It made me hard. I kind of wish she would do that now, only I know it wouldn't matter. Sex is the last thing I want tonight.

I watch television until the creaking floor tells me Anne is in bed. Then I turn the television off, go to the door, and pull my jacket from the rack. I need to walk off this anxiety.

The night is clear, one of those evenings when you can look up into the stars and know how small you are. The waning half-moon hangs to the south. Growing up in the sixties, I once believed I would go there before I died, dust coating my boots, gravity barely tugging. I used to dream of gliding over a cratered plain, thinking how wonderful it was to be alive. Of course, I also dreamed of falling, the fear boiling up inside me until I snapped awake in bed.

A car crunches past with a boom box throb. A hint of cannabis drifts. The windows are tinted, but must be cracked open. I swallow thickly and consider waving my arms. I would give my last dollar for a joint right now.

The car pauses at the stop sign at the end of our street and turns. By the time I reach the intersection, it's gone. *Where to now?* I think.

I see the history museum where Anne sometimes volunteers, a 1900's era mansion a few hundred yards up the hill. I know the security code. I know where the spare key is hidden. I can go there.

Squeeeeeeee ...

I punch a sequence into the alarm pad, only now

thinking that maybe they've changed the code since I saw Anne use it. Won't *that* be embarrassing.

A life-affirming series of beeps sounds. Silence descends. *Success.*

The house is dark, but for the red blinks of motion sensors. I look up the staircase. There are no sensors on the third floor, where restoration is ongoing. It's peaceful there.

By the time I climb all the flights to the third floor – high ceilings make for long staircases – I'm breathing hard. I can't help thinking that the spot on my lung has grown into full-fledged cancer, and the shortness of breath is the first gasp of my dying.

No, you're just out of shape, Anne's voice assures me. What would she think of me coming here? She could get into hot water with the Historical Society. Why do I do these things?

I don't turn around and march down the stairs. I don't even slow, really, but continue around a corner, using my palms to guide me in the dark. I come to a door and open it.

Moonlight filters through squat windows. The ceiling is not so high here, but the room is large, half the house's width and most of its length. Piles of wood and drywall break up the floor space. Sawhorses stand beneath the largest window. Carpenters have been ripping out interior walls. I remember Anne telling me this used to be a ballroom. Society people would gather here to dance and talk after long days of rigging account books, or bossing mill hunks around. If I stand very still, I can hear the music, the voices, the churning of skirts against stays. A flowery smell wafts. *Perfume.*

And then I see it; the shadows of saw horses and two-by-fours become people, men wearing topcoats, women in lace-trimmed blouses. They move past, bowing, nodding, arm-in-arm like couples carved on a music box.

I slink down until I'm sitting on the floor, back pressed to the wall, sanity slipping. It's not enough I have cancer, not enough they want to castrate me ... I hug my knees.

"Get up, silly." The voice is both real and unreal, the memory of a dream.

A young woman reaches down, wrist bent. Her dress is frilled, and floor length. I recognize her face in the moonlight. It's Amanda the resident ghost – according to volunteers who have heard her or felt her touch. Her portrait hangs downstairs.

"Dance with me," Amanda says. She has a pretty smile, a smooth complexion. Her hair is cut short. This must be before she married the embezzler who built a boat too large to get through the workshop door.

I take her hand. It's solid, warm. We join the mannequin flow. I've never danced, yet this waltz comes naturally. The music ebbs, and I see a string quartet in the corner. A man saws at a cello, his eyes like black marbles.

This is ludicrous. I stop. Amanda's fingers pull from mine like taffy. Another man takes my place, and she continues dancing.

I part a set of pocket doors. The rollers run smoothly, which seems wrong. There's another room on the other side, a billiard table. A man leans over one end, petite cue stick propped between knuckles. I smell sweet tobacco.

"Shall we make it interesting, Jameson?" This from a fat man by the wall. A pipe smolders from his hand.

"Indeed, sir," the first man says. "I welcome your green."

"A ten that you cannot sink the seven ball into the corner," the fat mans says.

"Done," the other says, and strokes through his shot. I wince as balls crack. The seven ricochets past the cup and back toward me.

The shooter stands. "It must be the table, or the floor."

The fat man laughs. "Something is always crooked with you, eh, Greer?" He looks directly at me. "Do you play, sir?"

"Me?" My voice echoes too loudly. The balls disappear, the men, the table, the music in my ears. Everything. I'm suddenly alone, back pressed to the wall, eyes staring past shadow scaffoldings of wood, to the waning moon. Even the moon is not constant.

Amanda whispers from deep within my head: "You know that you can't go back, Stephen, you can never return." And I do know it. Maybe I've known it all along.

The Stranger

by Gay Degani

Five long months have passed since he'd trudged along the Old Road back to his car against a ninety-mile-an-hour wind, eyes watering, ears ringing, his unzipped sweatshirt snapping behind him. He'd collapsed into the driver's seat and shoved his hand into his pants while the storm's fury rattled around him. He was gone before the oak tree fell on Jamie's bungalow.

He never forgets the ferocious wind that blew down from the north, the clear black sky, the brilliance of scrubbed air, the sharp cold in his chest when he breathed. He hasn't forgotten the sting of windburn on his cheeks as he lay in his own bed. And Jamie's silhouette in the window, dark against the glowing yellow of her living room, haunts him when he brushes his teeth, when he sits alone in his office at the community college, when he slams his car door and watches his daughter dash out down the front steps to greet him.

He's yearned more for Jamie than anyone before, delaying the endgame longer, embracing the task of waiting. He's kept her on the edge of his mind, his pleasure in the denial of his urges, that tension created by his unfulfilled physical need. He's survived on his mental projection of possibilities, refusing to give in. It's this discipline that is his most exquisite torture.

He finally returns to the Old Road after his grades are turned in and his wife and daughter are halfway across the continent visiting his in-laws. He parks the car in the same place as before, but decides on one more excruciating delay before yielding to his bliss. Instead of jogging along the asphalt as he'd done in January, he scrambles down a path into the arroyo where the late afternoon sun haloes the leaves of trees and glints off the thread of water at the bottom of a concrete channel. He's never gone this long before without giving up, giving in, ruining something that could have been perfect. His heart bangs against his ribs, his body buzzes in anticipation as he struts along the chain-link. In this wildish place on the edge of town, in its golden light, he prepares himself for his final move.

Dust kicks up under his feet as he marvels at his own restraint, how he's managed to stay away so long. Jamie's face comes to him, clear and sharp, tongue pressed against her front teeth, her hazel eyes wary, standing in his classroom, handing in her late assignment, her voice low and throaty, making her excuses. She isn't beautiful, merely pretty – and sad. He lusts for sad. And she isn't coy, never flirting with him, but he knows she's holding back, as disciplined as he, kindred spirits. He allows himself to imagine his finger tracing a line from her mouth, down along her nipples, first one, then the other, slowly to her cunt. His own body answers, his mind a remarkable instrument of persuasive creation.

A twist to his ankle shakes him out of his reverie and tumbles him against something rough and hard, scraping his hand as he tries to catch his fall. He looks up and gapes because his brain can't sort what he sees: a knot of snakes bristling from a giant head in the weeds along the path, its Medusa shadow stretching behind, his own shadow leaping away. It takes him a moment to recognize the stump of a tree, torn from the ground and abandoned on its side, its snakes nothing but curling roots.

He tries to laugh at himself, but the sound is forced, bitter. He spits out "Fool. Idiot. Jerk-off!" and kicks at the mocking stump, missing, and wheeling around, stomps away, up the path to the Old Road.

All these months, he's taken pleasure in denying himself, thinking of her as he watched his female students waiting in the hall before class, brushing past them without quite touching, venturing down the rows of desks while he lectured, standing close enough to feel their heat, but never more than that. Medusa, ravished by Poseidon in the temple of Athena.

Time for him to do his own ravishing.

The sun slants cool and low behind him, yet sweat beads his forehead. At the top, on the verge, he forces himself to lean over, catch his breath, and prolongs his moment of perfect anticipation until a shudder of need forces him to look up.

"No." He closes his eyes.

Opens them. "No."

On the night of the windstorm, Jamie stood in the window of a bungalow across the Old Road, but now, there's no woman in the window. There's no window, no bungalow. Only a crumbling brick foundation remains.

How did this happen? He crosses the road and studies the yard. Then he knows. Five hundred trees in the city had been uprooted by the windstorm. Next to where the bungalow used to stand, hidden behind a hedge, he sees another Medusa, another tree stump yanked on its side, its mass of roots facing away from him, a couple small stacks of cut oak nearby. He sways a little remembering that wind, what it had given him, the storm, the woman, the discipline. And then took away. He'd denied himself because of the rules, *his* rules. And he'd lasted five months because then, everything would be in place. She would be ready. He would be ready. And the endgame was always worth it.

But all those months to gape at a hole in the ground? He moves a hand to his crotch, fingers himself through the cloth of his pants, then gives up. This isn't how the game is played.

In the Dark

by Sally-Anne Macomber

To: Milton Flaxmill, Red Cow Publishing
From: Trudy Polaris
Date: June 20, 2014 12:07 a.m.
Re: Getting it right

Hi Milton,

I am completely in the dark at the moment. I am also munching cheese as I type, so now I have an excuse for all my typos!!

The tax break my husband has us on here is not proving as financially successful as we had hoped so I am sitting in my skiing gear – thermal extend-a-bra, padded ski pants, a beanie with an insulated pom-pom on my head – in the secret basement of our Tyrolean hideaway, hoping the Eurozone tax agents and the Tyrolean Electricity Commission and maybe a dairy farmer or two (who might still bear a grudge about that silly Bulgarian fetta escapade) will get the hint and leave us alone.

We have no money to pay them.

All we have is our talent and determination and a little fetta we are able to chip off the great wall of the stuff still sitting in the garden, which we do at night, with a serrated cheese knife, when all the watchers and spies and observationists have gone home. Which is after the sun goes down, so about 10:00pm or so here, now it's June.

Plus of course, I also have this email lifeline to you and *Nuclear Fission in The Pyrénées* which I am secretly hoping will prove to be the masterpiece we all deserve it to be, and which will earn me big dollars and get us out of this tax crevasse we're in.

But, Milton *mein Liebling* … on to more important things …

I have been playing around with fonts and am wondering if there is room in *Nuclear Fission in The Pyrénées* for a few of them. What do you think?

I was originally thinking about 20.

I was online – there is little else to do here in this basement, even though the sun is shining and summer is well on its way outside (when do I get to go outside though, I ask you, and feel the sun's warmth on my face and shed the thermal extend-a-bra, padded ski pants, and beanie with the insulated pom-pom on my head? I mean, I ask you, just when?!) – and I came across a free font site. (And not a font-free site, which is a very different thing!)

There are some amazing fonts out there! My God, so many! It makes my head spin to think of the design opportunities we are missing out on by not using as many beautiful fonts as we can.

So I have changed my mind and am now wondering if we could have a different font on every page?

This would mean we could also have different style fonts for each different chapter. We could have 1920's style fonts for *Above and Beyond Andorra* ('Gonggong Sans' is a firm favourite for this chapter, the serifs are so clean and brutal in that Deco way I love) and 1950's fonts for *Nuts in the Nuclear Age*. (Can't decide if 'Extraordinary Nevada Tahoe Marie Extra Bold Light' would be better starting off this chapter, or 'Mud Italic'. 'Mud Italic' is sort of woodsy in a Lincoln Logs hunting lodge kind of way, while 'Extraordinary Nevada Tahoe Marie Extra Bold Light' has a more streamlined Jet Age soda pop at the drive-in in an old Chevy feel.)

I want the title pages to all have the same font though – more seems a little indulgent, and I like the idea of the calm before the storm, before the fonts get completely frenzied – so I'm thinking maybe 'New Verity Nadir' is the best choice for the title pages. There's a bold-faced, bald clean clear truth to 'New Verity Nadir' that I think strikes at the heart of what *Nuclear Fission in The Pyrénées* is really all about.

Unfortunately, it's also a very small size font, so an appropriate size might be 1514 or pretty close to that.

And given the theme of the book, I've decided the title pages would work best in black, with the letters in white. So I have added the title in 'New Verity Nadir' below, size 462, white letters on black background, just so you can see it for yourself. You might need to make it bigger so you can see it properly. If you scroll your cursor (or curser? or cursur?) across the box below, you will see just what I mean.

███████████████████████████████████

Anyway, things are quietly happening here. A word from you now and then would be good, though. I like to feel connected.

Your writer gal-pal,

Trudy

Cobwebs

by Mandy Nicol

Mum doesn't want me to go out tonight because she thinks I met Charlie online. She thinks I'm being foolhardy. I've given up explaining that I met him at Angela's barbecue, that we've been keeping in touch by email, that I've had coffee with him a couple of times when I've driven to Melbourne to fit Angela's wedding dress. Angela's free wedding dress. The one I'm now glad my sister twisted my arm to make. Charlie hasn't kidnapped or murdered or fleeced me yet but Mum won't be convinced.

"Did you put hairspray in your bag?" she asks.

"What's the matter with my hair?" I pat my head, though I'm not sure what that can tell me.

"Not for your hair, Nadia. For an emergency. It'll work like capsicum spray if you get him in the eyes."

"For God's sake, Mum."

The exasperation in my voice stirs the dogs. Old Peregrine's kind eyes and Seph's bright and beady little buttons zero in on me.

"Just put a can in your bag, will you please?" asks Mum. "Better to be safe than sorry."

I go to my bedroom, pick up the hairspray from on top of my dressing table and toss it in a drawer – I figure she'll check. I look at my face in the mirror and that's a mistake because I look like a sad clown with those downturned glossy red lips. I hope it's the Mum effect, I hope I don't always look this sour.

And now I panic. What the hell am I doing? Having coffee is one thing but this is a date. A real date. He's driving over two hundred kilometres just to take me out to dinner. And he'll already be well on the way so I can't ring his mobile and say I've changed my mind. I don't know where he's staying, or even if he's staying. God I hope he doesn't think he's staying here. Why didn't I ask him?

I count the charms on my bracelet, make sure there are seven. Then I count them again. Yes, seven. I make sure the lucky horseshoe is there, which of course it is, because I've counted seven. Twice.

This is going to be so awkward. How are you supposed to act on a first date when you're thirty-four years old? Why didn't I think things through instead of jumping in and gushing *yes* as soon as he asked? We were outside a café in Carlton, saying goodbye, it was a casual invitation, I could so easily have said *thanks but no*. Why didn't I say no?

I flop back onto my bed and kick off the tottery heels. Why did I think me tottering around on high heels would be a good look?

I stare at the cobweb on the ceiling. I can't see a spider anywhere, never have, yet there's always a cobweb in the corner. I contemplate the invisible spider and gradually my heart stops banging around in my chest.

I lie on my bed for a long time. Until I hear tyres on the gravel outside, then a car door slams. I stand up, smooth down my dress, spray some perfume on my neck. I bend down to gather my shoes and I picture Charlie being greeted at the front door by Mum and a can of flyspray.

I scoot to the door barefooted.

To the Dogs

by Margaret Bingel

Jersey's Cats, Dogs, and Other Strays is always open early on Sundays because, being at the junction of three churches and a synagogue, when the faithful go and hear about God's love, their hearts tug either towards feeding the homeless, or adopting a pet. There are always volunteers to open early, so scheduling one or two to show up at 5:00am to greet prospective owners is never a problem. Reggie, the animal shelter's director for three years, loves taking the early morning Sunday shift regardless of his other volunteers' availability. He loves the looks the tired and world-weary give the animals on their way to worship, and the joy that spreads across their face when they take one of them home.

Reggie flips the sign to 'Open' and makes his rounds. Feedings, belly rubs, and investigating wounds on some of the new arrivals keep him busy for an hour. Strays often show up with more cuts than he likes, but he and the other volunteers always make sure the animals' needs are taken care of. After opening the door to the free play area, he watches the cats and dogs run out and start mauling the ropes and toys scattered on the floor.

With the animals playing, he hears the door chime and sees Sylvia, Karl, Meagan, and Sam walk in, talking about the end of the school year. Karl holds a cardboard jug of coffee, and Sylvia has a paper bag full of cups and stirrers.

Reggie follows them into the kitchen.

"I'm thinking 'beach' tomorrow, who's in?" Meagan asks. "We need to have some fucking fun, Jesus Christ."

"Oh my gosh, Meagan, watch your mouth, geez." Sylvia is always uncomfortable with Meagan's swearing. "Kids could be here."

"But they're not!" Meagan grabs a creamer. "I'm going to enjoy this cup of joe with Joe."

Sam rolls his eyes. He thinks Meagan spends way too much time on just a few of "her pets" as she selfishly puts it. He prefers to handle the snakes, one of the few who can stomach feeding them. (He keeps a boa at home.) It's not that he doesn't like Meagan, he just thinks she's unaware of anything that isn't cute and isn't her.

Around 8:00, everyone hears the door chime. Glancing about, Karl, not playing with any of the cats, steps out to greet the customer.

"Hi, welcome to Jersey's, may I help you?" he asks Ned.

Ned squints his eyes at the teenager. "I'm looking for a dog." He has been dreaming about one for months.

Ned follows Karl to the play area. Ned walks right in and stares at all the animals, chewing on toys, sleeping in corners.

"Feel free to walk around," Karl says with a touch of sarcasm. "Let them sniff you first, then you'll see if they like you."

Ned feels a humming under his skin. So many dogs! How will he every find the right one? He watches what looks like a pug sniff the ass of a chihuahua. He chuckles, but isn't interested. The animals are not what they seem, he thinks. They are waiting for someone. They are waiting to choose.

Suddenly, a cold, wet thing touches his hand. Jerking away, Ned looks down and sees a dog, sniffing him. Smaller than a medium-sized dog, she looks up at Ned with mournful eyes. He's locked in her gaze. The bitch wags her tail and pants, her mouth looking like a smile.

"What can you tell me about this one?" Ned asks Karl, reaching down to pet her. She sniffs his hand again, nuzzling his palm.

"That bitch?" Karl smirks. "She's some kind of beagle, we think. Nothing wrong with her, but she hates everyone. Howls at the kids when they come to pet her. I think she's yours."

Scratching her ears, Ned agrees.

"Her name is Nadia," Karl says, "and she's a runaway. Her owners have never claimed her. She's been here for two years, waiting for someone to let her guard down around."

But Ned isn't listening. He stops scratching Nadia's ears and she whines. When he looks down, he sees he's forgotten to tie his shoes, again.

A Frankenstein Storm

by Darryl Price

It's been storming something terrible all day today, hitting the windows like relentless sopping wet sheets. It's not scary. Just very, very lonely sounding, if you know what I mean. Monotonous, feels like I'm on a bed on a large boat of some heavy kind, or in a tub boat lost out to sea. There's one for you, Doc. Consider that a freebie.

Sometimes when I lie awake in bed at night I wonder about all those lives out there being lived among the so many beautiful lights. Someone once described them to me as being like campfires. I wanted nothing more in my life than to sit around those campfires and be part of that circle of knowing. But it seems I mostly lived my life in fast cars. Going places or returning from them. I've never felt warm or invited in this world, except the once, and as you know that didn't turn out so well for me.

It's not her fault. I swear. It's nobody's fault. It's just a bad wind came and blew my whole life down to the ground and I've been having a hell of a time ever since trying to pick up all the little scattered pieces. Sometimes I don't even know where to begin. I start and stop a lot. I used to keep a diary, but it was all stupid shit you know, pardon my English, Doc, like someone trying to write someone a folk song and failing at it miserably. It just didn't make any real sense to anyone else but me. Well. Me and her. She always seemed to get it.

I guess that's what I'm doing here, right? Beginning, or trying to begin. You guys are making a Frankenstein monster out of me! I'm only going to frighten little children, or myself if I look in the mirror. What I need is a sad soul hospital. You got any of those lying around? That's where it hurts the most. How you gonna fix that? I'm broke on the inside of my feelings.

Ok, I know you said I could write down whatever I wanted to, but I'm still trying to come up with those bizarre little mythological stories for you, since you seem to like those the best out of all of them. If it's proof that you want that I'm as sane as the next guy who's down on his luck, well, I don't know how to give you that, except to say that I believe it about myself, even if no one else does right now. And the reason I say that is everyone here looks at me strangely. What I wouldn't give for one kind look that doesn't come from anyplace but itself.

Would I even think like that if I were crazy?

Here's your story, now leave me alone: once there was a princess who could talk to butterflies. The only problem was that the butterflies never really had too much to say back to her, really, and so she never learned a lot about what they were thinking. One day she was sitting on the grass when a tiny little blue thing fluttered around her knees. Hey, she said, I want to ask you a question! The butterfly landed on her arm and looked up at her enormous head. Do you know where I can find some juicy red roses, he said. No, well, yes, I guess I do, but first you have to answer me a few questions, then I'll tell you. Oh I really don't have time for all this, the butterfly said. Oh but please, said the Princess in a great sobbing voice and so the butterfly agreed. You may ask only 2 questions, and then I really must be going. Alright she said. First what is the meaning of butterflies, and secondly, do you believe there is a god? The butterfly pumped his little wings up and down and said, the meaning of butterflies is really very simple, we mean whatever you think we mean, and as for god, we feel glad enough to be here in the modern world with the rest of you. But those aren't real answers, said the princess. You're just saying whatever comes into your mind so I'll show you to those roses. Oh very well said the butterfly. Butterflies mean all life is lived in a pretty good circle and god is whatever we put in that circle as we fly through our days together. Hmmm, said the Princess, I suppose that will have to do. It's better than the first answers you gave me. She gave the butterfly directions to the rose bush that grew on the other side of her house, but when he took off he actually went the other way instead.

Well I'm tired now, Doc. I'm going to knock it all off for the night. Hopefully by morning the bolts in my neck will be fully charged and I'll be able to walk out of here on my own two glued-together feet.

Good night.

Flying Solo

by Teresa Burns Gunther

It's a Tuesday evening and a busy week at work. But, restless at home, with nothing for dinner Rachel goes for a drive and finds herself standing at Sea Cliff on the rim of the Pacific staring out across its unknowable expanse to Japan. She always avoids the places tourists congregate but it's twenty-eight minutes before sunset and the sky is going wild and Sutro's at The Cliff House offers a view with benefits.

It's a quiet night and the host has a table for two by the window. Rachel orders a drink aware of her singularity, wondering if she'll always be a one: Table for one, single occupant, travelling alone. No one else is flying solo at Sutro's.

A middle-aged couple leans in at each other, eyes narrowed, mouths moving with words that look sharp, unhappiness for dinner.

At a table near the bus station a freckled woman cuts her children's food and mops up spilled milk. She talks, her smile feigning happiness while her husband ogles a duo of twenty-somethings, blonde and brunette, laughing and fluffing their hair, at a table one over.

Left of the sirens' table a balding businessman in a dark and tired suit is oblivious to their appeal and the blushing sunset. His square chin is lifted in a pose of amused disinterest at what is clearly a negative assessment coming at him from a large man opposite, a clearly dissatisfied customer gesticulating, complaints issuing from a florid face with drops of spit lit by the sinking sun.

A white-collared priest dines with an elderly couple in the corner. He sermonizes as he eats, oblivious of the woman wincing, her eyes darting away from the views of his masticated dinner in his too full mouth.

A pimply busboy leans against the wall watching the tables with eyes that see nothing; his mind gone travelling somewhere his body longs to follow.

Rachel thanks the waiter for the glass of scotch delivered neat with a coaster. She breathes in its peaty aroma and the thrill of a rare San Francisco June evening, fogless, still warm at 8:03 pm! She slips off her shoes, puts her feet on the other chair, empty and waiting to hold them. She drinks alone in a summer dress as the sun lingers inches above the horizon, fracturing the sky in a Hallelujah chorus of colors, ecstatic striations of gold and crimson that reach up across the sky, spill over the waving surface of the sea, and paint her white tablecloth pink as the noise of restaurant life becomes a cushioning hum.

Morgana Malone and the Miracle of Christmas

by Matt Potter

"Be holding this," Ludmilla says, and pushes a samovar into my arms.

The samovar is big and silver and crushes against my breastbone because it weighs a ton. (Or tonne, if you want to be metric about it. Or actually, 1.016 tons, if you want to be *accurate* and metric although it could be the other way around. Not that I adore the Imperial measurement system but since I lost my job at Grigor's therapy practice and don't have a lot of money and spend a lot of time alone at home, I'm on the internet quite often. And I found a website just the other day comparing metric to Imperial and it was *mesmerising*.)

Meanwhile, Ludmilla is busy piling things up on the kitchen bench. What looks like a pasta press. Then what she said is an exotic blini maker. (She didn't say *exotic*, I did, or thought it when she lugged it inside – 'gee, that looks exotic,' I thought – and she saw me looking at it and said, "No peeking – it makes blinis.") Then her famous borscht pot. And then another pot she's using to make 'sochivo' (aka 'kutia', just depends upon which part of Russia you come from. Although I think Ludmilla is not from Russia but is an ethnic Russian from the Ukraine or maybe even

Georgia, it's hard to work out just where she's from because when she's talking about her childhood she gets excited and spits a lot.)

Thinking of Ludmilla spitting makes me think of sweet Mr Rubinstein, who would come in every day for therapy. Or as he'd say, "because I am enjoying some chillink here in the waiting room." Mr Rubinstein of the eye patch and the toupée, who loved the widening grey-brown strip on my head. (I am growing out the orange I had it dyed because (1) I really don't like looking like a carrot and (2) I can't afford to get it dyed orange again by a professional hairdresser.)

My mind whips back to 'sochivo' or 'kutia', the special dish of boiled wheat sweetened with honey and sometimes dried fruit, which I know about because I looked it up on the internet. Ludmilla emailed me the links. She said it would be a nice gesture of international goodwill if I made it for the dinner party tonight, especially because I'm not Russian. "And I know you are not Russian," she said, "because no Russians are having orange hair."

(But I've never been that good at boiling wheat! So I'm going to pay her to boil the wheat instead. Or, give her a big discount on her first month's rent. Apparently making 'sochivo' can take hours.)

"What is your matter?" Ludmilla glares at me. "Your eyes are spinning spinning spinning inside your head and your brain is looking like it is cooking."

The samovar, I realise, with its cute green filigreed frog bobbling on the very top, almost touching my nostrils, is crushing the life out of me but there is no free space on any of the kitchen benches or the table to put it down and it's too magnificent and ornate and curlicued (and heavy and awkward) to put it down on the floor so I lean against the wall still clutching it but actually, it's the pantry door I'm leaning against and then I realise almost immediately as Ludmilla makes a beeline for me that I'm in her way.

"You are standing where I need to going," Ludmilla says. "Salt, salt, I need salt!"

I sort of lob out of her way – or shuffle, really, with the samovar in my arms – and then I realise I don't have any salt anyway. Because I never have salt.

"I don't have any salt, Ludmilla," I say, as she pulls the pantry door open and the 15-month calendar – January 2013 to March 2014 – smacks against the back of the door. "Remember last week when you were here, you had to use sugar because I didn't have any salt?"

Ludmilla stops in her tracks. "No salt?! You have … no … salt?!"

"No," I say, "I don't really cook with salt."

"No salt?!"

"No," I repeat. "No salt." Although, really, I'm not cooking with anything at the moment because I'm not really cooking because I'm not really eating.

Ludmilla closes the pantry door. "Then lucky lucky lucky you for I am moving in with you," she says. "So I know now why you be so skinny." And she stretches it out, *skee-ee-nee*, like I'm suddenly a lot taller too.

Although, if anything, if you looked at me – *really* looked at me – you'd say I was shorter.

"Where can I put this samovar, Ludmilla? It's pulling my arms out of their sockets."

"And lucky lucky lucky you our first meal together is for Christmas in July in June," she says. She steps over to the sink and looks through the window at the grey early winter sky. "No rain," she adds. "There is winter but there is no rain."

"Could you clear a spot on the bench?" I say, waddling over to the sink. This samovar is really killing me but if I drop it, it's going to dent the floor. Which is concrete but probably the dentable kind.

"But Christmas in July in June with *no salt*?" she says, turning to scowl at me, her mouth a frown and a smile at the same time, so really, just skewed. "Im – pos – si – ble!" she says, like she's just discovered the word and she's trying it out. "Impossible, impossible." She picks up her battered blue vinyl handbag from its perch on top of the exotic blini maker and slings it into the crook of her elbow. "*No* salt, *no* Christmas in July in June. So we buy salt."

The samovar rattles on the back seat as I drive Ludmilla in my faded watermelon pink Nissan Micra to the nearest supermarket. Ludmilla's first gesture as my new housemate is this Christmas in July party except it's not July yet, it's June, but it *is* the 25th. Accepting this party is my first housematerly act of diplomacy.

("Then we can be celebrating the big Australian tradition, Christmas in July," Ludmilla had said, when she told me it would be a good idea if I got a housemate. Like her. And soon. Like next week (which is actually this week now). When she came to my house to give me a free salt reading. At her own instigation. Except, of course, I didn't have any salt.

"But we don't do Christmas in July here," I'd said, licking the rolling pin before running it across the sugar I'd spread across the kitchen table. "Some of us barely do Christmas in December. We're just going through the motions 'til we can go to the beach for the summer holidays."

Taking the rolling pin from my grasp, she'd glanced at the sugar impressions made on the wood, then looked me up and down, raised an eyebrow, and harrumphed.

"And it won't even be July next week," I'd added, "it'll still be June."

"Christmas in July *in June*," she'd said. "I bring my samovar and we celebrate *big* Australian Christmas in July in June tradition.")

§

Ludmilla opens the passenger door and slings the 10-kilo bag of salt on the floor in front of the seat. Then, "What is this?" she says, and picks up the white envelope she was sitting on as we drove to the supermarket.

She holds it closer to read it, her thin lips mouthing my name on the front.

"It's from Grigor," I say. "That's his writing."

"Ach, but he writes not like a Russian," Ludmilla says.

"He's not Russian," I say. "His real last name is Smith."

"He writes not like a Russian," she repeats.

"Yes, his real last name is Smith," I say again. And then, before we go another round of *he writes not like a Russian / his real last name is Smith*, "I've been meaning to open it all week," I say. "It's just been lying there on the seat. I came out one morning and found it stuck to the windscreen."

Doors slam and I turn the key in the ignition. Just as I steer the faded Nissan Micra right, out of the car park, I hear ripping paper and turn to catch Ludmilla opening the letter.

"As you have ruined my life and made a mockery of my wedding," she reads. (Then to me but more to herself, "Who is this *mockery*?" she snorts.) *"Here is the bill for my ruination."* And then to herself but more to me, "There is a lot of serious numbers."

The samovar skids across the backseat as I pull over to the kerb, and right foot on the brake and with the engine still running, take the letter from her hand. My eyes run down the accompanying page of numbers. It's an itemised account of everything spent (and not paid for, by the look of things) for his wedding. The schnoodle, the platinum wedding rings, Grigor's rhinoplatsy, the vegan wedding bouquets … oh, everything.

So did Grigor marry Zebadie or was *that* passed on to someone else too?

"But this is *verrry* Russian thing," Ludmilla pronounces, her chin nodding. "What is *yacht*?" she says, but she says it like it's spelled, 'y-a-ch-t'.

I shake my head. Can he come after me for the money?

Ludmilla rips the letter from my hand. "Look," she points at the bill, "you know bad people, bad people be advantaged over you. So get rid of bad people."

I pull on the handbrake, turn the key and the engine shudders to a stop.

"Christmas in July in June is here," Ludmilla says. "Maybe you meet a nice *real* Russian man."

I look out the driver's window. It's not raining but everything is a watery blur.

"Okay, your friend Ludmilla, I help you. I cook you 'sochivo'," she adds, "for free. Okay?"

I turn to see her peering at me. And, smiling so her beige teeth show past her thin lips, she pats my knee.

I twist and look at the backseat, at the silver samovar resting between two seatbelt buckles. And wonder who should I smash over the head with it first: Grigor, or Ludmilla?

Nichole

by Gary Percesepe

O Sara!

It's June 26th and this date always reminds me of a woman I once knew. She lives in Brooklyn now, not far from you. I'd take you both to lunch when I'm in town next week, but I don't know how to reach her, how to find her. She's in Brooklyn, somewhere. I miss her. I miss her today.

I'd see Nichole once a week at the small literary magazine where we worked. The magazine had a good reputation. Thousands of hopeful writers sent their short stories to a post office box downtown. Nichole logged them in. The managing editor scanned the pile for names she recognized – writers we'd published previously, like T.C. Boyle, James Purdy, Gordon Lish – and for "agented work". The rest was slush. The slush was stood upright in two large boxes in the far corner of the magazine's one room office. There it would sit until one of the "readers" would take home a pile. Nichole and I were readers.

One day I read a story that knocked me out. The author had no credits. Straight from the slush, wrapped in a plain brown envelope, the story was about two lonely and alienated teenaged kids who are surprised one morning to find each other. A story I'd heard a thousand times. But it was the way the story was told – full of feeling, accurate, without a trace of condescension, right as rain. It filled the heart. I called Nichole.

We made a picnic in the park. I read the story out loud. Toward the end, the boy and girl meet at the high school, at first light. There is the sound of a lawn mower in the middle distance, and the smell of fresh cut grass. They are seated in silence on the steps of the school. The girl raises her shirt.

I finished reading. There was silence for the space of a minute. Then Nichole took off her shirt. She kissed me. "Shirt-raising fiction," she said.

I know, I know – you're smiling at that. Ha.

Wait a sec – there's someone at the door.

OK, I'm back. Delivery guy. Galleys for my story collection. So, anyway –

We fucked that day, outside at a state park, in a lovely meadow by a statue (oh so phallic) and we shared a bottle of wine and some cheese and crackers I had thought to bring. Or maybe she brought the wine? I don't remember. But I read her that story and then she did what she did with her shirt, and I was like, uh oh, and then – O Sara! – we began to make love and she forgot she had a tampon in and we laughed about that – I mean, really? – and I removed it, or she did and I was inside her, but we both could not stop laughing it was so fucking funny and by then I was thinking I wonder if this is right, I had been affair-less for so long, and I cared about N in all of the right ways, so we just held each other then and went on laughing about the errant tampon, and of course a few weeks later she came out to me, the first person she told, she read it to me from her JOURNAL, the pages she had written after the interview she did with Ani DiFranco and KNEW she was in love, and I was so happy for her, and she told all of this to me in my car, where she went on reading her journal – and she later wrote a poem for her poetry class at Antioch, a poem about making love to an older man who wears a wedding ring, and the poem was, in my memory, the most beautiful poem

I've ever heard, because it came straight from her innocent Italian heart. She said it had shocked her classmates when she had read it aloud in class, and she folded it in half and handed it to me (like a fool, I have somehow lost it). She had a heart-shaped face, and a big smile and a way of looking at you that drew you directly in – that made you feel like you were the only person on earth alive. When she moved to Brooklyn I would get cards from her, not Hallmark cards but these lovely handmade cards with crayon art and multicolored, with little tufts of lace or something glued in – the most creative cards, and every card, every fucking one of them would begin like this:

O Gary!

This is a convention i have adopted, in memory of her

And I learned early on that I could never give her a book to read unless I wanted to GIVE her a book, because that was her rule – she never returned a book, if you gave it to her it was hers – and she explained this to me one day and we laughed at that too – she was a woman with rules.

I gave her a print of a Picasso painting one day, from the blue period, the man with the guitar, and she kept that too – I brought her a big basket of pizzelles one Christmas, for her and her friends, vanilla ones and chocolate that Savannah and I had made – I liked to give her little things.

I bought her a dress one day when I was in Roma. She had wanted to go to Italy with me but then at the last minute she couldn't – I kept expecting her to show up at my room or to run into her at the Pantheon or the Spanish Steps, the whole week I was there. But of course she never showed.

She had, it appears, never worn a dress in her life! Ha! Oh, I loved to see that dress on her, she wore it ONE time, to an Italian lunch restaurant I took her to in Columbus, a place called Bravo! And we talked in Italian and English to the waiters, and I asked her what it was like for her to make love to a woman, to kiss a woman, and we had this funny conversation, the only one of its kind I remember, and it was so funny to see her in that little blue dress, with black leggings I also bought her, to cover her hairy legs, and of course I had bought it for her as a joke.

I wound up writing a poem for her, which I published somewhere or other. Nichole and I were friends, not lovers, and I valued that. I remember thinking at the time: where can I ever find a friend like this?

And then, years later, I met you.

One day I took N to my house and got her up on one of my horses, and we went for a long trail ride together, she on the big black gelding, and I was riding a lovely bay mare, and there were apple trees along our trail and I reached over and plucked an apple off the tree for her and then one for myself, and we rode in silence through the colored woods one fall, with Trouble, the big Irish setter, leading the way, running along ahead of us –

She sat in on some of my classes on friendship love and romance at the conservative college where I taught – and the other girls looked at her as if they were seeing someone from Jupiter – she was dressed in the classic Antioch thrift shop look, and the conservative big-time Christian girls in their plaid skirts and silk blouses and pearls – it was so funny. She couldn't find anyone to hit on, and was a bit disappointed. We were both misplaced souls, and it made us sad sometimes to know how we didn't belong anywhere we went, which is why maybe we went places together –

And the terrible day in November when all hell broke loose with M and the idiot husband who called the house and I thought I would lose my job, my marriage, my family, it was Nichole who first took me into her arms and held me when I thought I would have no life left to live and she said you will go on, you will live, you do not need that place, that ridiculous college, there will be a better one for you, and she was right –

I went to her Antioch graduation and saw her parents, and there was N, in a strapless black gown dressed as if going out to dinner in her native Philly, and her hairy armpits displayed to perfection and a string of pearls set against the black dress and her olive skin. I didn't speak to her that day, did not get to see her, stayed away because she was leaving and I couldn't bear to say goodbye to her, so I watched from a distance, and let her go –

Her cards: she would tell me about her love life, the women she was sleeping with, then who she was living with, what concoction she was cooking and the wine (she had little money and HUGE student loans for her Antioch degree in POETRY! – ha! she was the LEAST practical person on earth i have ever met, less practical even than M, which is saying something, as I thought M lived on dreams alone) – and one week I was in NYC and staying at the Chelsea Hotel and I remember Nichole came by to pick me up and we went to an Italian restaurant a block or so away (I MUST find that restaurant again, as I remember it so well, and placed it in another of my short stories, somewhere), and she walked me back to the hotel and we joked about going up but both knew that was a dumb idea and we didn't want it, either of us, though there was a tug when I watched her spin and walk away – but I let her go. Then one day the cards stopped coming –

O Sara!

She is somewhere in Brooklyn.

Can we ever know what we want?

Call me later –

xo

Samford Awakens from a Month-Long Coma

by Nathaniel Tower

Samford flickers his eyes open then snaps them shut, squeezing them tight against the buzzing fluorescent lights.

The last thing he remembers is charging toward the finish line of the One-Mile Run in the Clone Olympics. The crowd was roaring, and he was leading by over 100 meters, easily on his way to a world record.

"Did I win?" he mutters to the empty room. Well, not completely empty. There is plenty of medical equipment.

The lights buzz in response, brightening even through his closed eyelids.

A door pops open. Through small slits Samford watches the blurry figure in a white coat enter. The figure, whom Samford assumes is a doctor, jots notes on a clipboard. At least that's what it looks like.

After standing over Samford for a few minutes, scrawling notes, the doctor says, "And how are you, Samford?"

"Did I win the race?" Samford asks, his voice like gravel.

The doctor continues to write notes. Samford watches him reach for something metallic.

"This will only hurt for a moment." The metal object attaches to Samford's right eyelid and tears it open. Light floods his eye, and Samford thinks his head will explode from the overwhelming brightness. He tries to scream, but the doctor muffles his mouth with a gloved hand.

"It's better if you don't." He reaches for another metal object and places it on Samford's other eye. The pain of rushing light eclipses what he felt when the right eye was forced open.

Samford's body gyrates on the table. Unable to close his eyes, he pounds his legs and arms to tolerate the pain. For the first time since waking up he feels the shackles on his hands and feet.

"It's best that you not do that," the doctor says. He holds a small bottle above Samford's eyes. "If I miss, this could burn your face off."

Samford shakes even more violently at the toxic drops the doctor holds above his eyes.

"You are lucky I have good aim." Samford watches a thick drop release from the bottle and plummet toward his eye. The drop looks enormous as it makes impact, sizzling instantly and distorting everything Samford sees to red. The doctor repeats the process to the other eye.

Samford's vision flashes through the full spectrum of colors before the doctor releases the eye clamps and his eyes fall shut.

"Rest now," the doctor says. "I'll be back in a few hours to answer any questions you have."

The doctor is gone before Samford can force his eyes open again. To his surprise, his vision is clear and he has no more pain. He has no trouble keeping his eyes open either. In fact, he finds it almost impossible to close them, even for the momentary action of blinking.

Once he tires of staring at the lights and the tiny holes in the ceiling (what are those holes for anyway?), he squeezes his eyes closed for more than ten seconds. Of course, as soon as he drifts off to sleep, the door bursts open and the doctor comes in again.

Samford's eyes fly open. "So, did I win?" He's not sure why he is so concerned with a race that happened a month ago. At least he thinks it was a month ago. Not that he would really know. He's never been that competitive about anything before, except the number of women he can bang in a month.

"I'm afraid not," the doctor says.

"Who won?"

"No one. Don't you remember? The race was cut short. The snipers showed up. You were grazed by a bullet and collapsed on the field. It's too bad because you were winning by a lot. In fact, you were about to set a record. Does this ring a bell?" The doctor offers a smile, but it isn't the comforting type.

Samford thinks. "No. None of it. I just remember running, my balls flopping around, trying to beat the other clones."

The doctor stares at him, mouth open and brow raised. "What do you mean by the other clones?"

"It was the Clone Olympics. I had been kidnapped because I was some special clone. They trained me to win."

The doctor laughs then leans in close. "You're not a clone," he whispers.

"What the hell are you talking about? I have the serial number." He opens his mouth to try and recite the number but can't remember any of it. A string of gibberish emerges from his lips.

The doctor laughs again. "You silly humans. You have no clue. None of you."

Samford is too shocked to speak. His mouth hangs wide open, beckoning the doctor to explain.

"Let me explain," the doctor says before he begins pacing around the room, looking in drawers and underneath every visible object. It is several minutes before

376

the doctor starts explaining. Samford wonders if the doctor is checking for bugs.

"Okay, here it goes. All humans have a serial number implanted in their anuses when they are born. This has been going on since the '40s. It's the clones that don't have the serial numbers. That's the only way you can tell the difference."

"What about people born before the '40s?"

"They're too old to be cloned, so it doesn't matter."

"Why do we have serial numbers?" Samford asks, knowing the doctor will tell him anyway. He wants to look thoughtful to impress the doctor.

"It's simple, really. It's government tracking. But you probably had that figured out as soon as I told you. The government tracks everyone all the time. Everything about you. Your heart rate, how often you brush your teeth, your masturbation habits, the number of women you screw."

"Why?"

The doctor laughs again. *The laugh ends too soon for comfort, and the doctor continues.* "For control, obviously. The government is slowly gaining total control without you knowing it. Wanna hear something funny? All the politicians and all the world leaders and pretty much everyone famous: all clones."

"Why?"

"People think too much. Clones think as they are programmed."

"So who is in charge of everything? Is it a clone or a person?"

"Well, funny you should ask. The overseer of it all is –"

But the doctor's eyes roll back and he drops to the ground. The lights turn off. Samford's eyes are wide open but he can't see a thing.

Jacaranda Storm

by Kimberlee Smith

Been exactly a month to the day since Doreen appeared out of nowhere to disturb us in our little slice of nowhere, which my husband Dean and I have determined is what the living refer to as limbo, or purgatory, depending on your religious convictions. The way I grew up, there were two ways to go: up or down. Heaven or Hell. Can't say it's refreshing to have debunked that myth, but so here we are.

I'm Melodie and I died the day our daughter Etheline was born. I went by snakebite. Dean burned as if he went by way of Hell, in an explosion of fire and terror. Prop plane crashed into the tip of a mountain. Enough fuel to turn him to ash upon impact. I know because I was there, not in my body, but he didn't go down alone – he screamed until his heart gave out, thankfully right before it all blew up. But that's not the point now. Point is, this *thing*, Doreen, showed up after Dean and I were alone here for a couple months and were getting on each other's nerves, hoping for company of some sort. She wasn't company.

Tensions were rising; he was getting antsy to move on, to Heaven, maybe? In hindsight I'm not so sure that's where he's going when he moves on from this afterworld. And I've just wanted to stay here and keep an eye on our baby, watch her grow up in the care of my mum, Maybell. She's done as fine a job as can be expected. Sure, she drinks a little too much, but it's all she's got to keep her company other than the bub. She pushes Etheline in the pram every day, feeds her right, gives her a lotta love. Keeps her nappies clean, rocks her to sleep, sings her sweet songs.

So this craziness that called herself Doreen and said she had passed away and had actually been here before, but was just passing through on her way to visit her family that went before she did, was some sort of decoy … we don't know if she was either put up to testing us or was a menacing, devious spirit trying to get us to go with her. And I don't think she was going to what is often – and misleadingly as far as my experience tells me – referred to as "a better place," she was going *down*.

It goes something like this: She tells us she knows there is more to the afterworld than where Dean and I had been lingering for the past few months; that it's futile to spend eternity just looking down on our little girl, not able to have any connection with her at all.

"That'd just break your hearts every day, and wouldn't that be the worst choice?" she asks with cloudy eyes that look like smoldering coal and smiles with a gaping mouth like a cavernous hole, darker than her eyes.

"Doesn't do that poor bub with no mum and dad no good. And it don't do nothing for you two naïve souls but make you feel bad for yourselves. That don't gain you any points in this place," says Doreen with a snort. For a split second it looks like she has a bloody nose, but then Dean freaks out, trembling so hard his vibrations shake me like an earthquake, and he secrets to me, *That's fire coming out of her nose! Like a dragon!*

Bullshit … you sure? I volley the thought to Dean. He knows I'm begging for a different answer. But he thinks nothing to me, he just stares at Doreen and turns that rotten gray oyster color his apparition does whenever he gets out of sorts. This time it doesn't stop at that. He's like a not-any-longer human mood ring. He keeps turning until he's purple-black.

She wasn't able to read our thoughts, we believed.

"I got you and I got you two but good. You don't have any faith in this place, but I have been here before and you should take heed of my advice." Doreen is now weaving her hands throughout her midsection where she was chewed apart by a crocodile – or so she said – wildly weaving her arms in angry jerking movements, flailing and spinning.

"I ain't bleeding and it ain't fire! You don't know shit!" Doreen is screaming but her voice has dropped to a baritone and is echoing like, I don't know what else to call it but like the devil.

"No one ever said that, take it easy," I say, but then my electrical system short-circuits or goes into overdrive or whatever you want to call it when I cause the lightning and thunderstorms just by getting riled up. Doreen's been playing us all along, knowing just what we've been thinking ever since she appeared ... I don't want to say she *arrived,* because I have a feeling she's been here much longer than Dean and I, maybe forever.

"Doreen, I'm not leaving because I'm going to stay with my baby, watch her grow, at least for a while longer. There isn't anywhere better for us but here, as close as we can be to Etheline." I try to sound respectful and sincere, but with the storm all around it's not so easy.

"And enough with your fucking storms, Melodie. You think I've never seen that before? You think you're the first?" She's bleeding like a fountain now, ears, eyes, and nose. Her fists are whirring in infinity signs through what once was her midsection.

"You never been anywhere but here, you've never been on earth, you've never loved or been loved. You don't know the first thing about Heaven. You might know this place, but you don't know anything else," says Dean.

"Like Hell I don't," bellows Doreen.

The storms are going like this place is going to blow into oblivion. But then something beautifully unexpected happens. That storm quiets and then thousands of lavender jacaranda blossoms appear and whorl around Dean and me, intoxicating us in the perfume and velvet of the petals. It happens whenever there's a nostalgic loveliness in this foreign world. The phenomenon comes from – it has to – when Dean planted a garden of baby jacaranda trees for me as a surprise Christmas present, this past year right before I died. They are my favorite flowers.

Doreen stayed here and taunted us and spooked us until this morning, when she was taken against her will. We won this time. It seemed like she was sucked into a funnel, downwards, like what happens when you flush the loo. Just like Dorothy in *The Wizard of Oz*, all we had to do was believe we could go home again – to be with our bub from here, which is the best we can do – and the answer was there all along. We were being put to some sort of test. And we passed.

I'm not sure about Dean, because he'd been consumed by that rotten spirit Doreen since she presented herself to us, but more or less I've been in my own world since the day I arrived, following my mum real closely because she's always *always* with our bub. I can tell by what she's been doing recently – slowly closing up the house, overwatering the jacarandas, buying cases of throwaway nappies instead of using the ones she washes every day – that she's planning a trip. I think she's got nothing to lose, and she may well be right. I get the feeling she and Etheline are taking a car trip to find my daddy. A long drive that's long overdue. And I'm going to be there every centimeter of the way, Dean or no Dean. That's up to him.

What's Wrong with Her

by Vanessa Weibler Paris

"First was Lizzie," I start. "Really small eyes, super close together."

"I mean, how close could they possibly be?" Bobby asks, shrugging out of his jacket and tossing it on the back of his chair. It's a Christmas gift from his wife Jenny, and I wonder if the slick black leather will swallow the bar smoke. "There's a nose in the middle, right?"

"Close," I say. "And then Janie. Big gap between the front teeth."

"How big?" Bobby asks.

"Hmm," I say. "Well, Janie's front teeth were about as close to one another as Lizzie's eyes."

"Oh," says Bobby in response, and then, "oh."

"And then came Nancy," I say. I pause for a swallow of my beer. Guinness, heavy, practically a meal. It takes me a moment to force the word. "Harelip."

"Harelip?"

"I know," I say. "I didn't even know people still got those. Aren't they all fixed at birth? At least in first-world countries?"

"Poor Nancy," Bobby says, holding up his Amstel Light.

"Poor Nancy," I agree, clinking and swigging.

I almost can't believe I'm saying these things. I've spent my whole life as Slim Jim, unable to gain or maintain no matter what. I hide my body in a fog of baggy clothing and smoky bars, but I can't hide my face. Gaunt and angular, hollow-eyed and sharp-chinned. I once heard someone describe my features as "skin stretched over a skull." I feel sick speaking this way, of these women. But when you join a website called Ugly People Dating and then meet up with your best friend in the world to debrief your dates, of course he's going to ask: "What's wrong with her?"

"And then there was Maura," I tick off a finger. "Really bad skin."

"How bad could it –"

"Bad," I say. "I almost wanted to reach out and start squeezing, as if it would somehow make her feel better. Provide a release." Maura, beautiful blue eyes and a weak white smile surrounded by piles of soft red bulges. I'd wished I could free her lovely features from the spotty topography, removing them like Mr. Potato Head parts and pushing them gently onto a smooth new plastic face.

"Barbara," I tick another finger. "Facial scar, not even very big, not even that obvious. Car accident from when she was a kid. There was also Danielle," I say, adding before he asks, "who's just, you know, overweight."

Bobby coughs and busies himself with a chicken wing. He teeters on the edge of obese himself, having expanded slowly over the years. A pound this year, another the next. A stealth few ounces here and there. He would never complain about it to me, I know. He would never risk hurting me.

"Drummette?" Bobby holds out a baby drumstick, dripping with wet orange sauce. I like the drummettes; he likes the wingettes. We're not just best friends; we're each other's wingmen.

I take it gratefully, eat it skin-on. It's hot, hot enough to make my forehead sweat and nose run and throat cough. It's just right.

"So, the million-dollar question," Bobby says, pulling small pieces of meat free of the fat, then lining them up beside celery sticks on his plate. "Any second dates on the horizon?"

"I asked Lizzie," I admit. "She wasn't interested. But polite about it. And I called Maura. She never called back."

"Their loss," says Bobby, as I knew he would.

"But there is one," I say. And I tell him about Iris.

I tell him about Iris, whose dating profile picture was shaded, shadowed, sepiaed in silhouette. Iris, standard-sized and symmetrical featured. Iris, whose 'About Me' was left entirely blank.

I tell him about the texts swapped, the emails exchanged, the phone calls shared before we even met. About how I tried postponing the date, terrified to finally meet her, because I'd already fallen in love and didn't want it to end.

"So," Bobby says eventually, holding tight to the same celery stick he was gripping when I first began. "What's wrong with her?"

Iris had kissed me at the end of our date, my first kiss since I was a teenager at a spin-the-bottle party. She'd leaned in without any sign of revulsion, without closed eyes, and kissed me. And then she'd turned toward my ear and whispered hotly, *"I'm ugly on the inside."*

The BBQ

by Joanne Jagoda

I don't want to get up. It feels good to stay in bed. It's so quiet in this old house with the girls at their summer jobs. The graduation party was nice though not my style. Lillian pulled out all the stops as usual. Her caterer set up stations around their big yard with a sushi chef, a taco station and a bar where the kids got virgin daiquiris and pina coladas. The girls invited their friends, and I had a few teachers from school and a handful of old friends. Cassie and Robin were embarrassed that everything was so fancy but their friends got into it, playing tennis and swimming. They loved being waited on, and no one wanted to leave. I put on a good show but I was torn, missing my husband but thinking about David too. He knew about the party, but it would have been awkward to have him there. He's coming to dinner tonight to meet the girls.

Guess I better get my butt up and go to Farmer Joe's to pick up corn, tomatoes and lettuce. I'm going to grill chicken. Since Paul died I've had to learn how to barbeque. That was his specialty. I can see him in his 'Kiss the Cook' apron … tongs in one hand and a bottle of Corona in the other. I'll stop for rolls and a cherry pie at La Tartine on Judah Street. I've got to stop picking at my cuticles. I'm nervous about tonight. What if the girls don't like him?

That's dumb. He's so sweet and asks about them all the time.

Farmer Joe's had the best organic tomatoes today. I'll wash the salad, shuck the corn and marinate the chicken in that recipe I got from *Epicurious*. I'm going to use my new paisley placemats from Cost Plus.

"Mom, I'm home."

"Hi Cass."

"Your table is very ... uh ... Martha Stewart. Nice placemats and napkins."

"I guess that's a compliment, Cass. How was the lab?"

"Extremely cool. We injected Elmo and Burt with the vaccine, and had to observe them for hours. They tolerated the treatment well for rats. Oh yeah, 'Dude' is coming tonight."

"And you can call him David, not 'Dude'."

"OK, DAY-vid. What-ev ..."

"Please try to be nice."

"Mom, I'm not a baby. I get it.'"

"Robin do you have to let the door slam **every** damn time you come in?

"Ooooh ... bad language Mom ..."

"You're a pain, Rob. How was your day?"

"Not bad for babysitting a bunch of preppy brats. Oh yeah tonight we meet the 'Dude'."

"I just yelled at your sister about that. His name is *David*. And do I have to remind you to be civil too? And don't spoil your dinner with ice cream."

"Chill Mom. We're not six. Come on, Cass. Let's go upstairs."

"I'm going up to shower." Just a dab of this perfume he likes. And these high-heeled sandals are cute. I look acceptable ... oh hell, I look good. It's been a long time since I've felt this way. David has been hinting about taking a long weekend in the Napa Valley. I get all tingly just thinking about it.

"I'm starting the grill and you two get out of your jeans. I'll put on the chicken in ten minutes."

"We HEAR you Mom!" Robin yells down to the yard.

I'm going to sit in the car a minute. This is my big night. I've been waiting to meet the twins. Just one more step to getting closer to the family. These gifts I selected for them should do the trick.

Oh, there's the door. He's right on time. He looks cute in his jeans and a yellow polo shirt, and his hair is all messy from the convertible. I feel like I'm sixteen.

"Annie, you look delicious and your perfume … is mmmm. Here, these are for you."

"Oh, these wildflowers are gorgeous, thank you … and you brought wine too." He is holding two small blue boxes. I think they are from Tiffany's. Paul splurged on a Tiffany ring for our twentieth anniversary. "Girls, come meet David."

"David Lewis, meet my daughters. Cassie and Robin meet David." *Why are they so quiet. They usually don't shut up.*

"Hello young ladies. These are graduation presents for you. Go ahead … open them."

I know they don't recognize the Tiffany boxes. I hope they like what he got them. Ah, Cassie got a silver bangle and Robin's is a silver heart pendant. Why don't they thank him? Damn it girls, say something. Where are your manners?

Robin finally pipes up, "Uh thank you Du ... ah David. It's, uh pretty."

"Yeah, thanks, David. Come on Rob. Let's try them on upstairs."

"Girls, we're having a glass of wine on the patio. Dinner in thirty."

"OK, Mom."

"David, let's sit outside. San Francisco doesn't get many warm nights. Thank you for the gifts, from Tiffany's no less. How did you know what they'd like? Half the time I get them the wrong thing."

"I'll let you in on my secret. My sister in London has teenagers and they tell me what they like to get for their birthdays and Christmas."

She's so easy to fool. My sister hates my guts and doesn't have children. It was so easy to hack the twins' computers and see the search engines they look at.

Oh my god, he's turning the chicken just like Paul. I better have some wine or I'll lose it.

"David, I like this wine."

"It's a Mondavi Chardonnay. We'll go to their winery in the Napa Valley. Have you picked our weekend?"

Cassie and Robin huddle in their bedroom. "He's cute, Rob and don't you love his accent? Mom is gaga over him, and he's trying hard to get on our good side."

"Yeah, he's cute, but I get a creepy vibe from him."

"You've hardly said two words to him."

"How did he pick the perfect gifts for us? I was just looking at something like that online."

"Rob, it's a nice coincidence. Don't you believe in coincidences?"

"Girls!!"

"Anne, dinner was delicious. I never knew you were such a good cook. Girls, tell me about your summer jobs. Cassie, I heard you work in a lab."

"Actually David, we'd like to know about you," Robin interrupts before Cassie can answer.

"Well Robin, I'm from London and came to open a new branch office and –"

"But what does your company do?"

Anne forces a laugh. "Rob, don't bug David. Let's have dessert. I bought the best cherry pie."

Robin glares at her mother but stops asking questions while they eat dessert.

"Another slice David?"

"Uh, no," he pats his stomach and takes Anne's hand. "Cassie and Robin, I hope you won't mind me taking your mom on a getaway to the Napa Valley next month."

Robin's eyes grow wide. She stands up so fast her chair falls backward. "Mom, how could you?" Robin stomps out and Cassie follows her.

Anne shrugs and stammers, "You have to give them time David. You're the first man I've brought home since their father died."

David tries to grin and yanks Anne up from her chair. He whispers in a low voice, "I want to be with you. They'll have to get used it." She shivers when he nuzzles her neck.

"Well ... let's try for ... uh, late July. Maybe it's better during the week rather than the weekend if you can take off. That way I can spend the weekend with them."

"Sure, whatever you want."

That little bitch, Robin. I knew she'd be trouble. Now I have to re-arrange everything.

He looks at his iPhone. "How about Wednesday July 30th? We'll start off early and stay a couple nights. You'd be back on Friday."

"That'll work."

"We'll tour wineries, have gourmet meals, go for mud baths and leave plenty of time for uh … well, you know …"

Anne blushes and kisses him. He kisses her back hard.

"I'm heading out, Anne. Look … I really want this trip to happen. And thank you for dinner."

"I'll speak to them. They'll be OK with it." She closes the door after him and sighs.

I hope he isn't mad. He has to give them some time. Shit. He did seem a little put out.

"Mom, I'll help you with the dishes. Rob is upstairs pouting. David's cute and all, but he sure surprised us."

Robin bursts in and blurts out. "He's weird. There's something about him. How did he know to pick that particular jewelry? We had just been looking at those."

"Robin, he's got teenage nieces and good taste. Nothing wrong with that. I get it that he'll never be your dad, but I have fun with him. It was rude the way you left the table."

"I don't like him. Anyway, we're meeting Laurie and Kate at the Metreon."

The door slams.

Why can't they give him a chance? They wanted me to date. I'm so damn frustrated. I'm going to mop the kitchen floor.

I don't want to clean the damn floor. I'm going to have another glass of wine. I knew things were going too perfectly.

Authors

Rachel Ambrose is a twenty-something fiction writer from Connecticut. Her favorite season is winter, she enjoys well-made Manhattans, and she loves Southern fiction. Her work has appeared in *Crack the Spine*, *Exiles Literary Magazine*, and *The Colton Review*. Currently at work on her second novel, she blogs at http://victorywhiskeyjuliet.tumblr.com.

Lynn Beighley is a fiction writer stuck in a technical book writer's body. Her stories often involve deeply flawed characters and the unsatisfying meshing of the virtual and actual world. She has an MFA in Creative Writing and currently has 16 books published.

Margaret Bingel is just a writer, living in Manchester, New Hampshire. She spends her time working at her father's beer store, art modeling, and writing (when she can). She doesn't have a website or a blog yet, but who knows, maybe she'll have one in the future.

Guilie Castillo Oriard is a Mexican writer currently exiled on the island of Curaçao. She misses Mexican food and Mexican *amabilidad*, but the laissez-faire attitude and the beaches of the Caribbean are fair exchange. Plus, the bounty of cultural diversity inspires great culture-clash fiction. Guilie is currently revising and editing her first novel. Her short stories have appeared in *Fiction 365*, *Lady Ink Magazine* and *Pure Slush*. She blogs at http://guilie-castillo-oriard.blogspot.com.

John Wentworth Chapin lives and writes in Baltimore, where he is too frequently starting Project B before finishing Project A. John writes non-fiction as well as fiction. Find him on the web at http://johnwentworthchapin.com.

James Claffey hails from County Westmeath, Ireland, and lives on an avocado ranch in Carpinteria, CA with his family. He is the author of a collection of short fiction, *Blood a Cold Blue*. His website can be found at http://jamesclaffey.com.

Gay Degani has published online and in print including *The Best of Every Day Fiction* editions and her own collection, *Pomegranate Stories*. She is the founder-editor emeritus of EDF's *Flash Fiction Chronicles*, a staff editor at *Smokelong Quarterly*, and blogs at *Words in Place* where a list of her work can be found. She's had two stories nominated for Pushcart consideration and won the eleventh Annual Glass Woman Prize for her flash piece, *Something about L.A.*

Michelle Elvy is an editor and writer who has meandered from the shores of the Chesapeake to New Zealand's Bay of Islands. Michelle has published poetry, short stories and non-fiction about travel, faraway places, food, motorcycling, slow travel, the kindness of strangers and raising children in unusual places for numerous literary journals and magazines in the US, Canada, Australasia, UK and Europe. She edits at *Flash Frontier: An Adventure in Short Fiction* and *Blue Five Notebook*. She can also be found regularly at *Awkword Paper Cut*. More about manuscript assessment and Michelle's take on editing and writing at http://michelleelvy.com.

Gloria Garfunkel is a psychologist and writer with a Ph.D. from Harvard University in Psychology and Social Relations. A former psychotherapist, she has published many stories in literary journals and anthologies.

Teresa Burns Gunther has had fiction and nonfiction appear in numerous literary journals and most recently in *Northwind Magazine, Bookslut* and *Best New Writing 2012*. Teresa is the Editor of *The Lakeside*, an on-line literary magazine, and she founded Lakeshore Writers Workshop in Oakland, California where she leads creative writing workshops and classes and works one-on-one with writers. You can find more of her work at her website http://www.teresaburnsgunther.com/.

Gill Hoffs lives with her family and an ever-dwindling supply of Nutella in the North of England. Find Gill on facebook or as @gillhoffs on twitter, email her a dirty joke at gillhoffs@hotmail.co.uk, or leave a clean comment at http://gillhoffs.wordpress.com/. *Wild: a collection* is out now from *Pure Slush Books*. Her non-fiction book *The Sinking of RMS Tayleur: the Lost Story of the Victorian Titanic* is also out now from *Pen & Sword*. (See her site or http://www.pen-and-sword.co.uk/ for details.) Feel free to send her chocolate.

Joanne Jagoda of Oakland, California, took an inspiring writing workshop after retiring in 2009, and launched on a long-postponed creative writing journey. Since discovering her passion for writing, she has worked non-stop on short stories, poetry and non-fiction. Her work has appeared in a number of e-zines and print anthologies, including *Pure Slush* and *Idea Gems Magazine*, and she was a poet of the month for a Jewish news weekly in Northern California. When not taking writing and poetry classes, Joanne enjoys being a writer-coach for ninth graders, Zumba, and visiting her three grandchildren in Jerusalem.

Len Kuntz is a writer from Washington State and an editor at the online literary magazine *Metazen*. His work appears widely in print and online, and you can find more of his work at http://lenkuntz.blogspot.com.

Sally-Anne Macomber was born and raised in Toronto, Canada, and studied journalism at Concordia University in Montreal. Her work on high fashion and the demise of haute couture has appeared in various online and print publications in both Europe and North America. She turned to writing flash fiction in 2010, and hasn't looked back.

Jessica McHugh is an author of speculative fiction that spans the genre from horror and alternate history to epic fantasy. A member of the Horror Writers Association and a 2013 Pulp Ark nominee, she has devoted herself to novels, short stories, poetry, and playwriting. Jessica has had thirteen books published in five years, including the bestselling *Rabbits in the Garden*, *The Sky: The World* and the gritty coming-of-age thriller, *PINS*. More info on her speculations and publications can be found at http://www.jessicamchughbooks.com.

Gwendolyn Joyce Mintz is a fiction writer and aspiring photographer. Her work has appeared in various online and print publications. In other incarnations, Mintz is a writing instructor, a teddy bear maker and somebody's grandmother.

h. l. nelson is Founding Editor/Executive Director of *Cease, Cows* lit mag and a former sidewalk mannequin. Pub credits: *PANK*, *Hobart*, *Connotation Press*, *Metazen*, *Drunk Monkeys*, *Red Fez*, *Bartleby Snopes*. She's also editing an anthology which includes stories by Aimee Bender, Roxane

Gay, Lindsay Hunter and other fierce women writers. Her MFA is currently kicking her ass. Tell her what you're wearing: heather@hlnelson.com.

Mandy Nicol grew up in Melbourne, Australia, and made a tree change to country Victoria in the mid-nineties – the decade, not her age. She has various animals including a flockette of pet sheep that are thankful for her vegaquarian habits. She writes short stories and loves flash fiction. *Pure Slush* is the first venue to publish her work.

Derek Osborne lives in eastern Pennsylvania. His work has appeared in *Boston Literary Magazine*, *Bartleby Snopes*, *Literary Orphans*, *The Linnet's Wings*, *Pure Slush* and many others. To read more visit http://gertrudesflat.blogspot.com, or email him at derekosborne1@gmail.com.

Vanessa Weibler Paris lives in Erie, Pa., with a guy, a girl, a boy, a bunny rabbit and a dog. She writes things both real (for work) and pretend (for fun). Her favorite things include hot peppers, bad puns, small-world stories, and tales with a twist at the end.

Gary Percesepe is Associate Editor at *New World Writing* (formerly *Mississippi Review*) and a Contributor at *The Nervous Breakdown*. Author of four books in philosophy, Percesepe's poetry, fiction, essays, and interviews have appeared in *Story Quarterly*, *N + 1*, *Salon*, *Mississippi Review*, *The Millions*, *Brevity*, *PANK*, *Metazen*, *The Brooklyner*, and other places. His collection of short stories, *Why I Did the Grocery Girl*, is forthcoming from *Aqueous Books*. He has taught at Saint Louis University, Wittenberg University, and University of Dayton. He lives in Buffalo, New York.

Matt Potter is an Australian-born writer who keeps a part of his psyche in Berlin. Matt has been published in various places online, and he is, rather amazingly, also the founding editor of *Pure Slush*. You can find more of his work at his website: http://mattcpotter.webs.com/.

Darryl Price was born in Kentucky and educated at Thomas More College. A founding member of L. Jack Roth's Yellow Pages Poets, he has published dozens of chapbooks, and his poems have appeared in many journals. He currently edits *Olentangy Review* with his wife Melissa.

Stephen V. Ramey is an American author from New Castle, Pennsylvania. His work has appeared in many places, including *The Doctor TJ Eckleburg Review*, *The Journal of Compressed Creative Arts*, and *A Capella Zoo*. *Glass Animals*, his first collection of (very) short fiction is available from *Pure Slush Books*. Find him and more of his work at http://www.stephenvramey.com.

Shane Simmons is a self-confessed coffee shop writer who believes that regardless of quality, each paragraph penned should be rewarded with sweet treats (cake, muffins, Belgian waffles, etc). London-born, he ran away to Glasgow ten years ago, expanded his waistline and now blogs at http://scribblingsimmons.wordpress.com/.

Kimberlee Smith is a writer whose poetry, essays, fiction, and creative non-fiction have been published in numerous literary journals and anthologies. She was awarded a residency to the Jentel Arts Program in 2013. She lives with her two daughters, two dogs, three cats, two rabbits, and nine chooks on her farm in rural Connecticut. She received her MA in English from the University of Sydney, a certificate in the Creative Writing Program through UCLA, and her BA in Journalism from the University of Southern

California. She is enrolled currently in post-graduate studies at Columbia University in New York. She can do a headstand on a trampoline, kill a chook, and make hard cider from the apples in her orchard.

Andrew Stancek was born in Bratislava and saw Russian tanks occupying his homeland. His dreams of circuses and ice cream, flying and lion-taming, miracle and romance have appeared recently in print in *LA Review*, *Windsor Review* and *New Sun Rising: Stories for Japan*. Among the many online publications featuring his work are *Every Day Fiction*, *Gemini Magazine* (Flash Fiction Contest Grand Prize Winner), *fwriction*, *r.kv.r.y. quarterly literary journal*, *Tin House*, *Flash Fiction* Chronicles, *The Linnet's Wings*, *Connotation Press*, *THIS Literary Magazine*, *LA Review*, *Windsor Review*, *Thrice Fiction Magazine*, *New Sun Rising*, and *Pure Slush* online.

Susan Tepper is the author of four published books of fiction and a chapbook of poetry. Her most recent title *The Merrill Diaries* (*Pure Slush Books*, July 2013) is a Novel in Stories that follows a young woman's adventures in love and lust on two continents, spanning a decade. Tepper has received nine Pushcart nominations, and one for the Pulitzer Prize in fiction. You can visit her website here: http://www.susantepper.com.

Nathaniel Tower lives in the Twin Cities with his wife and daughter. After teaching high school English for nine years, he decided to pursue a career in writing / publishing / editing. His fiction has appeared in over two hundred online and print journals. His first collection of fiction, *Nagging Wives, Foolish Husbands*, was released in 2014 through *Martian Lit*. Nathaniel is the founding and managing editor of *Bartleby Snopes Literary Magazine and Press*. You can find out more about Nathaniel at http://nathanieltower.wordpress.com.

Townsend Walker lives in San Francisco. His stories have been published in over fifty literary journals and included in seven anthologies. One story won the SLO NightWriters story contest. Two were nominated for the PEN / O. Henry Award. Four were performed at the New Short Fiction Series in Hollywood. He is associate editor at *Grey Sparrow Journal*. During a career in finance he published three books, on foreign exchange, derivatives and portfolio management. Educated at Georgetown, NYU and Stanford, his website is at http://www.townsendwalker.com.

Michael Webb is continually surprised anyone is interested in what he has to say, and he blogs occasionally at http://innocentsaccidentshints.blogspot.com.

Other 2014 compendiums
from Pure Slush

Jan Feb March 2014
ISBN: 978-1-925101-33-1

July Aug Sept 2014
ISBN: 978-1-925101-47-8

Oct Nov Dec 2014
ISBN: 978-1-925101-48-5

For the complete catalogue of
fiction and non-fiction
print books and eBooks
visit the Pure Slush Store at
http://pureslush.webs.com/store.htm

www.ingramcontent.com/pod-product-compliance
Lightning Source LLC
Chambersburg PA
CBHW030352030726
47497CB00002B/306